Billionaire Mogul—Phoenix

Scarlett Avery

Edited by John Hudspith

Proofread by Jamie Betts, Melody Fuhrman, Chrissy Becker, Janet Mowdy, Doris Hires Collins, and Jacks Larson

ISBN 978-1-989778-99-9

No part of this book used automated software or AI in its creation. The content was written by a human (Scarlett Avery, the author). The cover was professionally designed and the interior was professionally formatted.

Dedication

For my readers who are unapologetic about their addiction to smut, but also need all the feels.

Get the BILLIONAIRE MOGUL—PHOENIX Secret Chapter

Join my mailing list and grab the Exclusive Secret Chapter or Storyboard for this romance.
Zero spam.
www.MyRomanceAddiction.com

Chapter 1

Michaela

I'm in blissful communion with my first steaming hot latte of the day when my friend breaks the silence with an ear-shattering screech.

"You're getting married?!"

I lower my cup. "What?"

Keira's eyes lift up to mine. "You're getting married."

My eyes drop to her cup. "Did you spike your latte with a copious amount of cognac? And if so, how come I didn't get any?"

"I can't believe you've been in LA for two days and you haven't even told me." She ignores my dig and keeps talking, still not making a shred of sense. "Sheesh, I thought we were friends, Mikki." She rolls her eyes. "I was wrong. I guess I can kiss my dreams of being your maid of honor goodbye since I didn't even get an invitation."

I'm hanging out with Keira Weatherly during the tail end of her convalescence. After a morning swim—I swam while she played referee on the side of the pool—we're sitting in her boyfriend's kitchen, enjoying a leisurely breakfast. Well, it was leisurely until she started talking crazy.

I knit my eyebrows in confusion. "Is this a joke?"

"It says so right here!" She points a frantic finger at her iPad.

"Where?"

"On JustSpotted.com's website," she says. "According to them— Wait a minute." She grips the device with both hands, brings it really close to her face, widens her eyes, and then pulls it away. She does that a few times before speaking again. "Holy deliciousness, Mikki. You're getting married to a really, really hot guy!"

I drop my cup on the saucer. "Keira, how can I be getting married when I'm not even dating?" I let out a sarcastic laugh. "Celebrity sightings in La La Land must be at an all-time low if a leading gossip site like JustSpotted.com is making up stories about me." I shake my head at the absurdity of it all.

I'm no stranger to being featured on celebrity sites or magazines. The press has dubbed me, *the goody-two-shoes hotel heiress*, because until recently, my life was devoid of drama. In the past, when the spotlight was on me, it was usually because of my social outings in New York or to dissect my fashion selections. I haven't crossed over to the dark side or anything like that, but thanks to my emancipation trip to Nepal, I've kicked the goody-two-shoes and Pollyanna image to the curb. These days, the press doesn't know what to make of me. Good.

"I must have a celebrity-doppelganger running around LA, fooling everybody." I run my hand over my super short hair. "That's the only logical explanation."

"Speaking of hair, JustSpotted.com posted old photos of you—"

"See! They got it wrong! They have photos of my identical-twin-from-another-mother, her long, dark locks flowing in the wind, passing as me."

Keira's lips turn up in an unimpressed frown.

Okay, so I'm not a poet.

"Mikki, even if you had a celebrity-doppelganger, the chance of the two of you having the same name is practically impossible," Keira says. "This article is about you and your husband-to-be—"

"For crying out loud, Keira, I'm not getting married!"

"Here"—she drops the iPad on the kitchen table—"you tell me you're not getting married."

I snatch it, ready to laugh my ass off, except I don't.

My jaw drops.

My mouth is agape and I'm certain my eyes are bulging out of their sockets.

What in God's name?

'MICHAELA KNIGHT SOON TO BECOME MRS. KÖNIG!'

I read the headline in shock.

Because I'm certain this is a joke at my expense, I click open another tab and type my name in the search bar.

I'm unprepared for the deluge.

'MICHAELA KNIGHT SPOTTED IN LA GETTING READY FOR UPCOMING WEDDING.'

'PHOENIX KÖNIG + MICHAELA KNIGHT. LONG LIVE THE KING AND THE QUEEN!'

'WHO'S WHO FROM COAST-TO-COAST EXPECTED

AT PHOENIX KÖNIG AND MICHAELA KNIGHT'S WEDDING.'

'PHOENIX KÖNIG + MICHAELA KNIGHT TOPPING THE CHART OF THE MOST GORGEOUS COUPLE EVER!'

'PHOENIX + MICHAELA. IS THIS FOREVER?!'

'KING KÖNIG TO TAKE A QUEEN.'

King König?

Phoenix König?

Who the hell is that?

I read page after page of results, utterly stunned.

As my eyes scan the headlines, my rage boils.

My stepmonster did it again.

"What a manipulative bitch," I say.

"So, you're not getting married?" Keira asks.

My eyes shoot up to hers.

"No, I'm not! I don't even know this Phoenix König guy!"

"Well, if you're going to get hitched to a stranger, he's a great one to pick. Holy hotness! He's totally fitness-model material. And did you see his eyes? Rhys has—"

"Oh my God, Keira! Stop it! I don't care about his eyes. I'm not getting married to a person I've never met before." I'm too perturbed to pay attention to the hotness level of a stranger I'll never meet. I have bigger fish to fry. My life is front and center of the gossip rags and someone is responsible for this travesty. "Obviously, my stepmother decided to use fake news to drum up business. Again," I mutter through gritted teeth.

"You think she's behind this?" Keira asks.

"Of course, she is!" I say, handing over the iPad. "Who else loves to meddle in my love life and can't resist the urge of pawning me as bait? Remember how well things turned out with pervy Freddy III?"

Keira grimaces. "Gross."

"Yup, the man is disgusting."

Halfway into our first coffee date, Frederick William Pliskin III asked me if I was okay being blindfolded with my arms tied behind my back and gagged with his jizz-filled underwear while he fucked me from behind. He also wanted to watch as his three cousins took turns fucking me—another of his kinks. Let me think... Hell no, fucking pervert!

My stepmother is incapable of picking a decent man. Given her taste in the men she selects for me, I have no clue how she ended up with my father. No matter how many times I ask her to mind her own business, telling her to back off is like waving a T-bone steak in front of a famished dog and expecting it to behave. Pointless.

"At least she's stepping up her game." Keira's words drip with sarcasm. "Unlike her multiple previous laughable attempts, this time your stepmonster picked a winner. Maybe marrying Phoenix König isn't a bad idea." She keeps scrolling through the iPad. "He's a local businessman— Scratch that!"

"What?"

"He's a tycoon!" Her hazel-green eyes are huge when they meet mine. "According to this article, he owns a shit load of real estate and—"

"Good for him." I dismiss her commentary with a shrug.

"No, seriously, Mikki, think about it. You'd get to move to the west coast, and we'd hang out more often. Who knows? Your future husband lives in Manhattan Beach and we'd end up being neighbors."

I roll my eyes.

"I love New York way too much to ever leave."

I can't see myself trading the fast pace of the concrete jungle for the mellow vibe of the City of Angels. I'm a New Yorker through and through.

"If we lived in the same city, it would be reminiscent of our time in Nepal—two badass rebels against the world!" she says.

"Nepal..." The memory washes over me like a caress and I offer my partner in crime a warm smile.

Keira and I met not long ago, but you'd never tell by how well we get along. Even if we live on opposite sides of the country, we're constantly in touch. We're the same age, and we both ran away from our lives when everything around us came crashing down.

That's how we ended up on the other side of the planet at the same time. For six months Nepal was her refuge. I was there for two. We left the monastery we were staying at with a greater sense of self-awareness, self-actualization and a lot less hair. Leaving that safe cocoon was bitter sweet. I returned to a city I love, a father I worship, and to a stepmother I loathe. Keira moved back to her hometown.

I pluck my phone from the table, my fingers already typing the gossip site's URL.

"I need to put an end to this madness. The celebrity blogger needs to retract this ridiculous wedding announcement before people start believing the lies. Then, I have to deal with my stepmonster."

"Oooohhh, the shit's about to hit the fan!" Keira says.

"Damn right. Someone needs to butt out and shut up!"

~

"Where are you going?" Keira asks when I reenter the kitchen to the main house an hour later.

Since she returned to LA, she's been living with her older

brother's best friend who's now her boyfriend. Rhys Hartford's guesthouse is quite posh, but pales in comparison to his magnificent, modern mansion, aka the main house.

"You're not dressed to hang out at the pool," she says.

After breakfast, I swapped the jeans shorts and yellow tank top I was wearing for a more fashionable getup.

"No pool time today, *chica*. I'm going to battle, so I had to dress the part."

Her eyes travel the length of my body.

"What does that mean?" she asks.

"There's no phone number to reach the gossip site. I sent numerous emails, but given their influence, I'm sure they're bombarded with messages. No doubt, mine is lost somewhere in their inbox. I tried to call my stepmother, but it goes straight to voicemail. Ditto for my father. Exasperated, I called my father's executive assistant. At least I was able to reach her."

"And?"

"Apparently, everyone is walking on eggshells on the executive floor."

"What happened?"

"My father and stepmother are locked in his office and they're engaged in a yelling match. From what I hear, it's ugly."

"Your stepmother is a piece of work," Keira says.

"Daddy has to be really pissed off to lose his composure in front of the staff. I can only hope he's finally tired of getting stepped all over. I love him to pieces, but marrying that woman was his biggest mistake."

Keira gives me another onceover. "Okay, there's a war raging in New York, but that still doesn't tell me where you're going."

"I'm not holding my breath when it comes to getting a response from the gossip site and since my dad is duking it out with his wife, I have to rely on Plan B."

"Which is?"

"I want to know why Phoenix König and my stepmother concocted this little scheme. What's in it for him?"

With a careful step and balancing on her cane, Keira comes to stand in front of me. The top of her blonde head reaches just below my chin. Barefoot, I'm an inch shorter than her, but since she's wearing flip-flops and I'm wearing high heels, I'm really tall right now.

"You called and made an appointment with the tycoon?" she asks. "He had time in his busy calendar to fit you in at the last minute?!" Her tone is laced with skepticism.

"I tried, but his guard dog—whoever is manning the switchboard is giving me the runaround. Even though I kept giving the person my name, she refused to believe me. I have a sneaky suspicion she thinks I'm a whack job."

"If your text and social media messages exploded, I can just imagine how it must be for someone like Phoenix König," Keira says.

At least she stopped calling him my husband-to-be.

I roll my eyes. "Puh-lease. This is part of a well-oiled publicity machine. Phoenix König must be enjoying every minute of this."

It's official.

The fake news of my pending wedding has gone viral.

Lucky me. *Not!*

It's a little freaky how fast fake news can travel. Suddenly, my phone was lighting up like the giant Rockefeller Center Christmas tree. I let it all go to voicemail. Until I have answers, I'm ignoring everyone. Too bad for me, the two people I'm dying to hear from haven't called me back.

"Innocent until proven guilty, remember?" Keira says. "It's the legal principle our great country was founded upon."

"Yeah, well, I'm about to administer my own legal principle."

"What do you have up your sleeve, Miss Knight?"

I adopt her formal tone. "I'm glad you asked, Miss Weatherly. I pinned down King König's HQ—"

"Oh, this sounds very James Bondish." Keira's eyes sparkle with excitement.

"Trust me, it feels like a covert operation," I say. "All that to say, I know where to find him. Thank you, Google! Now, I'm going to pay the king a little visit."

Keira shrieks. "You're going to drop in unannounced?"

"I am!"

She squints at me. "Is that a good idea, Mikki?"

"What other choice do I have?" I ask. "Sure, I could open a bottle of wine at nine o'clock in the morning and get drunk, but that won't do much to help me understand how I got entangled with this stranger."

"What if he can't meet with you?"

"If he's in connivance with my stepmother and willing to spread lies, he'll make time to meet with me," I say, lifting my chin up.

"You should wait it out," she says. "I'm sure you'll be able to get through to your stepmother eventually."

"She's barely interested in talking to me when she's in a chipper mood, unless it's to shove a 'suitable lifemate' down my throat," I say with quotation marks. "Given the drama in New York, I doubt she'll want to talk to me. It's not like Daddy knows anything about this farce. I want answers and I want them now. If not from her, then from this King Kong Tycoon."

Keira laughs.

While my cabbie weaves his way through traffic, I frantically research as much as I can on King Kong Tycoon. It wouldn't be wise to walk into battle without an ounce of preparation.

Keira was right.

My never-to-be-husband is a serious tycoon.

Given my family is also in the hotel industry, you'd think I would've heard of Phoenix König before. His name probably came up in conversation, but I forgot it as quickly.

The Königs play in a whole different league from us. In essence, it's like comparing a goldfish to a blue whale. Phoenix's family owns a plethora of commercial real estate and luxury residential complex buildings across the country, on top of owning the biggest flagship of luxury hotels in California, the second biggest in the nation. They also own many luxury hotels around the world. King Kong Tycoon's dad, Soren, is the CEO, but he runs the corporation along with his four sons—Phoenix, the oldest. Slate, the middle child. Wilder, the other middle child. Roman, the youngest.

I was dead set on finding as much dirt as I could on Phoenix, but I got sidetracked by the numerous articles about the patriarch's recent heart attack. As I was reading about the heart-wrenching ordeal, I tried, but failed to push aside traumatic memories of Daddy's close call three years ago. I don't think I could've survived losing a second parent.

A taxi ride later and I arrive at my destination. I pay the cabbie and get out of the car. Even if I'm wearing shades, I shield my eyes from the blinding sun as I crane my neck upwards to take in the grandeur of the Pompadour Hotel & Residences. Impressive skyscrapers rise above me. They're not nearly as tall as the average building in New York, but they still touch the sky. The Pompadour is an uber modern luxury complex composed of three sleek glass towers. It isn't only a pied-à-terre to the extremely rich and wealthy, it's also where the beast presides over his empire.

Let's see what you have to say King Kong Tycoon.

I stride across an ocean of asphalt to the Beverly Hills premier HQ, each step of my Christian Louboutin shoes stomping with the determination of a take-no-prisoner warrior.

Good God, it's hot.

I pinch the front of my dress with two fingers and fan myself, hoping to avoid walking into my meeting with the beast looking like a hot mess. Unsightly underarm sweat stains would make for a poor first impression.

It's like a freaking sauna.

I'm no stranger to New York's 90/90 summers—ninety-degree and ninety-percent-humidity—but LA is much hotter. I swear it feels like it's two hundred degrees. I can't fathom what it will be like by midday.

As I trek to the entrance, I take note of the hustle and bustle—the revolving door of new faces. That's one of the constants about life as a hotelier.

Everything about these buildings screams corporation. It's the antithesis of the Villiers Grand Hotel. Our family boutique hotel in New York brims with rich history and welcoming old-world charm. Even from the outside, the Pompadour seems a little too sleek, cold, and impersonal. I doubt it will be any different once I pass the threshold.

Pompadour. Hmph. Pretty pompous, if you ask me.

When I enter the hotel, the cool air hits me like a speeding freight train.

Thank you, God.

I pause long enough to scan my surroundings. My eyes bounce to every corner. A swarm of newly arrived guests take residence in the opulent lobby, and the hotel staff is busy attending to them.

How do I get to you, King Kong Tycoon?

I either have to ask a concierge for help or figure it out myself. The scale of this hotel is far more eye-popping than the Villiers Grand, but I'm willing to bet everything to my name, there's a dedicated set of elevators leading to the executive floor. As I debate, a group of four men talking, coffee cups in hand, pass right by me.

My bionic ears catch a snippet of their conversation.

"Yeah, we should be locking down the purchase on three old office buildings we'll convert into high-end hotels-slash-residencies in Dallas by end of day," one man says. He's wearing a purple shirt, black pants and tortoiseshell glasses.

"We should secure two soaring towers in Cleveland by end of the week," a tall blond wearing a flower print shirt says.

Bingo!

With the agility of a spy, I trail behind the foursome, balancing on my four-inch heels, as they lead me to the Promised Land.

Operation King Kong Tycoon commences.

I step into the elevator right before the doors close.

"Good morning," I say with a bright smile.

Four pair of eyes rake up and down the length of my body.

"Good morning," they say, practically all at once.

The lack of subtlety in their tone is as heavy as a brick. I'm surprised they didn't punctuate with, *And how you doin'?* a la Joey from *Friends*.

I'm not one to play damsel in distress, but it's the only card I have right now in my deck.

"I'm here to see Mr. Phoenix König. Silly me, I forgot which floor he's on."

"He's expecting you?" purple shirt guy asks. The tinge of suspicion in his voice doesn't go unnoticed.

Think.

Think.

Think.

"I'm here about..." *Dammit. Think faster.* "A family run boutique hotel on Park Place," I say. I cock my head to the side and knit my eyebrows together for effect. "It's one of those very hush-hush deals Mr. König wants to snag before anyone else."

Giving them the name of our family hotel would be like sounding the alarm. I want to catch Phoenix König with his bespoke pants down.

"Oh, yeah." The tall floral shirt guy nods. "Great address."

He fell for it?!

This covert operation is turning me into a real spy—one who thinks on her feet.

Go Mikki!

When I'm under pressure, I use Monopoly as my get out of jail card. Along with being the least landed-on spots in the game, Park Place is also the name of a park that's long gone. I Googled this useless piece of information one day for no good reason. I can't believe it's my lifeline.

Board game to the rescue!

It's with herculean effort I don't roll my eyes hard.

"Isn't it?"

The men nod.

"All five Mr. Königs are on the top floor," purple shirt guy says. "I guess I should say, all four Königs since Roman is still bedridden on the other side of the planet after the freaky accident." He presses the button before sliding a key card into a slot.

I read about that. Thank God he's still alive.

I smile. "Thank you."

"No problem." He winks. "Take a right when you get off the elevators. Lydia Gillanders is Phoenix König's executive assistant. She'll take good care of you."

"Got it! Thanks again!" I smile wide.

I didn't expect things to go this smoothly. This must be my lucky day.

I lean against the wall, eyes cast to my designer heels, pretending I'm unaware the men are eating me up with their eyes.

The ride to the top floor of this fourteen-story hotel is super short. These elevators seem to be powered by jet fuel. Nothing compared to the slower speed of our elevators at the Villiers Grand.

The foursome gets off on the twelfth floor, taking with them the awkward tension that was lingering over my head. I'm thankful they didn't drill me with questions about my fictitious hotel.

A nanosecond later, I reach the top floor. When the elevator doors open, I step out. Thank God there aren't any CIA-type security codes required. It would be a shame to get busted this early in the game.

I lean forward as I take in the lay of the land. I peek to my left, then my right.

So far, so good.

Only a set of glass doors separates me from my target—that and the gatekeeper.

You're close, girl.

I summon my lady balls and take a confident step forward. I stride down the hallway, praying all the angels in Heaven to watch over me.

Here goes nothing.

I pull open the glass door and step inside King Kong Tycoon's sovereign world.

No one.

The desk is empty.

I catch the name on a plate on the desk. Lydia Gillanders.

I'm at the right place.

My heart beats a little faster.

I just want answers.

I get on my toes to peek at the computer screen. It's as black as night.

Is Lydia on a break?

My eyes move to the heavy-looking wood door behind the desk where I'm certain my target is hiding.

What to do? What to do?

My inner wisdom speaks out, *"Patience, Mikki."*

As I pace the space, waiting for someone to show up, I run the possible scenarios of how things are about to go down in my head, and choose to eliminate the one where I get escorted out of the building by the police like a common criminal.

I got this.

Well, I hope I do.

We'll soon find out.

Another minute goes by.

Then another.

And another.

And another.

Dammit!

Where is Lydia?

Just when I'm about to run out of patience, the wooden door behind her desk opens.

Finally!

A tall man emerges.

"I want answers and I want them today, Slate," a deep, commanding voice from inside the office says.

"I'm on it, Phoenix," the man standing at the door says.

King Kong Tycoon is in his office.

I was worried my timing might've been off. After all,

Phoenix could've been trapped in an endless meeting or worse, absent from the office.

Score!

The man I now know as Slate senses my presence and shifts his attention to me. His arresting, piercing eyes meet mine. They're the clearest arctic blue eyes I've ever seen.

Wow.

The man is stunning.

His stylish dark-brown hair, his pristine, perfectly cut dark-gray suit, and his gorgeous shoes, scream power.

He's far more handsome than I remember from the photos I perused through on the way here. Then again, my focus wasn't on the König men's hotness meter, but rather, their profiles.

I should've paid more attention.

When I meet his eyes again, I snap back to the moment.

This isn't the time to get sidetracked by good looks. You're on a mission!

I offer the man still checking me out a coquettish smile.

He responds by flashing me a flirtatious, wide grin, flashing a set of gleaming white teeth.

He gives me a quick onceover and cocks an eyebrow, nodding.

I wink.

The megawattage of his smile grows to blinding levels.

Men are so easy.

I take this as my omen.

I don't think twice.

I charge forward like a linebacker running with the ball towards the end zone. The man stares at me, stunned, as I zoom right past him.

"Wait! You can't go in there!"

I ignore him.

Too late, buddy. I'm in!

Chapter 2

Phoenix

I'm startled when a whirlwind gusts into my office like a torpedo. Confused, my eyes bounce to my brother. He's as surprised as I am.

I shove out of my chair and shuffle to my feet, ready for the worst.

"May I help you?" I ask the woman who just barged in.

"My name is Michaela Knight. We need to talk," she says.

I study her for a beat, certain my eyes are deceiving me.

"You look nothing like Michaela Knight," I tell her.

"Interesting, you know who I am." She lets out a sarcastic laugh. "Until a couple of hours ago, I didn't know who you were," she says. "As for the way I look, the hair is a bit of a dramatic transformation."

No shit.

She moves her attention away from me, fumbling through her designer bag.

I lift my hands in surrender. "Whoa. No need to get violent."

She rolls her eyes at me. "I'm not looking for a gun. I'm

pulling out my driver's license to prove my identity. It's still my old photo, but at least you can verify my name."

The woman standing in front of me is unquestionably gorgeous, but her hair is a vast departure from the photos I've seen of her. She chopped off the curtain of dark brown, almost black hair. Without the long mane, her remarkable features stand out. She's now sporting a short, edgy haircut that makes her look much younger. If I didn't know better, I might be tempted to think she's barely legal.

"You're demanding for an intruder," I tell her.

"Hear me out before kicking me out," she says.

I consider her.

"Okay," I say with a nod.

She pulls out her wallet.

I doubt this tiny tornado is much of a threat. Given this morning's freak media show, I can't wait to hear what Miss Knight has to say in her defense.

This should be interesting.

I tear my gaze away from the feisty woman and shift my attention to my brother. He's just staring. I know that look. His lopsided grin is also a dead giveaway.

Yes, I have eyes. She's smoking hot.

"I'll catch you later, Slate," I tell him.

"Why don't I hang around? You might need a referee," he says.

"I got this," I tell him.

"You're sure?" he asks.

"Positive."

"You never know—"

"Slate."

"Okay, okay. I'm gone."

He closes the door behind him in slow motion, his eyes

taking in every inch of the woman dressed in a stunning hot pink dress.

I shake my head.

He grins.

"Here you go!" She flings her driver's license on my desk.

I pick it up, study it, verifying both her age and her identity.

"You *are* Michaela Knight." *Thank fuck she's legal.*

"Told you! Care to explain why you're dead set on fucking up my life?"

Her surly tone is borderline rude.

I drop the driver's license on my desk and inhale a calming breath. I close my fists and anchor them against my desk. From this vantage point, I get an eyeful of the swell of her tempting breasts. The neckline of her dress is sexy and classy. It commands attention without ever being trashy. The hot pink shade isn't as defining as red, but it still means business.

She looks up, fixing me with a pair of big, green eyes in a breathtaking shade I've never seen before in my entire life. Her barely there makeup is flawless and those damn black lashes are a mile long. Her perfect pale skin suggests she hasn't been in LA for long.

She clears her throat and takes a step back.

She squares her shoulders. "I asked you a question and I expect an answer."

I glance down.

My desk is an annoyance, a barrier I could do without.

I circle it and come to stand right in front of her. My eyes trail down the length of the pint-sized spitfire glaring up at me.

I approve of how beautiful she looks in this form-fitted dress that hits her just above the knee. I'm also quite partial to those sexy-as-fuck white high heels with a strap circling her delicate ankles. The immaculate white offers a flawless finish.

She crosses her arms over her chest, revealing more than a hint of cleavage. It's an effort not to stare.

"Well?" She has the audacity to tap an impatient foot on the floor.

My eyebrows rise to my forehead.

"You have some nerve," I say. "You trespass—"

"Newsflash! It's a hotel! I'm not trespassing."

Her voice doesn't match the rest of her. It's all expensive, smoky whiskey, while her look is all diamonds and champagne. If she wasn't snapping at me like she is right now, I'm sure I'd enjoy listening to her talk for hours.

Focus.

"You have no business on the executive floor," I say. "You're lucky I haven't called security to haul your fine ass out of here."

"Please leave my ass out of this conversation," she says.

"I said your *fine* ass."

"Too bad you'll never know."

Feisty.

The long list of things I'd do to her ass is one hundred percent X-rated, but this is neither the time nor the place.

"Ask nicely," I say.

"What?" She blinks in confusion.

"You're in my domain, Miss Knight. You want answers, ask nicely."

She shoots a *fuck you* glare at me.

"You're spreading lies about me. About us!" Her finger moves frantically between us. "Make it stop. Now!"

The muscles in my jaw flex.

This tiny woman has a fierce fighting spirit, the likes of which I've rarely seen in the women I date. She isn't accommodating. Nor is she a pushover. She stands on her own two feet. She's a real study in contrast. Miss Knight is nothing like what I expected.

"I'm not the one behind this grotesque PR grab," I say. "You are!" I point an accusatory finger at her.

She points one back. "No, you are! You're the manipulative asshole who's using me for God knows what reason. What did my stepmother promise you in exchange for being willing to destroy my life like this?" she asks through gritted teeth.

Her nostrils flare, her eyes shoot daggers at me, and her chest heaves.

Stop staring at her breasts.

"Did she trick you into believing you were getting a virgin bride?"

"What the hell kind of statement is that?" I ask, because it's so preposterous, I doubt I heard her correctly.

"Rich men seeking young, dumb virgins so they can shape them to their will—and manhood—and be the first to plant their seed into their womb," she says.

"You think I bought your virginity via your stepmom?" I barely manage to keep my voice calm and professional.

"Yes!" Michaela nods. "She keeps reminding me I have a precious commodity worth preserving for a dirty old man with pockets lined with money"—she rolls her eyes—"and, most likely a tiny, limp, shriveled dick."

The crude word coming from her mouth is an insult to my ears.

"She insists it's all part of a new woman's empowering movement. And, apparently, it's a lucrative market. I guess you must be her newest prospect."

For the love of fuck. What does she take me for?

"Well, I'm not a virgin," she says.

Good to know.

"I just don't bother correcting my stepmom because it's none of her business." She shrugs. "The joke's on you, dirty old man."

"Tread carefully, kitty cat," I say.

"Kitty cat?"

"You barge in here, ready to claw my eyes out like a kitten perched on a tree I'm trying to rescue—"

"I don't need to be rescued." She huffs. "I need answers!"

"First, I've never met your stepmother. Second, I don't buy women for sex or for any other reason. Third, I steer away from virgins. And fourth, I'm not an old man." *Dirty, yes, but old, no.* "I'm only thirty-one. Enough answers for you, kitty cat?"

Hesitant green eyes scan my face. But just as quick as a whip, suspicion flashes back at me.

"What's in it for you?" she asks. "Why are you lying to protect my stepmother?"

"I'm not! I've never met the woman."

"Well, this stunt has her signature all over it—" Michaela brushes a dismissive hand in front of her face. "It doesn't matter. How are *you* going to get JustSpotted.com to retract the fake announcement?"

I release a breath, my temper ebbing. "We can't."

"Hence why I didn't include myself in the statement," she says. "I don't have that kind of power, but obviously"—she extends her arms out, as if encompassing my luxurious office—"you do."

Even her mocking smile is charming.

"You must have a pricey PR firm at your beck and call. Get them to work their magic! We're not getting married!"

My brother Slate caught wind of the JustSpotted.com article before I did. He immediately called to warn me. I thought he was pulling my leg, but he wasn't. As I scrolled through the screaming headlines, I was certain Michaela Knight had played a part in this farce. Her outburst suggests she was caught off guard by the sneaky PR stunt as much as I was. The thing is, she doesn't have the full story. I do. And I'm about to burst her bubble.

"There's more to this than meets the eye," I tell her.

"No, there isn't! There's been a mistake. *You* just need to fix it."

"It's not entirely a mistake, Michaela."

Her long eyelashes flutter at the mention of her name.

Then, it hits me. This is the first time her name has passed my lips since she busted into my office.

"You're missing parts of the puzzle," I say.

She stares for a long beat, flabbergasted. And then she bursts out laughing. Full on belly laughs.

"You're cute and all, but either you're missing a screw or you're deaf. We. Are. Not. Getting. Married," she says, enunciating every word.

"Even though I don't approve of how things were done, I'm not one to renege on a deal, especially not this one," I say.

"I swear on everything that's holy, you're being a stubborn prick just to irritate the hell out of me," she says. "We don't know each other. We're not getting married. End of story." She jabs a finger at me, a harsh edge breaking through each word.

My eyes rattle back and forth like a ping pong ball from her manicured finger, to her sultry mouth, to her gem-like eyes. She really thinks she has leverage here. I'm on the bitter cusp of pulling her onto my lap to teach her who's in control.

"You have a mouth on you," I tell her.

"Congratulations on your power of observation! That still doesn't change the fact, we're not getting married!"

Exasperated, I ask, "Have you talked to your father?"

Her disdainful smirk falls.

She doesn't answer.

"Had you talked to your father before barging in here, trespassing on private property, flying off the handle, wailing about foul play, shrieking and keening like a goddamn banshee, you'd know what's at stake here."

She purses her lips together, conceding I've one upped her. "I tried to call him, but he's dealing with a situation."

"I'm willing to bet my fortune your father is behind this—"

"My—my father is behind this?" She stutters.

Ah. A tiny crack in her armor.

"I'm certain of it," I say. "He has the most to gain from this publicity stunt."

"You're not making any sense," she says. "My father would never do such a thing."

"He would if he was looking for extra leverage."

"Leverage on what?"

"Your father and I have a deal."

"A deal?"

"Yes. An ironclad deal, which is why I don't know why he felt the need to force my hand."

"What kind of deal are you talking about?" she asks.

"Like I said, you should've talked to your father before coming to me."

"Well, I'm here now and I'm asking you. Instead of answering my question, you're being elusive, which is characteristic of a manipulative liar."

"I'm not the one using undermining tactics, sweetheart. Your father masters the art of deception."

A thunderous storm rages in her eyes.

She leaps towards me like a bull in a ring charging at full speed towards the matador's red cape.

I'm quick.

I reach out to snatch her wrist before her palm hits my cheek and force her hand to rest against my chest.

She flinches at the contact.

So do I.

For a brief moment we both seem startled by the proximity.

It's a good thing I'm too fucking wound up right now to enjoy the warmth of her body against mine.

She breathes in and out, seemingly preparing for a second attack.

"I wouldn't do that if I were you," I say, my steady voice betraying the frantic palpitation of my heart.

"Stop it with your lies," she says. She tries but fails to break from my grip.

Even when she's immobilized, she's willing to fight with all her might.

"The ink is already dried on the contract," I tell her. "As of two days ago, my company owns the Villiers Grand Hotel."

The revelation takes the wind out of her.

"My father sold the hotel?" She's incredulous.

"Yes."

She studies me for a long beat.

I hold her murderous gaze.

Suddenly, a hysterical laugh leaves her lips.

"You're such a bullshitter!" Okay, I have no idea how to read this woman.

"And you're blind," I say.

"You're a pretentious asshole!"

Time to remove the kid gloves. "If you deigned to get off your high horse and open your fucking eyes, you would've noticed your father is drowning in debt. He owes a ton of money he can't repay," I tell her. "But no, you're here pretending to know what you're talking about, but in reality, you know shit, and you're only shooting your mouth off."

Her shoulders stiffen at the insult.

"That's right, sweetheart, you're not the only one who can throw the punches," I say.

For several long seconds we enter a Mexican standoff,

nostrils flaring, eyes trained on each other, breaths meshing together.

"I don't believe you," she says.

Niels Knight was supposed to step up to the plate and explain his precarious situation to his daughter. The onus wasn't supposed to fall on me.

Michaela is still staring at me like she wants to stab my eyeballs with a fork.

"Everyone has a price, Miss Knight." My words are cold. "Niels made a promise to your mother. A lot has happened recently, making it harder and harder for him to keep that promise. I'm unwilling to go into details—that's your father's job, not mine—suffice to say, his back was up against a wall. He needed a quick exit strategy. I just so happened to be in the market for a new hotel in Manhattan."

Her lips form into an O.

I didn't expect our first encounter to be sugary sweet, but this hostility is amped up by the fact she has no clue how much shit her father is dealing with.

"As far as merger-marriages go," I say, "it's part and parcel of everything else I've agreed to. Your father had a very long list of demands I was willing to meet."

"A merger-marriage?"

"Yes."

"What does that even mean?" she asks.

"The merger part is where I bail out your family hotel and fold it under our umbrella of hotels to prevent it from going into bankruptcy."

"Bankruptcy?" Her question comes out on a stunned breath.

I nod.

"The hotel is no longer ours?!" she asks.

"Not until the debt is paid off."

"But that'll take forever," she says.

"There are ways of shaving off a considerable number of years from the repayment plan."

"What kind of ways?" she asks.

"That's where the marriage part kicks in." I allow for a pregnant pause. "You and me... in holy matrimony." A little sarcasm never hurts.

She hitches a breath. Her green eyes are so huge right now.

"I'm tied to you by my father's debt?"

I tilt my head left to right. "Something like that."

She stares at me in shock.

"No. No way!" She shakes her head. "Nope. Not happening. We are never ever entering into holy matrimony. Not in this lifetime. Not in the next."

Let me break it down for you, sweetheart. "I'll be sinking in two hundred million dollars in exchange for your agreement to become my wife for three-hundred-sixty-five days."

Her jaw drops.

"Daddy sold me?!"

"He did what he had to do."

Silence surrounds us.

Myriad emotions flash in her green eyes.

I don't know her well enough to decipher them all, but what I see reflecting from her gaze indicates I'm her least favorite person on the planet right now.

I don't rush her.

I give her time to process everything.

Once she accepts her new reality, we can figure out the next steps.

"Let go of my arm," she says.

Not the reaction I expected.

"I said, let go of my arm." Her tone is slicing.

I do.

Her green eyes snap up at me in rebellion. "This meeting is adjourned!"

My eyebrows shoot to my forehead. "Are you kidding me?"

She doesn't respond.

She pulls the strap of her designer bag over her shoulder and squares her shoulders.

"Do I look like I'm fucking kidding?" Without waiting for an answer, she turns on her heel.

"Where are you going?" I call after her.

Michaela throws her parting words over her shoulder, still striding towards the door, "I'm sure you're pulling a fast one on me. My father would never sell the Villiers Grand. Never. He'd die before he ever let that happen. And, if he were in any kind of financial trouble, he would've told me about it. I wouldn't have to hear it from you—a complete stranger." She pauses and turns around to face me. "I'm sure you make it a sport to step all over the little guy, Mr. King Kong Tycoon."

Huh? King Kong Tycoon?

"But we're not going down without a fight. I don't know what kind of fucked up, twisted, and pathetic mind game you're playing, you cruel corporate sadist, but I'm out of here."

I'm so dumbfounded, words escape me.

Jesus.

Her tongue is sharper than an obsidian blade, her attitude as abrasive as sandpaper.

"I pray to God I never see your face again, Phoenix König." She flips me the bird, and she flies out of here like the flames of hell are licking her designer high heels. She slams the door behind her so hard, I'm surprised the windows don't shatter.

Who the hell does she think she is?

She storms in and out of here like she owns the goddamn building.

I should be pissed off. Livid, even.

That little cyclone did a number on me.

Every cell in my body is buzzing.

I'm pulsing with adrenaline. Arousal?!

My mind fights it, but my cock stiffens at visions of her stripped naked, bent over my desk, my tongue trailing all over her sinful body before I fuck her like it's my new mission in life. That would teach her a lesson. One I'm sure she would enjoy just as much as I would.

Chapter 3

Michaela

I storm out of Phoenix's office, seething with rage, nearing my boiling point like a freaking pressure cooker about to erupt. I swear, if it was possible, steam would be bellowing from my ears. I was so pissed off by all the garbage that came spewing out of that gorgeous man's sexy mouth, I nearly knocked Slate on his ass on my way to the elevators.

Fuck Slate!

Fuck Phoenix!

And fuck the Königs!

How dare Phoenix disparage my father like that?

The Villiers Grand is my heritage.

Mine.

Damn him for thinking he can get his paws on it.

I burst out of the hotel with the same urgency as if I were trying to escape the bowels of hell. I stop long enough to catch my breath. My teeth grind so hard I'm worried I'll crack one. I look up at the sky to where God resides and pray for calmness. My agitated state doesn't simmer much. If anything, flashbacks of my heated confrontation with King Kong Tycoon flare my rage. There aren't enough swear words—in every language—to sum up how I detest that man. If he thinks he's going to execute his evil plan, he has another think coming.

"As God is my witness, I'll never allow that man to get away with this! Never!" I say out loud, brandishing a fist in the air.

"That's right!" an elegant older woman sporting a stylish silver bob says, passing me. "Don't ever let a man have the upper hand."

"Whatever he did to you, nail the sucker's ass to the wall!" her blonde friend—or sister—says. "If you need a ruthless divorce lawyer, I have a list of the best ones in LA. Four divorces later, and I'm an expert."

Darn, that was supposed to be my inner voice.

"Err... thanks. I'm okay." I offer a small smile.

The women nod, sympathetic smiles stretching their lips as they keep walking towards the entrance of the hotel.

Twenty minutes in Phoenix König's presence and I'm already losing my everloving mind. I have no idea how to bottle this strong volcano stirring in the pit of my stomach.

The man drives me absolutely insane.

Marrying him?

Ha!

Not in a million years.

Throttling him?

I'd welcome the chance.

I can't stand King Kong Tycoon.

In fact, I hate him.

So why do I desperately need to change my panties?

Argh!

I'm aware passersby are shooting wary glances at me.

As more snippets of our heated war of words flash in front of my eyes, I gasp in horror.

Did I actually reveal I'm no longer a virgin?

What was I thinking?

That's the problem! I wasn't thinking. My mind takes a leave of absence when I'm close to that man.

I blame those damn mystical eyes...

When I wasn't spitting fire at Phoenix, I was lost in them.

I've never seen anything remotely close to that shade of blue in my life

Wow.

And talk about oozing sex appeal.

Damn those König men. They won the gene pool.

While we were sparring, I really, really tried to convince myself Phoenix König was my mortal enemy, but my body wasn't having it. His manly, expensive scent wafted into the air and traveled straight to my clit.

God, the man smelled so good.

It's like his scent put a spell on me. That must be why I was so out of sorts. It better be, because I have no logical explanation for my hardening nipples and throbbing pussy. And I can't even start to explain why I desperately wanted to know what his lips tasted like at the same time as I was fighting the urge to bludgeon him to death with that expensive-looking lamp on his desk. It was an internal battle like I've never had to wage before.

Trapped in his office was like being caged in a dungeon of lust. I've never loathed a man and found myself attracted to him.

Fuck my life.

In the end, it was all too much.

I had to leave his office before I did the unthinkable—combusted with desire or climbed the tall and utterly sexy man like a tree.

Focus, Mikki.

I ignore the intense way my body reacted to a man I should despise and shove down my inner voice—that isn't as quiet as I'd like and apparently, who's as horny as fuck. I reach inside my handbag for my phone.

Dammit.

My father still hasn't called me back.

What the hell is going on in New York that's monopolizing his time like this?

Is Daddy really having money problems?

Is the Villiers Grand on the verge of bankruptcy?

Is that why Thana and him are arguing?

Two hundred million dollars for three hundred and sixty-five days married to a pompous, pretentious ass? I doubt I'd even be able to last an hour.

Is that what it's going to take to save the hotel?

Was Phoenix lying or was he telling the truth?

Daddy wouldn't keep something this significant from me. I'm his only daughter. He'd confide in me. Surely, he'd seek my help?!

Gah!

I'm going to drive myself crazy if I keep having conversations with myself.

Daddy, you've got some serious explaining to do.

I circle around the hotel in search of a shaded area before I fry like bacon on a cast iron skillet. My phone rings, bringing my rushed steps to a halt.

I look at my screen.

"Daddy!" I practically shout when I answer.

"Hey, ladybug. How's LA?" he asks.

How can he be so calm?

"Daddy, please don't pretend you don't know why I left you fifty voice messages and sent you as many texts. What's going on? Why is my life all of a sudden breaking news? And more importantly, why is my name associated with a perfect stranger?"

My father lets out a long sigh.

I expect him to say something, but he doesn't.

"I just came from Phoenix König's office—"

"You went to see him?" my father asks. His tone is incredulous.

"Yes! I needed answers and I couldn't get through to you. What was Thana thinking? This fake wedding shenanigan is going to hurt the hotel's reputation. Once people find out it's a lie, we're going to come across like bullshitters."

My father doesn't respond.

My stepmother Thana Annunziata is the bane of my existence. She started at the hotel as the accountant after our long-time bookkeeper retired. It took her exactly a month and a half before she wiggled her way into my father's bed. In the two years she's been part of my father's life, I've made a valiant effort to get along with her for Daddy's sake, to no avail. Our personalities are like water and oil—they don't mesh.

"Thana is behind this, right?" I say when my father remains silent.

Daddy still doesn't answer, so I come to my own conclusion.

"I knew it! Phoenix lied to my face. He kept telling me he didn't know Thana, and he swore up and down you were the one behind this media circus. What a preposterous claim." I roll my eyes at the phone. "He also said all sorts of unbelievable—"

"Thana isn't behind this."

"Why is everybody protecting her?" I'm exasperated. "She did this!"

"No, I did." With those three words, my father pulls the rug from under my feet. "I'm the one who hired a publicist. Not Thana."

I'm stunned into silence.

"Right after signing the contract with Phoenix, I put my plan into action. The fact you were in LA made everything so much easier."

"Wh—what? How could you keep something like this from me?" I ask, sounding hysterical.

"Take a breath, ladybug."

"I can't take a breath when my whole world is crumbling around me."

"It was the only way out, Michaela."

I shake my head, even though he can't see me.

"Who are you and what have you done with my father?"

"Where are you now?"

"I'm sorry, Daddy, you just shattered my whole existence and you're inquiring about my location? What about answering my questions?"

"That's what I'm trying to do, Michaela," my father says. "I can hear traffic, which suggests you're outside."

"I'm outside of the Pompadour Hotel. I'm sure I don't have to tell you it's Phoenix's headquarters."

"No, you don't. I was there last month."

"You weren't at a conference?" There's no hiding the bitterness in my tone.

"I was saving the Villiers Grand," he says.

"I find that hard to believe."

He lets out a long, suffering breath. "There's a lot you need to know, but it's best if this conversation happens when you're in a more private setting."

"Daddy, you're scaring me."

"It was never my intention. I promised your mother on her

deathbed the Villiers Grand would be standing for generations to come. You echoed the promise."

"I did." I pause. "I'll make an effort to get along with Thana."

God. I'm sure drinking poison would've been less painful than speaking those words.

"Don't worry about her," Daddy says.

"Did something happen with Thana?"

My father ignores my question. "Everything I did was to honor my word to your mother," he says. "This was my only way out."

Since I always welcome any opportunity to avoid talking about my stepmother, I shrug off the change of subject.

"What Phoenix revealed is true?" I ask.

"When you get back to Rhys's guesthouse, get in touch via a video chat. I'll answer all your questions. I promise."

"Okay."

"I love you, ladybug. Never forget that."

"I love you too, Daddy."

He lets out a small laugh.

"What is it?" I ask.

"It's just the two of us against the world again."

"What does that mean?"

"It means you're going to hate my guts for certain decisions I was forced to make, but not this particular one."

"Daddy, you're speaking in a cryptic language."

"Call me when you get back to the guesthouse."

With that, he hangs up.

I just stare at my phone, dumbfounded.

Chapter 4

Phoenix

Michaela's expensive floral scent still lingers in the air, which explains why my concentration is fucked. Instead of attending to pressing matters and carrying out my role as the COO and acting CEO of an international hotel and real estate empire, I'm sitting behind my desk, flipping her driver's license between my fingers, grinning like a fool. Her departure was so abrupt, I nearly missed her phenomenal ass. Glad I didn't. Just like the rest of her, that juicy ass—I'm already in love with—was something else. That woman's body is built for sin, and the caveman in me wanted nothing more than to fucking devour every inch of her. Damn her for reminding me my right fist has been my best friend lately. God knows I'd enjoy having all that fire beneath me.

"I pray to God I never see your face again, Phoenix König."

I don't need to picture the rage on her face as she stormed out of here. I wonder if little flames were shooting from her nostrils. I can't wait for her to eat her words when she has to crawl back here with her tail between her legs. She was in such a hurry to jump right back on her broom, she forgot something she'll need. Frankly, I was so taken aback by her outburst, I wasn't thinking straight. Her ID was the last thing on my mind.

The little witch will be back.

I got ninety-nine problems... and she just became one more.

And, holy fuck, what a hot-as-sin problem she is.

Her vitriolic fury was the most pleasant part of my morning.

She's a study in contrast I'd love to unravel.

I haven't been this entertained in a very long time. She's like a new toy to amuse me for a short time.

After Michaela Knight delivered her middle finger salute, my day took a nosedive.

The temp replacing my executive assistant, who had to turn around the minute she walked in because her three-year-old son was having an epic meltdown in daycare, couldn't keep up. I don't blame her. Heck, *I* couldn't keep up. Never mind the endless calls, avalanche of emails and text messages, numerous requests from the press for a quote, and incessant congratulations from the staff, I had to face nine irate members of the board of directors. That meeting went just about as well as the one I had with Michaela, minus the sexbomb factor.

I'm still ruminating over the gorgeous rebel with the beautiful green eyes when a succession of three small knocks at my open door brings me back to the moment.

I glance up.

"Come in and close the door behind you," I tell Slate.

He complies before striding towards my desk. He unbuttons his suit jacket and takes a seat in one of the guest chairs.

"I'm glad I'm not in your shoes, big brother," he says, crossing a leg over the other.

"Thank you for the sympathy, little brother." I adopt his mocking tone.

"No, seriously. You're up to your eyeballs in shit and you now have another problem on your hands."

"Don't I know it!"

"From the looks of it, you and Michaela Knight are heading to the divorce court before even going to the chapel."

"Keep your fucking voice down!"

"Relax. One, the door is closed. Two, the board bought your story. Three, your executive assistant wasn't in when your wife-to-be barged in here, so Lydia can't contradict your story. Four, the temp arrived too late to witness the König vs. Knight boxing match of the year. In essence, I'm the only one who knows about your explosive first encounter with your soon-to-be-wife. It's *our* little secret." He gestures between us.

"Shut up, you idiot."

"Is that any way to talk to your ally in crime?"

I shoot him a warning glare.

He lifts his hands up in surrender. "Okay, okay. But in my opinion, you're worrying for nothing."

"I disagree," I tell him. "It pays to be cautious. The walls might have ears."

"You're in the clear, Phoenix."

He's over simplifying things, but then again, Slate always does.

"For now, I am," I say. "Niels Knight jumped the gun without warning. We agreed neither of us would breathe a word of the more *delicate* details of the contract until he spoke to his daughter. She was supposed to agree to this merger-marriage before it was made public."

"Niels is desperate to save his first wife's hotel from the claws of his crooked second wife." Slate sums it up perfectly.

My brother is abreast of my dealings surrounding the Villiers Grand Hotel. I made sure to brief him on my verbal sparring with Michaela right before we walked into the emergency meeting the board called.

"I know exactly what's at stake here," I say. "Granted, his wife is a conniving two-faced bitch, but a heads up would've been appreciated."

"After your eloquent explanation, the board of directors bought the *'it was love at first sight'* fairytale between you and Michaela. At least now they'll back off and stop scolding you for the media circus," Slate says.

Our board of directors is composed of nine men and women who have little faith in my abilities to run this company. I had to bite my tongue to remain silent during the meeting while they grilled me. Once they were done lecturing me—and busting my balls—I was able to plead my case. Sure, I occasionally land on the front page of the celebrity pages and it's too often linked to a woman, but I wash my hands of this morning's media fiasco. Still, I had to think on my feet because I was flying blind.

Convincing a board of directors composed of logicians who only care about the bottom line that a certified playboy like myself would fall madly in love with a woman at first sight and I'd want to marry her as soon as humanly possible because I just can't imagine living one more minute without her by my side, wasn't easy.

In business and life, I move at warp speed, which means it was no surprise I'd 'fall in love' in a New York minute. I might not have an Ivy League college degree or an MBA—by choice—but my keen ability to smell a fucking amazing deal a mile away and before our rivals, has earned me the respect of most of the board members. They can't bitch when I'm lining their pockets with money.

That's why I didn't hesitate when Michaela's father approached me a month and a half ago. He was dealing with an unbelievable situation. His terms were outrageous. And time wasn't playing in my favor. The coveted address of his Manhattan hotel made it impossible for me to walk away from the deal. It pays to be on the list of the Top 10 Richest Hotel Moguls in the country.

"Before the board becomes too suspicious and starts poking holes in my fake-whirlwind-romance to my soulmate, I have to get my fake-fiancée on board, and right now Michaela Knight wants nothing to do with me."

"You'll have to woo her," Slate says matter-of-factly.

"Like you fucking know what that means."

"I don't," he says, "but then again, I'm not the one campaigning for the position of CEO. You are, and you need her."

I rake my hand through my hair. "I hate being in this position."

"It's for the greater good." It's Slate's favorite go-to line since I told my father and brothers about my meeting with Niels Knight. "Back to you charming Michaela—"

"If I can get her to stop spitting fire at me like a goddamn infuriated dragon for longer than a second."

We both laugh.

"She's in LA," Slate picks up where he left off. "Find out where she's staying. Upgrade her accommodation to one of our luxury addresses. Take her out. Wine and dine her. Charm the hell out of her. Then lock that shit down, big brother."

"I don't have a lot of time to make our pretend union believable. Unfortunately for me, Michaela Knight is worse than a prickly porcupine. I can't imagine her warming up to me." I reckon wrestling a famished alligator might be easier than convincing Michaela to marry me after this morning's confrontation. "There's a lot at stake here. We can't lose our footing in this company."

"I agree," Slate says. "Dad is a hundred percent behind you. You have my vote. Wilder thinks you walk on water. Although physically incapacitated and stuck in a bed, Roman believes you'll kick ass. We all want you to have the position of CEO as much as you do."

"Replacing Dad is my ultimate goal. Niels threw a curve ball that could've derailed—"

"But it didn't. It's a minor shake up."

"It's a big fucking one."

"Nothing you can't handle."

I slam my hand against my desk. "It pisses me off I even have to jump through hoops like a circus seal to convince those tight ass stodgy old farts of my worth."

Until three months ago, my father, Soren König, was CEO of König Imperial Holdings, which includes the King Regency and the Pompadour 5-star hotels and luxury residencies. His recent heart attack changed everything. Thank God he's alive, but he can no longer keep the same hectic pace he thrives on. The onus is on me to preserve our legacy. It wasn't supposed to be this way. My older brother was the one groomed to replace Dad.

Since my great-grandfather started the company, a König has always sat at the helm. Even though he's in convalescence, Dad has a seat on the board. So do I. Slate, Wilder, and Roman also have a seat each. Thanks to our great-grandfather, who lost the controlling percentage to the public, the Königs are now in the minority—five against nine. The board never misses a chance to remind us. They always liked my father and my older brother.

They never warmed up to Slate, Wilder, or me. Since they consider Roman, the wild child who lands on the front of the celebrity pages a bit too often for their liking, they don't even bother to pretend to tolerate him. They might not say it, but it washes off them—having one less König to deal with at board meetings for the time being is a relief. Some days, it's like they expect us to kowtow to them before agreeing to some of our ideas. Assholes. To this day, they have the audacity to question our real intentions in working in the family business. They see us as four spoiled princes about to inherit the kingdom—with me being the most entitled one.

Like it or not, I'm stuck with them.

I have no other choice but to alter the board's perception and convince them I'm no longer a bed-hopper and—even though I'll never be Barron—I'm the *only* suitable contender. Niels Knight's desperation became my golden ticket when he barreled into my office unannounced, unwilling to budge until I granted him a meeting. Ironic... like father, like daughter.

In a pinch, he needed a little over two hundred million dollars—an astronomical sum for most. Pocket change for me. I was in a different kind of pinch. I needed an image makeover, stat. One look at Michaela's photo and I accepted Niels's merger-marriage request on the spot.

"Clearly, Michaela stormed in here without knowing what her father was up to." Slate's comment breaks me from my rumination. "I'm willing to bet my fortune, she knows by now."

"I hope so. I have no doubt Niels had his reasons for keeping this from her for this long, but now that the cat is out of the bag, he's forced to fess up. None of the women I date—"

"You mean, fuck."

"Thank you, choirboy."

He grins.

Asshole.

He's as much of a manwhore as I am. All four of us are. There's a reason the press dubs us, the filthy rich playboy kings.

"Like I was saying, none of my flighty one-night fucks would be able to step into the role of Mrs. König and dupe the board. Michaela Knight has the perfect pedigree—she's intelligent, elegant, poised, passionate, and incredibly beautiful. Another feather in her cap, she's used to the media's scrutiny."

She'd seamlessly fit into my world—into my wicked plan—like the queen she is.

"You have to find a way to lasso that filly—I mean, win over your runaway fiancée and put a ring on it," my brother says.

"You make it sound so easy."

"A little König charm and she'll be putty in your hands," Slate says.

"It's going to take a lot more than a little charm."

"Then turn the volume way up."

"That woman needs a *Master* to taper the hellion in her. The flare of rebellion in her green eyes as she flipped me the bird suggests you don't tame a woman like Michaela Knight. You fucking dominate her."

My brother nods slowly as a familiar cocky smile stretches his lips. "Good thing you hold a PhD in the subject."

I can't help my wicked grin.

Chapter 5

Michaela

My head spins like a cyclone all the way to Rhys's place. A thousand questions rattle in my brain. On numerous occasions I was tempted to call my father back because I didn't have the patience to wait, but I refrained. Something tells me once I have this discussion with him, my world will never be the same. It's like I'm a puppet on a string and I've lost all control.

The ride back seemed interminable. LA traffic and all.

Once I paid the cabbie, I slid out of the car and closed the door, the thumping sound as eerily scary as the lid of a coffin closing over me while I'm still alive. The moment I stepped into the main house to tell Keira I was back, she could tell something was wrong. There was no hiding it—stress was rolling off me. She had a thousand questions. I didn't have answers. I only have bits and pieces of information, and none of it makes a lick of sense. I promised her I'd spill my guts once I was able to get straight answers from my father.

Daddy, you have some explaining to do.

With my head hanging low, I make my way to the guesthouse. I kick off my high heels and shrug out of my pink dress in favor of shorts and a tank top. With my phone clenched in my hands, I walk to the living room, plop myself on the sofa, and video call my father.

When Daddy answers, his tired face fills the screen.

His green eyes, darker than mine, hold my gaze before his lips part in a sad smile.

My heart is beating so fast, I swear it's going to jump right out of my rib cage and start running back to New York City.

"I'm sorry, ladybug," he says.

I close my eyes. "Just rip off the Band-Aid."

"You have to look at me for this conversation, ladybug," he says.

I do.

He brings a glass to his lips and takes a sip of his red wine.

Wow. If my father is drinking in the afternoon at the office, this is worse than I thought—worse than I'm prepared for.

"The hotel has been on shaky legs for a while—"

"Why didn't you tell me?"

"I don't involve you in the financial parts of the business because I don't want you to worry. I'm supposed to take care of you."

"And you think I'm not worried right now? I'm going out of my mind with worry, Daddy. Fear has consumed me since we talked—"

"It was never my intention to put you in this position—"

"Perhaps you should've been honest with me from the beginning. I'm twenty-three years old. I'm a grown woman. I can handle whatever you're dealing with." *I hope.*

"I thought *I* could handle it—"

"How bad is it?" I cut to the chase.

He doesn't answer.

"Daddy, talk to me. Tell me everything."

"It's a colossal shit fest," he says.

Okay, not good.

"The short answer is, I'm a hair away from bankruptcy."

I stare at my father in cold shock while my heart tries to painfully reboot.

"Our loyal and dedicated employees count on me to put food on the table, pay their mortgages and send their kids to college," he says. "We have multigenerational families working in our hotel." Pride coats his words. "I couldn't let these people down. I couldn't let Mom down. Or you. I sunk every dime I had in my effort to keep from sinking—money from Mom's life insurance, my life savings, and the house is mortgaged to the hilt." He stares intently at me. "I even had to dip into the money Mom and I set aside for you. I had no choice if I wanted to cover the payroll." Another long pause. "I can't hold the staff responsible for my screw-ups."

"What about the house in the Hamptons?" I ask. "It's worth several hundreds of millions of dollars. Isn't there a way to use some of the equity?"

"I lied about the house in the Hamptons."

I flinch. "What do you mean?"

"I wasn't renting it on a long-term lease. I sold it four months ago to keep afloat."

I gasp in horror.

"You sold it without telling me?"

"I was drowning–back taxes, repairs needed for the upkeep of a heritage building as per New York State codes, and an inspection that didn't go too well." His eyes shift to a distant point. "On top of that, I'm still paying for your college degree and the colossal bill from my recent hospitalization, which are just about choking me." He purses his lips. When his green eyes meet mine, I can only read resignation and sadness. "As much as it kills me to admit this, the sale from of the house in the Hamptons was just a drop in the bucket. I was in way too deep for it to turn things around."

Oh God.

A lump forms in my throat at the thought of what I'm about to suggest, but I have to. What if it's a lifeline? "What about Mom's jewelry?"

"No. Never." Daddy shakes his head. He even adds a rapid finger wave. "That's off the table. That's yours."

"But, Daddy—"

"I said no, Michaela. I've lost my dignity and all my money. I've done enough to disrespect your mother's memory by nearly losing the family hotel. I refuse to pawn her jewelry. Those precious pieces are worth a fortune, and they're irreplaceable. Not to mention, many were your grandmother's and great-grandmother's. They'll remain in the bank's safe, unless you want to wear them. End of discussion."

I stare at him.

His lips turn up in a lopsided smile, but his eyes are veiled with sadness. "Your mother was always the brains of the operation, Mikki. If she were still alive, none of this would've happened."

You would never have married Thana.

"I've never been a numbers guy, which explains my predicament. I have nothing left to my name. I used every penny to save the hotel, but even that wasn't enough." Tears well in his eyes. "I thought I could dig myself out of this mess."

I suck in a shaky breath and lift my gaze to the ceiling.

Dear God.

"I'm sorry I failed you, ladybug."

My heart breaks at his words.

"Oh, Daddy, you didn't fail me. It's business. I wish you would've confided in me instead of shutting me out."

"I've already said everything I had to say on the subject."

His tone bodes no further discussion.

"Given her position and knowledge, didn't Thana try to do something to help?" I ask.

He lets out a sarcastic laugh. "Oh, she did something all right."

I frown my confusion.

"What does that mean?"

"Let me start from the beginning," he says.

"Please do."

"About five months ago, Thana started taking nighttime classes, claiming she wanted to be proactive to better help us navigate the ups and downs of the hospitality business. I didn't object. She knew things weren't looking too good. I thought she genuinely had my best interests at heart. Then all of a sudden, she declared she had to go to an intensive weeklong training in Tucson that was going to propel us forward. Once again, I was all for it. She left on Thursday, even though the classes started on Monday, stating she wanted to avoid being jetlagged by arriving a few days early. She didn't call much, but she sent a few text messages. I was too busy to make much of it. Monday morning rolls around, and my older brother barges into my office upon his return from a tech conference in San Diego, waving his phone, declaring he knew I had married a bitch, and he had proof she was two-timing me."

"What proof did Uncle Ian have?"

"Thana wasn't in Tucson. She was in San Diego with her lover."

"What?" I frown.

"She was cheating on me."

"Are you sure? I'm not trying to defend Thana, but that's a bold accusation."

"Ian caught her walking hand-in-hand with a man—"

"What if it was someone else?"

"Thana has a unique name. Furthermore, she's five-eleven, a natural redhead with long hair, blue eyes, and fair skin. Even with heavy makeup, it's a struggle to hide her freckles. What are the odds it would be someone else?"

Okay, he has a good point.

Still, I find it hard to believe Thana would cheat on my father. After all, my stepmother loves to remind me I'm stuck with her forever because Daddy is the love of her life.

"Your uncle didn't want to jump to conclusions," Daddy says. "It could've been a family friend. The guy's much older than me. I'm going to guess he's in his late sixties or early seventies."

"Wow."

Thana is thirty-five. Daddy is fifty-two. They've been married for a year and a half. They dated for five months before Daddy announced they were getting married. That was a dark day in my life. So much so, I went to Mom's grave to talk to her. Daddy had his heart attack five months after marrying Thana. Coincidence? I think not.

"Ian trailed behind the couple long enough to confirm his suspicions," Daddy adds. "Suddenly, the pair stopped and sat on a bench. Thana sat *on* the man's lap, her arms laced around his neck."

"Good Lord."

"Ian didn't think twice. He pulled out his phone and recorded what was unfolding in front of his eyes. He had barely pressed the button on his app, when the man planted an open mouth kiss on my wife's lips. The video clip showed tongue action and..."—Daddy purses his lips in a tilt of disdain—"the man rubbing her private parts over her dress."

I'm dumbfounded.

I don't hate my stepmother because she was replacing my mom in my father's life—well, that's a big part of it, but it's not the only reason. I can't stand Thana because she isn't trustworthy. She acts differently around my father than she does around everyone else. Especially the staff. Mom always treated employees with respect. Thana talks down to people and treats them like servants. When she took over running the hotel while Daddy was recovering from his heart attack, morale went way down. Since Daddy was battling for his life after a scary brush with death, I didn't want to add to his burden, so I kept my mouth shut. I always had visions of running the hotel side-by-side with my father, Thana's arrival changed that.

"Even though Uncle Ian was dying to expose her as the lying and cheating piece of shit she is, he didn't feel it was the kind of conversation to have over the phone. He wanted to tell me face-to-face."

"Did you confront her when she got back from San Diego?" I ask.

"I didn't."

"Why not? She's a cheater!"

His green eyes turn stone cold. "She's far more than that."

"I don't understand."

"You know the saying, *when it rains, it pours*—"

"She was cheating on you with several men?"

"That wouldn't have been as scandalous as what she did."

"Please don't tell me she fired staff without your knowledge."

"Thana was embezzling money from the hotel."

My mouth drops open and my eyes bulge out of my skull.

His loaded words are the equivalent of being pushed off the roof of a New York City skyscraper.

"Wh–what?" I ask when I'm able to pick up my jaw from the floor.

"She was skimming money from me and lying to my face," Daddy says.

Hearing it a second time doesn't soften the blow.

"How?"

"She had access to all the accounts and she had signing authority. Unknowingly, I had handed a coldhearted thief everything I owned on a silver platter. And the bitch took full advantage of it."

My eyes widen in shock. "You've got to be kidding me."

"I'm as serious as a heart attack—"

"Daddy! Don't say things like that!"

"Sorry, ladybug, it's just a figure of speech."

"In your case, it isn't."

"You're right. To answer your question, no, I'm not kidding. Since Thana took over running the hotel after my heart attack, she had her filthy tentacles everywhere. By the time I recuperated and I was strong enough to get back to work, she had a nice little setup that allowed her to skim money from me practically undetected. She was good at covering her tracks."

"How did you find out?"

"It turns out her cheating on me—and wanting to spend time with her lover—was a blessing in disguise."

"That doesn't even make sense. How can a cheating wife be a blessing?"

"After Uncle Ian left my office, it was a struggle to contain my rage and conduct business as usual. When I finally managed to regain my composure and lose myself in work, I received a phone call that unraveled my world."

"Who called you?"

"A new bank manager was assigned to our account," he says. "I thought it was a courtesy call, but it wasn't. He was calling to inform me I was overdrawn on the business account and I wouldn't be able to cover the employees' direct deposit wages and pre-authorize payments to vendors. I argued and told him he was mistaken. I explained I had deposited money on the previous Friday. He told me a large sum had been transferred that morning to a foreign account. I practically laughed in his face. He stood his ground, stating he was looking at the transaction on his screen. Everything in my body was tingling. I requested an urgent meeting."

"And?"

"I came back from the bank confused and angry. Things weren't adding up. I confessed everything to Ian, and he suggested I hire an investigator. That was two strikes against my wife, and he felt it was important to find out what other skeletons were hiding in her closet. Demanding an explanation from Thana was pointless. No way was she going to be forthcoming about the discrepancies in our bank accounts. I needed ammunition before confronting her."

"Private investigators are expensive. I thought the hotel was on shaky ground?" I ask.

"Ian fronted me the money," Daddy says.

Uncle Ian manages all the computer technicians and the team responsible for preventing hackers from stealing students' personal data at the NYU School of Law. No wonder he would know who to approach to secure the services of a reputable PI.

"Thank God Uncle Ian was able to help."

Daddy nods. "I'm not her only victim," he says.

"No way."

"The investigators tracked down three former employers she embezzled money from—"

"Why didn't those employers say anything when you called to check out her references?"

"They're all married men," he says.

"So?"

"Thana manipulated them into having an affair, which she meticulously recorded as an insurance policy. She was blackmailing them. They paid her off to buy her silence.

Since I was a widower, she used another tactic to steal from me."

"What an evil witch." I'm raging with anger. "She conned her way into our family."

"She did, but I'm her last victim," Daddy says.

"What do you mean by that?"

"By the time Thana came back from her little lovers' getaway trip, the investigators had placed surveillance equipment in the hotel and at our house. There were detectors on all the electronic devices—phones, laptops, and computers. Extra cameras were installed in every blind spot of the hotel. And, they requested access to our archive of surveillance footage. My wife had no idea she was walking into a trap. We were ready for Thana Annunziata to hang herself. It didn't take long for the truth to come out."

"What did they find out?"

I'm eager to know how the bitch duped my father.

"Hindsight is 20/20, but at the time, there was no reason for me to suspect my wife was backstabbing me. In her role as accountant, Thana had access to our bank statements, and she was the front person for our vendor relationships. Giving her more signing authority made sense—we were married. I trusted her. As I was getting back on my feet, I never changed the signing authority on our accounts. I didn't think I had to. According to the investigators' findings, she started skimming money from the accounts while I was still in the hospital, recovering from the heart attack—"

"What a lowlife!"

Daddy smirks and nods. "A little more digging revealed she was also faking vendor payments and pocketing the money."

I let out a strangled growl of anger.

Not that I condone violence, but right now, I just want to fly back to New York and kill the bitch.

I rub a hand over my face and let out a long sigh.

"I know, I know." My father's dejected expression says it all. "Thana was cooking the books, falsifying data to hide her treachery and theft. Since I was already on shaky ground, this was the kiss of death for the hotel. She stole a lot of money from us. A lot."

"How could she?"

"I've asked myself that question a million times, ladybug. I'm so angry with myself for being so blind. I admit, things weren't looking great, but her treason did me in."

I knew the woman was two-faced, I didn't know she was a criminal.

"You're going to press charges, right?" I ask.

"Without the investigation, I wouldn't have enough proof. But there's a mountain of evidence against her. I'm going all the way. I want Thana to pay."

"I'm a hundred percent behind you. Is she still living at the house?"

"When she got back from San Diego, I pretended like nothing had changed until the investigation was wrapped up. Since we hadn't been intimate in a while... it didn't change much—"

I lift a hand to stop him. "I don't need to know that part, Daddy."

"All that to say, it was a struggle to bite my tongue and not lash out at her, but I wasn't going to do anything to cause her to become suspicious."

"Please tell me you're going to ask for a divorce?"

"I'm done with her. I served her with divorce papers this morning. I'm giving her until tomorrow night to pack her shit and get out of our lives."

"Good for you." I nod my approval. "You're too good for her. She doesn't deserve you."

"No, she doesn't," Daddy says.

"I gather she didn't take being served with divorce papers well."

"She came barging into my office, livid. She had the audacity to deny her wrongdoings. I promised myself I would keep my cool, but I lost it and it turned into World War III. That's why you couldn't get a hold of either of us this morning. When Thana started throwing lamps, chairs, and whatever she could get her hands on at me, my executive assistant called the police. I'm glad she did. God knows how things would've turned out. We were both so angry."

"At least it's over," I say. The news of my father kicking Thana to the curb and out of his life should make me want to celebrate. However, Daddy shared so much heavy stuff, it's impossible to rejoice. "That's why you said earlier it was just the two of us against the world again."

"There's more."

That's not the answer I expected.

"Daddy, your cheater of a wife was stealing money from you. How can there be more?"

My father considers me for a long beat. "This is... pretty bad, ladybug."

"Daddy, you're scaring me. Whatever it is, just tell me."

"You know I'm behind this morning's PR stunt."

"You've already confessed that much."

"But you don't know why I did it."

"You're going to tell, right?"

"We no longer own the Villiers Grand."

Everything pointed to it, Phoenix alluded to it, and although not yet mentioned, it was implied in the conversation. Still, hearing my father say it without sugar coating it is like having my heart pierced by an arrow.

"Phoenix König was willing to buy the hotel as is," Daddy

tells me. "As it stood, I would've had to put in money I didn't have to get it up to par to secure the most from the sale." He pauses. "Phoenix is the only buyer I approached who was willing to accept all my terms—even the most outrageous ones." Another pause. "It may seem like I sold you to a powerful billionaire to save the hotel, but I have my reasons—"

"I'm not marrying that man," I tell him. "He's a complete stranger. How could you, Daddy? This isn't the early nineteen hundreds." The floodgates open. "You can't just marry me off like that. I'm not a commodity. How come I don't have a say in this? Why would you do that to me? Is it that you don't love me?—"

"I love you with every piece of me, ladybug. I did this for you—"

"No! Just no!"

"It's the only way, ladybug."

"I am not marrying Phoenix König," I say through clenched teeth like a pissed off three-year-old.

"Listen to me, Michaela!" The sudden edge in Daddy's voice causes my head to jerk back. "Phoenix agreed to one of my particular demands—one I was willing to die for to ensure it was part of the deal. If you back out, nothing—and I mean, nothing—will save the Villiers Grand. We can't do that to Mom."

Good Lord. My father has never guilt tripped me before today.

Chapter 6

Phoenix

After Slate left my office, I was caught on a conference call that droned on for a half hour longer than necessary, as my lawyers went through the lists of additional—and unrealistic—amendments-slash-demands to a contract for the potential purchase of twin family-owned hotels in Cleveland. The management is shit and as inflexible as an oak tree. The location isn't prime, but you don't build a hotel empire solely on five-star accommodations. Variety is the key to success. The plan is to turn those new acquisitions into four-star hotels. They'll pad our bank account just as nicely.

Alas, the two brothers who own the hotels think I'm shortchanging them. I beg to differ. It's a generous offer. They're nitpicking. Translation, they're grating on my last nerve. Sometimes, you have to know when to fold.

Once that was behind me, I dived right back into my day. I'm fully immersed in last week's sales figures of our Texas Pompadour hotels when the phone on my desk rings.

I pick it up.

"Yes?"

"Mr. König," the temp, says on the other end. "There's a Miss Michaela Knight on the line."

A cocky grin stretches my lips. "You can put her through."

I have something you need, kitty cat.

I must admit, I can't remember ever being equally amused, intrigued and attracted to a woman like this before.

Miss Knight breaks the mold.

"Is she the same Michaela Knight you're going to marry?" the temp asks.

The press is busy putting their twist on how a high-profile COO can keep a passionate romance a secret in this day and age. I doubt the press would've paid me nearly as much attention if it weren't for my former boy group days. Our publicist is losing her mind. She's itching to put out a press release with my side of the story in the hopes of containing the frenzy. Until I hear back from Niels or Michaela Knight—ideally, both—I'm keeping my mouth shut.

"I understand with social media the lines between privacy and what should be public are blurred. Just so we're clear, I don't discuss my personal life with my staff. Ever." My tone is curt. "You're a temp. Do you think that's an appropriate question?"

I might come across like an asshole, but I don't need too many people poking around and sniffing out my bluff.

"Of course, sir. I'm so sorry, sir. I should never—"

"Please put the call through."

"Right away, sir."

I grab my Montblanc pen and tap it against the desk.

"Hello, Phoenix," her melodic voice comes through the receiver.

"Michaela, darling. Don't tell me. You already miss me."

"Oh, get over yourself, you royal prick!" I can practically see her roll her eyes at the phone.

"Always so agreeable, kitty cat."

"Stop calling me kitty cat. I'm not a feline!"

"You could've fooled me. I'm still licking my wounds from your claws slashing my soul."

"From hotel mogul to poet? Don't quit your day job, König."

"For the record, I miss your sweet disposition."

"You're insufferable!"

"Yet, you call to hear my voice."

There's a stretch of silence on the other end.

"Did you hang up on me, Michaela?"

"No, I'm still here."

"How can I help you?" I'm twisting the knife in.

"You know exactly why I'm calling."

"I have many talents, sweetheart, reading minds isn't one of them." I'm not going to make it easy for her.

"I left my driver's license at your office and I need it back," she says.

"If you give me your address, I can have it delivered within the hour."

She doesn't respond.

"Michaela?"

"Yes."

"Did you hear what I said?"

"I did," she says. "I thought— Maybe it's— I mean—" She lets out a long sigh. "Can I come by and pick it up instead?"

"Suit yourself. I'll leave it at the concierge desk downstairs in the lobby."

"I was hoping I might pick it up from you."

"You're eager to see me again?"

"Are you sure your ego isn't too big for your office? Or even the entire hotel?" She's as quick as a whip.

"I have something you need and you're giving me attitude?" I pour salt on an open wound. "I don't have time for this—"

"Wait! Phoenix, don't hang up. Can we talk in person?"

"I'm afraid to let you near me," I say. "Your words were so violent, they practically gave me whiplash. I'm not sure if it's a learned skill, but you make quite the entrance and exit, Miss Knight. I'm still recovering from the way you torpedoed out of my office. I'm not sure I can take another serving of what you're dishing out today."

"Okay, I deserve that," she says. "Admittedly, I flew off the handle a little."

A lot.

"In my defense, I didn't have all the facts, so... I might've been at a disadvantage."

"Is that an apology?"

"I apologize for not having all the facts."

Oh, that's sneaky.

"Do you have all the facts now?" I ask.

"Yes."

"You spoke to your father?"

"I did."

"He told you everything?"

"He did." The fire in her voice is gone, snuffed out.

I can't even imagine how she must feel right now. She has a heavy burden to carry.

"I'm curious," I say.

"About what?"

"I'm still scratching my head, trying to understand the motives behind this morning's publicity stunt. I get that your father is walking a tightrope, but that was an impetuous move—one that could've made me reconsider our agreement. The contract was signed, sealed, and delivered. I gave him my word. I wouldn't renege on the deal."

"I can explain when I see you."

I nod, even though she can't see me.

I weigh my next words as Slate's advice rings in my ears.

"Are you free tonight?" I ask.

"Why?"

"Down, girl. It's just a question. You either have plans or you don't."

"I'm free."

"Let's have an early dinner. Six o'clock?"

"You're not afraid I'll try to stab you with a fork?"

"On second thought—"

"I'm not violent. I'm just vocal," she says.

"I don't have to fear for my life?"

"Not today..."

I chuckle.

"So, we're on?"

"Yes." One word that holds so many possibilities.

"Why don't we exchange phone numbers. That way you can text me your address, and I'll have a car pick you up."

"Oh, okay. Thanks." There's no hiding the trembling in her voice.

"I'd suggest a restaurant at one of our many hotels, but we need a private setting for this conversation."

"We do."

"You're docile all of a sudden," I say. "Such a contrast from earlier. I much prefer you submissive."

"If you're looking for a submissive wife, König, get a freaking mail-order bride!"

My fire-breathing dragon roars to life.

Chapter 7

Michaela

I'm sitting at the kitchen table in Rhys's guesthouse, folded over my laptop, my nose practically touching the screen, drooling all over the keyboard.

"Holy Mother of Hotness have mercy on my heart and my lady parts!" I say, as I scroll down another page filled with photos of the gorgeous man I despise.

My God, he wears a suit like it's nobody's business.

I'm unwilling to admit how many times I've fanned my face—and between my legs—since starting my detective work.

I didn't have nearly enough time this morning to do proper research on King König because I got sidetracked by the patriarch's heart attack. No way am I walking into a second meeting with Phoenix without knowing what I'm up against. I'm not naïve. I'm fully aware I'm no match for a mogul tycoon, and given everything my father revealed, my hands are tied. Still, a background check makes sense.

I click on the back button to return to the page of results.

As I scroll down, a headline catches my eyes.

'PHOENIX KÖNIG. BEST SHIRTLESS MOMENTS.'

Interesting.

I double-click.

My head jerks back at the magnificence before me.

The man commands respect and oozes undeniable masculinity and scorching hot sexuality in a white shirt and tailored black pants—no doubt bespoke—but shirtless... there are no words.

How can you bestow such good looks to one man, God? What about the rest of the male gender?

Geez.

No wonder I wanted the man I hate to manhandle me two minutes after meeting him.

It's so unlike me.

The number of gorgeous men who wear perfectly fitted suits is as common as potholes in New York City. Not to mention, a parade of wealthy men stays at our hotel on any given day. And let's not forget about my circle of friends and acquaintances. I'm no stranger to good-looking men. Which is why I struggle to explain this strong attraction for a man I should loathe.

No, a man I *do* loathe.

It's like this weird kinky love-hate pull I can't wrap my head around.

Must be the California sun.

The heat is frying my brain.

My phone vibrates on the table next to me, forcing my eyes away from my laptop and the Adonis god.

Speaking of the beautiful bastard...

King Kong Tycoon.

I couldn't resist. I saved his name as his cheeky moniker.

What can I say? The devil made me do it.

My eyes grow to the size of saucers when I read his text.

King Kong Tycoon: The car should be at your place in twenty minutes.

Shit! I lost track of time.

Michaela: I'll be ready.

King Kong Tycoon: Looking forward to getting to know you better.

I swallow hard.

Michaela: See you soon, Phoenix.

King Kong Tycoon: See you soon, my little feline.

I roll my eyes.

I clench my phone against my heart and lift my eyes to the ceiling to where I'm sure my mother is enjoying a martini while chatting up God's ear.

I'm doing this for you, Mom.

Conscious I have little time to waste, I jump to my feet and rush to the bathroom to brush my teeth. Then, I run to the bedroom to change.

We were supposed to meet for dinner, but Phoenix is eager to get some answers, so he suggested a late lunch instead. I was tempted to be spiteful and tell him my afternoon was booked solid, but I decided against it. Putting this meeting off is only delaying the inevitable.

My life as I know it is a thing of the past.

Done with.

Bye, bye, bye.

Finito.

No más.

Sayonara.

Au revoir.

Hasta la vista, baby.

I heard everything my father had to say, although it's not computing fully yet, I accept my new reality—I'm his only lifeline.

Sigh.

Deciding on something to wear when time is ticking would've taken me far longer back home given the size of my wardrobe, but here, I only have a few items of clothing to choose from.

In no time, I'm dressed and move my attention to my makeup and hair. I have a love-hate relationship with my short pixie cut. It's in the growing stages. Most times I don't recognize the woman staring back at me in the mirror because my hair was literally a curtain. Given I'm pressed for time, I'm glad I don't have to fight with a mane that always seemed to have a mind of its own. I touch up my makeup, applying a more in-your-face lipstick color and slide into my high heels. I give myself one last inspection and nod, satisfied with the end result.

Not bad.

Feminine, but screams of 'I mean business.'

I run back to the living room and snatch my phone from the kitchen table.

Three minutes to spare.

My fingers fly on the screen as I shoot Keira a quick text.

Michaela: I have to run out. I'll be back early evening.

Keira: What's with you today? It's like in those old-time cartoons when the Tasmanian devil enters the scene in a tornado swirl. You're like a whirlwind—In. Out. In. Out.

Michaela: Phoenix and I have to put our heads together to figure out how to manage the media. It's far more civilized to do this over lunch.

There's more to it, but Keira doesn't need to know. Not yet, anyway.

Keira: Ooooooh. You two hit it off?

Yeah, like a meteor hits earth at lightning speed before crashing in an explosion of fragments, causing devastation in its wake.

Michaela: You're reading into things. There's a lot to talk about. A face-to-face is easier.

Keira: How was the conversation with your dad? Is your stepmom behind this fiasco?

Michaela: I have to go.

Keira: When do I get the full story?

Michaela: Later. I promise.

Keira: You better.

Michaela: You have my word.

Keira: So you'll spill your guts to pay for your dinner?

Michaela: Deal!

Keira: Okay, I can wait a few hours.

I can imagine the grin on her face.

Michaela: I'll text when I'm about to come back.

Keira: Sounds good. Have fun.

I doubt it.

I'm sure Keira thinks I'm crazy, but I can't talk to her until I talk to Phoenix. I used the excuse of a heat-induced headache as a copout to stay locked up in the guesthouse. In reality, I wanted to Google the hell out of Phoenix König. Not that I had to since Daddy sent me a dossier compiled by the same private investigators who found dirt on my soon-to-be-ex-stepmother.

Pretty CIA.

When Daddy is facing a financial conundrum, he takes a page right out of a Mark Greaney thriller novel. I'm impressed. There's so much more than meets the eye about King König. I store my laptop and run out the door because the last thing I want is for the chauffeur to honk. Keira is already suspicious as it is.

~

As I sit in the back of the chauffeured dark-blue Bentley, my mind wanders. This morning I woke up with the intention of enjoying Rhys's spectacular pool and spending the day hanging out with my friend while working on my tan. Several hours later, my world is turned upside down. I'm on my way to meet a man I swore to never see again—a man who holds my fate in the palm of his hands.

The joke is on me.

If being in Phoenix König's presence for a mere twenty minutes sent my system into overdrive, I can't imagine what it's going to be like spending a few hours with him.

There's no turning back.

He holds the bargaining chips, and he has the power to play me like a puppet. I just want to understand what my future will look like.

After talking to my father, I oscillated between anger at Thana, bafflement at how Daddy shut me out of something pretty freaking important, and fear at how I unknowingly became the last pawn my father had to play. But, just like Daddy, I made a promise to my mother on her death bed. I will honor it even if it kills me.

I brush my hand over my dress, smoothing the fabric.

I shouldn't care this much about how I look, but that doesn't stop me from pulling out my compact to check my makeup. Again.

Stop it!

I don't give a flying flip about King Kong Tycoon's opinion of my wardrobe.

I'm about to slide my compact back into my handbag, when a sign catches my eye.

Marina del Rey Harbor?!

I stick my nose to the window and gawk at the incredible view.

We're meeting at a seaside restaurant?

Phoenix said he wanted us to meet in a private setting, this isn't what I had pictured in my mind.

As the car crawls to a stop, the door flies open.

I inhale through the nose and exhale.

This is it, Mikki.

I look up, expecting to meet the eager gaze of a courteous valet, but I'm dead wrong.

"You made it." Phoenix flashes me a warm smile.

For a few beats, I just stare at him, my mouth gaping.

His earlier business attire was flawless and screamed power. This more casual, but equally impeccable, head-to-toe black look is badassness personified. His shirt frames his broad-shoulders, making him appear imposing. His tailored pants accentuate thick thighs. And those shoes... I'm guessing also bespoke. I'm willing to bet money I don't have, the man has a spectacular ass. My eyes roam back to his gorgeous face and I thank God his shades hide his mesmerizing eyes.

"Cat got your tongue, kitty cat?"

I snap out of my trance.

"Of course I made it. As if your chauffeur was going to drive me anywhere else than our meeting destination?" There's an involuntary edge to my voice.

"You're in fine fighting mood, as usual," he says.

"What can I say? I'm always ready to rumble."

"That could be misconstrued as a double entendre," he says.

I clear my throat. "Don't get any ideas. This is strictly business."

"For once we agree." He extends his hand. "Shall we?"

I'm perfectly capable of getting out of the car by myself, but I'm not immune to his gallantry. I slide my hand into his.

Bad move.

I could've ignored the electric current rushing through my veins when he held my wrist captive against his muscular chest earlier, but now that his hand encircles mine, there's no denying the pulse of desire coursing through me.

What is going on with me?

He pulls me out of the vehicle and we stand toe to toe.

He shifts his attention to the vehicle and taps three times on the hood.

My getaway car rolls off, leaving me behind in the enemy camp.

Dammit.

Now I'm trapped.

Returning his focus on me, he slides his sunglasses to the top of his head.

Those eyes... I can't even pinpoint that shade of blue.

And that hair.

This man has zero imperfections. So unfair.

Phoenix gives me a onceover.

I return the favor.

I take him all in—inch, by inch, by inch.

My high heels do nothing to put a dent in the difference of height. Phoenix towers over me. Mind you, I'm only five-two, but this guy is well over six feet tall.

Height is sexy on a man.

And this man is a tall glass of smoking hot sexiness.

As my inner voice chatters on, a familiar smug smile tugs at the edges of Phoenix's mouth. "You like what you see, kitty cat?"

I roll my eyes hard.

It's the best I can do to avoid admitting I was openly gawking at him.

"It's okay," he says. "You can tell me if you do." His words drip with cocksureness.

Darn. He caught me red-handed, but I'm not willing to cave in that easily.

"I don't know what you're talking about."

"It's just the two of us, Michaela." My name shouldn't sound this good on his lips. "It'll remain our little secret."

I roll my eyes again. Speaking would only betray me.

"Fair enough. I'll go first." His gaze rakes over my body, eating me up with blatant appreciation. He leans in until his breath brushes against my cheek. His closeness is enough to send my deprived system into overdrive.

I close my eyes, relishing the sensation.

"You look absolutely beautiful."

To my detriment, I'm not immune to the raspiness of his voice.

I clear my throat and take a step back, distancing myself from him.

Call it self-preservation.

I could blame the scorching California sun for the reason my body is heating up like I'm swimming in a pool of lava, but I'd be lying to myself.

His blue eyes drop to my feet. "You wear those well."

I'm tongue tied, which is unusual for me.

I'm stumped as to how to reply. And I have no clue what to make of the glint in his eyes... the one that threatens to make me forget he's the enemy.

That unsettling feeling returns full force, so my claws come out.

"Save it, Phoenix. I'm here, aren't I?"

"I can't win with you." He lets out an exasperated breath. "Why can't you just accept a damn compliment?"

"Thank you. There. No need to butter me up, King Kong Tycoon."

"King Kong Tycoon?" He frowns his confusion. "The press has many labels for me, but that's one I've never heard before."

"It's an original. Just like yours truly!" I point at my chest.

"What's behind the mocking moniker?" he asks.

"Well, you're the giant ape in the luxury hotel industry, the press calls you King König, and apparently, you're a tycoon—"

"Apparently?" His eyebrows shoot to his forehead. "Just so we're clear, Michaela, I've earned my stripes."

"Noted."

"As for my last name, König *literally* means king in German."

"Oh. How did I miss that in my research?"

Crap. The admittance was an overshare.

He smiles.

In my haste, I forgot my shades. That's a liability because his smile is blinding.

"You've Googled me?"

I respond with a noncommittal shrug.

"And you think you know everything there is to know about me?" he asks.

"Something tells me you're a man of many, many layers."

Darn. That came out so breathy.

Unintentionally, I used my seductive voice. Clearly, she's in connivance with my inner voice to sabotage me.

"Good thing you have three-hundred-sixty days to discover my many layers..."

My precarious reality slaps me right across the face. I swallow a lump in my throat and force myself to appear confident, even though I'm fully aware that aggravating the man who can help save our family hotel might not be a good idea.

"Do you own the entire harbor?" I'm sure he doesn't, but I need to change the subject. Fast.

The edges of his mouth twitch, but he doesn't smile... except with his gorgeous eyes. "I'm *just* a multibillionaire—not quite a trillionaire yet," he says. "My brothers and I each own a boat. I figured it's the safest place for us to meet."

"You're not planning on kidnapping me and taking me to some remote private island until I agree to this merger-marriage, right? I don't want to disappear, never to be found."

He flinches, visibly baffled.

The fact the thought comes to mind indicates how surreal this day has been so far.

"You have a hell of an imagination," he tells me.

"You're a complete stranger."

"You're the one who wanted to meet in person," he says. "I was ready to leave your driver's license with the concierge, but no, you wanted a face-to-face, and now you're giving me attitude?"

"I expected to have my feet firmly planted on the ground. When the Bentley dropped me off, I thought perhaps we were meeting at a seaside restaurant, not on your getaway boat."

"Complete privacy is imperative. Meeting at a restaurant is far too risky. Hence, why we're here!" He drags a hand down his face. "Are we going to argue about everything?"

I square my shoulders. "Well, I've never been sailing before." I don't answer his question. Why make a promise I'm not going to keep, right?

"You've never been on a cruise?"

"It's never appealed to me," I tell him. "Too many people in a confined space."

"And no debauched spring break parties on a boat in the Caribbean or in Mexico while you were in college?"

"No. I'm a good girl—always have been." I flash him an innocent smile and bat my eyelashes. I'm only missing the halo. "Since I'm a virgin, I hope I can handle it."

He cocks an eyebrow. "Didn't you tell me you weren't a virgin this morning?"

I blush from ear to ear.

"I mean, I'm a sea virgin. I hope I won't get seasick." I try to save face. "I'd hate to embarrass myself."

"Don't worry. We're not setting sail. So you can toss the kidnapping plot out the window," he says. "We're just going to enjoy a nice lunch on the water, without having to worry about prying eyes, anyone within earshot, or paparazzi."

"Are you going to dazzle me with your cooking skills?" I ask.

"No. It wouldn't make sense to poison you this early in the game. I need you alive and kicking." He stretches his lips into an evil grin.

"Not funny!"

"I thought it was." The evil grin morphs into an arresting smile.

Bastard.

"The chefs at the Pompadour worked their magic. I don't think you'll be disappointed."

"Sounds like I get to live another day and I get to enjoy a spectacular lunch."

He chuckles.

"Let's go onboard and get this business meeting on its way."

"Okay."

We start walking.

"My boat is docked right at the end. Her name is *Daniela*. She's the one with the American flag and the flag with the king chess piece wearing a crown."

"You named your boat after your best hookup, König?" I laugh. "Man, she must've been something else." It's a low blow, but I can't help it.

His face turns somber.

Fuck, I put my foot in my mouth.

"No. I didn't name my boat after my best fuck." He takes a deep breath in. "It was my mom's name. She passed away—"

"I'm so sorry, Phoenix." I feel like the worst individual on the planet. I deserve the guillotine for that insensitive remark. "That was out of line."

"You didn't know."

I shake my head in response because it's best to keep my mouth shut.

He keeps talking, oblivious to my utter shame.

"My father, brothers, and I honor Mom's memory on our boats. Daniela Graciela Alandra Emiliana Peleritti was an Italian Argentine, born in Córdoba. Italians and Argentinians tend to give their kids multiple middle names. Hence, why Mom had three. Dad's yacht is named *Bella Daniela.* He used to call Mom, *Bella.* These days, Roman uses it since Dad doesn't use it as much. Slate and Wilder have their own yacht and use it in rotation. They named their boat, Alandra. The name means defender. Mom was the ultimate momma bear, even when we were grown men. She carried a great deal of guilt at not being able to *prevent* my older brother's death. Barron's boat was named The Peleritti. We sold it after he died —it carried too many memories."

I'm all choked up. "What a beautiful way to honor your mom."

"Yeah." A smile that doesn't reach his eyes appears on his gorgeous lips. "Let's go," he says.

"Okay."

We keep walking.

"There she is," Phoenix says.

Since my eyes are trained to my feet to avoid getting my heels stuck between the planks of the boardwalk, I'm unprepared when I look up.

Whoa.

"That's not a boat. That's a yacht!"

"Sixty feet of smooth sailing when I take her out at sea," he says matter-of-factly. "Come on, I'll help you onboard." Phoenix is already taking my hand into his.

Just like earlier, his touch ignites my body.

The effect he has on me screws with my head.

I balance my shoe on the first stair, grip the rail, and climb onto the luxury vessel.

If I could whistle, I would.

I may not like the guy, but he surely knows how to live.

The sleek, plush and streamlined interior of Phoenix's yacht matches the unquestionable elegance that's so prevalent at the Pompadour. The space is expansive and to my surprise, inviting. I have nothing to gauge this yacht against, but I suspect this baby cost an obscene amount of money.

"This is—" I search for my words. "It's so luxurious."

"I wanted it to be comfortable."

"Comfortable? You could live on this yacht year-round."

"I have," he tells me. "Not so much anymore. My brothers and I completed a luxury tri-tower residency complex six months ago. Along with the house we each own, we own a penthouse suite in the new residencies. We reserved the top two floors of each of the three buildings and never released them to the market. A König heir or one of our cousins occupies those coveted suites. Each top floor has two large penthouse suites. Irish twins Slate and Wilder share a floor in the same building. Roman and I live in separate buildings. For now, neither of us has a neighbor. The suites on the floor right below ours are an exact replica of our suites, we just don't call them penthouses."

"It's good to be Phoenix König. Heck, it's good to be a König, period."

I thought I had seen it all in New York. I was wrong. There's money and then there's König money. Phoenix's life is completely different from mine. I'm a bit intimidated by his wealth.

Can I really pull this off?

Can I handle playing the role of wife to a multibillionaire tycoon who sits at the helm of a multinational conglomerate?

"Most days it's good to be me." His response jolts me back to the moment.

"You're sitting on top of the world." I extend my arms in my attempt to encompass his universe. "What would a guy like you have to worry about?"

"Sometimes my name feels like a heavy weight I have to carry. Every day, I'm reminded I'm responsible for a legacy... and the livelihood of thousands of people who count on me. The implications of screwing up have a ripple effect."

His words hit me at the core.

Although our family hotel doesn't employ nearly as many people as Phoenix's, I get it.

I offer him a sad smile. "I understand. After all, that's why I'm standing here."

Chapter 8

Phoenix

Even if we're docked, nothing beats spending time on the yacht. The sun, the open air and the lull of the water against the boat help me forget everything else—even if it's for a brief moment. Suggesting this meeting place isn't only about seeking privacy, it's a refuge where I can leave my COO-slash-CEO hat at the door.

After a satisfying meal, an assortment of delectable desserts and the finest wine money can buy, Michaela sits across from me at the small dining table, her back facing the window, and the sun washing over her. She radiates.

I take another sip of the red Bordeaux, examining her over the rim of my glass. She's watching me watching her. We've been sizing each other up since we sat down.

A penny for her thoughts...

Mine aren't virtuous. She's very fuckable.

My cock hardens for what seems like the thirtieth time since she stepped out of the Bentley as my gaze falls to her pretty lips.

They're as tempting as the rest of her.

Her nude lipstick is long gone, revealing soft pink flesh.

What I would do to that mouth...

With my cock between her lips, she wouldn't be able to spit fire.

I stifle an evil laugh.

There's no shortage of gorgeous and willing women in LA. Until Dad's recent health scare, I made sure to take full advantage of the plethora of beauties the city has to offer. But I've never met anyone quite like the woman sitting across from me.

Michaela Knight is in a league of her own.

I'm not sure I'd say I have a type. However, I've never been with a woman with short hair. Perhaps it's because I've never met a woman as striking as Michaela. There's nothing detracting from her exquisite beauty.

And then there's the knockout body that gets my blood pumping like the turbines of a fucking submarine—breasts that would fit perfectly in the palms of my hands, a slim waist, curvy hips, and that perky ass I want to bite.

She looks delectable and utterly feminine in a bright yellow dress that accentuates her best assets. The dress from earlier screamed business. This one sends a more subtle message. One I like a lot.

The V-neck isn't pronounced, but that does little to rein in my less than holy thoughts. The bottom part of the dress hits below the knee like a fucking tease.

Lace, silk, or satin?

I'm dying to know her preference in lingerie.

Scratch that.

I'm dying to rip whatever she's hiding underneath with my teeth to get to the good stuff. If you're the lucky bastard to crack Michaela's tough as nails armor, I'm certain you'll discover honey sweetness hidden between her legs.

She's flawless and pretty in a way that doesn't require ten

pounds of makeup and revealing clothes that leave little to the imagination to stop traffic. Something tells me she's oblivious to the effect she has on the opposite sex.

I like this pretty new toy.

"Thank you again for the delicious lunch," she says, breaking the palpable sexual tension between us.

"I can't take credit for anything other than ordering my favorites. Our exceptional chefs did all the hard work."

"Well, thank you for ordering so well."

"You're welcome. I'm glad you liked it."

So far, the conversation has been casual and pleasant, but that's about to change.

Let's get down to business.

I drop my wine glass on the table.

"After speaking to your father, you must have a lot of questions for me," I say.

Her eyes snap to mine and she inhales a sharp breath. "I do."

"Ask away. I'll answer them all."

"There's one thing I'd like to say first."

"I'm all ears."

Her mouth twists in indecision. Like she's considering backtracking.

"There aren't any questions that are off the table, Michaela."

"It's not a question."

"What, then?"

"I just want to say thank you for not firing my father," she says. That's the last thing I expected. "Daddy likes to say he's more right brain than left, and Mom was the financial mind, but the hotel means everything to him. He's been working at the Villiers Grand since he was twenty-one. I doubt he could've handled losing the hotel and his purpose."

"Your father has a great rapport with the staff," I say. "I need him and I need your loyal staff to turn things around. In the grand scheme of things, a year isn't that long. A complete staff turnover would be like shooting myself in the foot. I'll have a team of top-notch directors and managers, but your father is an essential part of the hotel. We'll figure out what's the best role for him, but I have no intentions on giving him his walking papers."

"Daddy is so passionate about the hotel, you'd never know he married into the family business, as he likes to say." She laughs a little. "I'm sure you know my mom's great-grandfather started the hotel."

"I do. You can't buy that kind of heritage."

She nods.

Niels Knight and Charlize Villiers are from opposite sides of the track. He's from a working-class family. Charlize was the only daughter of a very wealthy hotelier. Niels started working at the concierge desk at night to pay off his student loans. The moment he met Michaela's mom, it was love at first sight.

When Charlize Villiers-Knight passed away seven years ago, he inherited the management of the hotel until Michaela turns twenty-seven, at which point she'd become the sole owner. Just like me, Michaela—born with the double-barreled surname Knight Villiers—has the responsibility of carrying the torch of her family's name and legacy.

"Your dad mentioned until your stepmom came into the picture, you used to manage the marketing and social media for the hotel."

"Yes. I have a bachelor's degree with a double major in art history and business. Once it became clear Thana and I would never get along, I needed an out. Until my trip to Nepal, I was working for a reputable art buyer as his assistant. He promised to keep the door open. I just haven't gotten around to calling him. As for my role at our hotel, I wouldn't say I was a whiz at marketing. I knew the right people, I hung out at the right parties, and I rubbed shoulders with lifestyle bloggers and socialites who document every aspect of their lives on social media. It was free publicity. Evidently, it wasn't enough."

"Your father was in over his head, which caused him to make a string of bad decisions."

"You mean like Thana?" she says, rolling her eyes.

"I'm not going to comment on that."

That marriage was a fucking bad decision on Niels part, but she already knows that.

"Did Daddy tell you about her lover?"

I nod. "He did, but I always do my due diligence."

Michaela lets out a sarcastic laugh. "At least now I understand why Thana was praising the virtues of holding onto my virginity," she says. "I never trusted her. And I was right. She's nothing but a con artist, a thief, and a pimp. How dare she give me life advice?"

It's a given I'd hire a team of investigators. I didn't want to leave any stones unturned. Along with a thorough background check on Niels and Thana, I also did one on her lover. I wanted to understand the implications of the upcoming FBI investigation.

Thana's lover, Dean Plimsoll, owns a sleazy virgin auction site. The asshole sells women's virginity to the highest bidder. From my understanding, he's on the FBI's watchlist for facilitating sex with minors. Even though his website claims all the girls he represents are at least eighteen and willing participants, that might not be the case.

Michaela's stepmother was using personal data from guests to flag prospective girls. She'd then feed the information to her lover for a cut of the profits. As if that wasn't enough, Dean was meeting many of his bidders at the Villiers Grand. I hope the two lowlifes get what they deserve.

"Do you think the investigation is going to tarnish the hotel's reputation?" Michaela asks. She's playing with her napkin.

I consider her for a beat.

I'm normally a straight shooter, but she's had a deluge poured on her today. Still, lying to her won't change the facts.

"Yes, I do. I have a stellar PR team, but they're not miracle workers. Given the situation, there's only so much we can do. Rebranding is the only way to go."

"We'd lose the Villiers family name?" Her tone is sheer panic.

"Yes."

"Oh God," she says. "We've lost everything. Mom must be turning in her grave."

The woman sitting across from me is nothing like the spitfire that torpedoed into my office. I reach across the table and place a hand on top of hers.

"No, you haven't," I tell her. "I know the name means a lot to you—"

"It means *everything*."

I nod. "I don't think we have any other choice here. That said, the building is still standing, the façade is classified as heritage architecture, and the hotel is located in a prime area of Manhattan. We still have a lot to play with."

"What's in it for you?" she asks. "Why are you sinking two hundred million dollars into a hotel with a shaky reputation and bleak finances? There must be thousands of other investments for you to choose from. And, how do I fit into your illogical plan?"

I knew the question was coming.

I remove my hand from hers and bore my eyes into hers.

"You mean, why did I accept your father's far-fetched request of a merger-marriage?"

"Yes. I don't understand. You can have any woman you want." She frowns. "Why me? I don't have anything to bring to the table."

"You have a lot more than you think, Michaela."

The line between her eyebrows deepens as her gaze darts between me and the napkin she's torturing.

"Please explain, because I just don't see it."

I hide nothing. I'm honest and transparent about my need for a fake-wife to secure the CEO position.

She listens, her expression unreadable.

I conclude by repeating what I told her earlier. "Two hundred million dollars to bail out your family hotel. In exchange, you become my wife for a year—"

"Why one year?" she asks. "You said the board wants to appoint a new CEO within six months."

"We'll raise eyebrows if we get divorced right after I'm appointed. We'll wait it out for an extra six months to appease any suspicions. At the one-year mark of our blissful marriage, I'm willing to forget all about the bailout money you owe me. We get a quiet divorce and you get to walk away with a hotel reshaped and debt free."

She lets out a long sigh

"I understand more than anyone on this planet your desire to want to keep control over your family business, but why not hire an actress or a model?" she asks. "Those women are groomed and trained to play a role. I'm not."

She's astute.

"Because it's too obvious, and well, too fake," I tell her.

The more the board made it their mission to prevent me from claiming the position that's rightfully mine, the more my mind concocted crazy scenarios. I ran down the list of possibilities of women I could approach, but none of them were suited to play the role. Most would end up becoming a headache to get rid of, and none of them had a nice piece of real estate I could hold over their heads. Desperate, I even went as far as contacting a few agents to scout an up-and-coming actress looking for the role of a lifetime. Nothing was going to stand in my way.

Niels's demand was my golden ticket. The timing couldn't have been more perfect. Could this plan backfire and explode in my face? Possibly, but I have something Michaela desperately wants. Pride runs through her veins, and I'm certain we can make this work. It's all about leverage.

"But we're strangers. We have nothing in common," she says.

"I disagree. We have a lot in common."

She lifts her chin up in defiance. "Name one thing. And us being humans doesn't count."

"Off the top of my head, we have five things in common."

"This, I have to hear." She sits back against her seat and crosses her arms over her chest, giving me an eyeful of the tempting swell of her breasts. It's an effort to pull my gaze up to hers. "One, our fathers survived massive heart attacks."

The edge in her expression vanishes. "Thank God for that."

"Yes. Dad isn't a hundred percent, but he's alive and in many ways, he's still the same stubborn man he always was." I can't help my smile.

"I can relate. Daddy is the same way."

"Two, we have the same middle name."

"You're lying."

I shake my head. "You're Michaela Kennedy Knight Villiers and I'm Phoenix Kennedy König."

Her eyes widen in surprise. "Seriously?"

"Your Google search fell short," I say.

"In my defense, I was pressed for time. You decided at the last minute to turn dinner into a late lunch."

"Fair enough," I say. I keep going. "Three, our last names not only sound regal, but we can trace our roots back to royalty—yours British, on your mother's side, and mine, German."

She cocks an eyebrow. She's impressed. "I'm guessing you did a background check on me."

"I have a large box filled with all your dirty secrets, Michaela Knight."

She shoots me an incredulous side gaze. "If that's the case, you need to demand a refund from whoever conducted that shoddy investigation. You got robbed. And duped. My life isn't nearly that exciting. Some might call me a goody two shoes. Until my trip to Nepal, I was."

Michaela's background is impeccable. She's as squeaky clean as they come. No bad publicity with her name on it. No drug arrests. No lewd behavior. No drunken foolishness caught on camera. No string of questionable and unsavory photos on social media with her private parts exposed. She's not a bad business decision waiting to happen. Dean and Thana's actions will cast a dark cloud over her name, but we can handle the punches when they come because she's not in the wrong, therefore she won't drag our family name to the bottom of the Pacific Ocean.

She's perfect for the role of my fake-wife.

"I wanted to get a reaction out of you," I tell her.

"Congratulations, König, you did. So, let's hear the rest of the things we have in common." She gestures with her hands, coaxing me to continue. The defiance in her tone... as present as her feistiness.

I lift a hand, flashing her four fingers. "Although my *king* will always trump your *knight*, our last names are also chess pieces."

"Good one!" She laughs. "Do you play?"

"Not very well. And you?"

"I do. Mom taught me. Some people meditate. Others exercise. Mom played chess to cope with stress. She was such a good player. I could never beat her."

"And that brings me to the fifth thing we share in common." I take in a deep breath. "We both lost our moms to cancer."

Her head jerks back, a shock-filled stare fixed on me.

"I didn't read about that..." Her voice comes out faint.

"With enough money, anything is possible. Dad worked really hard to keep it out of the press for privacy reasons. Any donation to cancer research is also kept quiet. And, there's so much information about our company, Dad, and the four of us floating on the internet, any old articles about Mom are most likely buried deep in the search results."

"How long ago did your mom die?" she asks.

"It's been four years. My older brother died a year before she did, of a drug overdose."

"Oh my God. I am so sorry, Phoenix."

"I appreciate the sentiment, but it's not your fault."

She offers a shy smile.

"Mom died within six months of being diagnosed for pancreatic cancer," I say. "Had it not been for the diagnosis, we would have believed she died of sadness. Barron's death died of a massive drug overdose nearly killed her."

Michaela places both hands against her heart. "Oh, Phoenix, it was so sudden."

"It was. Barron was seven years older. From the day he was born, he knew he'd step into our father's shoes."

While he was shadowing Dad and taking the company to

new heights, my three younger brothers and I were following our dreams. After we laid our brother to rest, we gave up the limelight and joined the family business. Losing a family member shifts your priorities. Losing two, even more so.

She closes her eyes for a beat. "Seven years after losing Mom to breast cancer, it's still so hard. The pain never seems to go away."

I shake my head, a lump rising in my throat. "No, it doesn't."

For a few long seconds, we're both silent.

"So, you see, Michaela, we have a lot more in common than you think."

She considers me.

"Phoenix, maybe I'm being naïve here, but is that enough to fool everyone?"

"My father and my brothers are one hundred percent behind me. The board bought my story... for now. My staff doesn't know much more than what's printed in the media. For the first time since my grandfather started this multinational company, a König might not be at the helm. That's a risk I'm not willing to take. If we allow an outsider to wedge himself—or herself—in that position, we'll have relinquished our power. As much as I hate it, the board has a strong say in the succession. They hold me by the balls."

The transition from pop star to hotel magnate was brutal. But here I am, the default first born, vying for a position I never in my life expected to want with this much ardor. The board is dead set on appointing a new CEO to replace Dad. They've made it clear they don't think I have the chops—or the model-citizen lifestyle—for the job. They're determined to keep me in my current position of COO and hire someone above me.

Fuck that.

I'm not going down without a fight. No way am I going to let an outsider reign over what's rightfully ours.

"I see," she says.

"Do you have a boyfriend in New York?" I ask.

Her eyebrows hit her forehead. "I didn't say yes," she says.

If she wasn't interested, she would've decamped out of here, flipping me the bird like she did earlier. But I'm not going to point out the obvious.

I soldier on. "If you're seeing someone, you're going to have to put an end to it. The sooner, the better. It's best to avoid any drama."

"I'm not seeing anyone."

I already knew that. I just wanted to hear it from her.

"Good."

"It seems you're quite the player," she says. "How is your current flavor of the week going to take the news?"

"If you're referring to a woman I might be involved with, rest your mind at ease. I'm a free agent."

"What about your weekly escort bookings? Won't they miss you if they don't hear from you for a while?" She flashes me a triumphant grin, like she one-upped me.

"I don't have to pay for sex, Michaela."

Her cheeks flush, but she follows with a quick rebuttal. "No little König babies running around or baby mamas looking for alimony or child support?"

"The media would've been all over that scandal," I say. "To answer your question, I always wrap it up and I always buy my own condoms to avoid surprises."

She grimaces. "Too much info."

"You asked," I tell her. "All right, we've established we're both single and neither of us have kids we know of."

She giggles.

"Two potential roadblocks we can scratch off the list. I

know your father never divulged his plans to Thana or your uncle Ian—"

"My father told you that?"

"Yes. He was pretty forthcoming."

"Wow."

"He has a vested interest in seeing this through. So do I. Are there any liabilities on your end I need to know about?"

"What do you mean?"

"Is there anyone who might become a whistleblower and tip off the media about our fake marriage?"

"Well, my friend Keira knows the truth."

I groan.

"I'm staying with her and she read the news before I did."

Shit.

"That could come back and bite us in the ass."

"She wouldn't say a thing."

"You're sure?"

"I'm certain."

"People can turn on a dime when money is involved or the prospect of their fifteen minutes of fame."

"Trust me, Keira has a hate-hate relationship with the media."

"You trust her that much?"

"I do. We were both running away from our reality. We met in Nepal. We were roommates at the monastery where we stayed. Since then, we've been really tight, even though we live on opposite sides of the country."

"I'm sure she's going to have questions when you get back to her place."

"I'm staying at her boyfriend's place."

Fuck.

"Does he know?" I ask.

"I'm not sure if she told him or not. He's in Las Vegas on

business for the next two days."

"What's his name?"

"Rhys Hartford."

I laugh.

"What's so funny?"

"I know him well."

"You're kidding?"

"I'm not. We're both members of the same... club. I also hang out with Rhys Hartford outside of the club.

Her eyebrows knit together. "What kind of club?"

"Let's talk about it another time," I say.

"Okay."

Thank God she doesn't press for more.

"We're going to have to deal with Keira and Rhys," I say.

More loose ends.

Every person who knows this is all smoke and mirrors is a potential leak, and if the board ever finds out, I can kiss the CEO position goodbye.

"Keira has known Rhys since she was a kid. He's her older brother's best friend. He comes off as trustworthy. Not to mention, the man runs a multibillion-dollar company. I'm sure he's no stranger to discretion. I don't see Rhys being a problem. The same for Keira."

I nod. "And you're sure she won't talk?"

"I'm certain of it."

I hate not being in control of every aspect of this charade, but I'm going to have to trust her.

"What about a best friend in New York?"

Her lips twist in disdain. "She decided to sleep with my boyfriend. So, we're not exactly on speaking terms," she says.

"Your ex is a cheater, your best friend is a backstabber, and you weren't getting along with your stepmother."

A grimace graces her beautiful features. She has the worst

poker face. "Pretty much."

"Nepal was your escape?"

"Yes. I was suffocating in New York."

"And you found what you were looking for in Nepal?"

Her expression turns amused before she nods. "I found my voice. I don't take crap from anyone anymore."

Without thinking, I reach out and stroke my thumb along her bare forearm, appreciating the silky softness of her skin under my touch.

She shudders. I expect her to pull away, but she doesn't. Instead, her green eyes hold mine.

"Were you forced to cut your hair to stay at the monastery?"

"No." She runs her free hand through her hair. "I wasn't trying to become a nun. It was my own decision. That said, Keira gave me the courage to do the big chop. She's also rocking a pixie cut, but she's a blonde to my nearly jet-black hair." She lets out a small laugh. "It's the second most rebellious thing I've ever done."

"Seems like you're still wearing your rebellious badge with pride."

"Today, I am."

We exchange a complicit smile.

Her demeanor changes just as quickly.

"What is it?" I ask.

She worries her lower lip.

"Come on, rebel. Talk to me," I tell her.

Glancing at her empty glass of wine and back up at me, she looks as if she's weighing her options.

"What about the press? How are we going to convince them we're so in love we *have* to get married? I mean, there aren't any photos of us together—no history of us even knowing each other. It's pretty hard to hide in the digital age."

She might not have formerly agreed to our merger-marriage, but her question tells me where her head is at.

"That's where the PR team comes in. They'll come up with an airtight story. As long as we follow the script, everything should be okay."

"This sounds very Hollywood. It's like we're actors."

"In many ways, we are. We're playing a role."

"Right." I detect a tinge of nervousness. Dare I say, self-doubt?

She's quiet for a beat.

Hesitant eyes meet mine. "Not that I had princess dreams of a regal wedding, attended by thousands, but I never imagined a merger-marriage would be the first time I walked down the aisle. And, I most definitely never imagined tying the knot with a multibillionaire."

"I never imagined walking down the aisle, period," I say. "I love my freedom way too much to put a noose around my neck. Luckily, the countdown starts right after we exchange the *I do's*. Something tells me we'll both be rushing to the divorce court when the year is over."

She nods. "Let's hope we survive the year."

After this morning, I have to wonder. But my eyes are on the prize, so I'm more than willing to put water in my wine.

"The incentive is strong for both of us," I say.

She nods again.

I seek out easy, no strings attached hookups with women who aren't looking for a forever guy. Sacrificing my freedom, and therefore cockblocking my ability to sink into a warm pussy whenever I want, will be an unbearable challenge. I'd never dream of entering a ball and chain arrangement unless it was well worth it. Securing the CEO position is the ultimate reward.

"Today was just about us getting acquainted with each

other," I say, "We can go over the contract and the prenup—"

"Very romantic," she says.

"Let's not pretend, Michaela. We both know what this is. I'd be an embarrassment as a COO if I entered a deal without an airtight contract. I highly recommend you hire your own legal counsel. I'm not going to blindside you, but you need the guidance and blessings of a lawyer on the terms of our arrangement and what you'll get out of it."

Given my legal powerhouse, I could screw her and Niels ten ways to Sunday. Her father is in the hole. Other than his house, he doesn't have a dime to his name. If I wanted to take advantage of them, it would be easy. That's just not how I operate.

"Okay," she says in a small voice.

I can't read her mind, but I'm willing to bet she's still struggling with her new reality.

"Once you're okay with everything, we'll set the ruse in motion. You're the kind of smart and sophisticated woman everybody will believe I've settled down with long-term. The PR team will start working its magic. The media gets a story we control. The board is thoroughly duped. I'm one step closer to my goal. Everyone wins."

"That's a lot of pressure," she says. "Wouldn't a quick Vegas wedding be easier to handle?"

"No one will believe a man in my position would settle for a Vegas wedding, unless you were knocked up. The board will see right through me. In order for this to fly, we have to put on a good show and play the part like we're campaigning for an Oscar."

A gap of silence stretches between us.

"Is there anything we haven't covered?" I ask.

She clears her throat. "There's one thing we haven't discussed."

"What's that?"

"After the wedding..."

"Yes?"

"I wanted to know—"

She lets out a sigh.

"I'm listening."

Her teeth dig into her bottom lip before releasing it. She then clamps her lips together and looks up to the ceiling as if calling for strength.

It's like she's having a conversation with herself.

"If you have a question, just ask," I tell her.

Twin blotches of color appear high on her cheeks.

What's up with the sudden shyness?

It hits me.

I pull her hand into mine and fix her with my gaze.

"You want to know about our wedding night?"

She nods.

"You want to know if I'm going to bury my big cock deep inside your sweet pussy and fuck you like no man has ever fucked you before?"

Her jaw drops, her eyes widening so much, I fear they'll take over her face.

"Only if you ask nicely, Michaela."

I promised myself I'd behave, but I couldn't resist.

I didn't think it was possible to render this woman mute.

Good to know.

A second ticks by.

Then another.

And another.

She's still staring at me.

She's not balking at the idea, though.

I cock my head, studying her in amusement. "Something tells me you'd enjoy it as much as I would... if not more."

She remains quiet.

I add fuel to the fire.

"Tell me this, Michaela. When was the last time you were fucked by a real man?" A veil of lust coats her green eyes. "Someone who knows what you need. Someone who'll tame that dragon roaring inside you. Someone who will take control from you, forcing you to surrender and submit. Someone who can give you what you crave, but didn't even know you desperately needed."

Still nothing.

"If you beg, I'll give it to you," I tell her.

The heat burning in her eyes dissipates.

She snatches her hand away from mine.

"In your dreams, König! Hell will freeze over before that ever happens," she says. "And begging for it?" She rolls her eyes. "Puh-lease."

No one's been taking care of her like she deserves. I'd bet my fortune on it.

"Care to make a wager?" I ask.

She hesitates.

"No!" She shakes her head. "I owe you enough as it is."

"Consider this a bonus. You wouldn't owe me anything extra for the pleasure."

She bats her eyelashes a mile a minute.

I'm on a roll. "I can assure you, Michaela, you wouldn't hesitate to beg for it."

She flinches, but regains her composure, lifting her chin in the defiant demeanor I'm getting used to. "Don't get any ideas about our wedding night. This is a fake wedding. We will not be consummating said fake wedding. I was just curious about our sleeping arrangements."

I fight a smile. "We have time to figure it out. I haven't decided if we'll stay at the penthouse or the mansion in Malibu.

Don't worry your pretty little head. I wasn't planning on touching you."

Something flashes in her eyes. Disappointment?

"I hope it doesn't mean you plan on cheating on me," she says. "I wouldn't want to be humiliated or made to look like a fool."

How am I going to live with this beautiful woman for one year without my balls exploding? Chances are I'll jerk off so much, I'll injure my wrist.

"I'm not a cheater," I tell her.

"If you're not going to get it from me... where are you going to get it from?" She keeps talking without giving me a chance to answer. "Are you telling me you're going to live a whole year without sex? I just can't see that happening."

"I could ask you the same question," I say.

She blushes.

Turning her cheeks that lovely shade of pink is becoming my favorite pastime.

"I'll do whatever it takes for the sake of the hotel," she says.

Nice way of skirting the question.

"I'm a big boy. Don't worry about my needs."

Before meeting Michaela Knight, that wouldn't have been a problem.

Now? Well... it's going to be a little more complicated.

My brain knows better, but my body...? Not so much. My cock wants nothing more than to seal this damn merger-marriage with a good, hard fuck. I'm desperate to release my cum inside a pussy instead of the palm of my hand. Hers would do nicely. Five months of celibacy will do that to a man. Even before Dad's heart attack, my schedule was so jam-packed, I couldn't even think straight.

But this meeting isn't about my cock. It's about her legacy and mine.

Michaela isn't a mail-order bride. This is a business deal. Therefore, this arrangement comes with certain self-imposed restrictions. But damn if I've gone from needing her to wanting her. I want to tame this firecracker more than I want my next breath. If she's this explosive, I can just imagine what it's like in the bedroom.

Sending her running for the hills wouldn't do either of us any good, König.

I coax the beast raging between my legs to behave.

She's staring at me with a cocked eyebrow, indicating she remains unconvinced.

"I will respect the boundaries of our fake wedding and I'll keep it in my pants," I tell her.

"I'm glad to hear we're on the same page," she says.

"The timeline is tight," I say, changing the subject. "Sleep on it and let's talk early tomorrow. How does that sound, Michaela?"

"Okay," she says. "By the way, you can call me Mikki. Everyone else does Do you have a nickname?"

"I much prefer Michaela," I say. "I don't particularly like nicknames, so don't ever get it in your head to call me Nix."

"Suit yourself." She shrugs. "I was just trying to create a rapport between us."

"There are much better ways of doing that."

She swallows hard and squirms in her seat.

I bite off a smile.

"Three hundred and sixty-five days, Michaela, and you'll save your family's legacy."

She offers a shy nod.

"The meeting is adjourned." I pause for effect. "But I'm too much of a gentleman to flip you the bird."

Her face drops.

She didn't see that one coming.

Chapter 9

Michaela

I'm back at Rhys's place.

I had a lengthy conversation with my father about my meeting with Phoenix. He's relieved we buried the hatchet long enough to set things in motion. Daddy reminded me time is of the essence because he's choking in debt.

Copy that.

Once I ended the call with my father, I joined Keira for dinner. We're sitting exactly where we sat this morning, but nothing is the same.

After a light dinner—because I was still stuffed from my delicious lunch on Phoenix's yacht—I spill my guts to my friend. She's the only person on this planet other than my father I can confide in. I'm so grateful I don't have to keep this fake marriage charade a secret from her. I can't imagine having to deal with all of this on my own.

Since my mind is still a bit jumbled from everything that's transpired in my life since I woke up, I blurt out everything in one go. I expected my friend to be shocked, but nothing like this.

"Say something," I tell her. She's staring at me like a deer caught in headlights.

"Holy shit. I mean, holy shit." Keira finally speaks. You woke up this morning completely unaware your life was going to take an unexpected turn."

"That's putting it mildly," I say.

"Well, at least you're marrying a hot guy and a former boy band member."

Keira is a singer, and she used to be a member of a really popular girl group. She was a little peeved I never asked Phoenix about his former career as a pop star. I read about the glory days of the boy group 4Destiny—4D, for short. Slate, Wilder, Roman, and Phoenix were at the top of their game when Barron died.

and I even drooled over a few videos while I was doing my recon. Finding out more about that part of his life was way down there on the list of priorities for our meeting.

"I haven't decided if I'm marrying him yet," I say.

"It doesn't sound like you have a lot of options, Mikki."

"That may be the case, but I want to make peace with the decision. It's the only shred of control I have left. When I'm ready, I'll give him my answer."

Keira shakes her head, her disbelief still written all over her face. "This is wild."

"Oh, it gets better."

Her head whips in my direction. "You've been holding back from me?"

"Phoenix knows Rhys."

"Seriously?"

"Yes. Something about a club. I asked him to elaborate, but he was evasive about it. I figured I'd get the scoop from you."

"Oh..." Keira's face turns as red as a tomato.

"Why do you look like the cat that ate the canary?"

She stares at me, wide-eyed.

I let out an exasperated sigh. "Keira, I've had enough surprises for one day. What club is Phoenix talking about?"

She shifts in her seat. "Okay, I'll tell you, but you can't tell Rhys I told you."

"Okay."

"That's not good enough."

"I won't tell him."

"Swear it," she says.

"Holy shit, woman. You're scaring me."

"There's nothing to be scared about, however, this isn't public knowledge, so it requires a high level of secrecy."

I lift one hand and place the other against my heart. "Cross my heart and hope to die."

She shifts her gaze to the left, then the right before fixing her hazel-green eyes onto me. "There's this hotel called the Quintus Hotel. It has many layers. From the outside, it's just another five-star hotel. That said, there's a secret passage that leads to a club that caters to LA's high rollers."

"Oh, like a business club."

"Well, that's one of the *many* layers. There's a gentlemen's club where members conduct business and there's also one exclusively for women. Given Rhys and Phoenix's power positions, I'm sure they rub elbows at that club to talk shop. But there's more. A whole lot more..."

She cocks an eyebrow, as if I'm supposed to pick up on her cryptic explanation.

"For the love of God, woman, stop speaking in codes. Just spit it out, already."

"I'm not sure you can handle what I'm about to share."

"If I can handle finding out my father practically sold me to an obscenely rich man to cover his debt and prevent our family hotel from going under and not fall apart, I can handle whatever you have to dish out."

"Dark Compulsion is an exclusive, member only *adult club* where high rollers meet for an illicit night and all sorts of kinky stuff."

My jaw drops.

Talk about ripping off the Band-Aid in one shot.

"Come again?" I ask.

"You heard me the first time," she says.

"Adult club? As in, sex club?"

"Yes."

My curiosity is piqued.

"Have you ever been?" I ask.

"I've been to the Quintus Hotel for dinner with Rhys. He wanted to introduce me to the kinky club, but my new role in his company, and the accident... delayed things." She taps her leg.

My face contorts. "Is it like a swingers club?"

She shakes her head. "Some married couples are into that, but that's not the essence of the club. It's a big building and there are many floors... there's a lot to explore. From what Rhys has candidly shared, it's not sleazy. It's very high-end. There are a lot of hurdles to becoming a Dark Compulsion member. Their screening process is top notch. Hence, the exclusive part. The members prefer their relationships uncomplicated, therefore a mutual level of understanding is paramount. You can't even get through the door without signing an NDA and leaving your phone in a secure holding area. So, club members get their kicks and at the end of the evening, they walk away. No drama. No expectations. No stalker behavior. No photos leaked to the press."

"I can just imagine what goes on in such a club."

"Rhys can't wait to take me. From my understanding, most

of his friends are members and they bring their significant other. You can tailor the experience to your needs and kinks."

"Wow!" I rest my back against the seat. "This isn't Kansas anymore."

"No, it's not," Keira says.

Realization hits me.

"Phoenix has a kinky side..."

"Chances are, he does," Keira says. I should be freaked out—concerned, even—but I'm not. "That's a good thing for you. In no time, you won't be able to spell the words *vanilla sex.* Trust me!" Keira grins from ear to ear.

I swallow at her admission, and my stomach flips as I flash-back to Phoenix's raunchy words when I asked about our wedding night. Conscious of my shortcomings compared to a master dirty-talker, I decided to press the eject button and get myself out of that erotic battle of words. Because, holy Jesus, I'm so not equipped to go toe to toe with that man. And damn his deep, baritone, sexy voice.

An afternoon with him and I'm dying to live out every one of his promises.

What's wrong with me?

My cheeks flush.

"Ooohhh, are you having a moment?" Keira asks.

I narrow my gaze at her.

"No, I'm not," I lie. "We still have to iron out the detail surrounding our sleeping arrangements, but I made it clear, sex isn't part of the deal."

She's incredulous.

"You're going to be married to one of the most eligible men in the country, you're going to live together, you're going to see him walking around in his boxer briefs—and potentially, naked—but nothing is going to happen between the two of you? For a whole year?"

"I'll do my best not to see him naked," I tell her.

"Why?" she asks. "I bet that man is something else naked." I'm sure she's right.

"First, he's still the enemy—"

"I thought he was saving your hotel?"

"It still doesn't mean I like him," I tell her. I continue without giving her a chance to respond. "Second, this is a business arrangement. Third, there's a time limit on this fake-relationship, so I'd rather keep my wits about me."

"Hmmm..."

"What is it?"

"Nothing."

"Just say it!"

"Is he going to hire escorts to take care of his needs while you're married?"

"No. He promised he wouldn't. And as strange as it sounds, I believe he'll keep his word."

Keira explodes in laughter.

"What's so funny?"

"You two are going to kill each other," she says. "All that pent-up sexual energy."

I roll my eyes. "You must be drinking the same Kool-Aid as Phoenix. Like I told him, I'm good. Thank you very much."

"So, you're not going to visit Dark Compulsion?"

"What's the point? It's not like anything is going to happen between Phoenix and me, and it's not like I'm going to get down and kinky with other men."

"Point taken." She pretends to drop the subject, but I know her better than that. "You're not even curious a little bit?"

I am, but I'm unwilling to admit it. "This is a business deal."

"Why can't it come with benefits?" she asks.

"Keira, I'm carrying a lot on my shoulders as it is," I tell her.

"My father bestowed on me the responsibility of saving a legacy that was started four generations ago. He made a string of bad decisions, and I'm the only one capable of digging us out of this colossal mess. Adding *benefits* to the mix is just going to fuck with my head. I can't afford that. I refuse to give Phoenix more than I have to."

Banging a sexy-as-fuck man with a kinky streak sounds like fun and games until someone gets hurt. I'll pass.

"You're right," Keira says and moves her attention to her wine glass. She circles a manicured finger over the rim in a deliberate slow motion, eyeing me from under her long eyelashes.

"What now?" I ask.

"You have a lot more willpower than I do," she says. "I was throwing myself at Rhys when I moved in with him."

"You two go way back. I'm marrying a stranger."

"You *are* marrying him?" Her grin is epic.

My jaw ticks. "As infuriating as he is, King Kong Tycoon is my only lifeline. I disagree with the way Daddy went about doing things. This reads like the plot of a bad mail-order-bride-slash-pioneer-frontier romance from two centuries ago."

"At least you lassoed a good one."

I giggle. "Yeah. My father spared me on that front. I could've ended up with a hideous man with a severe case of halitosis, body odor issues, a big fat wart on his forehead, hairy knuckles—and back—and scary looking unkempt feet."

I don't have to see Phoenix's feet to know they must be as good looking as the rest of him.

"Okay, that's hilarious," Keira says.

"Beggars can't be choosers."

"That is true. I guess your dad did right by you. Phoenix König is Prince Charming compared to your unappealing description."

"Even though there won't be anything hot and heavy going on between us, Phoenix is easy on the eye." And from the flutter of excitement between my legs, I have no doubt he would be easy on the pussy. I'll never know.

"A sexless arranged marriage with a dreamy billionaire for a year in exchange for two hundred million dollars that will save your family's hotel, which will revert back to your ownership once you sign the divorce papers."

Keira sums up my preposterous life.

"This isn't the picture-perfect wedding I envisioned for my first time walking down the aisle," I say.

"How many people walk down the aisle for the wrong reasons?"

"Good point."

"At least you know three hundred sixty-five days from your big day, your husband won't try to screw you over. How many women get shortchanged during their divorce? You're walking into this with your eyes wide open and a nice little contract tucked neatly under your arm like a boss lady."

I'm tempted to laugh, but I'm reminded of my precarious situation.

"Speaking of which, I need a California lawyer," I say.

"Rhys can hook you up."

"Daddy asked me not to spend any money on the corporate business card because we're maxed. Since working with Thana, aka returning to the toxic environment I fled, was out of the question and I hadn't gotten around to calling the art buyer I was working for—" *This is so embarrassing.* "I have no idea how I'm going to pay for the legal fees, Keira."

"I'll talk to my boyfriend. We'll figure something out."

I nod.

"Thank you."

My ringtone—a high octave pop Top 100 song—jars me out of a deep sleep.

Grumbling, I open one eye.

I'm surrounded by darkness.

My gaze lands on the clock on the nightstand.

Four a.m.?

I should've turned my phone off.

I curse and pull the sheet over my head, intent on ignoring whoever dared to wake me up before the roosters.

I will myself to fall back asleep when my phone rings.

Again?

Fuck.

Stop calling. I'm sleeping.

My phone rings a third time, causing me to growl like an angry bear.

This is a losing battle.

Who needs to talk to me this badly in the middle of the night?

With my face still squished into the pillow, I tap around on the nightstand until my fingers grip my phone. I bring the device right up to my face.

It's a struggle to open both eyes.

Daddy?!

Worried, I flip over and sit up straight in bed.

"Daddy," I say in a groggy voice when I answer his call.

My father doesn't respond.

Heavy breathing echoes on the other end.

I pull the phone away from my ear to make sure it's my father calling.

"Daddy? Are you still there?"

"I am," he says. "This is the worst day of my life, ladybug."

My heart leaps into my throat.

"What's going on? Are you crying?"

"I am," he says.

"Why are you crying?"

"It's gone."

"What's gone?"

"It's been burned to the ground."

"The hotel is on fire?"

"No. The house."

Sheer panic washes over me.

"Our house?"

"Yes."

I refuse to believe him.

"Our house is on fire?" By wording it differently, I'm praying I'll get a different answer.

"Yes."

Oh my God.

"But you're safe?"

"I wasn't inside the house."

Thank God.

"I was at the hotel. We were short staffed at the welcome desk."

"Where are you now?"

"I'm at Uncle Ian's. The police were at the house, so were the firefighters. They've extinguished the fire, but it's going to take some time for investigation. It's been a long night."

This cannot be happening. This has to be a nightmare.

"We have nothing left, Michaela," Daddy says. "The house is gone. Everything inside it. Gone. Incinerated. Your car in the garage is burnt to a crisp. The houses flanking ours are also gone."

I'm surprised I can hear him over the erratic beating of my heart.

"Are the neighbors okay?"

"By a miracle of God, no one was home. One family was cheering on their oldest son at a basketball game—the three other siblings were with them. The other family was at a school play."

"Thank God."

"People in the neighborhood said it was like an explosion went off."

I'm in so much shock, words fail me.

"I should've listened to your uncle," Daddy says.

"Why do you say that?"

"Ian told me not to let Thana near the house after I served her with the divorce papers. He told me I needed to pack her stuff and ship her shit to her lover's house. I didn't listen. I should've."

I'm dumbfounded.

"Do you think she'd do this?" I ask.

"I didn't think she'd cheat on me, and I never expected her to steal me blind."

"Daddy, arson is a big accusation."

"She threatened me this morning and again via a storm of nasty text messages after the police escorted her out of the hotel."

Dread washes over me.

"You never mentioned this."

"People say shit when they're angry. God knows I didn't mince my words."

"She actually said she was going to burn down the house?"

"She said she was going to make sure I had nothing left. She was going to strip me of all my possessions, one by one."

I'm shaking like a leaf.

"Oh my God. What about the hotel?"

"Thana is in custody."

"The police arrested her? Already?"

"Yes," Daddy says. "The text messages were sufficient for probable cause."

"What a bitch." I really want to use the C word, but I refrain.

"I never saw her for who she was," my father says.

"Don't even go there, Daddy. Thana is a mental case and quite astute at duping people. She's a con artist, through and through. You weren't equipped to see it coming. No one was."

"I hear you, but I'm still angry at myself. And I'm devastated. We lost our photo albums. All the memories with Mom... Gone." My father's voice breaks.

My heart weeps.

"Let me get on the first flight out of here and I'll be in New York as soon as I can—"

"No!"

I flinch.

"You can't come back, Michaela," he adds. His answer comes as a surprise.

"What are you talking about, Daddy? Of course, I have to come back."

"There's nothing you can do here."

"But I can be there for you."

"Listen to me, Michaela. You have one thing left of value. I know I said it yesterday when I fessed up, but now, it's truer than ever."

I swallow hard.

"You need to stay in Los Angeles and see this deal through with Phoenix. This merger-marriage is everything. Everything! Make it happen! Ian will help me with the house, the investigation, and the hotel. Your job is to marry Phoenix. That should be your one and only focus."

My father's words are so cold and calculated.

"But—"

"No buts! Do you hear me?"

Who is this man?

I bite my lip as tears burn my eyes.

"Answer me!" he says. "Do you hear me?"

"I—I do."

"Good. I'm going to let you go so you can get some sleep. You need to get up in a few hours and lock this deal down." He pauses. "I might sound like an intransigent monster... desperation will do that to a man."

With that, he hangs up.

In the dark, my entire body shakes as I clench my phone against my heart.

Yesterday, I knew who I was.

Today, I've lost my compass. Everything that characterized me is gone—the hotel, our home, everything I possess, money... and possibly my dignity. Even my father isn't the same man.

I thought I was strong enough to handle this, but now, I'm not so sure.

I toss my phone on the bed, pull my legs to my body, and drop my forehead to my knees. I let the tears stream down my face as I mourn the loss of my independence.

Saving the hotel is one thing, but now, it's like indentured servitude.

Phoenix König owns me.

I'm his payment on my father's debt.

How did my life come to this?

Chapter 10

Phoenix

A knock at the door breaks my focus.

I lift my eyes from my iMac to meet my brother's expectant gaze.

His trademark sly side grin is firmly planted on his face.

"Good morning," Slate says.

"Morning."

"I thought you might want a cappuccino," he says, striding into my office. "Two shots of espresso, two raw sugars, and extra hot, of course—" He freezes. "Looks like you've been at it for a while!" He jerks his chin to the two empty cups sitting on my desk.

"I've been here for two-and-a-half hours," I tell him.

"You got here at six?"

"I did. So far, it's been a productive and lucrative morning, but a boost of caffeine won't hurt." He hands me the coffee. "Thanks," I say before taking a sip.

"Are you working on a big deal you haven't told us about?" he asks.

"No, you're aware of the bids we have on the radar." I take

another few sips of the hot coffee. “I had a lot of loose ends to tie up from yesterday because I didn’t come back to the office after my lunch with Michaela.”

“How come?” Slate asks.

I drop my cup on my desk. “After walking Michaela to the Bentley, I decided to return to the yacht. The plan was to kick back for a few hours and watch the sunset before heading to the penthouse. I fell asleep. The sun breaking through the windows woke me up at five o’clock this morning. After a pit stop at my place to shower and change, I headed to the office. I figured, might as well attack the day.”

“Carpe diem, like Dad says.”

“Exactly.”

“Another bonus of starting the day early is I was able to talk to Roman,” I say. “He called me an hour after I got in—”

“At four a.m. Hawaii time?”

“He couldn’t sleep.”

“The nightmares?”

“He didn’t say as much. He blamed it on being in a strange bed—”

“Bullshit,” Slate says. “The manwhore is a professional bed hopper.”

“True.” I laugh a little. “He’s been bedridden for over a month since the accident, so clearly, he thinks I’m stupid. The nightmares are the culprit for his sleepless nights even if he’s lying to himself.”

“Shit,” Slate says. “I can’t imagine watching two buddies get engulfed by rogue waves and feeling totally helpless while struggling to save my own life.”

I nod. “That kind of trauma changes you. Only time and therapy will help him cope.”

Without the nurses and doctors watching over our brother,

we'd still be oblivious to his nightly turmoil. He's been guarded on the subject.

"True," Slate says. "How is he doing physically?"

"A little better every day. After another barrage of tests, the doctors are confident he'll be able to walk again. No permanent spinal injury."

"Amen to that!" Slate says.

"Thank God, indeed." I echo my brother's sentiment. "He's going to start working with a physical therapist next week—only the upper body. At least it's good news."

"It's excellent news!"

"He called Dad to tell him after he hung up with me. I told him I'd relay the message to you and Wilder," I say. "The other reason Roman called is because he wants me to put him back to work. He's dying to sink his teeth into a project—anything to prevent him from losing his mind to boredom."

"Typical König," Slate says.

"That, he is."

"Are you going to get him started on one of our new acquisitions?"

I shake my head. "I put my foot down. I told him it wasn't going to happen."

"I'm sure you're his favorite person in the world," Slate says.

"He told me to fuck off. I told him I still loved him."

Slate bursts out laughing.

"Until Roman is able to get on a plane and return home, I told him his only job is to focus on getting better. None of this"—I open my arms—"means shit if he's not one hundred percent." I hold Slate's gaze. "I suspect that's the real reason he wants me to keep him busy... more than the boredom of being bedridden with limited mobility."

"Going back to the reason you got here so early, how did it go with Michaela?" Slate asks.

"It's safe to say she was overwhelmed."

"Understandably so," Slate says. "Is she onboard?"

I share the highlights of my lunch with my maybe-bride.

"I told her to sleep on it. I'll call her by the end of the day," I tell him. "We both have a lot to lose if she decides to walk away from this deal. Putting pressure on her won't get me an answer any faster. I want her to be certain about this because we're going to have to *sell* this fairytale romance hard."

"If she's onboard, you need to step up your game," my brother says.

I knit my eyebrows together. "What do you mean?"

"Not everyone is buying your story."

My jaw clenches. "A member of the board approached you?"

"No. Given you've been at work since early this morning, I assume you're not up on the latest celebrity news."

"What are they saying?" I ask.

"You just have to worry about one asshole," my brother says, pulling out his phone from the inside of his suit jacket. He taps on the screen and hands me the device.

'PHOENIX KÖNIG AND MICHAELA KNIGHT IN LOVE? I CALL BULLSHIT.'

Annoyance consumes me as I scroll down the unnecessarily long blog post.

"Fucking *Payne* in the ass," I say, handing him back his phone.

"I particularly like the part where Payne says, *'Boy band singer turned COO—and interim CEO while his father recovers from a heart attack—thinks the public is stupid.'*" My brother's tone drips with sarcasm as he reads a snippet of the blog post out loud.

Payne Meldrum is a fame hungry celebrity blogger who has no problem using any means necessary to drive an insane amount of traffic to his website. He laughs in the face of journalistic integrity and uses rumors as facts. Heck, he'll create rumors if he has to. Most of his articles are dubious, but in this case, he's right on the money.

I meet my brother's gaze. "I don't need him poking holes in my story."

"I hear you, but to Payne's point, there's absolutely zero history of you dating Michaela."

"I'm fully aware of that," I tell him.

"You need a kickass PR campaign because Payne isn't going to back down." Slate states the obvious. "Knowing him, he's just getting started. When that ambulance chaser smells blood, he's worse than a vampire."

"Don't I know it!"

I reach for my Montblanc pen and tap it against my desk, a habit I have when I'm thinking hard or when I'm annoyed, like I am now.

"If only Niels had picked up the phone to talk to me," I say. "That stunt was unnecessary."

"You can't go back, Phoenix," Slate tells me. "You have to work with what you have. At least you can use your frequent trips to New York in the past few months to justify the hush-hush nature of your 'relationship'," he says in air quotes, "but you're going to have put on a show from now on."

"First, Michaela has to agree—"

My phone vibrates.

My attention swings from my brother to my screen.

"Speak of the devil..." I say.

Little hellion: Fine. I'll do it.

"Good news?" Slate asks.

I hand him my phone. "She's in!"

He grabs my device and lowers his eyes to the screen. His disapproving frown speaks volumes.

"Not exactly hot and heavy. Not even heartfelt in the least," he says.

"In her defense, it's not like I serenaded her with a four-string quartet before dropping to one knee and declaring my undying love," I tell him. "It was a pretty cut and dried deal. I expected her to drag things out until the last second before the clock struck midnight. It's barely eight in the morning and I got the answer I was hoping for. I'm not going to complain. There was always the chance she might turn me down."

"Thank God she didn't," he says. "Now, you have to move onto phase two."

"Which is?"

"You need to raise the heat level between the two of you."

"It's already pretty fucking high. She's constantly spitting fire at me."

He shakes his head. "You're talking about the *hate* level. I'm talking about the polar opposite."

I lean back into my high-back leather chair and cross my arms over my chest.

I consider Slate for a long beat, mulling over his advice.

A few long seconds tick by.

Slate doesn't speak.

Neither do I.

I lean forward, pick up the receiver to the landline sitting on my desk and press a button connecting my executive assistant.

"Lydia," I say when she picks up. "I need you to clear my

schedule for the rest of the day and cancel all my appointments."

"Consider it done," she says. "What should I schedule instead?"

"An urgent lunch meeting with Heather Mortimer."

"Got it!" she says. "I'll call our lead contact at the PR firm."

"Please ask the chefs to prepare an unforgettable meal. I'll let them pick the menu. They know what I like."

"Not a problem," Lydia says. "What time would you like lunch?"

"Let's say one o'clock. We'll use the large conference room."

"Very well," she says.

"I also need you to request my lawyer swings by. Any time after five will work. He's on standby for this appointment." Might as well strike the iron while it's hot. I want a prenup in Michaela's hands as soon as possible.

"I'm on it," Lydia says. "Anything else?"

"Please expect my fiancée to drop by this morning."

"Of course, sir."

Lydia is the epitome of efficiency. She's also discreet. Where some people had a thousand questions after yesterday's media frenzy, she didn't. She simply congratulated me when she came in later that morning.

I hang up the call and meet my brother's gaze.

"How's that for turning up the heat?"

Slate lets loose a cocky smile. "It's a valiant effort."

"Fuck off!"

"On a serious note—"

"What now?"

"Are you going to tell Michaela about MC?"

My mood shifts from pleasant to murderous in the blink of an eye.

"Why the fuck would you ruin my day by bringing up Marie-Clémence?"

He lifts his hands in surrender. "It wasn't my intention. Shy of a miracle of God—or a divorce—MC will always be intertwined in our lives. At least for the foreseeable future."

"Perhaps, but why does Michaela need to know about her? It's not like MC and I were ever married."

"It's something you might want to put on the table."

I drop an elbow against the desk and stroke my clean-shaven chin as I ponder my brother's suggestion. Images flash in front of my eyes as I'm transported to my last vitriolic encounter with that bitch.

"That would be giving Marie-Clémence Pisier too much importance," I say, through gritted teeth.

Chapter 11

Michaela

I drag my exhausted body from the Bentley to the front of the Pompadour Hotel. After my father shattered my existence with yet another devastating blow, I cried until I had no more tears. The two hours of broken sleep did nothing more than confuse the hell out of my system.

When I woke up at six-thirty, I was completely disoriented. One look around the bedroom, and I was reminded of my grim reality. Since I didn't have the courage to face Keira, I sat in bed, reliving yesterday over and over in my head. Finally, I had enough. I picked up my phone and composed twenty different text messages until I settled on one. With a heavy heart, I offered my freedom in exchange for a piece of property. Considering his position and responsibilities, I was surprised Phoenix had room in his schedule to meet so quickly.

What's the point of avoiding the inevitable?

When the elevator doors open on the top floor, I smooth down my dress before taking a step forward. As I was selecting what to wear this morning, it hit me. My only remaining possessions are hanging in the closet of Rhys Hartford's guesthouse closet. A sense of sheer panic choked the breath out of me at the thought, and I wanted nothing more than to dissolve into tears again. But I didn't. I couldn't.

So, here I am striding down the same corridor as yesterday, but instead of being fueled with indignation and fury, I'm consumed by worry and fear.

I pull open the glass door and step inside Phoenix's world.

The woman sitting behind a desk glances up at me and lifts a finger, indicating she won't be too long.

I nod, and my heart beats a little faster.

I take a long step back to give her privacy.

Not that I'm eavesdropping, but this close, I can't help it.

Everything about Lydia Gillanders screams poised, but her surly tone with whoever she's talking to indicates this has been a shit morning.

Welcome to my world.

As I wait while Phoenix's executive assistant finishes with her call, I remind myself why I'm doing this.

I promise I won't let you down, Mom.

As soon as the woman hangs up, I step up to her desk. I'm going to guess Lydia is thirty-something. Her salon-blonde hair is sleeked back in an office appropriate style. The turquoise sleeveless, form-fitting dress with a flattering neckline she's wearing accentuates her well-toned and well-tanned arms, her bright red lips and her light brown eyes. There's no denying it, she's very attractive. Too attractive. The big fat rock on her ring finger squashes the snarky and catty thought that pops to mind —King Kong Tycoon is probably not banging his pretty executive assistant.

Good.

Lydia glances up at me. "I'm sorry for making you wait. It's been a crazy morning so far," she says, pressing a button on the phone console.

"Not a problem," I tell her with a smile.

She offers a tight one.

Her eyes meet mine. "How can I help you?"

"My name is Michaela Knight—"

"You're the fiancée!" A warm smile stretches Lydia's lips.

"I am." I pray my voice doesn't betray my nervousness.

She leans against her desk.

I mimic her.

"No wonder the boss has been keeping you a secret. You're absolutely gorgeous. Good thing the boss saw you first. He would've had to fight the three other König heirs for your attention."

I blush from ear to ear. "Thank you."

"He's expecting you." She jerks her thumb over her shoulder.

"Thank you."

I make my way to the wooden door I burst through yesterday on shaky legs.

What a difference a day makes.

I ready myself to knock, but the door swings open.

And there he is... my future husband.

Chapter 12

Phoenix

I freeze when my eyes land on Michaela's face.

Gone is the luminescent serenity I remember from yesterday.

Her green eyes are veiled with… sadness?

"Good morning," I say.

"Good morning." Her tone is as flat as a board.

Where's the fire? The sparks? The spirit? The mini volcano?

"Everything okay?" I ask.

She bites against her lip and glances over her shoulder in Lydia's direction.

"Come in," I tell her.

"Thanks."

Almost as if pulled by a magnet, my eyes land on her gorgeous ass as she struts into my office.

Damn.

"Let's sit over near the large windows," I say. "The sofa and the armchairs are far more comfortable than the guest chairs."

"Okay."

She takes a seat, elegant and poised, before crossing her legs at the ankles.

I sit across from her in one of the leather armchairs.

I set things in motion. "Thanks for getting back to me so quickly."

"Might as well get it over with." She punctuates her flippant remark with a one-shoulder shrug.

I frown.

I understand this isn't her dream wedding and we're good at getting under each other's skin, but if I didn't know better, I'd say those words drip with disgust. Resentment, even.

"Michaela, you're here on your own accord, but you're giving off the vibe you'd rather not be here at all. I don't understand. Your text suggested we were on the same page, but it seems we're oceans apart."

She averts her gaze. "We are on the same page."

I study her striking profile, as she fidgets nervously with her fingers.

"What's going on?" I ask.

She shrugs.

"I asked you a question, Michaela."

This time she shakes her head.

I stand up, circle the coffee table and sit next to her on the sofa. I reach out for her, but she pulls her arm away before scooting closer to the armrest, creating distance between us.

Is she afraid of me?

"If you want out of this agreement, tell me now," I say.

"I'm going through with it."

"Your body language betrays your words."

"I'm in."

"I don't expect you to jump for joy, but why the gloom and doom?"

"It's not you."

"Then, what is it?"

I'm not backing down until she gives me a straight answer.

She lets out a suffering sigh. "We lost everything in the middle of the night."

"What are you talking about?"

I listen, stunned, as she recounts the conversation she had with her father.

"Other than Villiers Grand, we have nothing left," she says, looking up at me like a skittish kitten.

Jesus. "I'm so sorry, Michaela."

"Myriad emotions collide inside me as I wrap my mind around this tsunami of drama. Overnight, I went from Prada to nada."

It's all stuff, so it's replaceable. Still, I can't imagine what it feels like to be in her position.

"Does your father know the right people to help him with this ordeal?" I ask.

"I don't think so," she says.

"I'll make some phone calls to my people in New York," I tell her. Surprised green eyes snap up to mine. "We have a team of lawyers, investigators, and other experts who can help your father navigate through this. These specialists will make the process easier for him and ensure he nails Thana's ass to the wall if she's behind this. If he goes at it alone, it might be frustrating and costly."

She hitches a breath. "Really? You'd do that?"

"Really," I say. "I'll also hire a team of security guards for around the clock surveillance for the hotel. Even though Thana is in custody, who knows what her lover is capable of."

"That was also a big concern for me, but Daddy doesn't have the means to afford that," she says, emotions bubbling up.

"I do."

With her lips pursed, she offers a tight nod.

"You're going to be my wife. I take care of what's mine."

"Under other circumstances, I'd take offense to that last part, Mr. Alpha Possessive Caveman, but I'm way too grateful to argue. Thank you so much, Phoenix." Her shyness is as evident as her sincerity.

"Don't mention it," I say. We sit in silence for a few beats as she fidgets with her fingers. "Change of plans!" I say.

Surprised green eyes meet mine.

"Let's postpone the meeting with the publicist."

"Oh, no," she says. "We don't have to do that." She looks absolutely terrified. "I'm okay meeting with the publicist. That's why I'm here."

"Stop worrying," I tell her. "You've dealt with enough in the past twenty-four hours. One extra day won't derail us. Let's skip the formal meeting, take the day to yourself, and let's go out for dinner tonight."

"You're sure?"

"I'm positive."

"Okay."

"How about eight p.m.?"

"Eight works."

"I'll ask my executive assistant to book a full session at our spa—you'll get the works. We have an upscale boutique here at the hotel, but since you'll need to buy a new wardrobe, I'll have a car drive you to Neiman Marcus, Beverly Hills."

"Err... did you miss the part where I said we have nothing left? I can't pay for new clothes. I'll have to make do with what I brought with me."

"I have an account at Neiman Marcus. Everything will be billed to me—"

"Phoenix, I can't accept this," she says.

"Michaela, you've agreed to become my wife and you're facing a dire situation. This is the least I can do."

"But you're already helping my father deal with the house fire. I'm sure the experts you're going to call on charge a hefty fee. The same goes for round-the-clock security services."

"You're right, but there a few things you're forgetting."

"What?"

"One, I'm the giant ape in the luxury hotel industry, the press calls me King König, and apparently, I'm a tycoon," I borrow her words from yesterday. I

'm rewarded with a huge grin.

I wink.

"Two, we're talking about *you*."

"This feels like charity," she says.

"I disagree."

She considers me.

"This would be our first time stepping out as a couple," she says with air quotes.

I have no clue where she's going with this, but I'll bite.

"Yes." I nod. "The sooner we make an official appearance, the better."

Her eyes narrow into translucent green slivers of determination. The dragon awakes. "Is this something else I'll have to add to the two-hundred-million-dollar-plus tab I owe you?"

I can practically see the icicles hanging from her tone.

"Can't you just accept a fucking gift?" I say.

She lets her head hang on a frustrated sigh.

"Look at me," I tell her.

She does.

"This is never going to work if we constantly go at it like two heavyweight champions looking to throw the knockout punch." My tone is razor-sharp. "It's us versus them, Michaela. Them being the board, the press, nosy celebrity bloggers, and anyone else who can pull back the curtain on our charade. I need an ally. If you can't handle that, and if you're always going to claw my eyeballs out, we should both walk away from this deal right now." I pause. "It might not be love, but right now, it feels like I'm entering a twelve-month sentence. You either want to save your legacy or you don't."

Chapter 13

Phoenix

I'm seated at the bar at Luogo Sapori, a Santa Monica five-star family-owned restaurant, awaiting Michaela with a full view of the door. My upbringing demands I wait for her before I start to drink, but given the day I had, I need this.

"There's something about the way you drink a martini that's so fucking sexy and so undoubtedly manly," a warm female voice says from my right.

It's not Michaela.

The overpowering perfume lingering in the air doesn't match the lovely flower scent of the little dragon with the piercing green eyes. The voice of the woman speaking, isn't hers.

Evelyn Pussett.

"Cheers!" A woman I was hoping to never see—or hear from—again lifts her wine glass in salute.

I selected this restaurant in the hopes I wouldn't bump into anyone I know.

That worked out well.

"Evelyn," I say with a small nod.

"Phoenix König. It's been a while. I was hoping for a second round." Her voice is a syrupy seductive purr that's been perfected over many years and at the expense of many of her victims—men. "I'm sad it never happened." She pulls her lips down in a frown.

"You're more delusional than I remember," I say before taking another sip of my drink.

She ignores my jab. "I thought we shared something pretty hot."

I drop my glass on the bar and turn my head just enough to lock eyes with the tall, slim woman.

She's wearing a striking short sleeveless dress with V-neck front in a screaming orange shade. Her long blonde hair, draping over her shoulders, now reaches down to her waist. She's not only a natural blonde, but she's one of the rare women who wears her fake breasts well. She doesn't feel the need to flash her double D's, nor does she walk around without a bra.

"It was a hookup. Plain and simple, Evelyn."

"But it could've been so much more." Her lips curve into a flirty smile.

"You mean, had I not walked back into the bedroom when I did, you would've had your way?"

She swats my arm.

I clench my teeth.

"You totally blew that out of proportion!" She rolls her hazel-brown eyes. "I told you a million times already."

"Stepping out of the bathroom and catching you with a safety pin in one hand and a pack of condoms in the other is pretty self-explanatory."

She sweeps her hair over her shoulder and stands a little straighter. "That's not what happened," she says.

"You weren't trying to get pregnant so I would become your

ATM machine for the next eighteen years?" I ask, my tone as sharp as a serrated blade.

"No." The insincerity in that one word is nauseating.

Evelyn and I met last year at a late summer wedding in Carmel-by-the-Sea. She was a friend of the bride. A buddy of mine was getting hitched.

In a crowd of stunning women, Evelyn was hard to miss. She's statuesque, gorgeous, smart, and charming. She's also a great manipulator. As an assistant casting director, she didn't come across as a woman who was waiting for a man to save her.

What was supposed to be a few hours of carnal sex, turned into a lot more. We didn't leave her hotel room until the next day. I fucked that woman's ass so hard, and so many times, I thought my cock was going to break. She never asked for a respite. On the contrary, she kept begging for more. She's one dirty girl. I also fucked her pussy, but Evelyn needs a big cock pumping her ass to come undone. I was happy to oblige.

There was no hiding my identity, so she knew exactly who I was, but she didn't seem fazed, which is why I didn't expect her to pull that sneaky move.

"Are the rumors true?" Evelyn asks, changing the subject.

"Which rumors?" I ask.

"Did you get her pregnant? Is that why you're forced to marry that Michelle... or is it Miley... Marielle, maybe?" Evelyn waves her glass in front of her face in a dismissive gesture. "What's the name of the girl you're marrying?"

"You mean, *woman*?"

"Girl. Woman. Same thing."

Right. "Her name is Michaela."

"Is Michaela pregnant?"

None of your fucking business.

I face her to give her a piece of my mind, but I'm interrupted by a pair of lasers beaming at me. A man I recognize stares in our direction, annoyance and anger written all over his face.

I'm willing to bet everything to my name, Evelyn hooked up with the newly appointed Mayor of Los Angeles's brother. I've met him at numerous charity functions. He's an arrogant motherfucker. His ego is bigger than my brothers', my father's, and mine, combined.

I answer Evelyn's question with one of my own.

"Is that your date?" I jerk my chin.

She doesn't even bother turning around. "We're together," she says with nonchalance. "He thinks I look good on his arm and therefore, it's good for his public image. He has big political aspirations."

"You're aiming high," I say.

"He's okay, but"—she looks left to right before leaning in and murmuring in my ear—"you're a much better lover. And *much* bigger, too... and what you do with your tongue. Oh, fuck... no one's ever done that to me before."

I'm sure she meant it as a compliment, but she comes across like the two-timing bitch she is.

I come to the guy's defense. "That's a low blow to a man's ego."

"I make him think he's a stallion, when he's anything but. He's happy, and he rewards me with a monthly allowance. Everyone wins."

"Great relationship goal." Sarcasm drips from my words.

"It works for me," she tells me with a defiant chin lift.

"Good for you."

"So, you still haven't answered my question. You made it pretty clear you weren't the dating or marrying type. This is quite the turnabout."

I laugh. A day of fucking and she thinks she knows me. How presumptuous of her. "You have no—"

In my peripheral vision, I catch a flash of legs and a pair of heels that pull my eyes to the door. I do a double take.

Jesus.

"The cat got your tongue?" Evelyn asks.

Everything—and everyone—in the room disappears as my gaze travels up and down the length of her body.

Wow.

Michaela stops traffic in a jaw-dropping hot pink sequined short-sleeved dress. It's short enough to reveal her shapely legs —a lot of leg, in fact—but it's still elegant and chic. The seductive neckline that shows just a tasteful hint of cleavage draws my attention to her tempting breasts. The close fitted design of the dress hugs her in all the right places. And those strappy high heels in the same pink shade accentuate her calves so perfectly. Her short dark hair is styled in an edgy, yet sophisticated way. The glint in her ears indicates she's wearing the same small diamond studs she was wearing earlier today.

She's mouthwatering.

Scratch that.

She. Looks. Banging.

My cock strains against my pants as I take her in. It's a struggle to remember this is a business arrangement and not a real date. Everything about her is an open invitation... one I'll be forced to ignore.

Dammit.

"That's one hell of a dress," Evelyn says. "I guess Mindy isn't pregnant."

My annoyance flares.

"Get it in your head, Evelyn. Her name is *Michaela*. Not Mindy. Not Michelle. Not Miley. And not Marielle!"

"I forgot," she says with a shrug.

Right.

"If you'll excuse me." I stand from the barstool. "My girl is here." The moment I'm on my feet, Michaela spots me. Her eyes cut to Evelyn before meeting mine.

I read judgment in her gaze.

It's like her eyes are shooting ice pellets at me.

I purse my lips and offer a subtle headshake, so she knows this isn't what she thinks it is.

Her face is impassable, but there's a storm brewing in those big green eyes.

Shit.

"I guess a leopard can change its spots." Evelyn is still running her mouth. "Who knew?"

I stare her down when I say, "It's a question of finding the right one. It can happen just like that!" I snap my fingers.

Evelyn is incredulous.

"Michaela is the right one for me." If I'm going to play a role, it should be an Oscar performance.

"Mazel tov!" Evelyn lifts her glass in a mock non-celebratory cheer, a tight, fake smile plastered on her face. "I wish it could've been me."

I'm so glad it's not.

"Enjoy your new man and the allowance," I tell her. "My fiancée is waiting."

At the mention, my eyes drop to Michaela's left hand.

We need to fix that.

Chapter 14

Michaela

Who the hell is that blonde?

And why is she standing so close to Phoenix?

Whatever is going on between them looks very intimate—too intimate, if you ask me.

Oh shit.

I bet he's fucked her. That explains it.

Did he have drinks with her before meeting with me?

With his eyes locked onto mine, Phoenix struts towards me with such confidence, you'd think he owns the place. I straighten my shoulders as he approaches, both hands clenching my new bejeweled black clutch. I congratulate myself on my selection of heels. Five and a half inches don't put me eye to eye with him, but at least I no longer feel like he towers over me. I pin him with a critical stare—a mix of bitterness, bravery, and... jealousy?!

No. No. No.

That's not even possible.

I'm not jealous. I'm pissed off because he promised he

wouldn't humiliate me or make me look stupid. We're not even married, and he's already breaking his promise.

Men!

"Michaela." He offers a warm smile.

"Phoenix." I allow my eyes to brush along his tall frame. I should be appreciating the view, but I'm too ticked off for that. So, I let my claws out.

My eyes travel to the blonde shooting daggers at me before returning my attention to him. "Will your *ex* join us for dinner?" I ask, a mocking grin plastered on my lips.

He narrows his eyes at me. Under the lights, they glint like two dark sapphires. "She's not an ex," he says.

"And I'm the first female Pope," I say with a wry smile. "I didn't expect your love life to slap me across the face tonight."

Tension settles between us.

A muscle in his jaw ticks and his nostrils flare.

I brace myself for his retort, but to my surprise, he closes the gap between us and leans in until his lips flirt with my earlobe. "I have a past, Michaela. There's nothing I can do about it. She's part of it," he says. "I'm not a cheater," he reminds me. "Stop worrying about her. She's not worth it, trust me." He pauses. "Tonight, is about you. *You're* my present. This is our first date in public. We're supposed to be madly in love."

I'm sure I wouldn't be nearly this affected if he hadn't murmured those words in his trademark deep, smokey voice.

I clear my throat and take a step back, pulling away from his magnetic field of lust.

"Thanks for clarifying that," I say in a small voice.

He gives me a onceover. "I'm glad to see you gave my Neiman Marcus account a good workout."

"I didn't go overboard," I say, worried he might think I took advantage of him.

"I didn't mean it as a criticism. You look stunning," he says.

My cheeks flush. I'm certain they compete with the color of my dress.

"Thank you," I say. "I love the dress and the shoes." Our gazes drop to my feet in unison before we lock eyes again.

"So. Do. I."

I get that he's the lead singer of a former boy band and all, but the man's raspy voice is too sexy for words.

"The shopping spree was very generous of you," I say.

"I'm the lucky guy who gets to admire you!" He winks. "And by the way, hot pink is your color."

"It's one of my favorites."

"You wear it well..." He gives me another appreciative onceover, so slow it's like a caress. Then, a cocky grin forms on his kissable lips. "I can't wait to discover your other favorites..."

It could be my perverted mind, but I'm certain I heard a double entendre in his words.

"The experience at the Pompadour spa was unparalleled." I veer the conversation to mask my nervousness. "The stylists who did my hair and makeup worked their magic."

"They had a great canvas to begin with."

Oh wow.

"Thank you again for everything," I say.

An afternoon at the spa and shopping at a high end shop won't make up for my predicament, but it was a welcome treat. For a few hours, I was able to forget everything.

"It's my pleasure. Consider it one of many shopping sprees to come."

"Phoenix!" I frown. "No. It's not necessary."

"You're not going to win this argument, Michaela," he tells me. "I'm fully aware of what you bought today. You only purchased a few pieces. That's not a wardrobe."

It was way more than a few pieces, but he's right, it's not a wardrobe. I was overwhelmed, and that says a lot, considering I'm well versed in the art of power shopping. But today was such a sobering experience. Back in New York, I had a walk-in closet stuffed with designer clothes that's now all turned to ashes. It's only when you lose everything, you realize how much you had.

"You're impossible!"

"Get used to it," he says.

Another reminder things are about to change between us.

"Mr. König, are you ready for your table?" a man I didn't see approaching asks.

It's like when I'm close to Phoenix, I'm oblivious to everything around me.

"Hungry?" he asks me.

"I'm famished," I say.

"Shall we?" He extends an arm.

I glide a hand over his forearm. To my surprise, Phoenix drops his other hand over mine.

My gaze snaps to his.

He cocks a challenging eyebrow.

"Yes," I say.

He rewards me with a smile that could light up Las Vegas. And Paris. And New York.

God, the König charm is potent...

"If you'll follow me," the man, I assume is the maître d', tells us.

As we trail behind him, it's impossible to ignore the curious looks—and murmurs—as people turn and stare as we venture further into the restaurant.

"You're drawing attention," Phoenix tells me.

"Uh... no. These women are drooling all over *you.*"

"You're blind to your beauty, Michaela."

I love hearing my name on his lips?

"Women are looking at you with envy, and men are looking at you, wishing you were hanging from their arm instead of mine. Tough luck."

I'm stunned.

I'm unprepared for that pantie-melting side of King Kong Tycoon.

"You're buttering me up again, König?"

He slides a hand to my lower back, a move that sets my pulse racing.

Good God.

"No, kitty cat, I'm telling it like it is. You have the kind of undeniable beauty that could start a war between men."

Boom! My ovaries just exploded.

"Here we are, Mr. König," the maître d'hôtel says.

"This is perfect," Phoenix says before pulling out a chair for me.

"Thank you." I lower myself to the seat and place my clutch on the table.

Phoenix unbuttons his suit jacket and sits across from me.

I glance furtively around us.

Our table for two is tucked into the corner of the restaurant and offers an enviable view of the room. It's a great vantage point, but it also means there's nowhere to hide. The bottle of champagne already chilling in a bucket sends a clear message.

Showtime!

"Should I pour the champagne, sir?" the maître d' asks.

"I assume this is okay?" Phoenix's eyes drop to the bottle.

"Champagne is more than okay," I say. "Especially, when it's Krug's Grande Cuvée."

When we're short staffed at the Villiers Grand's restaurant, I cover for the wait staff. We carry an assortment of expensive champagne, so I know how much this bottle cost.

"Nothing is too good for my girl," Phoenix says, a mischievous glint in his eyes.

It's with great effort I don't roll my eyes.

That said, I'm not one to be upstaged.

I channel my inner starlet. "Baby, you take such good care of me. How did I ever get to be this lucky?"

He chuckles.

The maître d' pops the cork. For some strange reason, I'm tempted to shout *Opa!*, but I refrain.

"I'll send your waiter over," he says, pouring the champagne in our flutes before submerging the bottle in the bucket of ice.

"It's been a long week for both of us," Phoenix says. "Let's start with the platter of antipasto."

Whoa!

I'm careful not to let on how surprised I am by his selection, considering he doesn't know my food preferences yet.

"We'll order our main dishes later," he tells the man. He moves his attention to me. "Are you okay with that, *sweetheart*?"

Game. On.

"*Baby*, you know I'll never refuse a charcuterie platter."

"Should we opt for an extra platter of cheese?"

"Absolutely!" I say. I peer up at the maître d'. "Personally, I think cheese should be a food group," I say with feigned seriousness.

"I agree," the maître d' says. "I'll have the platters sent to your table *pronto*."

"Thank you," Phoenix says.

With that, the short, bald man vanishes in a puff of efficiency.

"The service is impeccable at the Luogo Sapori," I say.

"You're sure this restaurant doesn't fall under the König umbrella?"

"I wish," he says. "Everything is irreproachable here. I've been coming here for years and I've never had one complaint. Wait until you taste the food. You're going to be blown away. And I say that from the viewpoint of a man who hires some of the best chefs in the country. I've thrown big money at the grandmother who's still the main chef, but she refuses to come work for me. Something about maintaining the legacy and heritage. Whatever."

Phoenix lifts his champagne glass.

I mimic him.

"Here's to us!" he says.

"Here's to us!"

We clink our flutes and take a long sip of our champagne, eyeing each other from over the rim of the glasses.

The effervescent liquid hits my taste buds. *What a decadent treat!*

"This is exquisite." The words slip from my tongue.

"Worth every penny?" Phoenix asks.

"Definitely."

My gaze sweeps across the room, taking in our surroundings until my eyes fix on the blonde who was practically draped all over Phoenix when I arrived.

Her lips contort in an expression of contempt.

She gives me that look. It's like she's saying, *"Who the fuck do you think you are, bitch?"*

I flash her a triumphant smile as I lift my champagne glass.

That's right, he's mine.

As soon as the thought pops into my mind I want to slap my forehead.

He's not yours, silly.

This is fake.

A business transaction.

An arrangement.

This fierce sense of possessiveness is foreign to me. It makes no sense whatsoever considering I've only known Phoenix less than forty-eight hours.

My eyes meet his.

I study his handsome face as he holds my gaze. His strong, chiseled jaw is dusted with dark stubble, setting off the unique shade of his magnificent blue eyes, and his lightly tanned skin tells me he spends more time behind a desk than on a beach. My eyes travel as I continue my inspection. His arms bulge under his fitted black tailored suit jacket and since he's *sans* tie, I get a nice peek of his chest.

Devastatingly handsome.

Beautifully muscular.

And impeccably dressed.

This is suit porn at its best.

I'm willing to bet Phoenix König is something else in bed.

No wonder that blonde wants to pierce my heart with a poisoned dagger.

"You're done checking me out?" he asks.

I suck my bottom lip under my teeth to curtail a smile, dropping my gaze to my flute for a beat before glancing up at him.

"You're hard to miss." That comes out a little flirtier than I intended.

A smile tickles the side of his mouth. "Is that a compliment, Michaela?"

We run hot and cold, but right now, we're running scorching hot.

"Maybe." One word. More than that and I'll compromise myself.

He considers me for a beat. "I won't tell anyone if you don't."

"Our little secret?" I play along.

"Exactly."

I laugh.

"You're warming up to me, kitty cat?" he asks.

"Don't count your chickens before they hatch, König."

The air between us is crackling. It's quite the departure from the cold front that's been blowing between us.

A waiter approaching, carrying a massive tray, interrupts our banter. After placing a mouthwatering display of food on the table, he places his hands behind his back and bows his head. We barely have time to thank him before he disappears.

The efficiency here is commendable.

"*Buon appetito!*" Phoenix says.

"*Buon appetito!*"

"Dig in!"

"You don't have to tell me twice."

"You're not going to argue with me?"

Before I can answer, a man dressed head-to-toe in white with spiky blue hair approaches our table.

"Fuck," Phoenix mutters.

I frown my confusion.

I lean into the table. "Who is he?"

The man speaks before Phoenix is able to respond. "Looks like *Phoenix's Prodigious Phallus* is spoken for."

My jaw drops.

Phoenix's eyes burn with fury as he moves his gaze away from mine.

"What kind of stupid nickname is that?" Phoenix asks.

"According to my *many* sources, it fits," the man says.

I can picture *Phoenix's Prodigious Phallus*, and in my filthy mind it's pretty impressive—like the rest of him.

"Are you done annoying me?" Phoenix asks.

"That's silly, King König. I'm just lubing you up. I haven't even dropped to my knees to give you a blowjob yet," the man says.

I believe that's my job—

Whoa!

Where the hell did that come from?

Getting up close and personal with Phoenix's Prodigious Phallus isn't part of our arrangement.

"What do you want, Payne?" Phoenix asks.

The man hovers over our table. "Enough foreplay," he says. "In the name of journalistic integrity—"

"Integrity?" Phoenix says. "You wouldn't know how to spell the word even if Google slapped you across the face with the search result."

"Well, my millions of followers would disagree with you," the man says. "I *am* a bona fide reporter." He flashes Phoenix a condescending smirk.

This sparring between the two men doesn't go unnoticed. All eyes are on us.

Great.

"You mean, you post garbage on your celebrity blog," Phoenix tells him.

I remember reading Payne Meldrum's snarky article when I was getting my hair done. It was pretty condescending.

Payne ignores Phoenix's dig. "What a coincidence we'd end up at the same place at the same time. Lucky me. I get to witness the love story of the year unfold in front of my very own eyes."

The sarcasm is thicker than a cloud of smoke.

He shifts his attention to me, long enough to give me a onceover.

"She's gorgeous," he says. "Why have you been keeping her a secret?" he asks Phoenix.

"My relationship isn't up for discussion, Payne," Phoenix says. "Unlike the salt and pepper grinders, it's not on the table."

"So, you're Michaela, aka, the fiancée?" Payne continues his interrogation, unfazed. "Where's the ring?" he asks, his eyes zooming to my left hand. "Let me guess. It's being sized." He rolls his eyes. "You two are rushing to get married, but you're not wearing his ring yet? Right. I smell a publicity stunt."

What an asshole.

"Payne—"

"I'm sure the concept of privacy is foreign to you," I say, interrupting Phoenix, "however, it's still a value many of us hold sacred." I pin the short man leering at me with a stern glare. "Would you suggest we start making out on the table for you to believe we're in love?" I ask. "Or perhaps I should straddle my fiancé's lap and grind against him like I'm riding Ginuwine's *Pony*. Or would you rather we text you a clip of the kinky sex video we shot last night and call it a day?"

Payne's irritating smirk falls.

I'm on a roll.

"As for my ring, my fiancé wanted me to have the ring of my dreams—one I'll be proud to wear on this finger *forever*." I flash my hand and point to my ring finger. "So, he bought six different eye-popping styles that would make a bona fide princess green with envy." I read this story online not long ago and I can't believe it's come in handy. "Phoenix surprised me with them this morning over breakfast." I place a hand against my heart. "It was so romantic." I pause and sigh theatrically. "Having to wait a few days until the ring is sized to perfection is a small price to pay for long lasting happiness." I plaster a disingenuous grin on my face. "It shouldn't matter if you believe Phoenix and I are in love, because it's really none of your business, but apparently, you decided to make it your business. Do you have any other questions for us, Payne, or can we enjoy our dinner in peace?"

The annoying celebrity blogger's eyelashes—coated in gaudy electric-blue mascara that matches his hair—flutter like the wings of a chicken about to set flight as his eyes ping pong from mine to Phoenix's.

He's stunned.

Frankly, so am I.

Since yesterday, it seems I no longer have any filters and I have no problem putting people in their place. I don't know what kind of beef Payne has with Phoenix, but I didn't come this far to let this asshole jeopardize everything. I don't make it a habit to lie, but desperate times call for desperate measures.

"Wow!" Payne says. "I admire your lady balls."

"I'm quite attached to them." Sarcasm drips from my words.

"Consider me your *consigliere* now," Payne says with a respectful bow.

"My what?" I ask.

"It's a nod to the *Godfather* movie," Phoenix says.

"Exactly!" Payne says. "Which means, I can't publish tomorrow's blog post on King König and his queen without photos!"

"Don't bother taking photos if it's to ridicule us again," I tell him.

"As your *consigliere*, I'm now your ally," he says.

This guy is so flighty.

It's scary to think how many people he influences every day. However, the show must go on.

I meet Phoenix's gaze. "Is it okay with you, my love?" I ask him.

He cocks an eyebrow, visibly impressed. "As long as it's okay with you, sweetheart."

I nod.

Payne snaps away.

"Well, I'll be out of your hair," the blogger says after snapping what seems like a hundred photos. "Too much gossip, too little time."

With that, he's gone.

Unbelievable.

My eyes meet Phoenix's.

It's not like I can ask him questions since everyone in the restaurant is staring at us, including the blonde who insists on giving me the evil eye.

"Well, that was interesting," I say, before gulping down the rest of my champagne.

A single quirk of one corner of Phoenix's mouth suggests he approves of my performance. "You're full of surprises."

I lean into the table. "We're a team."

I'm mesmerized as he reaches for my hand and lifts it up to his lips before dropping a soft kiss against it. The delicious sensation is so unexpected, I hitch a breath. "We're a team," he says.

Chapter 15

Phoenix

The ride from Santa Monica at this time in the evening is a breeze. There's so much to say, but Michaela and I spend most of the journey soaking up Los Angeles at night. Even though my driver is paid for his discretion, I didn't want to chance it.

With little traffic to contend with, the Bentley closes in on the Manhattan Beach neighborhood where Michaela's friend lives in record time. After passing the security checkpoint, the chauffeur crawls through the gated community until we stop in front of Rhys Hartford's impressive mansion. I get out and round the hood to her side of the car. I open Michaela's door and extend my hand. She accepts it and I help her out of the vehicle.

"Thank you," she says, stepping onto the pavement.

"My pleasure," I say.

The warm night air envelops us as we stroll down the long path paved with waves of cobblestones to the guesthouse in silence. Suddenly, a movement catches my eye.

A woman with short blonde hair lurks in front of a window of the mansion's top floor.

I tip my head in greeting.

She returns the favor and smiles.

"Your friend is watching us," I tell Michaela.

Her eyes shoot up to the house and she waves.

Her friend waves back.

"Right before leaving the restaurant, I texted Keira to tell her I was on my way," Michaela says.

"We've talked about this before, but she's trustworthy, right?" I ask.

"You have nothing to worry about," Michaela says. "Keira is a friend, not a foe. She's on my team. She knows what the Villiers Grand means to me."

"Good. I'm sure she's going to have a lot of questions for you tomorrow morning—"

"Keira sure is going to give me the third degree." She laughs.

I chuckle.

"You were fantastic tonight," I tell her when we stop in front of the guesthouse. "You handled Payne Meldrum with such finesse. I was awestruck. I would've chewed him up, but you pulled out the kinder, gentle side of him. I didn't even know he had one."

"It wasn't too much?" she asks. "I mean, after all, I kind of lied about the rings."

"It was over-the-top, but you had me convinced."

"*Phoenix's Prodigious Phallus*?" She flashes me a cocky grin. "That's quite the title. Is it a myth?"

There are so many devious ways I could answer that question, but I decide to be good. "I'm going to leave that one alone."

Michaela cocks an eyebrow. "Are you going to leave me guessing?"

I could put an end to the suspense by unzipping my pants, pulling them down with my boxer briefs, and showing her the proof, but that might be pushing the envelope. Not to mention, my mother raised me right.

I weigh my words.

"Is that your way of saying you changed your mind and you're no longer stuck on us entering a sexless marriage?"

She looks me up and down, stopping at my crotch. "Regardless if *it's only* a myth, it's a catchy nickname."

Oh, she's asking for it.

I narrow my gaze at her.

She responds with a broad smile.

She's good at poking the bear.

Two can play that game.

"Celebrity blogging is a simple business model—more views equal more money. Payne will use just about any sneaky trick in the book to spin any shred of truth into an attention-grabbing headline that's nothing more than blatant clickbait. Although in this case, *Phoenix's Prodigious Phallus* is accurate. At least now you won't have to wonder anymore. You know it's *not* a myth, kitty cat."

She rolls her eyes hard.

"So, there's no bad blood between you?" she asks.

"Payne is annoying as fuck, but I ignore him unless he's hovering over my table while I'm trying to have dinner. He likes to give everyone equal opportunity, so he'll attack successful people, athletes, and celebrities. It doesn't matter to him as long as he profits from it. I'm just another guy with a name who's on his radar."

"I thought it might have to do with your boy band days," she says.

Of course, she read about my heydays.

"Picture it," she says with a theatrical hand gesture, "an excited Payne, before he became a celebrity blogger, waiting for hours with other eager fans to get your autograph after one of your sold-out concerts he couldn't get tickets to. Alas, you refused him because you were rushing to a press junket. He vowed there and then to one day destroy you for snubbing him."

"That's a hell of an imagination."

"I have an overactive mind."

"No shit. You know of my first career?"

She nods. "I watched *all* your videos. Those were some smooth moves, bad boy König."

I hang my head low. "In my defense, that was a long time ago. My brothers and I were young, and we were rebelling against the expectations set upon us at birth."

"You mean in terms of joining the family business?"

"Exactly."

"I understand that very well."

"I loved my older brother—the four of us did—but there was always an underlying message looming over our heads as we grew up. My father never came out and said it, but his actions spoke volumes. He had a favorite son. Barron excelled at pretty much everything in life, but he wasn't musically gifted. The guy couldn't carry a note to save his life, and he had two left feet. Slate, Wilder, Roman, and I didn't succeed because we were the best singers. We were on top of the world because we could put on a kickass show. That, and we could rip t-shirts or shirts off our bodies on cue. Combined with the blue eyes and winning smiles, we were set."

She laughs.

"Mom used to say we inherited our musical talent and stage presence from her side of the family, but for some mysterious reason Barron wasn't born with those genes." I laugh a little, thinking of the two people I miss every single day. "In any case, you did good tonight. You had my back."

"No problem," she says. "I didn't expect those reporters when we left the restaurant."

"Neither did I. My guess is Payne must've posted something on social media and that tipped off a few more piranhas who were hoping to get a scoop or a statement."

We left Luogo Sapori like freaking celebrities, with our hands lifted, shielding our eyes from the blinding flashes of the cameras as reporters shouted questions at us.

"Payne." Michaela shakes her head. "What a *pain* in the ass."

"My guess is his parents knew exactly what kind of human being they were bringing into the world when they named him."

"Oh my God, that's so funny and so accurate."

We laugh.

"You think on your feet," I tell her.

"Someone had to put Payne in his place."

"Let's stick to your ingenuous story about the rings. You'll have to let me know what style you prefer, and I'll get my contact at Harry Winston to deliver it in your size. He's discreet, so all this will be hush-hush."

Her eyes grow wide. "Phoenix, a Harry Winston ring is way too expensive for a fake wedding."

"You haven't met the members of the board yet. If you think Payne is a hard ass, you're going to get your bubble burst when you meet the group of nine men and women who are the thorn in my side. There's only a handful of people who know this relationship is fake. To the rest of the world, our union has to look real... all the way down to the engagement ring and wedding band."

She blinks.

"We have to go all the way on this, Michaela."

"Okay."

"This brings me to something very important..."

"What?" she asks.

"We need to coordinate our stories. Since we're not going to be joined at the hip twenty-four seven, we need to make sure neither of us slips up when recounting the details of our whirlwind romance."

"You want to do this now?" she asks.

"Not tonight. Tomorrow we should really put our heads together before we meet with the publicist."

"Tomorrow sounds good."

I take a step closer. "There's something else..."

"What?"

"Our first kiss."

"Oh."

Under the lights, it's impossible not to notice how her eyes practically take over her face.

She wasn't expecting that.

It's been on my mind since she stepped into the restaurant, but now, it's an obsession.

"The first time I kiss you shouldn't be when the priest gives me his blessing to kiss the bride." My voice comes out like a seductive murmur and my eyes drop to her lips. "If we don't practice, it's going to be obvious it's the first time. I'd hate to blow our story to pieces on the day we tie the knot."

"Oh."

"You did a stellar job acting the part tonight, and I willingly followed your cue. But can we fake a convincing kiss?"

"I don't know," she says in a low voice.

"We shouldn't chance it."

"What do you suggest?"

I move close enough to smell the many layers of her lovely perfume.

Delicate. Refined. Sophisticated.

Her.

"Practice makes perfect," I tell her.

"You mean, we should practice right now?"

"Why not? The more mileage, the smoother the ride."

"Isn't it the more mileage, the clunkier the ride?" she says.

"It depends on the caliber of the vehicle."

A sly smile stretches her lips.

She knows I just one-upped her.

"I'm going to guess, you're in a caliber all on your own," she says.

"There's only one way for you to find out."

"I guess so." She tucks a strand of hair behind her ear. "Do you want to come inside?"

"We should get used to kissing in public."

The truth is, stepping inside her guesthouse is a guaranteed way for my cock to accidentally slide inside her pussy. She's made it very clear that isn't on the table. There's no point in testing the limits of my willpower.

"You want to kiss out here?" she asks, her eyes looking behind me in the direction of the garden and the pool.

"It's just the two of us."

"True."

"It doesn't have to be hot and heavy, it can just be a chaste kiss, but I should know how your lips feel against mine," I say, placing my hands on either side of her face.

Shock radiates from her eyes. Her chest heaves, pulling my attention to her tits.

Fuck, those are gorgeous.

"Okay. Let's practice."

"That sounded a little too clinical for my taste. It's like you just agreed to getting your teeth cleaned."

She laughs a little.

"Can I kiss you, Michaela?" I ask, my thumbs stroking her cheeks.

She bites her lower lip as she leans into my caress.

"Yes, please."

"I like that answer, kitten."

"Kitten? What happened to kitty cat?"

"She retracted her claws."

She laughs again.

I take my time admiring her beautiful features.

Daring eyes hold mine.

"Are you going to kiss me or not, König?"

She keeps piling on the surprises tonight.

I lean forward slowly, torturing her a little before granting her wish... and mine.

The moment my lips meet hers, I throw the idea of a chaste kiss out the window.

The sparks that have been zapping between us ignite.

The world narrows to this moment—to our lips locked together. When she melts into the kiss, my hands lower to her nape, bringing our bodies closer together. I'm ravenous as I ravish her mouth. Her little seductive moans are intoxicating. My teeth close over her bottom lip and tug at it with a sharp nip. When her tongue slips out to soothe it, I slip my tongue inside her mouth, angling her head to gain better access.

Fuck this kiss.

I'm buzzing.

It's been so long since I've held a woman in my arms.

Michaela responds with reckless abandonment. I knew all that fire she was spitting at me could be channeled to something so much sweeter.

"Christ," I say, tearing my lips away from hers.

Fueled with the desire to explore and devour every inch of her, I walk us backward until she's pinned against the house's façade. I crowd into her, blocking off the view from the main house so her friend can't see us. Kissing in public is one thing, what I have in mind is another. I lift one arm so it's resting on the wall beside her head. Her skyscraper heels give her height, but she's much shorter than the women I usually go for.

We're so close, our noses touch, and our breaths mingle as the heat from her body radiates through mine. Even in the outdoors, her scent fills my nostrils and damn if it doesn't make my mouth water.

She looks up at me, almost helpless. Her usually translucent green eyes, now dark with desire, bounce between mine before dropping to my mouth.

My lips twitch, relishing the moment.

I lift a hand, brushing my fingers along her chin.

Her breath hitches and her eyelids lower for a beat before fixing her gaze onto me.

My fingers skim down the smooth skin of her neck.

She shivers.

I allow a finger to travel between her breasts before cupping one in my hand and squeezing hard.

"Oh God, Phoenix."

My cock swells in my pants.

I drop my head to her neck and breathe her in.

"Fuck, you're sweet," I tell her.

"You're torturing me."

"I know."

"If you keep it up, I'm going to melt."

I flash her a wolfish grin before pressing my hungry mouth to hers like I've been aching to do since she stepped out of the Bentley and onto the dock yesterday afternoon. When she parts her lips and invites my tongue inside with a sexy-as-fuck moan, it takes everything for me not to lose my shit.

I've kissed women before, but nothing comparable to this.

I press my body against her belly, making sure she knows Payne's nickname for me isn't a myth. She catches me off guard when she grinds against my erection. My cock is as hard as steel and it's a struggle not to lift her into my arms, step between her parted legs, and seek the relief I desperately need.

This is so fucking hot, I can barely remember my own name.

They say it's a fine line between hate and desire. It's the only way I can explain the mounting feverish hunger for this woman.

I lose my fucking mind in the kiss.

Our tongues tangle in a wicked, sensual dance, as she matches my fervor.

I pull away from her and stare at her. "Fuck, kitten," I say. "You're not holding back."

"Neither are you."

Needing more, I crush my lips against hers as I deepen my voracious kiss.

She moans into my mouth, an invitation for me to continue my assault.

And so, I do.

While still kissing the hell out of her, I press my cock harder against her center.

More urgent.

More ferocious.

More demanding.

Goddammit.

The temptation to slide my fingers between her pussy lips and finger-fuck her is so overwhelming, I'm nearly dizzy.

I curse this fake marriage.

If our tongues mesh so well together, I can just imagine our naked bodies seeking pleasure from each other as I fuck her like she's never been fucked before.

Too bad it's not meant to be.

My phone buzzes with an incoming text in my pocket. I ignore it, but it's a reminder things have gotten a little out of hand.

Shit.

Panting, I break the kiss.

"We're like fire and fuel," I say, brushing my lips against hers. "We combust upon contact."

"Dear God." She places a hand against her heaving chest. "That was a little too intense. It's supposed to be pretend."

My forehead touches hers and I breathe in her unique scent. "That was as real as it gets, kitten."

I kiss her again. It's soft, but firm. Still, it's nothing like the searing kiss we just shared, but I couldn't resist.

Reluctantly, I drop my hands and pull away from her.

She struggles to catch her breath as she frantically pulls at the bottom part of her dress.

"No one will know," I say.

Shy eyes meet mine and she bites her lower lip. "I've never done anything like this before."

"You mean, making out outdoors?"

"Yes. Or kissing like that."

"Like what?"

"With such..."

"Abandonment?" I finish her thought.

"Yes." She winces at her admission and averts her gaze.

Her cheeks match the color of her dress to perfection. She brings her fingers to her lips devoid of lipstick. They're swollen and red from my assault.

Look what I did to you, kitten.

I'm not going to lie. I love knowing I've unraveled her.

"It was a commendable first kiss," I say.

She arches an eyebrow.

"But since I'm a perfectionist, we're going to need to practice a lot more than that."

"You demanding tyrant," she says.

"You have no idea how demanding I can be, Michaela," I tell her. "Given the nature of our arrangement, you'll never know."

No answer.

I didn't expect one.

Chapter 16

Michaela

An incessant ringing jars me out of my sleep.

I groan, disoriented and irritated someone would dare to interrupt my deliciously naughty dream.

As I find my bearings, I'm shocked to find my fingers buried deep inside my pussy. I'm even more shocked when realization sets in.

No way was I fantasizing about Phoenix.

On a curse, I remove my slick hand from between my legs. I shift my gaze to the nightstand when my phone rings again. I grab it and flip so I'm lying on my back and answer.

"Hey, Keira," I say.

"You're up?"

"Barely."

"I can tell by your morning voice," she says.

"What's up?" I ask.

"I have a delivery guy here with an enormous bouquet of flowers."

I sit up straight in bed. "Someone sent me flowers?"

"I'm going to play psychic and guess they're from your husband-to-be," Keira says.

"Oh wow."

"King Kong Tycoon has great taste."

"What do you mean?"

"I have no idea what these are, but the bouquet stands out, and it's unique," she says.

Would it be wrong to admit a shudder of excitement washes over me?

"Do you want me to send the delivery guy over to the guesthouse?"

"Can you accept them on my behalf? I'm not exactly presentable right now."

"All right, I will," Keira says. "But get your pretty ass over here pronto so we can have breakfast and you can tell me what you did to deserve such a stunning bouquet."

"I'll be right over."

I end the call, a huge smile stretching my lips.

After a quick morning routine, I take a shower, get dressed and I'm out the door.

Memories of our fiery kiss tiptoe through my mind when I pass in front of the spot where Phoenix assaulted my lips just a few hours ago.

My mind kept reminding me it was all for show—just a practice run—but from the way my body ignited under his touch, I know it was way more. I'm still unsure who that brazen woman was who so greedily grinded her body against a near stranger without an ounce of shame, out in the open for public scrutiny.

Fuck, that was a hell of a phallus.

Kissing Phoenix shouldn't trigger this wave of confusion. I need to keep things straight. I can't afford to have a fuzzy mind around this guy. He's too dangerous. And too much of a great kisser.

Damn him.

With each step I take, more snippets from last night's kiss flash in front of my eyes.

I don't want Phoenix to kiss me again.

I don't want Phoenix to kiss me again.

I. Don't. Want. Phoenix. To. Kiss. Me. Again.

I stop halfway to the house and I bring my fingers to my lips as if they're still burning.

How could I have enjoyed it so much?

Why does he have to be who he is?

Such injustice, God.

Another time, another place, and that kiss might've meant something.

The irony.

This isn't a Hallmark movie.

My new reality is as far removed from a fairytale as can be.

I, Michaela Knight, am a pauper, pawned by her desperate father, in debt to King Phoenix König to the tune of two hundred million for a year of pretend.

Nothing more. Nothing less.

As I reach the main house, my phone rings.

King Kong Tycoon.

I should change his name.

Nah. Not yet.

I laugh under my breath.

"Good morning," I say, accepting the call.

"Good morning, Michaela."

That voice.

"I hope I'm not waking you up," he says.

"In a way, you are."

"I'm sorry," he says. "Should I call back a little later?"

"I'm already up. What I mean is, Keira called me when the delivery guy showed up at Rhys's house. I'm on my way there now. Apparently, someone sent me flowers."

"Guilty as charged," he says. "You haven't seen them yet?"

"No. Keira accepted them on my behalf because I was still in bed when the delivery guy showed up."

"You in bed... that's quite the visual, Michaela."

I can just imagine his hooded blue eyes staring at me with desire while the muscle in his jaw ticks like last night. As if on command, my pussy clenches.

God.

Enemies? Lovers? Future fake husband and wife? I have no fucking clue what we are anymore. I'm not sure I really care either. Not after last night's kiss.

I clear my throat. "Thank you so much for the flowers," I say, veering the conversation to safer ground before I throw caution to the wind and rush back to the guesthouse to rub one out. "That's so unexpected. Keira can't stop gushing all over them. I can't wait to see them."

"I selected a bouquet of dahlias."

"Dahlias are gorgeous."

"They're unique... like you. I got the hot pink ones because it's your favorite color."

Warmth curls in the vicinity of my chest.

The giddy feeling lasts a second.

Fake marriage.

Get it together.

"You're calling because you want us to meet today."

"Yes," he says. "We have a lot of ground to cover." I'm grateful he slips back into business mode. "Do you have plans this morning?" he asks.

"No. I was just going to hang out with Keira."

"I hope your friend won't hate me, but I'd love to steal you away. Let's have breakfast together. Something laidback before we jump into contract terms."

"Okay. I'm sure Keira will understand."

"Excellent! I'll send the Bentley over. The chauffeur will leave now. He should be there in forty minutes, if traffic permits."

"That works. I'll be ready."

"Your engagement ring should be delivered by the time you get here."

My head jerks back in surprise. "Oh wow. That was quick."

"You texted me your top selections last night, and I immediately forwarded it to my contact."

My heart is beating way too fast for me to form a response.

A hurricane of emotions riots through me.

This is really happening.

"We have to get the ball rolling, Michaela," he says, as if he can sense my turmoil.

I nod even though he can't see me. "Of course." The words come out faint.

"You're still with me on this?" he asks.

I pinch my lips together, wanting to escape from all of this, but I can't.

"Michaela?"

"I'm still in." *I know what's at stake.* "It's a lot to take in at times," I add.

"We're a team," he says, borrowing my words from last night.

I can't help my laugh. "We're a team."

"All right, I have to go. I'll see you soon, Mrs. König."

"See you soon," I say.

Then, it hits me.

Wait? What?

"Phoenix, I'm not changing my last name."

No answer.

"Phoenix?"

I pull the phone away from my ear and stare at my screen, dumbfounded.

He hung up.

Chapter 17

Phoenix

My gorgeous bride-to-be is fresh-faced this morning. She requires very little makeup to highlight her stunning beauty. She's all business in a pretty, flowy lilac floral dress that reaches her mid-calf.

My fingers itch to undo the buttons running up the front of the dress to take a peek at what she's hiding underneath. I have no doubt her body is clad in mouthwatering lingerie.

Her dainty feet are trapped in the same pair of sexy-as-fuck white high heels with a strap circling her delicate ankles she wore when she barged into my office two days ago to rip me a new asshole.

A little over forty-eight hours ago, we were strangers. Now, we're planning a wedding. Un-fucking-believable.

"This takes breakfast to a whole other level of perfection," Michaela says. "Where do you find your chefs? Do you poach them from the top restaurants in the country?" She leans forward and drops her coffee cup on the table.

"We don't need to resort to such underhanded actions," I

say. "We attract the best and we treat them right. My father lives by this motto. It's the same for my brothers and me."

"Hence, your undisputable success."

"Something like that."

We hold each other's gaze for a few long beats.

There's something about this undeniable pull that's beyond her unquestionably seductive physical features that jack up my libido. And it has nothing to do with going without sex for too long. It's debatable, but in this case, it's way more than that. With other women, the surge of attraction is never this all-encompassing. Not even with Marie-Clémence or Evelyn.

Michaela crosses one leg over the other.

The flash of skin is enough to awaken my cock.

She unfolds her legs and crosses them again.

Tease!

It's almost as if she can read my thoughts, and she's determined to test my resolve.

A surge of lust shocks my veins, and my cock throbs.

Fuck. Me.

Every inch of me wants to dive in the warmth between those toned legs.

I gawk, not bothering to hide my appreciation.

Our eyes meet.

Palpable heat snaps the air between us, searing and hot.

After last night's kiss, I'm not sure how we're going to survive a sexless, yearlong marriage. I guess I should speak for myself. I'm still unable to read her.

Her pink lips stretch into a knowing smile. "You're staring."

"So are you."

She laughs.

It wouldn't be hard to keep admiring her like this for the rest of the day, but that's not why we're here.

I grab the iPad and hand it to Michaela.

"Look at this. Payne changed his tune."

"'*HAIL TO THE KING! King König soon to turn his hotel heiress fiancée into a bona fide queen.*'" Michaela reads out loud. "Wow. What a departure from the article he published a couple days ago."

"Thanks to you." I point at her.

She beams.

"Since we also played things up for the cameras as we were leaving the restaurant, we struck gold. There are a few other notable articles on us stepping out last night. All good, but nothing compared to Payne's article, which has gone viral."

"This is great news, Phoenix. You were worried the media might not buy our story, and they'd take malicious pleasure in poking holes into our romance. It seems they bought it, hook, line, and sinker."

"I'm relieved they did," I say. "The publicist is ecstatic. Instead of putting out an official statement with our side of the story, she's going to let the good publicity do its thing. The less we say, the better."

"I agree," she says. "That's a big win for us."

"It's a major win because the plan is for us to get married this Sunday."

Her jaw drops.

Her long eyelashes flutter like crazy.

She opens her mouth to say something, but nothing comes out.

Her shoulders slump.

The helplessness and worry I read in her gaze is the polar opposite of the fierce determination I've seen shining from her translucent green eyes.

"I admit, the timeline is short," I tell her.

"Ridiculously short," she says, her gaze filling with anguish.

I nod.

"Is that even enough time? Doesn't it usually take a year to organize a wedding? Six months at the very least?"

"So many of our hotels offer wedding services. It's a matter of pulling together a few key individuals to make it happen in a flash. As for the venue, we'll get married at Dad's mansion."

Wide incredulous eyes stare at me in disbelief.

"My life changes in four days." There's no way to miss the resignation underlying her words.

I stand up, round the coffee table, take a seat next to her on the sofa, and place a hand over her trembling ones.

"I know I'm pushing hard," I say. "I thought I had everyone convinced of our *love story*, but after this morning's early meeting with the board, I have to press on the accelerator. One board member in particular isn't buying it. Truth be told, the guy hates me. He's cracking the whip for the board to find a replacement for my father. If the board isn't slowing down their mission, neither can I."

"I understand," she says. "This is what I agreed to."

Over a copious breakfast we shared the basics—family history, where we went to school, favorite color, hobbies, likes, dislikes, allergies—none for either of us—and the list goes on. Since we already shared a lot when we were on the yacht, we have enough to cover our tracks. With time, we'll fill in the blanks.

Now, we move onto the more contentious points. I reach inside my jacket for an envelope and hand it to her.

"What's this?" she asks.

"The contract."

"I see." She unfolds it.

Her eyes bounce from one line to another as she takes in all the clauses.

"Do you have a pen?" she asks.

I reach inside my jacket and produce my Montblanc pen.

"Thanks," she says, grabbing it. "I'm not changing my name," she says, crossing out the clause. "Earlier, you hung up before I could contest."

This woman...

She scans past her monthly cash allowance—fifty thousand dollars. She skips over the clause giving her a chauffeur on demand *and* the car of her choice. She bypasses the clause that allows her to keep her diamond ring. And it's like she barely notices the terms of our divorce that guarantees the Villiers Grand Hotel will be hers free and clear three hundred sixty-five days from our wedding day. Michaela Knight Villiers goes straight for the clause about the last name.

My obstinate queen.

"You're the only woman in the world who would have an issue changing her name to Mrs. König," I say.

She lifts a stubborn chin. "Why bother going through the hassle of changing my name for one year? Not to mention, I don't want to lose that connection with my mom." Emotions coat those last words.

"In terms of the hassle, I have people to take care of that," I tell her. "You won't have to chase after documents. That's their job. Yours will be to sign a few documents. Once we get divorced, I'll get my team to take care of the paperwork to revert your name. That said, I understand and respect your desire to keep your mother's last name. What if we compromise on Mrs. Michaela Kennedy König Knight Villiers? It's a bit regal, but you can pull it off. It ensures you won't lose your name on any official paper and Mrs. König won't sound foreign to your ear."

She studies me.

"I can live with that," she says.

"Good."

Satisfied, she keeps reading.

"There's a clause about children?!"

"Just in case," I say.

"In case of what?" Her face pinches with confusion. "It's not like I'm the Virgin Mary. There will be no Immaculate Conception."

"You and I know the marriage is fake. My lawyers don't. This is a standard clause."

"Oh. I see."

Her attention returns to the contract.

"There's nothing shady about the contract, but like we've discussed before, you need the advice of a lawyer," I say when she reaches the last line. "Did you find one?"

"Rhys is working on it," she says.

"I'll need the signed contract back by Friday midday."

"Okay. Where will we live?" she asks.

"We'll stay at the penthouse and we can spend weekends on the yacht or at the Malibu mansion."

"Okay."

"Hopefully you're not a slob," I say.

She shoots me a death glare. "I'll have you know I'm a very tidy person. Some might say I'm a bit of a neat freak."

"I'm not surprised." I give her a onceover. "It shows."

"You set me up, didn't you?"

"And you fell for it." I shrug. "Do you have any other questions for me?"

"One last thing," she says.

"I'm all ears."

"What color are your eyes?" she asks.

That's the last question I expected.

"Will that make or break our arrangement?"

"It's not going to change anything, I'm curious."

"You noticed my eyes, kitty cat?"

She arches an annoyed eyebrow. "I'm sure you know your eyes are a unique color."

"Like my mom, I have hazel-blue eyes," I tell her. "Roman has one blue eye and the other hazel-blue. He has heterochromia," I say. "And, you're right, hazel-blue is unique—much more than green eyes."

"Not bad," she says with nonchalance.

"Not bad?"

"Okay." She pauses for a beat. "You have attractive and mesmerizing eyes."

"A compliment?"

"I'm stating the obvious."

"You know what else is unique about me?" I lower my eyes to my crotch.

"Err... I'm good."

I couldn't resist.

"Speaking of Roman, how's your brother?"

"He's doing better." I pause. "Guilt still eats at me, though."

She frowns. "What do you mean?"

I hesitate.

"Maybe I shouldn't have asked the question."

I exhale. "Two and a half months ago, I sent Roman to the Maldives to determine if we should keep a couple of hotels we have there or if we should sell them. Numbers are one thing but getting the lay of the land offers perspective. It was a productive trip. Within a week of him landing on the island, we made the final decision to sell. Then, he was off to the Seychelles to check up on our three hotels there."

I have her full attention.

"On the way back to LA, he stopped in Hawaii to meet up with a couple buddies of his for a short surfing holiday. As the baby of the family, Roman is a daredevil. Mom and Dad let him get away with murder. Since he had four older brothers, he always felt the need to *ten-up* us. That character trait never subsided. Pe'ahi—located on the north shore of the island of Maui—is more commonly known as Jaws and got the threatening name due to the size and ferocity of the swells."

"Yikes!"

I nod. "I don't have balls big enough to take on Pe'ahi."

"But Roman does?"

"It wasn't Roman's first time surfing there." I swallow hard. "However, this time, things went horribly wrong. He got caught in one of those monster waves and nearly died. His two friends didn't make it."

"Dear God."

"Since Dad was recovering from a heart attack and was prohibited from flying, Slate, Wilder, and I made the trip to Maui. It was frightening to see Roman all battered and bruised. My baby brother was in a coma for ten days and he sustained life-threatening injuries, but he's still with us. Losing another family member would've destroyed us all."

She places a hand on my arm. "Mother Nature was having a bad day, Phoenix. You're not responsible for Roman's accident."

Logically, I get. Most days.

I move away from a topic sure to bring down the mood. "About the honeymoon—"

"We're going to have a honeymoon for a fake wedding?" she asks, eyebrows pinching together.

"Yes and no."

"You lost me."

"Dad usually attends the HEEA Europe Awards. It's a prestigious hospitality industry award. He had a checkup a couple days ago and although he's recovering nicely, his doctors don't think it's wise for him to fly just yet. My brothers are already booked to attend other important industry events, so I'll be the one representing the company. The awards take place next week in Paris. I figured we'd kill two birds with one stone—the awards and our honeymoon."

"A fake honeymoon in the most romantic city in the world?" She shakes her head. "We might as well play out this plot to the hilt."

"My sentiments exactly."

Malice sparkles in her eyes. "Will we take selfies in front of the Eiffel Tower or should we Photoshop all our honeymoon photos?"

"Smart ass."

"You have to admit, it's pretty ironic. Paris is synonymous with love *not* merger-marriages."

"I reckon you'd be surprised how many people hold hands for show. Your former stepmother is a great example."

"The conniving bitch did a great job fooling us all." She doesn't hide her disdain.

"Now, for the last item on the agenda." I veer the conversation. "The ring."

"I stand my ground, a cubic zirconia would've been a safer bet." Her lips curve in amusement.

"I play big and I win big, kitty cat."

I pull a navy-blue box engraved with two iconic letters from my pocket.

"Oh gosh!" She gasps. "I'm willing to bet that's not a cubic zirconia."

"I surely hope not because that is a lot of coin to drop on a synthetic stone."

Her eyes bounce to mine, her excitement evident.

The moment is strangely intimate, considering her earlier jokes at the fake nature of the relationship. Dropping to one knee seems a bit much, so I play it down.

"You're in luck. My contacts at Harry Winston had the cut

you selected…" I crack open the lid on a 5.15 carat elongated cushion cut diamond ring set on a platinum band circled with small, brilliant diamonds.

Michaela's mouth drops open.

"Oh, Phoenix…" She brings one hand to her chest. "It's absolutely gorgeous. I know I selected it, but seeing it in real life, takes my breath away." I can't explain why pride floods my chest at her words. "Two carats would've been more than enough. You didn't have to supersize it."

"I'm glad you like it," I say. "As for the size, a queen marrying a king deserves a ring that makes a statement," I tell her. "Expect the matching wedding band to be as queen-worthy."

She giggles.

"If you keep spoiling me like this, I'm going to forget it's pretend."

Our gazes lock.

An awkward moment passes between us.

She can't take back her words.

A flash of uncertainty glints from her eyes.

"Silly me!" She slaps her palm against her forehead. "Of course it's pretend."

I follow her cue.

"Let me make it official," I say, reaching for the diamond ring.

"Okay," she says on the heel of a nervous laugh.

She extends her left hand. I take it and slip the ring on her finger.

"Oh wow!" Michaela says. "It sparkles like crazy and it takes a life of its own on my finger." She smiles down at the ring.

"It's feeding off your dragon fire."

"Sweet talker."

"It fits?"

Her eyes lift to mine. "It fits perfectly."

Another awkward moment lingers between us.

"Honestly, it's absolutely beautiful, Phoenix," she says. "Thank you." That came out with a touch of shyness.

"No, thank you for agreeing to all of this."

We exchange a warm smile.

"This dazzler should shut up naysayers," she says, breaking the spell.

"*The wedding* will shut them up," I say.

She exhales a long, shaky breath. "This feels so real," she says, placing one hand against her belly.

"Nervous?"

"Very. Butterflies are flapping their wings in my belly," she says. "If I'm this freaked out now, I can't imagine how it's going to be on the day of the wedding."

"I have faith in you."

"In that case, I guess I can't let you down."

"No, you can't because we're a team."

She rewards me with a genuine smile.

"Just in case things get too overwhelming on our wedding day, we should practice that kiss again," I say.

She shoots me a dubious side gaze.

"If we ace the kiss, that's one less thing to worry about."

Of course we're going to ace the damn kiss. This is totally self-serving.

"Okay, we'll go with your twisted logic."

"Please don't sound so enthusiastic."

With the hand adorned with a diamond, she reaches for the lapel of my jacket and tightens her grip. "Are you going to kiss me or not, König?"

A smug grin stretches my lips. "And you said you wouldn't do it."

She frowns her confusion.

"If it's good enough, you'll beg for it, kitten," I say. "Seems like last night's kiss left a lasting impression because you're begging for more."

She opens her mouth to respond, but I reach out, grab her by the back of her neck and pull her to me. I stifle her smart retort by crushing my lips against hers.

She moans and throws herself into the kiss, clutching at my jacket and pressing her body against mine.

The lovely floral scent I remember all too well wafts over me.

All coherent thoughts go flying out the window.

I fucking own her mouth, greedily taking it over and over again.

From the desperate way I'm kissing her, you'd never know I devoured her mouth like a glutton last night.

I agreed to her no sex stipulation, but since she didn't say anything about kissing, there's no way I'm putting on the brakes.

I'm unhinged.

Goddammit, I want more.

I tear my mouth from hers.

I pull back an inch so I can see her face clearly.

"Tell me to stop."

She says nothing. She just stares at me, her chest heaving.

If I were a better man, I wouldn't even need to ask. I'd respect her wish, but fuck, this woman...

"Tell me to stop, kitten."

I wonder if I look as crazed as I feel and sound.

"Don't stop." Her voice is husky and barely louder than a whisper.

Two words.

A world of possibility opens up to us.

"You're sure?" I ask.

"Yes. Forget everything I've said so far. Just kiss me."

In a mad rush, I remove my suit jacket and fling it somewhere in my office.

"Come here," I say, before lifting her from the sofa and dropping her on my lap.

Like a good girl, she straddles me.

"You make me fucking crazy, Michaela."

"This doesn't make any sense. We barely know each other. And I'm supposed to hate you."

"You can hate me and still want me," I say. "Based on last night, when we channel that hate-lust energy between us, it's combustive."

"This is so confusing.".

"Why waste time over-analyzing it?" I lift my hips, pushing my cock against her, and a groan slips from her lips.

Cradling her face in my hand, I devour her lips.

She tastes as sweet as the breakfast pastries she ate.

I skim my free hand from her knee, up her thigh, to the hem of her pretty dress.

She shifts on my lap, grinding down against my monster erection. I growl into her mouth as my tongue glides along hers.

This shouldn't feel this good.

She places her hand against my chest and pushes away from me. Concerned eyes meet mine.

"What is it?" I ask.

"What if someone comes into your office and finds us like this? Is the door locked?"

All the doors on this floor lock automatically. Furthermore, they're all equipped with a keyless touch-pad lock. It's a bit Fort Knox, but no way am I going to get fooled again.

"Does it matter?" I ask.

"Good God!" She winces. She shifts off my lap, but I clamp hard hands on her hips, preventing her from climbing off me.

"My staff know better," I tell her. "Even if I were to leave the door open, no one in their right mind would dare to walk in without knocking. Not even my brothers. They know better than to waltz in without my agreement."

"What if Lydia hears us?" she asks. "She sits right outside your office."

"She's stuck in a meeting until lunchtime. There's nothing stopping us, kitten."

Her eyes bounce around before settling onto mine.

She lets out a low laugh. "You make me do reckless things, Phoenix König."

"It's the only way to live, Mrs. König."

"I'm still Miss Knight."

"Only for four more days."

We exchange a complicit smile.

"Can I keep kissing the hell out of you?" I ask.

"I'm not going to stop you."

Thank the fuck God.

I kiss her hard enough to bruise her pouty lips.

She doesn't protest nor does she pull away. She meets my passion, tongue stroke for tongue stroke.

I take her hand and place it on my bulge. She whimpers into my mouth as her fingers cup my erection. My cock pulses and twitches at the contact.

"You do this to me, kitten."

"God, that's hot," she says as she strokes my cock.

With my free hand, I unbutton the front of her dress, revealing a cock-hardening lavender lace bra.

"Fuck," I say, as my eyes land on the swell of her breasts and her protruding pink nipples peering from the sheerness of the lace. "Jesus, you're so beautiful."

Unable to resist, I reach out and trail a finger across her skin.

She gasps when my finger caresses one nipple, then the other.

My lips crash against hers again and I kiss her with fervor as my hand slips under the hem of her dress. The warmth of her smooth skin burns my touch. Searing a line of fire along her skin, I travel between her legs until my fingers brush against the silk fabric of her panties.

I prefer to keep my sex life in a more private setting. Hence, why I'm a member of an exclusive adult club. It never even entered my mind to get down and dirty in my office. Yet, here I am defiling this beautiful woman.

"Phoenix..." She moans and pushes her body against my hand, urging me further.

"I love hearing my name on your lips," I tell her. "It's a lot better than King Kong Tycoon."

She responds with a shy smile.

"Say my name again."

"Phoenix."

"Again."

"Phoenix," she says in a breathy voice.

"One more time for good measure."

"Touch me."

That's not my name, but I can roll with that.

"I am touching you, kitten."

"I—I want more," she says.

"You're going to have to be more specific."

"Touch my..." Her eyes lift to the ceiling.

"Tell me."

"Touch my pussy."

"That's exactly what I'm doing." Yeah, I'm playing hardball.

It would've been presumptuous of me to peg her, but I'm guessing my assumptions are correct. She doesn't have that much experience.

"No, not like that," she says.

"Ask and you shall receive."

"My... my clit."

"Better. Now ask like a good girl."

"Please, touch my clit."

"I didn't hear my name in that sentence."

"Jesus, you're such an ass—"

She gasps when I put pressure against her pussy by lifting my hips.

"The sooner you give me what I want, kitten, the sooner I'll return the favor."

"Phoenix, please, touch my clit."

Finally!

A feral groan escapes my lips in reply.

I resume my assault on her mouth as I slide her panties to the side.

She's soaking wet.

She widens her legs and gasps when I drag a finger through her drenched pussy. There's no going back the second her desire coats my fingers.

Fuck, yeah.

Her heady scent flirts with my nostrils, and my mouth waters for more than I'm allowed to take. I'd be lying to myself if I said I'm not dying to take everything from her. Is it a mistake to confuse things between us by taunting her this way? Yes, I can't deny it. Should I draw a line in the sand? Probably. Do I care? Not at this particular moment in time. My desire to tame the dragon inside her supersedes common sense.

Fuck, I want her.

I slide my fingers to her hard little clit, coating it in her arousal.

"Just like that. Just like that. Just like that."

My cock swells at her words.

Not wanting her to come just yet, I slow down the tempo when her legs start to tremble.

"Don't stop," she says.

"I'm not done with you yet."

I part her pussy lips as I glide a finger through her wetness.

Christ!

It's like my boxer briefs are choking my fucking balls.

"Oh God," she says as her back bows.

I place a finger against her lips. "Shhh. We don't want anyone to know I'm doing dirty things to you, kitten."

"I—I'll keep quiet."

"Are you sure you can do that, or should I stop?"

Fire sparks from her translucent green eyes. "Don't you dare, König."

"We're on the same page?"

She nods eagerly.

I ramp things up and slip two fingers into her needy pussy as I continue to skate over her clit with my thumb.

She closes her eyes and drops her head back. "Good God," she says.

I pepper her neck with kisses. The temptation to bite against her milky skin and leave my mark is strong, but I resist. Barely.

"Give me your mouth," I tell her.

She does as she's told.

My tongue moves in sync with my fingers. Each stroke ratchets my desire for her. Each stroke a reminder I haven't shot my load inside a warm pussy in far too long.

My body hums with need for this woman.

I'm so close to flipping her onto her back and shoving my cock inside her pussy and fucking her like a savage until I fill her with my cum. I hold back. As it stands, we've already crossed the line of decency. Anything more would be foolish.

"I'm sure your sweet little pussy is addicting," I say as the slick wetness from her pussy coats my hand. I lean into her neck and murmur against her skin, "I'm willing to bet my fortune, you're fucking tight."

She responds by riding my hand with urgency.

Damn fucking right.

I respond in kind.

I finger-fuck her like my life depends on it.

Her hips rock in mesmerizing circular motions.

"Oh, Jesus, Phoenix," she says, combing her fingers through her short hair.

With her eyes closed and her dress undone, she's a vision.

She lowers her hands, places them on my shoulders, and bounces on and off my fingers.

The unexpected perversion is almost enough to make me come.

Fuck!

I pray the sucking noise of her slick pussy riding my fingers remains trapped within the walls of my office.

"Oh yeah, oh yeah, oh yeah!"

She's loud.

Her muscles contract in her pursuit to get what she needs, but she's not the one in control. I am.

Placing a hand on her hips, I halt her movements.

Wild eyes search mine. "You can't do that."

"That's where you're wrong, kitten. You broke our agreement."

"I'm sorry. I won't make another sound." If her plea doesn't do something to me.

I consider her.

"I promise," she says.

I resume my mission.

So does she.

In no time, she's nearing the edge.

Her hands fly to her mouth, muffling a sound.

Good girl.

"Dear God," she lets out in a low voice, her legs trembling.

"I want that pretty pussy to come all over my fingers until your slick release drips down my hands," I order.

She rolls her hips against my hand, keeping time with the demanding rhythm I've set for her.

With each gyration of her hips, she pants faster and faster.

"Work that pussy for me."

She reaches out and claws at my shirt, her fingers tugging into the crisp white fabric. As if that's enough to prevent me from pushing her off the edge.

Silly kitten.

Not on my watch.

I strip her of the remainder of her control, finger-fuck her harder, and apply precise pressure on her clit. Her pussy clenches in strong pulses, each throb sending a vibration straight to my balls.

"Come for me," I say against her lips. "But remember, not a sound."

"Okay, okay."

I thrust deeper and harder into her drenched pussy, wishing like fuck it was my desperate cock instead of my fingers as she clamps down on me. Her hips gyrate with velocity as she grinds her clit in jerky movements against my thumb.

My balls are filled with so much cum, and the need for release, nearly blinds me. How I manage not to come inside my boxer briefs is beyond me.

Her body tenses, her eyes roll to the back of her head, and she hitches a sharp breath as I send her flying off the cliff.

"Oh, my—"

I press my mouth against hers, swallowing her climax cries as she shatters all over my lap.

Dammit that was beautiful.

When she comes down from her high, I remove my hand from her pussy. Bewitched, I watch as pleasure continues to ripple through her.

I don't rush her.

"You okay?" I ask after a long beat.

She opens her heavy eyelids and stares at me with lust-filled glassy eyes. Her chest heaves as she tries to catch her breath.

She nods.

Under her watchful gaze, I slip two fingers still soaked in her pussy juices into my mouth and suck them clean.

Her eyes widen and her jaw drops.

She's so fucking tempting.

"Tell me, kitten," I say, moving my lips to her ear and biting the lobe.

She gasps.

"Are you still campaigning for a sexless marriage or are there ways to sway your decision?"

Chapter 18

Michaela

"Holy mother of big rocks!" Keira says, examining my engagement ring like an expert cutter would on 47th Street—aka New York City's Diamond District.

I'm back at Rhys's place.

I'm still not used to sporting my new accessory *du jour*. Therefore, when I joined Keira near the pool, where she was reading, I didn't expect the diamond on my ring finger to catch the light like it did and send my friend into freakout mode.

"Clearly, this is the real deal," she says, her huge hazel-green eyes meeting mine.

"It's Harry Winston, real."

Her eyes are even bigger now. "Mother of God, that's as real as it gets."

"Indeed."

"You are marrying a billionaire, after all. It goes with the territory."

"That's what Phoenix said. I'll be honest, I stopped breathing when he slipped the ring on my finger."

"I would've totally passed out," Keira says. "So how was the meeting with the soon-to-be-husband?"

My cheeks burst into flames.

"It went well," I say in a high-pitched voice.

Keira's brows draw together in confusion. "What was that about?"

"It was an intense meeting." *...to say the least.*

"I bet you had a lot to hash out."

"Amongst other things."

"I want to hear all about it," she says. "But food first. Are you hungry?"

"No. The chefs at the Pompadour outdid themselves. I'm still stuffed from the delicious breakfast."

"In that case, I'll eat, while you spill your guts," Keira says.

"Deal!"

I balance on my high heels and follow behind her to the kitchen.

She's still using her cane, but she's walking with more ease today. Knowing Keira, she's dying to wear heels again.

When we get inside, I drop my bag and take a seat at the kitchen island as she prepares her lunch.

In no time, she whips up a yummy looking tuna sandwich, complete with a side of crudités and a bowl of corn chips.

"Oh, by the way, Rhys found a lawyer to go over your prenup," Keira says, as she takes a seat across from me.

"I can't thank you enough for going to bat for me."

She stretches across the island and places a hand over mine. "First, we're friends. Second, you've gone through so much in the last few days, if anyone deserves a break, it's you."

"It's been a brutal few days." I place my other hand on top of hers. "Thank you, from the bottom of my heart," I say, as emotions take over me.

We exchange a warm smile.

"I'm just glad you have an expert in your corner to make sure King König doesn't stiff you," she says.

"I only have a basic understanding of contracts, but from what I can tell, he's being more than generous."

"Phoenix kept his word about the Villiers Grand, right?" she asks.

"He did."

"I'm sure your dad will be relieved."

"That's why he orchestrated all this."

I had a quick conversation with my father this morning while I was waiting for the car to arrive. Daddy didn't omit to remind me time was of the essence because he's drowning in debt. I assured him the Villiers Grand Hotel would fall under the König umbrella when I say I do. By Monday of next week, he'll be able to breathe easy.

As Keira eats her lunch, I share the most salient points of the contract.

"There's a clause on children?" She nearly chokes over a bite. "Well, that was a waste of good ink," she says. "It's not like you're going to touch each other."

"It's standard for a man in Phoenix's position." I shrug as if it's no big deal. It's best not to go there.

"Come to think of it, it makes perfect sense," she says. "When do you go wedding dress shopping?" she asks.

"Phoenix will make arrangements with a stylist at the Pompadour boutique. I'm sure she or he will have a selection for me to try on by tomorrow since the wedding is Sunday—"

"Wh—what?"

She's incredulous.

"I might've forgotten that part."

"Yes, you did," she says. "That's kind of important."

"Everything is so surreal. I might have omitted that detail as a way of pretending it's not actually happening."

"The enormous rock on your finger says it's most certainly happening."

I nod. "Four more days..."

"Wow!"

"We're going to keep it intimate. Phoenix's father, Slate, Wilder, and his extended family members on his dad's and mom's side will be there. Roman can't fly, but he'll join us virtually. On my side, we don't want to risk getting exposed. So, it will just be Daddy and Uncle Ian—"

"Does your uncle know the truth?" Keira asks.

"No. He doesn't. He thinks I'm in love. He's been following the buzz online. He's too close to Daddy not to invite him. He'll be present, but oblivious."

"It's easier to keep him in the dark," Keira says.

"One less person to worry about," I say. "In any case, you're invited, of course. I hope Rhys will be in town."

"Oh, trust me, I'll make sure he's present."

"Good. I can use two more friendly faces in my corner."

"You should thank your lucky stars your father picked the Bugatti of fake husbands."

"He did... in more ways than one."

Keira cocks an eyebrow. "Why do I sense you're hiding something from me?"

I pick up a discarded pen sitting on the kitchen island, tapping it a few times on the surface as I weigh my words.

"I'm waiting," Keira says.

I let out a frustrated sigh. "Phoenix is sexy as hell. He has the most incredible eyes I've ever seen. He's gorgeous. He's demanding in an all-encompassing-take-charge kind of way. He's annoyingly sure of himself and drips with confidence. He redefines suit porn. When he smiles, I freaking need shades. He's gorgeous. Even his hands are freaking sexy. I'm sure it's the same for his feet. In other words, he's exactly the kind of man I would avoid in New York," I tell her. I'm not sure I took a breath, but evidently, I still have more to say because I keep sharing. "And who the fuck has hazel-blue eyes? How am I supposed to not get distracted every time I lose myself in them?"

Shock flashes over Keira's face and she stares at me like she's never seen me before.

Honestly, I don't blame her.

Since Phoenix came crashing into my life— Okay, I guess it's the other way around because I barged into his office unannounced. Regardless, in the short time I've known him, he has an undeniable effect on me. And I hate it!

"Did he drug your coffee?" she asks.

"Why would you say that?"

"Not only was that verbal diarrhea a departure from your earlier description of him, but you used the words 'he's gorgeous' *twice*, and you mentioned his eyes, *also twice*."

"No, I didn't."

She shoots me a sideways glance like I grew another head. "Yes, you did."

I brush a dismissive hand in front of my face. "I was just agreeing with you. Thank God he's a Bugatti and not *Consumer Reports'* worst compact luxury sedan on the market."

"Yup," she says, "that man is a fine ride."

I let out a little laugh. "Oh, he's a fine ride, all right."

Shit.

Keira's eyes widen. "If I didn't know better, I might be tempted to think you're speaking from experience." She pauses, giving me a chance to say something.

I don't. I already put my foot in my mouth.

"Michaela?" Keira says.

"Yes?" I play dumb.

"What aren't you telling me?"

"The man is dangerous."

Keira sits straight on her stool and narrows her gaze. "Did he put any pressure on you in regard to the contract?"

"God, no." I drop my head in defeat. "I... I..." In the heat of the moment, what happened in his office was hot and heavy, but now, I'm a little—a lot—ashamed.

"You what?"

"That stupid kiss..."

"What kiss?" Keira asks.

"Last night. After he walked me to the guesthouse, we kissed. It was supposed to be a practice run for the cameras so our first time wouldn't be awkward. I was ill-prepared, Keira. The moment he dropped his lips onto mine, I could barely remember my own name."

She stares at me, her shock evident.

"At least I can justify last night's kiss as an integral part of this whole charade." I keep talking. "What happened this morning at his office is beyond me. I'm still grappling with what I allowed him to do to me."

"Good God, Mikki, what happened?"

"It was dirty."

"Dirty as in another tongue-lashing between you or dirty as in tongue-on-tongue action?"

"Tongue, mouth, hands... and his cock."

"Fuck. Me."

"Trust me, I was two seconds away from begging him to do exactly that."

"Start talking!"

I spill my guts.

"Holy slut!" Keira fans herself when I finish recounting my X-rated story.

I wince.

"My only saving grace was I didn't have to do a walk of shame. Lydia wasn't at her desk when I left. She heads a monthly morning meeting with the company's other executive assistants." I cover my face with my hands. "Still, this is so embarrassing. I don't even recognize myself."

"Oh, no, girlfriend. I mean slut in the best possible way," Keira says.

I look up at her and frown. "You don't think less of me?"

"Michaela, at the fault of sounding like a broken record, I'm going to repeat myself. Your soon-to-be husband is smoking hot. No one can blame you for making out with him."

"A lot of good it did me to swear up and down on a stack of Bibles I wouldn't allow him to touch me. My hormones tried to pull the emergency brake, but his potent male swagger and general deliciousness pretty much pulverized my walls."

We sit in silence for a beat.

"I guess the sexless marriage goal is well and truly fucked after this morning," Keira says.

"I told Phoenix it couldn't happen again."

Keira's jaw drops.

"You can't put the genie back in the bottle, Michaela. You realize that?"

"This morning was a lapse in judgment."

She's dumbfounded.

"You're actually serious right now?"

"I am." I offer a firm nod. "Moving forward, there's no room in our fake relationship for that kind of naughtiness. It felt too real, Keira. I don't want to end up with the short end of the stick a year from now. Phoenix is a member of a private adult club. He's used to casual hookups. I'm not. I already know it's not meant to be a forever story for the two of us. Why be a glutton for punishment?"

~

Once I was done oversharing, Keira declared I needed to work on my tan before my wedding day. I rushed to the guesthouse to change into my bathing suit, and I'm just about to run out the door, when my phone rings.

I look at the screen and accept the video call.

"Hey, Daddy!"

"Hey ladybug, how did it go this morning?"

"You look even more exhausted than you did this morning," I say instead of answering his question. The fatigue lining his features is so pronounced.

"Phoenix's expert called to talk about the fire, and then the police called because they had more questions. It's been a stressful morning."

"Oh, gosh, Daddy, you're dealing with a lot," I say. "I'm sorry I'm not there to lighten your load."

"We've already talked about that at length, Michaela. Your only job is to get to the altar," he says. "I'll deal with the rest."

A bitter laugh rumbles up from deep inside me. "Got it. Let's get down to business, then."

My father gives me a warning look, but I ignore him. I understand the urgency, but I resent how he makes me feel like I'm a commodity.

"You'll be glad to know Phoenix and I ironed out all the important matters. Now, it's a question of meeting with the lawyer Rhys found me."

My father lets out an audible exhale. "Keira's boyfriend was able to find someone to look over the prenup?"

"Yes. The lawyer will go over the prenup, the contract, and any other legalese before giving her blessing," I tell him.

"Since Phoenix won't be footing the bill, will you be able to negotiate a payment plan of some sort?" There's no mistaking the worry in his voice.

"Rhys wanted to pay for it in full, but I refused. He'll front me the money and I'll repay him back over time."

"Okay," Daddy says.

Silence stretches between us.

"Phoenix is a good man, Mikki."

I lose my temper. "How would you know, Daddy? He's just a business deal to you and a dossier an investigator collected!"

"Phoenix is solid." He stares straight into my eyes. "He'll be good to you, ladybug. In my heart, I knew he was the right choice."

That sounded kind of cryptic.

I hold his gaze when I say, "At least he's not a monster."

"I deserve that," my father says on the heel of a small laugh devoid of any humor. "You have no idea how guilty I feel about putting you through this, but—"

"I'm the only way out of this cluster fuck of a mess."

He glares at me.

I cock a defiant eyebrow.

"When is the wedding?" Daddy asks, moving right along.

"This Sunday."

His eyes widen in surprise. "That's fast."

"I thought that's what you wanted."

"I thought it would be a few weeks. Not a few days," he says.

"Phoenix doesn't see any point in stretching things out."

"I'm sure he knows what he's doing."

"Phoenix's executive assistant will make travel arrangements for you and Uncle Ian. He'll hire a private jet for the two of you."

"That's generous of him," my father says with a touch of humility.

"It's going to be a private affair at his father's mansion."

"It's a good idea to keep it intimate," Daddy says.

A crippling thought enters my mind as a pang of pain stabs at my heart. I place a hand against my chest and fold over a little.

"What is it, ladybug?" my father asks.

I pinch my lips and lift my hand to cover my mouth as emotions bubble up.

A tear trickles down my cheek.

Then another.

And another.

"Jesus Christ! Did Phoenix do something to you? Did he force himself on you? That's not part of the deal. He gave me his word he would treat you with respect." Anger colors my father's voice.

"No." I wipe away my tears. "So far, he's been a gentleman." I inhale a shaky breath. "It just hit me."

"What just hit you?" Daddy's voice rises.

"I've known since the day Mom passed away, she wouldn't be at my wedding, and I know this is a fake wedding—" I sniffle. "Still, it's a hard pill to swallow not having her there."

My father's eyes close for a beat. When he opens them, they're glassy.

We stare at each other in silence, overcome with emotions.

His gaze flinches as he blinks away tears before he speaks. "Oh, ladybug, you just broke me," he says, his voice trembling. "I've been single-mindedly pushing my mission forward. Securing the Villiers Grand's future became top priority—my *only* priority. I was so afraid I had fucked up your heritage, so ashamed I had let the woman I loved with every part of me down, I didn't even stop to think about Mom not being here and how that would affect you." He takes in a long, deep breath. "I'm so sorry, ladybug."

The sincerity in his gaze—and voice—touches my core.

Now we're both crying.

"One thing I know about my beautiful wife is she'll be watching over her baby girl," Daddy says in between tears.

In that simple statement, it's as if Thana was never part of our lives.

I nod in response because my heart is too heavy to speak.

"Charlize will be all decked out, with her nails done, her makeup expertly applied, and her long silver hair dyed brown and styled—coiffed, like she used to say." He offers a sad smile. "She'll be wearing a fancy dress and an elegant fascinator as a nod to her British roots. You know she'll be holding a glass of champagne, looking down from heaven above, giving God the play-by-play." He pauses. "She might not physically be with you on Sunday, but she'll be right here." He taps two fingers against his heart.

Now, he's the one to break me.

I bawl like a child.

Chapter 19

Michaela

I pray to God the pageant smile frozen on my lips fools everybody.

I'm going to be sick.

I'm going to be sick.

I'm going to be sick.

I'm this close to throwing up. Cold sweat prickles down my back even though it's another beautiful, sunny California day. My throat is parched, as if I've been wandering in the desert for days. My stomach is in knots and my skin burns with awareness. The butterflies that have been fluttering away in my stomach since walking down the aisle hanging from my father's arm are now engaged in the type of wild dance that could ward off evil spirits.

I'm absolutely terrified.

I've long stopped hearing the priest's monotone voice. I'm trapped inside the confinement of my head.

I got this.

I can do this.

I knew this day was coming. I woke up with the full understanding there was no safety net. I either jump or run. As tempting as it was to become a runaway bride and make headlines, I decided against it.

So, here I am.

Dear God, I'm really getting married.

As I stand in front of God, my dad, Uncle Ian, Keira, Rhys, and all the people from Phoenix's side, I become keenly aware of the vows I just took. The second Phoenix slipped the wedding band on my finger, a violent wave of nausea threatened to shoot out of me like a projectile. The weight of all those perfect, shimmery diamonds on my finger is as heavy as a prison sentence. And then there are all those eyes shining with hope, witnessing this sham of a wedding.

The end justifies the means.

Phoenix cocks an eyebrow and mouths, *"You're okay?"*

I give him a tight nod in response, my pageant smile still firmly in place.

He squeezes my hands before bringing them up to his lips, kissing them gently.

I guess he knows I'm bullshitting.

His action elicits a round of chuckles from the crowd.

The priest clears his throat and adjusts his glasses.

He's not amused.

Clearly, we're breaking a religious protocol or something.

"Sorry," Phoenix says to the priest.

For the first time since slipping into this outrageously expensive designer white gown, I smile. A real smile.

The priest carries on.

Phoenix winks and I respond with another genuine smile.

Even in my sheer terror, I must admit the man is drop dead gorgeous in his bespoke black tux. He's something else in a suit, but the tuxedo takes the concept of suit porn to unprecedented levels of hotness. Under the bright LA sun, the hazel tones in his eyes turn into a seductive and enchanting kaleidoscopic range of colors, making the blue in his irises stand out.

My fake husband is a glorious package.

"You may kiss your bride." The priest's words come crashing through my consciousness like a wrecking ball.

Oh God.

This is it.

It's official.

I'm a wife.

Phoenix flashes me a dazzling smile that nearly takes my breath away. He cups my face and stares into my eyes for a few long seconds.

"You're all mine now, Mrs. König," he says. "Finally, I get to kiss *my* wife."

I'm taken aback by the sincerity in his declaration, unsure if it's an act or not.

I don't have time to overthink it.

Phoenix brings his lips to mine and kisses me. It's nothing inappropriate, but it's still enough to consume every part of my body.

It's a dizzying feeling and one I could get used to.

The thought terrifies me.

Get it into your head. Three hundred and sixty-five days left...

Chapter 20

Phoenix

The intimate wedding and garden reception under a big, fancy canopy were a coup—simple, elegant, and upscale. The chefs at the Pompadour pulled out all the stops.

Thank God the official photos are behind us.

I swear the photographer must've snapped a thousand photos. Not that I'm complaining too much. We're paying a premium for one of the top photographers in L.A. So far, it's clear the guy is worth his weight in gold. Him and his team are still buzzing about, setting up their equipment in preparation for the cake cutting.

After the obligatory rounds of *thank you for coming*, my wife escaped upstairs.

My wife.

Those are two words I never thought would ever slip from my lips.

Even though I'm a willing participant in this fake marriage, I'm not too proud to say I nearly lost my shit during the ceremony. Knowing the countdown officially started when the priest uttered, *"till death do you part"*, is the only thing that prevented me from panicking at the idea of tying the knot with a woman. Michaela owns my balls for only one year. After that, I'm back to being a free agent. Thank God I have an exit strategy already in place.

Speaking of the little dragon, what's taking her so long?

I stride back inside and climb the stairs two by two to the top floor of my father's Malibu Colony Beach mansion and make my way to the guest room he assigned to her.

As far as Dad, Slate, Wilder, and Roman are concerned, Michaela and I have a platonic marriage.

I didn't feel the need to update them on the latest developments.

I knock.

She cracks open the door and pokes out her beautiful face. She's still radiant. And all but her lipstick, her subdued makeup is still flawless. "What are you doing up here?" she asks, gathering the fabric of her white silk robe.

"Is that any way to talk to your husband?" I ask.

"You don't have to act when it's just the two of us."

"I disagree. It's best to stay in character."

She rolls her eyes.

"What are you doing?" I ask, peering over her head.

"I'm changing," she tells me.

"Why? You stop traffic in your wedding dress and tiara."

The stylists at the Pompadour's boutique worked their connections to track down a stunning designer dress at the last minute. They're definitely getting a bonus. When they suggested a tiara adorned with Swarovski crystals as the ultimate regal accessory to complement a princess dress, Michaela hesitated. I told her she should go for it. I'm glad she did. She looked like a queen walking down the aisle.

"Thank you for the compliment," she says. "And thank you again for my perfect dress and all the incredible jewelry." She brings a hand to her 2-carat diamond studs. I also got her a magnificent wide diamond bracelet made in Italy. "I truly felt like a princess today."

"I'm a generous husband, but then again *my queen* deserves it," I tell her.

She purses her lips. "Well, *your queen* loves the way her king spoils her."

I shouldn't like hearing those words this much.

"So back to my question. Why are you changing?"

"It's tradition to slip into a less princesscy dress for the party."

"Okay." I push open the door and let myself into the room before closing it behind me.

"Phoenix, you can't be in here," she says. "People will notice we're both missing."

A muscle in my jaw clenches and my cock twitches in my tuxedo pants as I take in every delicious inch of her. My eyes travel down her body, stopping a little too long on her exposed legs and her dainty toes painted in a soft shade of pink.

"Come on, kitty cat, loosen up. It's tradition for the groom to escape for a little alone time with his bride."

She crosses her arms over her chest and shoots me an incredulous stare. "According to which manual?"

"*Phoenix König's Guide to the Perfect Fake Marriage.*"

We both laugh.

"People have been buzzing around us all morning like busy bees," I says. "Now that it's just the two of us, we can talk openly. You can change. I won't look."

"Fine."

Every muscle in my body locks tight as she sashays to the other side of the room, giving me an eyeful of her fine ass. The temptation to find out if she's wearing virginal white panties and a matching bra underneath the robe is overwhelming.

"Do you think we pulled it off?" she asks, leaning against the dresser.

I mimic her by leaning against the door.

"I'm certain we did," I say. "Your uncle and my extended family are clueless."

"Uncle Ian was miffed I kept our relationship a secret," she says, biting a perfectly manicured nail. "I told him I was so swept away, my feet weren't touching the ground and my head was in a blissful cloud. Hence, why my mind was so preoccupied and I failed to announce my new relationship status to the world."

"Damn, woman, you deserve an Oscar once this is over."

"At the very least."

"The official wedding photos will hit the internet within the hour. That should seal the deal in the public's eye."

The publicist refused to wait. I wasn't going to argue with her.

"No hiccups so far?"

I shake my head. "It's smooth sailing... let's see if it still holds true later at the party."

"We got this."

I nod.

This woman who was a stranger less than a week ago is now my most formidable ally.

"We did it as a team," I say, pushing off the door and stalking to her.

Without her high heels, she's just a tiny dragon.

"We did," she says with a smile, looking up at me.

My eyes drop to her chest. The outline of her breasts is visible under the silky fabric of her robe.

No bra.

I watch with fascination as her chest lifts each time she takes a breath. This close, her tempting perfume envelops me.

As if drawn to her like a magnet, I lean in and inhale her scent. A hint of headiness mixes with the floral notes of her perfume.

Heaven.

Something stirs beneath my skin and I already know I'm in trouble. But fuck if that stops me. I lean the rest of the way, tangle my hands into her short hair, and stare down at her.

She stares back.

Unable to resist, I place a soft kiss on her mouth. It's meant to be nothing more than a thank you, but when our lips touch, I can't pull away.

She moans into my mouth, as if testing my resolve.

I'm just a man.

I'm not that strong.

With a growl, I turn us both around and cross the room until her back hits the wall.

The kiss is as reckless as it was the last time I had my mouth on hers behind closed doors. Swept up in a cyclone of desire, I ravish her mouth. Her taste explodes on my tongue, turning the fire already raging inside me up twenty notches.

Damn.

I deepen the kiss.

She responds with as much ardor.

Our tongues mingle in a sexy dance as our hands roam all over the place, our breaths heavy.

She places her hands against my chest, pushing away from me.

"What is it?" I ask.

"You promised we wouldn't do more than kiss." Her voice trembles.

I kiss her ear, then her neck before saying, "We are kissing."

She twists out of my grip and hooks closed fists at her hips, her mouth screwing up into a defiant expression.

"That's not the kind of kissing we agreed to," she says.

"I'm aware I'm married to a woman I can't fuck, but kissing should at least be on the table," I tell her. "And none of that chaste stuff either. I'm talking about kissing you thoroughly like you deserve."

"Don't say things like that, Phoenix." Her usually translucent green eyes are as dark as a forest, her pupils dilated with lust.

You want this as much as I do, kitten.

"Why not?" I ask.

"Because. You shouldn't."

"That's a weak excuse," I say.

She sinks her teeth into her full bottom lip and sucks it into her mouth, seemingly pondering on her answer. "Things could get complicated."

I run my eyes over the curve of her cleavage. Lifting a finger, I draw a line between her breasts before cupping one of them.

She shivers.

She may protest, but her body isn't.

Every muscle in my own body aches with the need to sink my cock deep inside of her. I'm sure I'll pay the price for my greed. Once won't be enough and I'll have to find my way back inside her sweet pussy. Good thing I'm a master negotiator.

"After what happened in my office, things are already complicated, kitten," I say. "We can keep pretending there's nothing between us and grow frustrated with each passing day —with me acquiring a bad case of blue balls—or we can live out this attraction." I allow for a pregnant pause. "I vote for the latter."

Her eyes flick from mine to my lips and back up again.

"They'll hear us."

That's the hold back?

She needs a little nudge.

"Given the sheer size of the mansion, the music playing and the animated conversations outside, I doubt anyone will hear us. And, let's not forget, the free-flowing champagne plays to our advantage. If we were able to get away with our naughty fun at my office, this will be a piece of cake. And, if we were to get caught, it wouldn't shock anyone. We're newlyweds madly in love, remember?"

Her eyes shift from left to right.

She's thinking.

I can help.

I lay my cards on the table. "Since Wednesday, you've been an obsession. You have no idea how many times I've jerked off to the image of you climaxing all over my fingers. I want you naked, and writhing, and moaning, and of course, coming again."

"Phoenix..." My name is a plea on her lips, and it's my undoing. "Don't say that."

"You're repeating yourself, Michaela, but your protest does little to veil the lust I read in your eyes."

She bites against her lower lip so hard, I fear she'll draw blood.

I soldier on. "I want to fuck you so bad and shoot my load so deep inside you, I can't think straight. I've never—and I mean, never—wanted a woman like I want you." I wrap an arm around her waist and pull her to me until her body is flush with mine. "I can't fake this," I say, pressing my hard-on against her.

Helpless eyes stare wide behind a curtain of long, fluttering, dark lashes.

"And *you* can't fake this." Without warning, my hand travels underneath her robe to the middle of her legs. "For fuck's sake. You're naked."

Her cheeks flush. "The thong I was wearing was uncomfortable, so I removed it. I was just about to slip into another pair of panties when you knocked."

"Bless that thong."

My fingers slide between her drenched pussy lips.

A gasp escapes from her lips when I part her robe, revealing her naked breasts.

"Holy shit! You have the most magnificent tits."

She giggles.

I make love to her perfect tits, licking and sucking each nipple into my mouth, causing her to make desperate, needy, little sounds that are music to my ears. I circle my tongue around a puckered, pink bud one last time before biting against it as I slide a finger over her hard clit.

"Dear God," she says.

"You're so damn wet for me," I say, my voice strained.

My cock is about to fucking explode.

"This is over the top," she says.

"Everything about us is over the top," I remind her. "From the way we met, to the reason we were brought together, to our speedy wedding... it's pure madness. But us together, fuck..." I brush the back of my fingers along her cheek with my free hand while the fingers of the other skate over her clit in slow tortuous circles. "Your body was waiting for me. Tell me you don't want me to make you lose your fucking mind like I did in my office."

"Cocky much?"

"Let's stop pretending," I cut to the chase.

"I'm going to blame the champagne for this decision."

I pull my hand away from underneath her robe and step back.

Confusion colors her eyes.

"What did I say?" she asks.

"If you can't make this decision on a clear head, I'm going back downstairs."

Her eyes flinch, her surprise evident.

"All right—"

"Wait," she says and grabs my arm. "I want you to make me come again."

"That's it?"

"I want *you*, Phoenix."

With an agonizing grunt, I rip my tuxedo jacket off my shoulders, tossing it aside. I make quick work of my bowtie and in a flash, I unbutton my shirt, step out of my shoes and remove my socks. My pants and boxer briefs are next.

I stand in front of her naked and ready.

"Jesus Christ." The words drop from her lips as her eyes zoom in on the proof of my desire for her.

I'm so hard, my cock is pointing north.

"I told you I wanted you."

"Phoenix, that..." She points to my monster erection, "...is very impressive."

"You don't know the half of it. Wait until I'm pounding your sweet pussy, then you'll know firsthand."

She stares at me in shock.

"Are you on birth control?" I ask.

"Yes, I'm on the pill."

"You got my medical test results before signing the contract... and vice versa. We're both clean." I lower my eyes to my throbbing cock, before meeting her gaze. "Chasing after condoms right now would be a real fucking pain."

She laughs.

"I've never had unprotected sex before," she says.

"Neither have I. You're my first—my first wife *and* the first woman I'll fuck bare."

"That's a lot of pressure."

I reach out for her. She doesn't resist. "Something tells me you're up for the challenge, Mrs. König."

"I think I can handle it, Mr. König."

"You think or you know?"

She ponders on my question.

She lifts a defiant chin, fire burning in her eyes. "I can handle your big cock, Mr. König."

"Fuck. Me."

"I thought the idea was for you to fuck *me*?"

"Oh, kitten, you're asking for it."

"Promises, promises."

She drops her robe and stands before me in all her glory.

Goddammit.

I take it all in—the seductiveness of her slender curves, her gorgeous, fuckable tits, her toned legs, the sensuality of her stomach, and her pussy hair, trimmed in a shapely martini glass.

My cock salutes in appreciation.

My gaze slides back to her breasts. Holy fuck, her creamy-pale breasts with soft pink nipples are perfect. They're a nice size that will fill my palm and just big enough to titty fuck.

My mouth waters.

"I caught a glimpse of your beauty the other day, but seeing you naked... Your stunning body renders me stupid."

She beams.

I take my time drinking her in, unrushed.

"I'm sure it's a cardinal sin not to fuck your fake wife in a bed covered with smooth Egyptian cotton sheets on your wedding day, but if we lie down, we're likely to never go back downstairs. Not to mention, sporting freshly fucked hair, is wrong on so many levels."

"So, so very wrong," she plays along.

"You're okay with a fast and furious ride?"

"Yes." She licks her lips in anticipation.

Such beautiful submission.

My lips find hers and my tongue delves in.

She digs her fingers into my hair, and pushes her mouth onto mine, losing herself to the kiss.

I kiss her with hunger as my tongue forces her lips apart.

Fuck, kissing her might be my new favorite pastime.

After a few long passionate seconds, I pull away from her.

"I want you to come on my face, my cock, and my fingers, but we don't have the luxury of time."

My words shock her.

"Your mouth should come with a warning."

"Oh, kitten, I've been tame so far." My voice is deep and coated with lust.

"I'm scared of what you're like when you're unleashed."

"Don't worry, you'll soon find out." I lift her in my arms.

She circles her legs around my waist and snakes her arms around my neck.

I take a few steps until her back hits a wall.

I position her body right over my cock and growl at the unexpected wetness.

She gasps.

I'm unprepared for this mind blowing sensation. I don't even play with a woman's pussy until I'm all wrapped up.

I might die before the cake cutting.

Slowly, I slide my cock inside her pussy.

She's dripping.

"Jesus, kitten, you're so tight."

"Oh, God, you're huge."

I slow down my cadence to give her time to adjust to my size before feeding her a few more inches of my cock.

"Holy Jesus, you're so deep," she says.

"I'm not even all in."

Incredulous eyes find mine.

"You're kidding?"

"I never kid about my cock."

"I'm not sure I'm up to the challenge."

"You're selling yourself short."

Without giving her a chance to respond, I thrust inside her with such force her back slams hard against the wall.

She cries out in surprise.

"Now, I'm all in."

"Dear God!" Her head lolls back against the wall.

She's so tight, her pussy squeezing my cock like a vice. There are no fucking words to describe what her hot wetness is doing to me. The sensation is so primal, yet so foreign.

"Enjoy the ride," I tell her.

"Oh Jesus," she says.

"I respond better to Phoenix."

"Fucker," she says.

"Your wish is my command."

I *fuck her* hard and desperate.

The frantic cadence is nearly delirious. I swear I'm about to lose my mind.

It's been a while, but fucking this woman bare is the real reason I'm certain my heart is about to burst out of my chest.

"Fuck. This— This is so fucking hot," I say.

"This is the hottest thing I've ever done."

I sneak a peek to where our bodies are joined and my eyes lock to the way her pussy consumes every inch of my cock.

Needing more, I slide my arms under her legs, forcing them further apart. In this position, I can dominate her fully, leaving her no choice but to submit to me.

Because I'm a greedy bastard, I don't hold back. I thrust hard, pushing my throbbing cock inside her hot pussy over and over, burying myself to the hilt.

I press my forehead to hers. "I fucking love your pussy."

"I fucking love your cock."

My mouth crashes against hers, and I kiss the hell out of her. "I love it when we're on the same page," I say when I come up for air.

"So do I."

Sliding in and out of her slickness without any barrier feels like I'm swimming in sweet honey.

Goddammit.

I'm relentless, voracious and unyielding in my need to dominate her. I fuck her like she's never been fucked before.

She doesn't complain.

She takes it, over, and over, and over again, matching my feral nature.

I didn't expect this from her.

Behind the sweet angelic face, hides a dirty girl.

My dirty girl.

Each one of her desperate moans acts as fuel on a raging fire.

I ram into her as if it's my sole mission in life.

My heart is pounding like a drum, and my balls contract so hard, it's like they're going to rip open from the weight of my cum.

Shit.

I have no idea how I'm going to go back to fucking with condoms once this arrangement reaches its term.

I push the disturbing thought aside and lose myself inside her.

We both gasp from the force of my thrusts.

She pulls at my hair as if searching for relief.

That does little to rein me in.

I'm too far gone.

I need her pussy like I need my next breath.

"You feel so good, kitten."

I slide in and out of her pussy, raw and rough.

"Oh shit. Oh God. Oh fuck!"

"Shhh," I tell her.

"Sorry," she says.

I lean in and kiss her lips.

"I'm honoring my wife's pussy by fucking her like she deserves?"

"Oh, yes, you are. You really are."

I pound her without mercy.

I fuck her so hard, my balls slap against her sweet ass.

My ragged breaths echo around the room as I fight to maintain control.

"I—I'm close," she says between breaths.

Thank the fuck God.

No way am I coming first.

"Yes, yes, yes! Oh, God, yes!"

"Don't hold back on me, kitten."

"Phoenix! Fuck! Phoenix—"

My lips capture hers, eating her cries of pleasure.

Chasing my own climax, I pound into her with such force, her back slams against the wall.

Once.

Twice.

Three times.

My body tightens, my balls draw in painfully and my legs threaten to give out from underneath me as I deliver one last forceful thrust. The muscles of my ass lock up so hard, I choke. "Christ, kitten..." I bite down on her shoulder, as I shoot my warm load deep inside her. Unwilling to come down from my pinnacle, I keep fucking her through the river of cum spewing from her pussy and sliding down my legs.

Holy hell.

If it wasn't from the way my body was trembling, I'd be tempted to believe I've crossed to the afterlife.

The sound of our exhausted breaths takes over the room. I shift her body so I'm holding her full weight in the palms of my hands. She wraps her legs around my waist, pulling me closer to her.

I'm in no rush to break our embrace.

She lets out a little purr of contentment that tingles all the way to my balls.

I swear, I could go for a second round right here, right now.

I drop a light kiss on her flushed cheek. "You okay?"

"I'm more than okay. That was... that was... there are no words."

I chuckle. "We're good together?"

"We are."

"This was a little rushed because I wanted you so damn much, but I'll make it up to you later." I murmur my promise in the crook of her neck. "I can't wait for you to come all over my tongue."

Her breath hitches. "Phoenix, I can't do this again. It's way too intense."

"That's the way it's supposed to be."

"Until now, I couldn't spell mind-blowing sex even with the help of Google. I had no idea it could be like this," she says. "There's no way I can handle this kind of wild ride more than once every other day."

I pull away from her just enough so our gazes meet. "Every other day?"

"Yes. I need a day—even two—of rest."

"What kind of inept lovers have been fucking you, woman?"

"I haven't been with many men and it's been a while, not that you need to know. Also, not everyone has your stamina or your size, King Stallion."

If that doesn't make me laugh.

"Well, in my kingdom things are different," I tell her.

"My body won't sustain it."

"The fuck it will."

"Phoenix, between your punishing thrusts, the position you had me in and your *Prodigious Phallus*, I doubt I'll be able to walk elegantly in my heels. Everyone will know something happened between us."

"And that's a problem how? You're my wife."

She shakes her head.

I pull out of her and drop her to her feet.

I cup her face in my hands.

"If you think I'm not going to taste your pussy and give you at least three other orgasms before the stroke of midnight, you're dead wrong, Mrs. König."

She considers me, lips pursed, and malice shining bright in her eyes.

I brace myself for the flames that are about to erupt from her mouth.

"Well, when you put it like that—"

A knock at the door has me jumping out of my skin.

Shit.

Michaela draws in a harsh breath as one hand flies up to cover her breasts, while the other cups her pussy. When her panicked gaze meets mine, I do a hand gesture, coaxing her to find out who's at the door.

"Who is it?"

"Hey, sis, it's Wilder."

"Oh, hey, Wilder. What's up?" Michaela asks.

"Abuelita Noelia sent me to find you," he says. "You and my brother better come back downstairs because she's looking for you all over the place."

"Is your grandmother okay?" Michaela asks.

Wilder chuckles. "That eighty-three-year-old woman is an

oak tree. She's looking for you to have a little chat to bestow *womanly wisdom* for your wedding night. She even enlisted one of the cousins to help with the translation. She says you're absolutely gorgeous, but your Spanish *isn't very good looking*."

"That's a funny saying," Michaela says.

"*Abuelita* adapted that saying from Celia Cruz," Wilder says. ""*My English is not very good looking*" was the Cuban queen of salsa's go-to phrase whenever she addressed a non-Spanish speaking audience."

"I see."

"In any case, you two better come down, *pronto*. And for the record, I'm just the messenger, so don't kill me for putting an end to your husband and wife fun."

I can just picture his shit-eating grin.

Idiot.

I roll my eyes.

Michaela cringes.

Mom's youngest sister, Aunt Angelina, lives in LA. She's part of our big day, accompanied by her husband Blaize Bickford-Smith, and my cousins Callum and Ainsley—she's here with her new husband. Dad chartered a jet to fly the rest of Mom's family from Argentina for the wedding. My grandma, uncles, aunts, and cousins survived my mother's and Barron's death. Even if this is a fake wedding, not having them here would be wrong. Explaining a divorce is much easier.

"How did you know I was up here?" I ask Wilder.

"Bro, I have eyes. Your wife is stunning. Smoking hot, in fact. If you weren't up here with her, I was going to seriously start questioning your sanity and your manhood."

"I apologize for my brother's lack of tact," I tell Michaela.

She winces.

"You two are terrible actors, by the way," Wilder says.

I was certain we fooled everybody.

"What are you talking about?" I ask.

"Regardless of what you professed, one look at Michaela, and I thought, *platonic, my ass.* Seriously, the chemistry between you two reverberates against the walls. It's electrifying." He launches into a falsetto.

"Idiot! You're not auditioning for a talent show."

"Yeah, yeah, yeah," he says. "In any case, you can thank me later."

"Thank you for what?" I ask.

Then, it hits me.

I'm having a conversation with my brother and I'm still buck naked while he's standing on the other side of the door.

Unbelievable.

Under other circumstances, this would be quite comical.

I shake my head at the ridiculousness of the situation as my gaze moves to Michaela's naked body and then her terrified face.

The poor thing is as white as a sheet.

"You're lucky I came to warn you." Wilder keeps talking.

"About what?" I ask.

"I gave you a minute to hit your apogee before knocking, it would've been rude otherwise"—it's now he chooses to be a fucking poet?—"but you two are fucking loud. I mean, really fucking loud. I could hear you when I reached the top step and as I was making my way to Michaela's room. And, that says a lot since this mansion is enormous."

"Oh God." There's no hiding Michaela's mortification.

I'm right there with her.

I have a close relationship with my brothers. Not this close.

"Jesus Christ," I say.

"It's a good thing everyone is outside enjoying themselves. Your secret is safe with me, lovebirds," Wilder says. "But I'd recommend you keep the bumping uglies for later, get dressed and get your ass downstairs. Make sure to bring the consort to the king, aka my lovely sister-in-law. See you kids later."

A booming laugh resonates on the other side of the door, as his steps recede.

Michaela's face turns a bright shade of pink that's eerily close to the bouquet of Dahlias I got her a few days ago.

Wilder can be such a fucker when he puts his mind to it.

"Come on, let's get dressed before Abuelita Noelia comes up here," I tell Michaela once I'm certain Wilder is gone.

"Okay. I might need a shower first, though."

"No, you don't," I say.

"But—"

"I want my cum inside you. It's dirty and sexy, and it'll get me all worked up for round two."

Her jaw drops.

Chapter 21

Michaela

Keira's eyes widen in delight as she takes a bite of cake. She points an animated fork to the piece of cake on her plate as she chews, nodding in approval.

"Good God, this champagne cake is delicious, and moist, and buttery," she says after swallowing.

Just like the rest of the day, the cake cutting went without a hitch.

"If I ever get married, I'm so hiring the chefs at the Pompadour Hotel." Her gaze slides to Rhys who's laughing it up with Dad, Uncle Ian, and my father-in-law.

Complicit giggles erupt from both of us when our gazes meet.

"You're so obvious," I tell her.

"Says the new bride. You couldn't stick to the script. You had to break with tradition and nix the tossing of the bouquet," she says. "Even with my injured leg, I was ready to duke it out to catch it."

"You don't need a bouquet. That guy is so into you," I say.

"You think?" she asks the question she already knows the answer to.

I give her a, *are you fucking with me right now* look?

"Okay, maybe he likes me as much as I like him." She glances over at Rhys again. She has it bad. "Like I was saying, I want to hire the Pompadour chefs because the food is out of this world and this cake is positively the best thing I have ever eaten in my entire life."

"I agree," I say, shoving another forkful into my mouth.

We're both on our second serving of cake.

"I know your husband is a billionaire and owns a fleet of luxury hotels, but I still can't get over how his dream team put together an outstanding wedding in a matter of days," Keira says, her eyes scouring the garden. "And you didn't even have to lift a finger."

"This fairytale wedding surpasses any of my wildest dreams." *Too bad it's fake.*

Abuelita Noelia waves and winks as she strolls by, hanging from the arm of one of Phoenix's Argentinian cousins on her way to the dessert table.

Guilt washes over me.

She really believes I'm her new granddaughter-in-law. The worst part is, she's the sweetest woman, even if she thinks my Spanish *isn't very good looking*. I force a smile and wave back.

"I still can't get over Abuelita Noelia giving you *the talk*," Keira says.

"Neither can I. Bless her for feeling the need to assume the role of sage adviser since my mother, my mother-in-law and both of my grandmas have passed away." According to Abuelita Noelia, I look as innocent as a virgin debutante, therefore, she wanted me to be prepared for my wedding night. I had to bite the inside of my cheek not to laugh during her Sex Ed 101 talk. I commend Phoenix's cousin for not cracking up. One of them was indulgent enough to double as a translator.

"At least now you're armed with a crash course on how to please your husband on your wedding night." Keira laughs her head off.

I lean into her and murmur low in her ear, "Between us girls, I already crushed the course. And FYI, my husband is very, very pleased with my performance." I pull away from her and let my words sink in.

Her eyes widen so much, they practically take over her face.

"No, you didn't!"

"Yes, I did."

"You changed your mind—"

A man I didn't notice approach, interrupts Keira. "Do you already have second thoughts about the wedding?"

I turn to face him.

He lifts his champagne flute as a salute, but the gesture lacks sincerity. Just like everything about him.

"Oh, hello—" I pause for effect. "I'm sorry, I don't remember your name." *Lie.*

"It's perfectly normal, we just met. My name is Potter. Potter MacCaak," the silver bearded fifty-something man says.

Potter Willis MacCaak, aka a vocal and aggravating board member, aka the biggest thorn in Phoenix's side. We just met and already I don't like him. He's very cagey.

"Oh, yes." I offer a tight smile. "There's so much happening today, it's hard to keep it all straight."

"It's understandable," Potter says. His lips curl up, but the smile never reaches his dark-brown eyes. "It's quite the party. Great turn out. A lot of notable people are attending."

"I'm touched so many people came out for our big day." I step into my starlet role before changing the subject. "Where are my manners? Potter, I'd like to introduce you to my friend, Keira."

"The pleasure is all mine," he says with a formal nod before extending his hand.

He's weird.

"Pleased to meet you," Keira says, shaking his hand.

"Have you known the lovely Michaela long?" Potter asks.

Her cautious gaze slides to mine.

I keep a poker face.

"Michaela and I have an incredibly tight relationship," Keira says. "She's one of my favorite people."

Great answer. She didn't even have to lie.

"I see." Potter nods again. "Do you also live in New York?" he asks

"No, I live in LA."

"Really?" Potter frowns.

I can see the wheels churning in his head, attempting to poke holes in our story.

"Thanks to modern technology, it's like we live in the same city," Keira tells him.

"Were you in the know about the secret relationship?" Potter asks Keira.

"The whole point of something being secret is that, well, it's secret," Keira says. "That said, girls talk. So, yes, I was in the know. It was like Fourth of July fireworks when Michaela and Phoenix first met. It's no wonder they just *had* to get married."

Bravo, Keira! Bravo!

Technically, she's still not lying. Explosions definitely detonated when I barged into my husband's office six days ago.

"Well, for the rest of us, the relationship came out of nowhere," Potter says. "A bit suspicious, if you ask me."

Good thing no one asked you.

"To answer your earlier question, Potter"—I cut in—"I

don't have second thoughts about marrying the man of my dreams." I intend to drill this into his thick skull even if it kills me.

"Will the honeymoon be as speedy as the wedding?"

I glare at him.

Why is he being such a busybody?

"You're very interested in our relationship," I say. "More than any other board member. In fact, more than anyone else here."

"I'm just pointing out the obvious," he says, his eyes dark and narrowed.

I fix him with a hard stare. "I don't have to remind you Phoenix is juggling a lot since stepping in for his father on top of his other responsibilities as COO. That said, my husband is whisking me away to the city of love for our short honeymoon."

"Vegas?" Potter smirks.

No, asshole. "Paris."

"Ah. The other city of love."

Since when is Vegas associated with love?

"Everything is so ephemeral in Vegas, I'm sure you and Phoenix would feel right at home there, but Paris isn't bad." It's an effort not to roll my eyes. "You wouldn't happen to be pregnant?"

What the fuck?

Potter's eyes drop to my belly. "That would explain the speedy wedding."

Irritation grits at the surface, but I bite down the litany of insults ready to irrupt from my lips.

Do not verbally assault the board member.

I pray for calmness.

"It's true Phoenix can be a bit of a hot head, but I never pegged him for a man willing to have his balls chained to the wall." Potter has more to get off his chest. "If you're pregnant, it's a big day out for you and the baby. Who cares about the women he sees on the side, right?"

My jaw drops.

What a repugnant douchebag.

He leans into our circle and whisper shouts, "You know he's been around. I mean, a lot. The man has quite the unflattering reputation. This quickie marriage won't stop his philandering."

I'm just about to give this idiot a verbal lashing, when Phoenix comes and stands next to me. He wraps me in his arms and brings my body close to his before placing a soft kiss on my lips.

"I just needed to kiss you," he says.

I offer him a tight smile.

Recognition flashes bright in his blue eyes.

He shifts his attention to the sorry excuse of a man standing in front of us.

"Potter, are you pestering my wife?" Phoenix's tone is so cold, you can practically see his breath.

"Not at all," Potter says. "We're getting better acquainted."

"In other words, you're being your normal charmless self," Phoenix tells him.

Phoenix is a strapping man and easily towers over Potter by a solid six inches, if not more. The pesky board member is no match for King König. He seems oblivious to that fact. Either that or he likes living on the edge.

Potter takes a step towards Phoenix and pumps his chest in defiance, poking a menacing finger in my husband's face. "It's no secret you don't like me—"

Phoenix swats his hand away. "No, I don't. I don't trust you either," he says.

"Too bad for you, Phoenix, I'm going nowhere, so—"

"Potter." Soren interrupts the nasty man as he approaches

our circle. Wilder and Slate flank their father. "You seem obsessed with my daughter-in-law. Not that I blame you. She's precious. My son married well."

Potter takes a step back and adjusts his suit jacket before offering an insincere smile. "He did," he says. "And since Michaela is a new member of the König family, it's only normal I get to know her better."

"I understand." Soren nods. "But this isn't an inquisition. Today is a day of celebration."

There's no denying God favors the König men. How else can you explain this level of manliness? They take hot to the next level. All four men are very tall, well-built, sporting strong jaws, blessed with refined, straight noses, and gifted with excessively handsome good looks. Their blue eyes, in various shades, are weapons of seduction few women could resist. And those dazzling smiles... wow, wow, and wow! I'm sure Roman is equally handsome in person.

Phoenix would make beautiful babies.

Wait. What?

What the hell is wrong with me?

No babies will come out of this fake marriage.

"My sentiments exactly," Potter says. "Which is why I was hoping Michaela and I could become *friends*."

I'd rather lick asphalt.

"There's plenty of time for that," my father-in-law says. "Like I said. Today is a day of celebration. Let's leave the lovebirds to bask in the glory of their big day." That's not a suggestion.

Potter's suspicious eyes bounce from Soren's, to Phoenix's, to mine.

"Of course," he says.

"I was just telling Slate and Wilder I have an amazing

bottle of whiskey I'm dying for you to try. Vintage. Exclusive. Refined. Rare."

"That sounds like my kind of drink," Potter says.

"I thought so," Soren says. "Let's head to my office and crack that baby open." His tone leaves no room for argument. "We'll grab a few other board members on our way."

The recent heart attack might have slowed down the patriarch of the family, but it hasn't dulled his edge. The man is as sharp as ever. Thank God.

"I'll catch you kids later." Soren winks at me. I offer him a small smile of appreciation. "Son, dance with your beautiful wife."

"I'm right on it, Dad," Phoenix says.

Keira and I giggle.

The König men laugh.

Potter looks constipated.

"Keira, is it okay if I steal my bride?" Phoenix asks as the four men stroll towards the mansion.

"Of course," she says. She leans in. "That guy is a jerk."

Phoenix lets out a wry laugh. "He wants my balls on a silver platter."

"I thought your balls belonged to me," I say.

"Ooohhh..." Keira is visibly impressed.

Phoenix shakes his head. "You're asking for it, kitten."

I grin, proud of my retort.

Chapter 22

Michaela

While we were swaying to the beat of a mellow song, I made the mistake of revealing I couldn't go along with Phoenix's earlier demand. His blue eyes veiled in a threatening shade of dark, navy-blue, similar to an ocean before a violent storm. He then grabbed me by the hand and pulled me off the dance floor. It's not like I could protest without raising a few eyebrows.

So here we are, leaving our own party in a mad rush.

"Phoenix, you're walking too fast," I say, doing my best to keep up with his long, determined strides. He's holding me by the hand and dragging me behind him.

"You disobeyed me," he tells me from over his shoulder.

I wrinkle my nose at his words.

"You need to understand there are consequences, dear wife."

"You're taking this *obey thy husband* a little too far," I tell him. "Not only is it archaic, it wasn't even in our marriage vows!"

He ignores my protest. “Before I left the bedroom, I told you what I expected of you, Michaela.”

I roll my eyes even though he’s so steadfast in his mission, he can’t see me.

“I can’t believe we’re arguing about this.”

“How dare you clean yourself up after I told you not to?”

“Your demand was unreasonable,” I say, exasperated. “I wasn’t going to sit down with Abuelita Noelia smelling like... like sex. And, slow down, already!” I pull against his hand.

Without warning, he stops.

I practically bump into him.

He turns around and looks at my strappy high heels.

The next thing I know, he’s sweeping me off my feet like a king would his queen.

“Your heels are sexy as fuck, but they aren’t made for walking.”

“Well, I was unaware a midnight stroll was part of the program.”

“Last minute addition,” he says and keeps walking.

My need to win this argument fades the minute my head rests against his strong chest. I wrap my arms around his neck and indulge in the moment.

I could get used to this.

He carries me like this until we reach a building that’s detached from the mansion.

He drops me to my feet with care and reaches in his pocket for something. He points whatever he’s holding to a set of beautifully ornate heavy metal doors. “Get inside.”

Lights turn on automatically when I step inside.

“The garage?” I ask, turning around to face him.

“No one will think of looking for us in here.”

“I’m not sure that’s a good thing.”

A dangerous smile crosses his face. "You'll change your tune soon enough, kitten."

I avert my gaze. I have to, because what I read in his eyes both scares me and turns me on like crazy. I scan the expansive space, nodding as I take in luxury car after luxury car. The lighting is a bit too harsh and too bright, which makes the walls look even whiter. This isn't just any old garage. This rivals the pristine showrooms you'd expect to see in Beverly Hills.

"Dad has an enviable car collection, and my brothers and I keep a few of the valuable vintage rides we acquired during our boy band days here," Phoenix tells me.

"You brought me here to show me your luxury cars?"

"Not even close." Heat emanates from his eyes.

I swallow hard.

"Why are we here?" I ask, a tinge of worry coloring my words.

He approaches me.

I take a step back.

"I want you right here," he says and points to the floor.

I return to my initial spot.

"Better," he says. He reaches out and runs a finger along my neck.

I shiver.

"I've been hard since you came downstairs, as tempting as a sexy angel in a white, fitted one-shoulder dazzler."

After Wilder came looking for us, I convinced Phoenix to go ahead without me, stating I needed to touch up my makeup and hair after our scorching embrace. That was only part of the reason.

"Looking at your fine ass sway under this cock-hardening dress was torture. Don't get me started on the high slit." His eyes drop to my leg. "Fucking hot," he says, meeting my gaze. "Here I was smug with the knowledge we shared a dirty little secret. Then, I find out the truth." He takes me by the chin. "When I tell you I want my cum to remain inside your pussy, I mean just that." His voice is a low rumble.

Why did I even bother with panties? They're soaked through.

"Phoenix—"

He places two fingers against my lips, silencing me.

With his eyes burning into mine, he traces a line from my chin down my throat, and then to the center of my chest. He snakes his fingers under my bra and runs his thumb over my hard nipple.

My body trembles at the contact.

"My beautiful wife... so disobedient."

I'm too turned on to speak, let alone think.

"Remember what I promised you?" he asks.

My eyes shift from left to right, playing back his words in my head.

"Let me help," he says. "I promised you three more orgasms—one of them, courtesy of my tongue."

If I thought I was wet before, now it's a river down there.

"Shouldn't we wait until later?" I ask in a feeble voice. "When it's just the two of us?"

"Guess what, kitten? It is later, and it is just the two of us," he says. "You're going to enjoy your punishment as much as I'll enjoy administering it."

With one hand gripping my wrist, he places the other against my chest, and forces me to walk backward until I'm standing near a yellow vehicle. I look over my shoulder. Not that I'm a car aficionado, but even I know this Italian-made luxury ride cost a fortune.

"Once you come all over my tongue, I'm going to fuck you raw on my vintage yellow Ferrari."

"Oh God."

"Is it a first for you, Michaela?"

"So far, this is a day packed with firsts."

"Good." I really should be concerned about his wolfish grin, but my clit is throbbing with way too much anticipation to care at this point. "On your back."

He helps me get in position.

The cool metal of the luxury sports car's hood does little to dampen the fire burning inside me.

Without warning, Phoenix walks away.

I scramble to sit up. "Where are you going?"

"Stay down!"

His domineering nature is such a turn on.

"Okay," I say, resting my back on the car.

He's back.

My core tightens as I take him in.

God, he's breathtaking.

The first three buttons of his crisp white shirt are undone. He's no longer wearing his tuxedo jacket, and the bowtie is gone.

I wish he'd lose the shirt altogether.

Everything was so fast and unexpected earlier, I didn't get enough time to admire his chiseled muscular body or salivate all over the mouthwatering V-muscle leading to his perfect, thick cock.

I look down at his hand and frown.

"The moving blanket will protect my clothing," he says without me having to ask.

"Smart." I'm impressed.

"Scuffed shoes and ripped pants stand out. We don't want to be that obvious."

"No, we don't."

"Feet on top of the hood."

"With my heels still on?"

"Yes."

"Won't it damage the paint?"

His gaze bores into mine. "Trust me, kitten, your sexy-as-fuck silver strappy heels aren't going to stay on that hood for long."

I obey.

Phoenix drops the moving blanket to the floor.

For a long beat, he just stares at me.

My body heats up like a furnace under his lustful gaze.

Just when I'm about to beg for him to put an end to this insufferable torture, he reaches underneath my dress. His fingers travel up my trembling thighs until they brush against my covered pussy. My very wet pussy.

"You're an eager little kitten."

He takes his time teasing me.

I squirm under his touch.

"I can already smell your hunger," he says, moving his fingers to the waistband of my panties.

Dear God.

This man's mouth...

He tugs my panties, and I lift my bottom off the hood so he can slide the elastic over my ass. He pulls them all the way to my ankles before untangling them from my heels. The delicious sensation of my slickness dragging between my legs nearly makes me lose my mind. He brings the seamless panties to his nose and inhales my scent.

"I shouldn't want to taste you this badly, kitten." His hands running up my thighs. "I'm willing to bet my fortune, you'll taste sweeter against my tongue than you did when I licked your juices off my fingers when you were in my office."

My chest heaves, my breasts swollen underneath the fabric of my matching strapless white sheer bra at his admittance.

"God, I want to feel your tongue down there."

My eyes widen in shock. I didn't mean to say those words out loud.

He flashes me a wolfish grin. "Down there? Where's that?"

I drop my eyes between my parted legs.

"Words, kitten."

"My pussy."

"What do you want me to do to your pussy?"

"I want you to do what you promised."

"What was that?"

"You promised your tongue on my pussy?!" That came out sounding more like a question than a statement. In my defense, the supreme self-assuredness oozing from him is intimidating.

A smile curls his lips.

"I love those dirty words on the lips of my prim and proper wife, but no, kitten, I'm not going to just put my tongue on your pussy, I'm going to fucking devour the pussy that now belongs to me like a ravenous beast. I'm going to make you come so hard you'll be praying to God, the saints, and all the angels in Heaven. Fuck, I'll make sure you think you're flying to Heaven."

I swallow hard.

"Spread them wide for me."

He doesn't have to ask twice.

He kneels in front of me and bores his eyes into mine.

He runs his fingers up the length of my thighs in a languid caress.

My body shudders.

"Your pretty pink pussy is mine for the next three hundred and sixty-five days," he says. "I'll touch it, ravish it with my mouth and fuck it when I want. And, more importantly, I'll make you come as many times as I want."

A low moan escapes me as my thoughts melt into a pull of lust.

I swear I just climaxed.

His fingers slide from my pussy to an untouched part of me.

I gasp.

"And this..." He circles my sacred spot, and I tighten my ass cheeks in fear he'll go further. "Tsk. Relax."

I try, I really try, but my body is still tense.

"Phoenix, I've never..." I let my words trail.

"You will with me."

I just blink at him in shock.

"I'm not going to fuck you there until you're ready, but you'll take my cock in your ass and you'll thank me."

Instead of running out of the garage screaming in fear, my pussy flutters in excitement.

What's wrong with me?

How can he have this much power over me?

"For the record, I didn't hear you protesting," he says. "Don't kid yourself, Michaela, you're a dirty girl."

Gripping each of my ankles in his hands, he widens my legs apart.

"I want you here," he says, sliding me down the car.

Pressing his palms against the inside of my thighs, he spreads me wider, leaving me completely exposed to him. With his eyes locked onto mine, he presses his tongue against my clit.

I let out an agonizing sound as my back arches with pleasure.

"Oh, fuck, you taste good," he says.

He pushes two fingers inside me.

I groan.

His fingers thrust in and out of me as his tongue skates over my clit in slow, languorous circles.

My vision blurs.

When he applies more pressure by closing his lips over my clit, my eyes roll to the back of my head.

"Oh Phoenix," I say. "Oh, yes."

He picks up speed, lapping harder and faster.

"Oh shit..."

He pins me down with one hand splayed open across my belly, forcing me to stay put.

The combination of the wicked things his tongue is doing to me and the hedonistic sounds he makes, nearly sends me over the edge.

Sweet mother of God.

His demanding pace is dizzying.

"Shit. I'm—"

I clasp my hand over his head and pull at his hair. I can't decide if I want him to stop or continue.

My body gives in.

My hips jerk off the Ferrari, taking him with me.

It's over for me.

"OhmyGod, ohmyGod, ohmyGod." I chant to a higher power as I ride out my orgasm.

I'm so loud and some part of my brain registers it's very unladylike, but frankly, I don't give a damn.

Phoenix curls two fingers, finding a spot deep inside me I didn't even know existed, and it's like fireworks detonate at my core. My muscles clench hard and to my shock and awe, a gush of liquid projects from my pussy.

Phoenix's startled gaze meets mine. "Fuck, yeah. That's it, kitten, feed your king," he says before putting his mouth on me again.

He continues to lick the flood from my pussy.

I'm horrified and embarrassed, but Phoenix seems unfazed. With his eyes still on me, he laps up my abundant juices.

I come.

And I come.

And I come.

The flow is so strong, it's like a geyser. My body convulses and trembles each time my pussy muscles clench.

Holy shit. I didn't know my body could do that.

I thought my earlier orgasm was mind-blowing, but this... this is transcendental.

I'm certain this is what an out of the body experience feels like.

How am I going to walk away from this man?

Phoenix stands up.

My eyes widen at the mess I've made.

His shirt is drenched.

I open my mouth to apologize, but I'm distracted when his hands find his belt.

"I dying to get inside you again," he tells me.

"Your shirt," I say, pointing at it.

He looks down.

"Who cares about my shirt? That was fucking hot. Not every woman gets to come with such force, kitten. I love how your body reacts to me."

So do I.

He unbuckles, unzips, and pushes his pants and boxer briefs to his knees.

His thick erection pops to life when he stands back up.

That man's cock is a gift.

I lick my lips.

"You want it in your mouth?" I want to French kiss that cocksure smile off his face.

I nod.

"I promise I'll fuck your mouth soon, but not now."

Before I can shoot off a smart reply, he grabs my hips and flips me over onto my front, flattening me against his pricey car.

I squeal.

He grabs me by my bare thighs and hitches me against his body.

"Open your legs." He kicks my feet apart, leaving me no choice.

My feet don't touch the ground for very long. With the precision of a nuclear warhead, he rams into me in one forceful thrust, causing my body to slide up the wet car.

"Oh God." Just like earlier, his cock stretches me past what I'm used to.

"Stay down." He places a hand against the back of my head.

My cheek presses against the cold metal of the Ferrari, making this dirty encounter even raunchier than it already is.

"I can't get enough of your tight pussy." He accentuates each word with a powerful thrust. He grabs a handful of my short hair and pulls as he fucks me deep.

I shouldn't love it this rough, but I do. I really do.

"Fuck, I love punishing you by stretching your pussy. I could do this all day long and all night. Maybe next time, you'll think twice before disobeying me."

"This is what you call punishment?" I say. "Bring. It. On."

"Kitten, you're going to learn to watch your mouth."

He grants my wish.

He's like a piston, thrusting into me hard and stealing my breath.

He slams in and out.

Over.

And over.

And over again.

I don't complain.

I don't even ask him to slow down.

Dear God, I didn't know I needed this.

"Take me. Take every inch of my cock." He slams into me even harder.

The sound of skin slapping is pure bliss.

I whimper.

"God, you feel so good, kitten."

He thrusts again and buries himself so deep, it's like we'll be fused like this forever. Not that I'd mind.

"You want my cum filling you up or do you want me to mark your back?"

I have a choice?

"I— I—" For the love of God, he's fucking me so hard, I can't speak.

Slap!

"When I ask you a question, I expect an answer," he says.

"My pussy."

"Put it in a sentence."

"Come inside my pussy."

My heart is beating like a drum.

"Say please!"

"Please come inside my pussy."

"Who's fucking you?"

"Stop being such a demanding asshole!"

"That's not how this game is played, kitten."

Slap!

Slap!

Slap!

Slap!

Slap!

"Holy fuck!" My ass cheeks are on fire.

"Now give me what I want!"

Even I know when to bow to the king.

"Phoenix, please come inside my pussy."

"My little kitten retracted her claws." He leans forward,

pressing his front to my back, resting his weight on me. He places his lips against my ear, breathing hard. "You dirty little thing, you need a nice hard fuck."

I nod.

Why am I only finding out now how much I love a domineering man?

"Words1"

"I do."

"No other man is going to fuck your tight little pussy like I will. No other man will own this pussy like I do. No other man will worship it as much as me."

I hate him for telling me something I already fear.

"Are you ready for me to shoot my load inside your sweet pussy?"

"God, yes."

"You have to come first, though."

He reaches around for my clit, flicking it, massaging it, and toying with it until my legs shake. When he closes his fingers around my throbbing clit, I see stars.

My body tenses and my breath hitches.

I tilt my head and let out a blissful wail of agony and pleasure as wave upon wave of climax rip through me.

"Good girl. Now you're ready for my cum."

He doesn't give me time to answer.

Phoenix pounds into me a few more times before his body tenses.

"Oh, fuck, kitten."

And then he comes, pouring his release deep inside my pussy.

I'm full of him.

We lay on the hood of the Ferrari, panting.

My eyes fly open as a frightening thought infiltrates my mind.

"How are we going to sneak back into the house undetected?" I ask. "There's no mistaking what we've been up to. Your shirt is drenched, so is my dress."

"We have time to figure it out."

"What do you mean?"

"Hold onto your horses, kitten. I'm gearing up my engine for another round."

I swallow hard.

Chapter 23

Phoenix

Even though she's expecting me, I rap my knuckles on Michaela's door.

She opens it.

She looks as fresh as a bouquet. She's only wearing a touch of makeup, and the large diamond stud earrings I gave her yesterday lighten up her angelic face.

"Good morning," I say.

"Good morning," she says.

She lets me in.

I close the door behind me.

I turn to face her and take her in.

"You look absolutely beautiful," I say.

Her sexy body is adorned in a long floral dress with bold printed bright pink flowers against a white background. The spaghetti straps and seductive V neckline accentuates her slender neck and showcases the swell of her luscious tits.

Damn.

Since she's not nearly as tall as she was yesterday, I can only assume her heels aren't skyscrapers.

"Thank you. It's one of the new dresses I bought thanks to your generosity," she says.

"Stop saying that," I tell her. "It's my pleasure. I benefit from everything you wear as much as you do."

She laughs a little. "You're so cocky."

I stroke my clean-shaven chin, a sly grin already firmly in place. "We haven't known each other long, but I'm pretty sure you figured that out when we first met."

She rolls her eyes.

"Speaking of which, we've officially known each other for a week."

She's stunned.

"It hit me as I was walking to your room."

"Talk about a whirlwind week," she says.

"From strangers to newlyweds in less than seven days."

"Unbelievable."

"Did you get a good night's sleep?" I ask.

"I did. Hands-down, that is the most comfortable bed ever." She points to the king-size bed. "It was like sleeping on a cloud."

After what we shared yesterday, not sleeping in the same bed seems ridiculous, but there are enough moving parts to our fake story. Wilder may be in the know about the changes in our arrangement, but Slate and Dad aren't.

"You can't take the hotelier out of Dad. He doesn't kid around when it comes to a good night's sleep. All the mattresses in the mansion are the same custom-design signature beds we have at the Pompadour. Guests love them so much, they're always begging to buy them. It took us a while to make the decision, but in the end, we caved in. For the last two years, we've been selling them on our website. You wouldn't believe how many orders we get each and every week. So much so, we had to hire staff to man a dedicated department."

"You're kidding?"

"I'm not."

"Incredible," she says. "I guess I don't have to ask how you slept."

"I didn't have a good night's sleep, to be honest."

"How come?"

I approach her.

"I was forced to sleep alone." I lean in and drop a soft kiss on her lips. "I would've rather slept in the same bed as my wife." Her cheeks turn a lovely shade of pink. "It would've made it a hell of a lot easier for my morning wood."

I grab her by the waist and pull her body against mine, pressing her against my erection.

"Phoenix. Your father is somewhere in the house and the staff is buzzing about," she says. "Not to mention, last night was pretty wild and intense."

She's right.

After a second raunchy round in the garage, stepping back into the mansion would've been *mission impossible*. Lucky for us, Wilder came to the rescue. I texted him to grab a couple plush terrycloth robes embroidered with our family crest from the home spa. The few guests who saw us walking back inside assumed we had gone for a swim.

"I'll behave," I say. "Ready for breakfast?"

"I'm starved."

"I could eat a restaurant out of business. I went for a swim early this morning."

Her eyes widen. "How could you get up to exercise when we went to bed at three o'clock in the morning?"

The festivities lasted until the wee hours.

"It was either that or jerk off to release the tension. Turns out, after a vigorous swim, I still had to take care of my cock in the shower. I blame not being able to fuck my wife first thing this morning for my predicament."

She brings her hands up and covers her face. "The things that come out of your mouth."

"You asked." I grab her hands, forcing them away from her face and bring them to my lips. I drop two soft kisses against them.

She laughs.

"In any case, on my way back to my room, I stopped by the kitchen for a bottle of water and a banana. The kitchen staff went overboard. Brace yourself for quite the feast."

"I'm looking forward to it."

"We're gathering in the theater room—it's a carbon copy of a VIP viewing room you'd expect to find on the executive floor of any big Hollywood studio. Dad asked Louis to make sure the staff sets up breakfast in there—"

"I still can believe your father has a long-time, trusted British majordomo who oversees everything, including managing the household staff."

"Dad would be lost without Louis."

She shakes her head. "You billionaires live large—" She frowns.

"What?"

"We're watching a movie while having breakfast?"

"No. The room is fully soundproof. Therefore, it ensures complete privacy."

She tilts her head to the side. "Why is that important?"

"Dad wants to have a conversation."

"That sounds serious."

"He has a few concerns."

"About what?"

"I'll find out at the same time you do," I say. "Wilder and Slate will join us. As much as Dad wants your father to join us, it might be tricky to explain to Uncle Ian why he's not invited to breakfast."

"I thought we pulled it off."

"So did I."

"I'm sorry." Remorse morphs her beautiful features.

"Why are you apologizing?"

"Obviously, I didn't live up to my end of the bargain. I let you down."

I bring my fingers to her unpainted lips and trace their contour.

"You were amazing yesterday. Heck, you even had me fooled, and I was in on it."

"Clearly, it wasn't enough."

"Michaela, let's not jump to conclusions. We're going to go downstairs together, enjoy a delicious, hearty breakfast and hang out with my father and brothers. Once we know what's at stake, we'll face it *together*. We're a team, remember?"

"Yes, we're a team!"

I take her by the hand and lead her to the door.

With our fingers interlaced, we trail down the stairs and stride towards the theater room, greeting staff and accepting congratulations on the way.

We're the poster couple of wedded bliss. Almost.

Slate arrives at the same time we do, a smile already tugging his mouth when he sees my wife.

"Good morning, Michaela," he says before kissing her on the cheek. "You look lovely, as usual."

"Thank you and good morning to you, Slate," she says.

"You look well rested," he says. "I gather you approve of our mattresses."

"That's putting it lightly," she says. "Did you sleep well?"

My brother's smile slips.

"Until six o'clock, yes."

"Oh. You couldn't fall back asleep after waking up?" Michaela asks.

Slate turns his attention to me, his gaze narrowed.

Is that anger I read in his eyes?!

"What the hell was that about this morning in the pool?" he asks. "I was convinced you were trying to exorcize some kind of demon, or was that your way of purging all the alcohol from your system?"

No, it was my attempt to curtail my overwhelming desire for my wife!

"And did you have to play music that loud while you were at it?"

Okay, the music might've been a bit too loud, but he doesn't have to chew my ass off.

"What? I don't deserve a good morning?" My tone is sarcastic.

"Not when you awake me before the fucking roosters," Slate says.

"You didn't have to sleep here last night!" I tell him. "I specifically remember Dad's invitation extended to my wife and me. You could've gone back to your place. Wilder did." None of the guests stayed at my father's mansion. He made arrangements at one of our many hotels for all the out-of-town guests.

"What crawled up your fucking ass this morning?" Slate fires back.

The door to the theater room flies open.

"Boys!" Dad steps out. "You're grown men. Stop acting like children." Slate and I simmer down. "Come inside. Now!"

We obey.

Wilder is already here.

After a round of good mornings, Dad invites us to grab some food.

He doesn't have to ask twice.

The five of us make our way to a table weighed down with a scrumptious feast. With generous plates in hand, we all sit at a round table the staff placed in the room. Dad and I flank Michaela.

"You two are trending," Dad says.

"I haven't checked social media yet," I tell him. "After my swim, I jumped on a conference call with my executive assistant. I had to give my approval on a few things relating to the Paris trip. Since Michaela and I leave tonight, time is of the essence."

He nods. "Did you catch any of the headlines?" Dad asks Michaela.

"No," she says. "The media can be cruel when it comes to dissecting fashion, especially when it comes to a wedding. I'd rather keep my head in the sand for a little longer."

"You don't have anything to worry about," Dad says. "The media crowned you, reigning queen."

"Are you kidding me?" Michaela asks.

Dad chuckles.

"The publicist texted me to let me know you've been voted *Most Beautiful Bride of the Year* by a number of influential publications," he says.

"I have?" Michaela asks, her green eyes widening in surprise.

"Yes." Dad grabs his phone from the table, unlocks it, and hands it to her.

'Michaela Knight, now Mrs. Michaela König, sets the standard for years to come when she said "I do" in a show-stopping, elegant white gown designed by Valentino. She wore it and the Swarovski crystal tiara like a queen, a nod to her aristocratic heritage.'

She reads the press coverage out loud. "Gosh, that's a lot of pressure," she says, lifting her eyes from the screen as she hands Dad the device.

"Not really, since you already hold the title, sis," Wilder says.

We all laugh.

"Why did you call this meeting, Dad? What's up?" I cut to the chase.

"Potter," Dad says, placing his phone on the table.

"We all know he's annoying as fuck, but what did he do now?" I ask.

"I wasn't kidding last night when I said he was a little too obsessed with Michaela—"

"Understandably." Wilder cuts in. "She's gorgeous."

"That she is," Dad agrees.

"I scored a hot wife!" I wink at her.

"Stop it," she says. "You guys are going to make me blush."

"You already are, sweetheart," Dad tells her. "Back to Potter." Dad veers the conversation. "At some point in the evening, Niels came up to me completely frazzled."

Michaela sits a little straighter in her chair. "What happened?"

"Niels revealed some disturbing things..." Dad lets his words trail.

"Like what?" I ask.

Dad's eyes bounce around the table, meeting our gaze before speaking. "Potter cornered him and bombarded him with a million questions about the Villiers Grand." Shock slams into me. "Potter had a keen interest in understanding Niels's motive to sell the hotel to us instead of selling it to High Stone Holding."

My eyebrows shoot to my forehead and my fork freezes halfway to my mouth.

"Get this, Potter stated it would've been a more lucrative deal for Niels and for Michaela since High Stone Holding approached him, whereas Niels approached us," Dady says.

There's a deafening silence in the room.

My brothers and I exchange a knowing look.

Potter is plotting against us. That, I'm certain of.

What does he have to gain from fucking us over?

"Daddy never mentioned anything about being approached by another company," Michaela says. I'm not surprised he'd keep quiet about that encounter. "Isn't High Stone Holding owed by the Madigans?"

"Yes." Slate answers her question. "They've been part of the top three hotelier dynasties for several decades and they've been fighting dirty to outrank us from the number two spot for as long."

"And by dirty, Slate means by any means possible," I say. "Ripley Madigan, the head of the family, is the kind of man who's willing to prostitute anyone to get what he wants." Bile rises in my throat at the memory of the six months Marie-Clémence played me for a fool.

Michaela frowns her confusion.

"Niels was surprised by the level of details Potter knew." Dad keeps talking.

"Did the Madigans really approach Daddy or was that Potter taking a wild guess?" Michaela asks.

"They did," I say. "Several times and they were waving big money at him, but—" I stop.

"But what?" she asks.

My eyes bounce from Slate's, to Wilder's, and to my father's.

"But what?" Michaela places a hand on my forearm. "Tell me."

I push my plate away, my appetite suddenly gone.

"Tell her," my father says. "She has a right to know. You're married now, so she's safe."

"Okay, this is scaring me," Michaela says. "What's going on?"

I reach out and smooth the frown line between her eyebrows. My eyes bore into hers for a prolonged beat.

"Just tell me, Phoenix."

"The marriage wasn't optional for your father because he wanted to make sure you didn't get screwed over. Additionally, in his eyes, the marriage protected your legacy against backlash from the scandal around Thana's lover." I pause. "When Ripley Madigan approached your father, he thought he had struck gold. It was the perfect timing, and he figured one of Ripley's three twenty-something sons could be a decent candidate as a husband." Another pause. Of course, those are his legitimate sons. Rumor has it, he has as many as a dozen illegitimate kids. "Ripley refused the option of you marrying one of his sons. He wanted to keep you all to himself—"

"He's old enough to be my grandfather." The note of hysteria in Michaela's voice is unmistakable.

"Ripley is sixty-eight years old," Dad says. "The difference of age is preposterous."

"And he already has four very young *girlfriends* on the side, along with his wife of forty years," I say. Since the vermin blindsided me a few years ago, I paid astute investigators to dissect his life after the meeting with Niels. They couldn't dig up all his skeletons—because an unscrupulous guy like Madigan has a boatload of them—but what they reported back was enough to prevent any nasty surprises before accepting my now-father-in-law's proposal. "He has a penchant for selecting virgins, days after they come of age. It's like he grooms them and stashes them somewhere with the clock ticking, counting down to their eighteenth birthday. He usually phases them out when they turn twenty-one—"

"I'm twenty-three," she says.

"True." *And she's not even a virgin.* "According to your father, Ripley was willing to make an exception to his rule because you bring far more to the table than his dumb virgins do," I say. "Ripley's words, not mine."

"His wife doesn't care?" Michaela asks.

"My guess is his wife is willing to turn a blind eye to maintain the lifestyle she's accustomed to. And here's the kicker, the girlfriends live together in a neighboring house, so it's not like Mrs. Madigan is oblivious to her husband's cheating ways. There's more. Ripley *offers* his girlfriends to business partners to seal deals."

Michaela turns as white as a ghost.

"His girlfriends are always well taken care of when things go his way, so they're okay with being *prostituted*," I say in quotation marks. "It's a win-win for everyone involved."

She gasps.

Anger bubbles inside me at the horror reflecting from her eyes. I hate seeing my little dragon this vulnerable.

"Ripley is into sordid and demeaning sex." I keep talking. "Your father refused to hand you over to a pervert. Ripley put pressure on him. Niels wouldn't cave in. He simply wouldn't budge from his position. Then, Ripley pulled out the big guns. He started blackmailing your father."

"What?" Michaela is incredulous.

"Ripley knew how desperate your father was. He also knew about Thana and her lover—I mean, he knew everything."

"Oh God." Michaela winces.

"Your father couldn't figure out how Ripley was able to get his hands on that kind of private information," I say. "Panicked, he came to me. When he explained his situation, I filled him in on Ripley's sexual deviances. I told him he was right to trust his instincts. He wanted to save you from a grim future with a bad man." I grab her hands into mine. "He wanted you to marry someone who wouldn't corrupt you, soil your soul, or take advantage of you. I gave him my word I'd do right by you."

Her eyes well and a tear rolls down her cheek.

I wipe it away with my thumb.

I cup her face with my hands, leaning close enough to kiss the tip of her nose.

"You and me against the world, hellion."

She looks up at me and smiles between her tears.

For a long beat, no one speaks.

Dad clears his throat. "Going back to Potter." He breaks the silence. "Most of the information surrounding the deal was never divulged to the board. The four of us made a quick decision on the Villiers Grand, informed Roman, and then presented the deal to them as a *fait accompli*." They weren't pleased and they had objections. A lot of them. We expected as much. They shut the fuck up when we presented them with our aggressive one-year expansion plan. "Not only was the purchase of your hotel hush-hush, it was done at lightning speed. So, it bears the question, how did Potter know so much?"

"I knew there was a reason I didn't trust that guy," Michaela says.

"You're spot on," Slate tells her. "He's been on the board for a long time, but lately, you have to wonder if he's still on our team."

"It seems his new purpose in life is to hamper our efforts every chance he has," Wilder says.

"It's like he wants our demise." My jaw clenches. "Mine, specifically."

"Can't you get rid of him?" Michaela asks.

"It's not that simple," Slate tells her.

"That's too bad," Michaela says. "If he's on the board, he should be a friend, not a foe."

"You'd think," I say, cracking a wry smile.

Wilder frowns. "If no one at this table revealed anything to Potter—and I'm certain Roman would never betray us—does it mean we have a leak within the company?"

"That's the billion-dollar question, son," Dad says.

"What did my father tell Potter?" Michaela asks Dad.

"He didn't say much because he was afraid to jeopardize our deal," Dad says. "He played it smart. I told Niels if Potter ever asks any other questions about your hotel, to refer him back to me personally. I'll deal with him."

"Did you drill the asshole last night when you went to your office to open that bottle of whiskey?" Wilder asks. My brothers cut their time with Potter short, choosing to return to the party instead of being trapped in Dad's office with a man they loathe.

"I didn't," Dad says.

"Why not?" Slate asks.

My father cocks a warning eyebrow.

Undeterred, Slate soldiers on. "Don't you want to know how the hell Potter got his hands on that information?"

"Son, you seem to forget who the hell you're talking to." Dad points a finger at him. "Watch your tone!"

Slate shrinks in size.

"Just like the game of chess, in business, it's about outplaying your opponent," Dad says. "It's the same in the game of poker. For now, I'm keeping my cards close to my chest."

"What does that mean?" Slate asks.

"I don't know what Potter is up to yet—"

"Nothing good."

"I agree with Wilder," I say.

"Everything points to it," Dad says. "Until I'm dialed in on what he has up his sleeve, it's best he doesn't know I'm—we're—onto him. Understood?"

We all nod our agreement.

"Let's all be careful around Potter," my father says before turning his attention to my wife. "And you, Michaela, whatever you do, avoid him at all costs."

"Okay," she says, the tremor in her voice audible.

Chapter 24

Phoenix

The jet just reached altitude and we're cruising across the sky.

"This is living large, King König," Michaela says, bouncing in her seat as if she's testing the springs.

"You approve?" It's a struggle to contain my amusement. She's like a kid on the morning of her birthday.

"Most definitely," she says. "The smell of leather is unmistakable. White. Nice touch. I appreciate how buttery soft these are." She caresses the chair's armrest. "Way better than vinyl or that horrible fabric they have on some commercial flights—so unhygienic. On top of that, we don't have to worry about airborne germs like we would if we were flying coach. Even if we were sitting in first-class, we'd still be breathing the same recycled air. Not here. It's just us and the small crew."

"It's one of the many perks of owning your own private jet."

"That, and the legroom." She extends her short legs and wiggles them in the air.

My gaze travels from her painted toes trapped in strappy

heels, runs up her legs, pausing at the hem of her dress before my eyes scrape back up to her face.

"You can recline the seats fully," I tell her. "There's no space restriction."

Her eyes snap up at mine.

"There's a footrest. It's perfect for catching some shuteye during long trips." I point to the armrest.

She takes me up on my offer.

"Do we get blankets?" she asks.

"And pillows and sleep masks."

"God, this is incredible!" she says. "I love your life."

"You mean you love *our* life."

She blushes. "Yes, for as long as it lasts, I freaking love *our* life."

I can't help my smile.

The flight attendant approaches us with a tray.

"Congratulations again, Mr. and Mrs. König," she says.

"Oh, champagne!" Michaela grabs a flute. "Thank you on both accounts."

I grab the other. "Thank you."

"It's my pleasure," the flight attendant says. "I'll leave the appetizers on the table. Let me know when you're ready for dinner."

With a smile, she turns on her heel.

I lift my glass. "Here's to Paris!"

"Paris, here we come!" Michaela says.

"And here's to my father-in-law and his unbendable demands," I say.

Something unreadable veils Michaela's eyes.

I brace myself.

"What is it, hellion?" I ask.

"I won at the lottery." Her eyes well up. "You're a good man, Phoenix König." She blinks the tears back, but one rolls down her cheek. She wipes it away with the back of her hand.

I reach out and squeeze her knee for comfort.

For a few long breaths, we stare at each other.

No words are needed.

After this morning's meeting, Michaela was pretty shaken up by my revelations. She's grateful she's not indebted to an evil psychopathic asshole without a conscience. Her father would've laid his life on the line to make sure she didn't end up as Ripley Madigan's property.

My need to protect her is stronger now than it was when I gave Niels my word.

I fight for what's mine.

"Five glorious days in Paris," Michaela says, breaking the silence.

"I wish we could stay longer, but there's too much going on in LA and... you know"—I lean in—"this is kind of last-minute."

"I haven't been to Paris in so long, you won't hear me complain." I want to ask her when she last visited the French capital, but I refrain. This is the kind of information people in love know. The flight attendant, captain and the first officer signed nondisclosure agreements, but why chance it? *There's still so much to discover about you, Mrs. König.* "Other than the gala, what else is on the agenda?" she asks.

"I have to pop into our three Pompadour hotels to take in the lay of the land and meet with upper management. It was on Dad's agenda, and now I shoulder the responsibility. It's going to be grueling, but I don't have much of a choice."

"Oh, okay," she says. "It sounds like I'm going to spend most of my days alone."

I sense her disappointment.

"Paris is a beautiful city. Since you haven't been in a while, there's a lot to see and do—so many amazing restaurants to discover. Feel free to give my Black American Express card a good workout."

"I guess," she says with a shrug.

"Let me get this straight," I say. "You were less than eager to take on my last name––which most women would trip all over themselves to agree to––and now I suggest shopping, upscale restaurants and sightseeing in Paris and you're lukewarm at the perspective. You're an enigma."

"Don't get me wrong, all those things sound appealing, but it's a reminder I don't have anything to challenge me," she says. "A life of daily shopping, spas, and lunch dates at LA's hot new eatery—or at the Pompadour—will become boring real fast."

I chuckle.

"What's so funny?" she asks.

"After our lunch last week on the yacht, I knew expecting you to wait for me at the penthouse like a good little wife at the end of a demanding day with my slippers, a cigar, and a tumbler of fine scotch was fooling myself—"

"Newsflash! This isn't the fifties!"

"I'm yanking your chain, kitty cat." I wink. "All that to say, I made an executive decision about you."

She cocks an eyebrow. "What kind of executive decision?"

I reach to the seat across from me and grab my Louis Vuitton briefcase. I rummage through it and pull out a stack of business cards.

I hand them to her.

Her gaze bounces from the cards she's holding to my eyes.

"Michaela König, Art Director and Principal Art Buyer, König Imperial Holding." She reads out loud.

She blinks at me.

"Congratulations on your new appointment," I say. "I hear your new boss is a pleasure to work for."

She narrows her gaze. "Let me guess. *You're* my new boss?"

My lips break into a triumphant grin. "In the flesh."

"You've got to be kidding me."

"You just said you're not one to sit idle. You worked for one of New York's top art buyers in your attempt to distance yourself from Thana—"

"I was his assistant. You just promoted me to director. That's a huge leap."

"You can handle it," I tell her. "It's the same thing you were doing in New York, but now you represent one client and you call all the shots. You'll even have an executive assistant."

"I hope I'm not taking someone else's position?"

"Actually, you are."

Her face drops.

"Please, tell me you didn't demote or fire someone on my account. I couldn't live with myself if you did that."

I love her altruistic nature.

I reach out for her cheek and caress it. "I'm not that kind of asshole boss, kitty cat."

"Thank God. I couldn't stay married to you if you were."

"The woman who held the position before you was expecting another child. She left a little over a month ago. She now has four boys under the age of eleven, and she wanted to be a stay-at-home mom to raise her family. We were supposed to fill the position before her departure to ensure a smooth transition, but with Dad's heart attack and recovery, Roman's surfing accident, and my extra responsibilities, it slipped to the bottom of the list of priorities. Additionally, after meeting with your dad for the first time a month ago, I told the director who was responsible for finding a replacement to put the hiring on ice. From your profile, I knew you'd be the perfect candidate."

She shakes her head. "Anything is possible in your world."

"Pretty much," I say. "If you accept the position, you can get started when we land in Paris—"

"What?!"

"While I'm in meetings, you can visit the galleries for inspiration, that way you can hit the ground running when we get back to LA. We're in the middle of a big renovation of a new Pompadour luxury residency-slash-hotel in Santa Monica that will require a lot of new art—paintings, sculptures, pricey vases, you name it. You can work with the decorator to make it happen."

"Just like that?"

"Just like that."

"Wow!"

"Take it or leave it, Mrs. König?"

She considers me for a beat.

"It looks like you're my new husband *and* my new boss."

I grab her hand and interlace our fingers together, boring my eyes into hers.

"Fair warning, I'm as much of a demanding boss as I am a husband." I arch a brow. "You'll be evaluated *nightly* on your daily performance to determine if you deserve my tongue, fingers, or cock. On days you really impress me, you'll get all three. If you blow my mind, you'll get a good spanking before I allow you to ride my cock."

Her cheeks bloom into a bright shade of pink.

"Now, let's talk about my other expectations."

She gasps.

Over the next hour, I brief her on our hotels. She listens intently. I keep it specific to the Pompadour brand so as not to overwhelm her. Her position is nothing she hasn't done before, and I'm certain she'll ace it. We end our meeting as dinner arrives. The food is excellent, as always—another perk of having your own jet. The meal ends with more champagne and a remarkable array of scrumptious French desserts.

"The champagne is going straight to my head," Michaela

says. "I blame the altitude for feeling this light-headed. I didn't drink that much, did I?"

"This is our second bottle."

"Oops!" She giggles. "That explains it." She drops her glass on the table.

I follow her lead.

Her eyes roam the space before meeting mine. "I can't believe you have a bedroom at the back of this plane."

"These seats are comfortable to sleep in, but the bed comes in handy."

"I see." Her eyes roam again. "I guess if you were to join the Mile High Club you wouldn't get into hot water or legal trouble since you own the plane."

That gets my attention. "What are you suggesting?"

She shrugs. "Nothing."

"Do you want an introduction to the club, kitten?"

"I was just making conversation," she says in a dismissive tone.

I study her.

She kicked off her high heels a long time ago.

She traded the long maxi dress she was wearing this morning for a short flirty one.

I'm quite partial to this one.

She rubs her bare legs together and bites against her lower lip.

If that isn't an invitation, I don't know what is.

"Have you ever..." her words trail.

The sexual tension crackles between us.

I bring my lips to her ear. "Have I ever fucked a woman on this plane?"

"Yes."

"The answer is no. This is a company plane. My father,

brothers, and our vice presidents use it. Everything that happens on board is strictly business."

"Of course," she says.

She stares out the window, but she keeps rubbing her legs together.

I observe her, twisting my black titanium wedding band around my ring finger, pondering on how far to take things.

She adjusts herself in her seat.

She's desperate for salvation.

Fuck it.

I get up.

"Let's go," I say.

Her head whips in my direction.

"To the bedroom?" She whisper-shouts.

"No, that's too obvious," I tell her. "We're going to the bathroom."

"Like that's not obvious at all," she says.

"Maybe, but it will be a lot kinkier."

Her eyes sparkle with interest.

I reach out a hand to help her up.

She accepts it.

She stands, but nearly falls back into her seat.

"Careful!" I catch her just in time and bring her close to my body.

"Thanks."

"You're drunk?"

"No, just a little tipsy." I frown. "I'm fine." She places a hand against my chest. "You were taking me to the bathroom, remember?"

"Eager much?"

She leans into me. "You promised kinky. Based on yesterday, yes, I'm very eager."

"Such naughtiness coming from such a sweet mouth."

She gives me a *guilty as charged* look.

I lead the way to the back of the plane and close the door to the bathroom behind us.

"Oh, this should be good," she says.

Lust veils her eyes.

"You look innocent enough. You're anything but," I tell her.

"Let's get one thing straight. In the little time I've known you, you've corrupted me."

"I'm so proud." I wink.

"Since we've been married, you've done a pretty good job of making me lose my mind. When do I get to return the favor?"

"You already have."

"No, I haven't."

"Yes, you have."

"When?"

"I fucked you hard yesterday, and I came hard—every single time."

"That's not what I meant," she says in a flirtatious tone.

"What did you have in mind, kitten?"

She reaches out and cups my cock.

I growl.

"As much as I like you wet—and fuck do I love when you get that wetness all over me like you did last night—this setting is a bit too intimate for that."

Her breath catches and her cheeks flush at the eroticism in my statement.

The pulse at the base of her neck throbs.

Tick, tick, tick.

Her eyes flash with burning lust.

My hungry gaze captures every nuance of her beautiful face before homing in on her lips. I grab her by the neck and take her mouth in a slow, sensual kiss. She parts her lips for me, so my tongue dances with hers.

I'm unhinged.

We both are.

It shouldn't feel this good. This right. This perfect.

I kiss her with abandonment.

She responds with fierce passion.

I fucking love it.

I could fuck her around the clock—for breakfast, lunch, dinner, dessert, snacks, and coffee breaks—and I'd still want more.

I twine the fingers of one hand in her hair, tilting her head back and exposing her neck, licking up her smooth skin, ending with a growl near her lips.

"You're okay with us keeping it to a fast ride?" I ask against her mouth.

"God, yes," she says.

I lift the fabric of her dress.

My hand inches up between the silky smoothness of her thighs until my fingers brush over her panties.

Fuck, she's wet.

I push the fabric aside, and when I glide a finger through her slick pussy, she moans as she kisses me harder.

Jesus Christ.

I need to be inside her. Now!

I slide my hand from between her legs and bring it to my mouth before wrapping my lips around my finger dripping with her sweet juices. I suck it clean under her heated gaze.

"Better than any dessert prepared by a top master pastry chef," I tell her.

She moans, biting against her lip.

"Turn around," I say. "Hands on the counter and legs spread open."

"Wait!"

"What?"

"I meant it. I want to take care of you, Phoenix. It's not fair if I don't reciprocate."

"That's not how it works, kitten. It brings me pleasure to take care of you."

"Don't you think it's the same for me?" she asks. "You're not even giving me a chance to—"

I tease her pussy again as she whimpers, folding over against my chest.

I bring two fingers to her mouth. "Show me what you want to do to my cock."

Huge green eyes stare at me from behind fluttering lashes.

"You either want my cock or you don't?"

She parts her lips.

I stick my fingers inside her mouth and she licks them clean, fixing her hooded gaze on me.

My cock strains against the zipper of my jeans and my heavy balls swell and tighten as they fill with cum.

"Strip!"

"But—"

"I'm also going to get undressed," I tell her. "Let's avoid walking out of here with cum staining my jeans or your pretty dress."

She giggles.

In a flash, we're both naked.

"Now, where were we?" I stroke my massive hard-on.

Her eyes follow my hand.

"I was so overwhelmed yesterday, I didn't get a chance to admire you." She licks her lips as her eyes roam over my body from head-to-toe. "God, you're gorgeous, Phoenix." The words come out as a near whisper. "I've never been with anyone who looks like you. Ever," she says. "I thought being with such a perfect man would make me feel self-conscious… but you make me feel so incredibly sexy and desired. Along with being married, this is all new to me."

"I don't make you feel sexy, kitten. You *are* sexy." I drop a hard kiss against her lips. "Seriously, you're stone cold gorgeous. I'm just feeding off your sexiness."

She places a hand over mine.

My cock pulses.

Together, we stroke my cock.

It's fucking hot.

"You're so huge."

"I am, but you've already proved you're up to the challenge."

She licks her lips again.

"You want it in your mouth?"

She nods.

"Let me hear you say it, kitten."

"Yes, I do."

"What do you want to do to my cock?"

"I want to suck it until you come."

"What if I want to fuck your mouth instead?"

Her eyes widen in surprise. "Okay."

"You're going to swallow every drop of me?"

"I've never done that before." Her voice trembles.

"I get to christen your mouth?"

"I can't believe you said that."

"That's exactly what's going to happen," I tell her. "And I expect you to swallow every last drop of your husband's cum like a good wife."

She holds my gaze, but doesn't respond.

"I will." Two words.

"Good girl," I say. "On your knees."

She trails her hands down my body as she lowers herself to the floor.

I let go of my cock and it throbs and pulses between us.

Her eyes drink me in.

I grunt as her fingers wrap as far around my erection as they can.

She stares in fascination at the gap still remaining.

I'm a very big boy.

She strokes my cock from base to tip.

Fuck, yeah.

She runs her thumb over the head. "Your cock is so perfect."

"And you're so fucking perfect on your knees, hand on my cock, luscious tits out." I reach out for her nipples.

She gasps.

"And, these babies are so hard for me."

She grabs my ass with one hand and squeezes my cheek hard in response.

Damn.

With her eyes peering up at mine, she sticks out her tongue. She gives me a slow, teasing, languorous stroke up and down my fat cock.

I bite against my lower lip so hard, I swear I'll draw blood.

Unrushed, she lavishes a few minutes on just the crown, driving me out of my mind with the eagerness to feel her plump lips sliding over my entire cock. Her mouth is fucking incredible—soft, silky, hot, and exactly what I need. She runs her petal-smooth lips along my cock. The sublime sensation shoots straight to my brain and I squeeze my ass cheeks, tilting my hips forward to feed her more of my cock.

A throaty laugh escapes her.

A low growl escapes me.

I almost forgot how smooth and soft a woman's tongue was

and how mind-blowing it feels when she traces the lines along the sensitive underside of my dick. And then there's the teasing way she traces delicate circles around my bulbous crown.

Fuck, I've missed this sight.

It's been too long since I've had a woman's lips wrapped around my cock. And I couldn't have asked for a more beautiful pair of pouty lips than my wife's.

With her eyes pinned to mine, Michaela opens wide and swallows my swollen crown.

"Goddammit!"

Her eager tongue explores my slit.

Damn, I love how she does that.

She repositions herself and does it again.

I clench my ass tight at the sensation of the pointed tip of her nipple scratching my knee.

Unable to resist, I reach down and pinch her nipple before twisting it hard.

She gasps.

And then, she responds in kind.

Both hands land on my ass before squeezing my cheeks tight. Bobbing her head up and down, she swallows several more inches of my cock in one go. She lets out a vibrating hum that tingles my balls in the most delicious way.

Hell, yeah.

Threading my hands through her hair, I hold her down over my cock. "Take me deeper."

She obeys.

Her head bobs up and down.

Up and down.

Fuck.

The pace is dizzying.

My jaw drops open in disbelief—or maybe pure enjoyment—as she works her pretty little mouth up and down my big cock, one hand gripping the base, her eyes closed like my dick is her fucking salvation. My hips and legs are practically trembling with the suppressed need to take control and fuck her mouth.

Patience.

For several long seconds, there's nothing else but my cock between her wet lips.

I'm riveted by the sinful sight of her head bobbing in front of my hips, turned on by her moans, at the way she worships my cock. My eyes travel over her heavenly body, her pale skin—she's still sporting a New York City tan—the curve of her small waist, and the perfect ass I can't wait to claim.

She shifts.

It doesn't take me long to pick up on what she's doing.

I frown my disapproval.

I fist her short hair tight. "Don't you dare."

Her eyes hold mine.

"Did you think I wasn't going to notice you squeezing your thighs like that, kitten? *I* make you come."

With a frown, she whimpers her displeasure.

I pull her hair tighter, forcing her to open her mouth around my cock.

"What's that?"

She shakes her head, her eyes imploring.

"That's what I thought." I tap her cheek a few times. "Finish me off!"

She resumes her mission, sucking me off like a starved woman in front of a sumptuous buffet.

"Goddammit."

She moans, her hand pumping up and down the inches of cock her mouth can't handle.

"Such sweet submission," I say.

Her soft lips drag up and down my cock, her tongue

swirling in circles over the head. The slurping noise ratchets the hedonistic experience. She cups my balls, popping me out of her mouth, and licking my head like a fucking lollipop.

Every nerve ending in my body shoots off like a rocket.

Jesus Christ, she's good at this.

My balls swell with cum, and the hold on my control is fraying faster than the fuse on a stick of dynamite.

I want to come so fucking bad.

I tighten my grip around her hair, forcing her to swallow me whole and thrust my hips forward.

She lifts her eyes to meet mine. The glee of malice shining bright in them as she kneads my balls is unmistakable.

My dirty wife.

I go crazy.

I fuck her mouth, pumping in and out between her plump lips, losing myself.

I hit the back of her throat.

She gags, her eyes watering, but she doesn't tap out.

"You okay?" I ask, in between labored breaths.

She nods.

I'm so far gone, I don't think I could stop fucking her sweet mouth, but I'm a gentleman.

"You sure?"

She nods again.

Fuck, yeah.

I pick up my cadence, hitting the back of her throat every single time.

Fuck. Fuck. Fuck.

The pressure inside me builds up like a storm, pushing me towards the edge of the cliff, and I keep pulling back, pulling back, pulling back, because I don't want this to end.

I fuck her mouth without mercy.

She takes it without complaining.

She takes me in deep. Eye-popping deep.

My heart batters thunderously against my rib cage with every forceful thrust.

I can hardly breathe.

I'm having a fucking heart attack.

I'm going to die thirty-five thousand feet high in the sky.

My hands are shaking when I pull my cock from her silky, smooth lips.

"Open wide," I say. The urgency to come is overpowering.

She does.

She even sticks out her tongue without being asked.

With trembling legs, I pump between her lips one last time.

My balls draw up and my cock twitches on her tongue before I explode.

Oh shit.

Oh fuck.

Oh Christ!

Oh, kitten.

OhmyfuckingGod!

My vision clouds and I go temporarily blind. I throw my head back, barely containing my climactic cries. I release myself almost violently, shooting my hot cum down her throat like a power hose.

I lower my head to admire my handiwork through hooded eyes.

Like a good girl, Michaela swallows every last spurt.

Damn that woman's mouth.

If we weren't already married, I'd have to ask for her hand in marriage.

My heart is pumping louder than a drum, my chest heaving hard as I attempt to regulate my breathing.

Fuck that was intense.

Reaching out, I caress her cheek.

She's on her knees, submitting to my every demand, yet she holds all the power.

"You're still with me?" I ask.

She doesn't answer.

Instead, she cups my balls in her hands and kisses each one with extreme tenderness. When she's done, she sits on her knees, her hands placed on her thighs, her eyes staring up at me. Her lips are swollen from my assault.

"Was that okay, dear husband?" she asks. Her words are a brazen mixture of innocence and insolence.

She's fucking perfect.

Chapter 25

Michaela

The life of a billionaire's wife is extra sweet.

Just like flying in style on a private jet, landing at Paris' Charles de Gaulle Airport is very different when you're part of the top echelon. Customs isn't a never-ending line of cranky, tired travelers arriving from crammed commercial flights, desperate to get to their hotel or home. There was practically no wait time for us. We were in and out in a flash.

Money is a beautiful thing.

The same level of luxury applies to the drive from the airport to the hotel. Sitting in the back of a chauffeured Mercedes-Benz beats sitting in the back of a tiny taxi by a long shot.

Been there, done that.

Then, there's the accommodation.

The hotels I could afford when I visited the city tended to be small in size, with diminutive rooms designed for sleep and nothing more. Everything about the Pompadour Saint-Honoré is grandiose.

Where the Pompadour, Beverly Hills is sleek and modern, this location is encrusted in olde worlde charm. The exterior of the building is exactly what you'd expect to see in a city like Paris. The juxtaposition with the ultramodern interior décor is striking. The luxury hotel is located on Rue Saint-Honoré in the 1st arrondissement—one of the city's wealthiest neighborhoods. It's a convenient walking distance from the Louvre, the upscale shops on Champs-Élysées, and steps away from Place Vendôme. The beauty of this prestigious hotel is unparalleled.

"How do I look?" I ask Phoenix, stepping out of the bedroom and into the living room. Our penthouse-style suite is so massive, there's an actual living room outfitted with sofas, chairs, a bar, large screen TV and a kickass sound system.

He turns around from the window where he's standing, drink in hand.

He gives me a onceover. His blue eyes are electric as he appraises my dress.

"You don't like it?" I ask.

He studies me.

I grow self-conscious under his gaze.

His long strides carry him to the bar cart. He drops his tumbler on the glass surface then slides both hands into his pockets before strutting in my direction.

He gives me another onceover, this one so slow, it feels like a caress. "Jesus."

"Is that a good Jesus or a bad one?" I ask, nervousness coating my words.

Phoenix's eyes roam over my body, taking in every inch of me.

I work my lower lip, awaiting his verdict.

"That's a 'Jesus, I can't wait for this damn gala to be over, because right now, I'm seriously debating skipping it altogether so I can spend the rest of the evening sinking my very hard cock into your hot, wet pussy'."

On their own accord, my eyes land on his crotch before meeting his gaze.

He isn't joking. He's hard.

Unbelievable.

"You seem to have a minor problem," I say.

"There's nothing minor about my cock and we both know it."

We laugh.

"All kidding aside, I look the part?" I ask.

"You nailed it, Michaela."

"You're not just saying that?"

He closes the gap between us. "I mean it, kitten." He rubs up and down my bare arms. "You're going to steal the show tonight."

"I feel quite pretty."

"Fuck, pretty. You're breathtaking." His eyes drop to my feet. "The crystals on the shoes complement the diamond chandelier earrings and bracelet I gave you as wedding gifts."

I bring my hands up to my earrings.

Another onceover. "You look like a queen. *My* queen."

"Thank you for the compliment. It means a lot."

Tonight, marks our first official outing as husband and wife, and I'm really nervous. We're not talking about a casual dinner party among friends. We're heading to the opening gala for the Hospitality Experience Excellence AWARDS.

No pressure.

"You're going to make me the envy of every man tonight," he says. "Something tells me I might have to beat a few of the men back with a stick if they stare too long at my beautiful wife."

The tinge of possessiveness makes me giddy.

After a long eleven-hour flight, we arrived at our suite at one o'clock in the afternoon, Paris time. Phoenix had to attend to business. I took a power nap. Then, I spent two hours at the hotel's spa and salon for hair and makeup. Once the stylists worked their magic, I was ushered to the hotel's boutique to select a pretty dress. After trying on six stunning selections, I picked this showstopper. I didn't want a long gown, so I went with a form fitting deep purple strapless dress that hits me above the knee in a shimmery satin fabric. I paired it with Giuseppe Zanotti black strappy heels.

Given Phoenix's reaction, I'm proud of myself for going with my gut.

"If we're exchanging compliments, you look dashing." I run a hand along his torso as I drool all over my husband. My gaze trails down his long, muscular body before meeting his blue eyes. "You wear a suit like it's nobody's business."

"Thank you." He winks.

Phoenix is clad in a trademark bespoke suit, a shirt and shoes. Tonight, he opted for head-to-toe black. No tie. He looks fierce. Seriously, this unbelievably handsome man could easily double as a model. To say this level of hotness is distracting isn't an understatement. Not one bit.

"There's one thing missing on your outfit," Phoenix says.

I frown and I lower my head for one more inspection. "There is?"

"Hold tight." Phoenix rushes to the bedroom.

"What are you doing?" I shout.

"Wait there. I'll be right out," he shouts back.

"Okay."

He's back, holding a square red box with an iconic luxury brand scripted across the lid—Cartier.

I stop breathing.

"I got you this," he says.

"Phoenix, you didn't have to."

"I wanted to," he says.

"You're impossible." That's the best I can come up with because I'm still shell-shocked. Whatever is hiding in that box is going to knock me on my ass. I'm sure of it.

"I bought it for you in Beverly Hills and kept it in the safe in the bedroom when we arrived. I wanted it to be a surprise."

"Congratulations, it's a big fucking surprise."

He laughs.

"The minute I saw it, I knew it had your name all over it. Now, that I see you in all your glory, it's perfect." He flashes me a pantie-melting smile, blinding me.

Phoenix opens the box.

My hands fly up to my cover my mouth and I gasp inside my palms.

Oh, my freaking God.

Myriad emotions ricochet through me at the sight of the most beautiful piece of jewelry I've ever seen in my life other than my wedding ring and the rest of my wedding collection. It's like a thousand little diamonds are winking at me under the light.

My eyes bounce from the dazzling bling to Phoenix's expectant gaze.

"Please tell me those aren't diamonds," I say, placing a hand against my beating heart. Perhaps not the most eloquent words, but Holy Jesus, this necklace must have cost a fortune.

"We've had this discussion before, Michaela. As my wife, you deserve the best."

"Phoenix, this is stunning."

"And it will look even better around your neck." He traces

my breasts with one finger. "It complements the bodice of the dress and it will accentuate the swell of your tits."

I shiver under his touch.

"Turn around. Let me put it on."

"Okay."

He slips it on.

I place a hand against the necklace as if it's going to fall.

"All done," Phoenix says, closing the clasp.

"Let me go see myself in the mirror."

"Use my phone," he says, producing it.

"Oh, my Lord!"

"You like it?"

"No. Nope. Not at all. I. Love. It."

"I'm glad you do," he says. "One more thing."

"You didn't buy me more jewelry." My tone is warning.

I can't handle more. This is already overwhelming.

"No. It's more of a request," he says, tracing my jawline with his finger.

Something wicked flashes in his eyes.

"What kind of request?" I ask.

He leans into me.

This close, his expensive cologne tickles my nostrils. God, I can't get enough of his *Eau de Alpha* scent.

"Hand over your panties." He whispers his command against my lips.

I lose my ability to speak.

Wh—what?

I just stare at him, my lashes fluttering like crazy.

"You heard me," he says when I remain silent.

"You— Huh? My panties?"

"Yes, I want you to remove your panties and hand them to me." And if he doesn't extend his hand, waiting.

"Phoenix, I can't walk around commando."

"No one will know."

"But I'll know and you'll know."

"That's the whole point. This is just between the two of us." His grin is dangerous.

I'm still staring at him.

The air between us crackles with a palpable charge as I consider his demand.

"I promise to behave," he says, sweetening the pot. "Knowing you did that just for me is a huge turn on and it'll get me so worked up that by the time we get back here, I'll fuck you like an animal and make you come so hard you'll forget your name."

Well, when he puts it like that.

I lift the bottom of my dress, but he stops me.

"Let me." Phoenix kneels in front of me, his molten eyes searing into mine.

He lifts the hem of my dress, latches his fingers around the elastic, and drags my panties down my body.

"Ah," I say. The cool sensation of my slickness running down my thighs is unexpected.

He leans forward and drops a soft kiss on my bare pussy.

I gasp.

He does it again.

And again.

The fourth time, he snakes his tongue between my lips and swirls it around my hard clit.

Crap. He's not playing fair.

My pulse thuds inside my throat, beating hard as naughty memories of our smoking hot make-out session in the bathroom of his private jet assail my memory.

Without warning, he pulls away.

Fuck.

"You're so wet, kitten."

The hunger I read in his eyes causes my pussy to pulsate.

"Step out of the panties."

I balance myself on his shoulder so as not to lose my footing in these strappy high heels.

I lift one leg.

Then, the other.

Phoenix brings my panties to his nose and inhales my scent.

Hooded eyes lift up to me. "You're going to be dripping and so fucking ready for me, kitten."

Yes, and yes.

"I can't wait to fill you up with my cum."

Neither can I.

My thighs tremble as if to announce an oncoming climax.

Good God.

I curse this stupid gala.

Phoenix offers a wolfish grin. "Looks like you're ready to get fucked."

Yes, I am.

"Patience, kitten."

But my body is desperate for release now.

He stands up and tucks my wet panties inside the pocket of his suit jacket. "This should be a great gala."

I have no words.

I'm still wrapping my head around what I just agreed to. I want this man so much, I'm willing to bend to his filthiest kinks.

I, Michaela König Knight Villiers, have officially crossed to the dark side.

Unbelievable.

~

The Hospitality Experience Excellence Awards are held at The Mandarin Oriental—a hop and skip away from the Pompadour. It's so close, we stroll to the hotel instead of jumping into a chauffeured car or taxi. Walking hand in hand with my husband in the city of love, all decked out for a glamorous evening, is what dreams are made of. A voice in my head screams at me, reminding me this is as fake as plastic. The other voice tells me not to give a damn it's all smoke and mirrors. Sometimes, make-believe is *everything* a girl needs.

Once inside the hotel, we head to the registration desk.

And we're off to a rip-roaring start!

With VIP passes in hand, we enter the main ballroom. As we step inside, it hits me full force, as my eyes bounce from one corner of the elegant room to the other.

God, I'm as skittish as a virgin on prom night.

This is beyond nerve-wracking.

As if Phoenix senses my panic, he squeezes my hand tight. "You belong on my arm as my wife. As my queen."

I nod.

My lips part, but I wouldn't call it a smile. The nerves in my belly are still rattling like chimes caught in a violent storm.

"You got this, beautiful."

"I have a new nickname?"

He leans in close and drops a soft kiss against my cheek. "Kitten is a bit too personal when we're out in public."

I let out a small laugh.

We keep walking.

My heart leaps into my throat and my step falters.

"Are you okay?" Phoenix asks.

I shake my head.

His gaze drops to my feet. "Did you hurt your ankle?"

I shake my head again. "I should've never agreed to your outrageous demand," I say in a low voice. "There are a lot of people here tonight. Now, I'm worried others will know I've gone commando."

He laughs.

The kind of unrestrained laughter that causes people to glance our way.

Great.

"This isn't a laughing matter," I say in a hushed tone. "This is a disaster waiting to happen—a very embarrassing one."

"You're worrying your pretty little head for nothing," he says. "Do you think you're the only one? I doubt it."

Right on cue, a tall brunette in five-inch heels with a serious pair of breasts and generous round hips walks by. The silver sequined dress she's wearing—which is practically see-through—confirms what Phoenix was just saying. My jaw drops at the sight of her visible butt crack.

Good God.

"Told you." Phoenix chuckles. He presses a kiss to my forehead, and I lean into him. "Now that I've eased your mind, let's go work the room, Mrs. König."

"Okay," I say, my voice still a bit shaky.

Phoenix's warm hand splays against my back as he guides me further into the ballroom. We each snatch a glass of champagne from the tray of a passing waiter.

I need liquid courage.

Careful not to gulp the effervescent drink in one go, I allow my lips to touch the champagne.

Wow! I mean, wow!

"I know we're in France, but this is amazing," I hold my glass at eye level to appraise the exceptional bubbly.

"The HEEA never skimps," Phoenix tells me.

"Makes sense." I nod. "With that in mind, why isn't the HEEA opening ceremony held at one of your hotels?" I ask. "Many of the König hotels are serious contenders at the Hospitality Experience Excellence Awards. Not that the Mandarin Oriental is anything to sniff at, but it doesn't compare to the Pompadour or some of the other luxury hotels under your umbrella."

A cocky smile touches his lips. "Look at you."

I'm confused. "What?"

"We've been married for only forty-eight hours, and already, you're a proud König and fiercely protective of the family brand."

"I'm just stating the obvious."

"To remain impartial and to avoid setting expectations, the HEEA holds the opening and closing ceremonies at a hotel that isn't in the running. So far, our hotels have never been considered because year after year we win awards in multiple categories." Pride drips from his words.

"I see."

"There's someone I'd like to introduce you to," Phoenix says.

And with that, my official wife duties begin.

With a smile firmly in place and my heart pattering, I shake hands, accept congratulations and make small talk with people I'm likely to forget before the end of the evening. To my surprise, my nervousness fades.

The wives—or lovers—of a few incredulous tycoons who obviously know Phoenix's reputation ask to see my ring, almost as if to confirm this isn't a hoax. The joke is on them, but still, I oblige.

We move around the room, and it doesn't go unnoticed the respect Phoenix has from his peers—many among the richest men on the planet. I know it's ridiculous, but I'm proud of him. And I'm damn proud to be seen with him. For the hundredth time since breakfast yesterday morning at Soren's house, I thank God my father didn't sell me to a monster.

The parade of strange faces seems endless as we do the rounds, but I don't complain. This is my end of the bargain, and I execute my role with grace. Years of shadowing Mom and Daddy at our hotel prepared me for tonight.

Phoenix's hand stiffens against my back.

My gaze lifts up to his.

His eyes stare straight ahead.

They're devoid of any softness, and his face looks like it's carved from granite.

Confused, I follow his stone-cold gaze.

A tall man dressed in a sharp navy-blue suit stands next to a pretty brunette with shoulder-length hair wearing a fitted soft yellow sleeveless dress that hits her mid-calf. She's model-tall and wears the beautiful dress to perfection. When my gaze lifts to the man's face, my head jerks back. Not because he's engaged in a deadly stare-down with Phoenix, but because there's an air of familiarity about him.

I study the man, taking in his dark, almost black eyes, his dark brown hair, and his tight beard.

I know those eyes.

I'm certain I've seen him before, but where?

My attention shifts to the woman holding his hand.

To my surprise, laser focused hazel-brown eyes are trained on me. There's something about the way she's glaring at me with her pursed red lips and cocked eyebrow that rubs me up the wrong way.

Is that smugness?

I don't even know her. Why such animosity?

I respond with my best resting bitch face.

Wow, I'm almost out of practice. I haven't used this contemptuous expression in a long time since I no longer have to deal with my duplicitous stepmother.

The bitchy woman squints her eyes at me.

I glare right back.

With an eye roll, she averts her gaze.

Is that all you got?

"Ah, the hit couple the press can't shut up about," the man says, approaching us, his words cold and calculating.

"Brock," Phoenix says.

"I thought you'd be on your honeymoon, König, not working a room," the man I know now as Brock says. "I read all about you tying the knot. Neither MC nor I could believe it. Mister Single Forever finally settles down."

"Oh, we're friends now?" Phoenix says. "Pardon me, I didn't get the memo."

Brock shakes his head. "Man, you hold a grudge."

A harsh sound comes from Phoenix's lips. Not a laugh. More like contained derision. "Whatever helps you sleep at night."

I'm going to take a wild guess here. These two hate each other.

"Let it go." Brock smirks. "Festering all this anger and animosity could be detrimental to your health, König. You should be careful. After all, heart problems run in your family. You wouldn't want to end up like your old man."

Brock's nasty retort hits me like a slap in the face. Judging from Phoenix's deadly expression, I'm not the only one. If looks could kill, Brock would be six feet under right now. Phoenix's jaw is locked so tight, I fear he'll shatter his teeth.

"Watch your mouth, Brock." My husband's voice is low and laced with a warning.

I'm sure cursing is frowned upon at an event as elegant as this one, but Phoenix's eyes scream, *"Fuck you, asshole."*

Brock turns his attention to me. "And you must be Phoenix's new wife. Since your husband seems to have left his manners at the door, allow me to introduce myself. I'm Brock

Litoris and this is my lovely wife Marie-Clémence Pisier-Litoris," he says, gesturing to the bitch by his side.

Brock Litoris. The name doesn't ring a bell, but this close, I'm certain I know this guy from somewhere. That said, right now, I'm too distracted by those outrageous last names to figure out how I know him. Litoris and Pisier-Litoris? Seriously?

Marie-Clémence offers a tight nod in lieu of a handshake.

Fine by me.

I respond in kind, my smile as fake as hers.

"You can call me MC," the bitch says in a pronounced French accent. "So many Americans can barely manage proper English, let alone another language—one as rich and complex as French. Your school system is such... a failure." She purses her lips in disdain. "The new generation can't write or read cursive anymore. Such a tragedy. All that to say, Marie-Clémence can be so challenging for most."

I've never wanted to bitch slap a woman this much in my life.

"En ce qui me concerne, j'ai étudié pendant deux étés à Nantes, donc je parle un français plus que correct. Votre nom ne sera pas un souci pour moi. Marie-Clémence est très facile à prononcer." I put the condescending woman back in her place.

Her eyebrows hit her forehead.

She's flummoxed.

You didn't see that one coming, bitch.

Brock doesn't hide his shock.

I look up at Phoenix and smile wide.

He manages to school his expression, but his arched eyebrow and slight tilt of his lips betray him. He's pleased I one-upped snooty Mrs. Pisier-Litoris.

There's so much we still don't know about each other.

"Ah. You speak French," Marie-Clémence says.

"I'm one of those Americans who manages more than

English. I read and write cursive perfectly as well. Our school system hasn't failed all of us."

Judging eyes run up and down the length of my body.

I part my lips in a triumphant grin.

Michaela, one. Bitchy French girl, zero.

"Phoenix got himself a smart little one," Brock says. The idiot keeps accumulating the insults. "It's a pleasure to meet you, Michaela." He extends his hand.

Phoenix snakes an arm around my waist, pulling me closer to his tense body. A warning.

I stare at Brock's extended hand for a beat before meeting his pitch-dark black eyes.

"I'll be honest, Mr. Litoris, after that dig to my husband and your cold, callous remark about my father-in-law's recent heart attack, I'm less than enthusiastic to shake your hand," I tell him, snubbing his welcoming gesture. My mother must be turning in her grave at my effrontery and lack of manners, but everything about this man makes my skin crawl.

I curl my hands around my evening clutch to drive home my point.

Bitchy French girl's gaze flashes to my hand, and her eyes nearly take over her face at the sight of my wedding ring.

I can't help my smug smile when my eyes travel to her left hand.

Size matters.

You want to turn this into a cockfight? Bring it!

"Wow, for a little woman, you're a spitfire," Brock says, sticking his hand in his pocket.

Demeaning asshole.

I pull my lips up in a forced smile. "What can I say? I'm feeling protective of my husband," I say, patting Phoenix's chest.

I mean every word I just uttered. This isn't an act. I'm not privy to their dynamic, but I'll go to bat for Phoenix.

"And here I thought you got yourself a wife. Instead, King König got himself a tiny guard dog." Brock flashes a set of teeth that's way too white.

I despise this vile man.

"They say Chihuahua's are the worst." Mrs. *Piss-Clitoris* adds her two cents.

"I reckon, snakes are far worse... you don't see them coming until it's too late." Phoenix shoots back a slicing remark at Marie-Clémence.

I sense bad blood between these two.

"There you go again bad-mouthing my wife, König," Brock says.

"She brought it on herself... with a little help from you. But then again, you two feed off each other."

"Michaela, I'm sure Phoenix has told you all sort of erroneous things about my wife and I—"

"You give yourself too much importance. My husband has never mentioned your name." My gaze slides to the woman with a stick up her ass. "Or hers."

"I'm surprised Phoenix never mentioned us. The three of us have history together," Brock says.

It doesn't take a genius to figure that out.

"Like I said, you give yourself too much importance, Mr. Litoris."

He glares at me.

"Come on, Brock, there's nothing here for us." *Pissy Clit* pulls on her husband's arm. "There are far more important people in the room to mingle with than to waste our breath on Phoenix and his *little* wife."

The fury flooding Phoenix's gaze is unsettling.

"You're right, honey," Brock says. "After all, Ripley sent us here to sniff out new opportunities."

As in Ripley Madigan?

With a condescending stare, Brock sweeps his beady black eyes over Phoenix's body. I receive the same disdainful treatment.

"One-upping our unworthy adversary is the name of the game... something we do very well." He flashes his too white teeth. "Let's go close some deals—"

"Don't you mean, con people?" Phoenix says.

"You've always been a sore loser," Brock says.

"Rich coming from a guy who uses duplicitous tactics to get his way in life." Phoenix's words are sharp as an axe.

Whoa. It's a veritable minefield between these three.

Without so much as a goodbye, the aggravating couple turns on their heel and melts into the crowd.

It doesn't take them long to find another prey.

Vultures.

I look up at Phoenix.

Angry heat radiates from his blue eyes, his nostrils flaring like an enraged bull.

"Do you want to talk about it?" I ask.

My question snaps him out of his trance.

His eyes meet mine. The storm that was raging in them subsides. For the first time since the Pisier-Litoris duo came onto the scene, a true smile softens his stone cold features.

He leans into me and places a gentle kiss on my temple.

"Thanks for having my back, beautiful," he says. "You were amazing."

"We're a team."

"Yes, we are," he says.

"They're nasty people."

"You don't know the half of it. You played them well. I can

promise you this…" He pulls me closer to him, "you're going to get a big fat treat when we get back to our suite, Mrs. König."

"Oooohhh!" Excitement blooms in my tummy. "What kind of treat?"

"A big fat cock hungry for your pussy."

Heat gathers at my center, sending a ripple of delicious tingling sensations straight to my nipples and my clit.

Is this gala over yet?

Chapter 26

Phoenix

It wasn't hard to convince Michaela to ditch the gala. Thank God. Breathing the same air as Brock and Marie-Clémence is hazardous to my goddamn health. The thought of spending any more time under the same roof as those two was nauseating. I might have to tolerate them during the awards, but tonight, I'd rather not be in their presence.

I suggested returning to the hotel for dinner, but Michaela had a better idea. We hopped into a taxi and made our way to the fashionable Marais district in the 4th arrondissement. Hand in hand, we strolled to *L'As du Fallafel* on Rue des Rosiers—the city's best Israeli-style falafel and shawarma sandwiches. It just so happens to be a favorite for both of us. Armed with a gargantuan variety of delicious pita sandwiches, a platter of kefta, and enough homemade fries to fill a bucket, we returned to the Pompadour. Still dressed to kill, we headed straight to the large balcony adjacent to our suite to devour our dinner.

It's a beautiful, warm night, and the spectacular view of

Paris under an indigo sky is incomparable. A chillout lounge vibe spills from the exterior speakers, adding to the ambience.

"That was ridiculous," Michaela says, popping the last bite of French lemon tart into her mouth. "The pastry chefs at the Pompadour are going to make it impossible for me to stop stuffing my face with yummy sweet goodness."

"Desserts here are decadent," I say. "I could've asked our chefs to prepare something comparable to our Israeli feast, but nothing beats the real thing. Not to mention, I never miss the opportunity to stop by *L'As* every time I'm in town."

"The last time I was in Paris, I ate at *L'As* nearly every day. It's so good," she tells me.

"I still can't get over your mastery of French," I say, changing the subject.

"I have an accent, I forget how to say certain words, and I'm not always the best with complicated French conjugation, but I speak it well enough to shut that woman up and put her back in her place," Michaela says.

"It was priceless," I tell her. "Did you learn French in school?"

"I've been studying French for years. After graduating, I spent six months in the Pays de la Loire, in western France. I stayed with a lovely family. I chose that particular area because it's one of France's wine regions. I was getting ready to step into the family business full-time. Then Thana happened and my dream went to hell."

He nods. "Thana, the two-timing witch."

"Yup!"

We each take a long sip of our Sauvignon blanc, eyeing each other over the rim of the glass.

"Speaking of another she-devil, can we talk about Brock and Marie-Clémence?" Michaela puts an end to the mellow mood of the evening. I knew this was coming. "We're bound to bump into them again in the next few days."

"You're right. As much as I'd like to, we can't escape them."

"Did you and Marie-Clémence date or... sleep together?"

No waffling. She goes straight for it.

"We had a thing for about six months."

"How does Brock fit into the mix?"

I consider her question.

"I don't want to pry, but whatever happened between the three of you must've been pretty significant. The palpable animosity hung thick in the air. Shouldn't I know why?"

I wish I didn't have to go down memory lane, but she deserves an explanation.

"Marie-Clémence was a makeup artist. She mainly worked TV shows. Now, her full-time job is being Brock's wife. We met at a function. There was an instant attraction. We started seeing each other. It was casual, and she knew what to expect. Not that I dated, but I was in no headspace for anything more. Barron's death forced me to step into a role I wasn't prepared for. I had big shoes to fill. And, I was still grieving for Mom. MC seemed understanding enough at the time." I pause. "Brock was Barron's assistant. He was twenty-seven when I took over my brother's position and he had big aspirations, which I wholeheartedly encouraged. As I was learning the ropes, I relied heavily on him. That was a big mistake."

"He wasn't supportive?"

"He was very supportive. I just didn't know it was a façade. While he was smiling at me, he was backstabbing me to advance his career."

"What?" Michaela is incredulous. "How?"

"A lot of the deals we were vying for seemed to slip from between our fingers right when it was time to close. I thought it was me. I was certain I was making rookie mistakes and losing those prospects right before they signed the contract. Dad assured me it had to be more. This went on for a while. Time and time again, we were losing out on amazing properties. And the worst part is, we were losing out to the Madigans—"

"That must've been so maddening."

"It was infuriating, and it was driving me out of my mind because I couldn't figure out why it kept happening," I tell her. "The board was growing increasingly impatient with me. I didn't have an explanation. Everything became clear when I returned early from a business trip to London. Because I was so dead set on proving myself to the board, I asked my chauffeur to drive me to the office instead of going back to my place. I wanted to fine-tune a few proposals for upcoming meetings. Since it was nine o'clock at night on a Friday, the executive floor was deserted. As I was approaching my office, I heard moans. I thought it might be the cleaning crew. I was just about to enter my office to find out what the hell was going on when a woman's voice stopped me dead in my tracks. It was a voice I knew too well. A voice that was calling out Brock's name, pleading with him to make her come all over his face."

A violent torrent of emotions swirls through me, flashing back to that day.

"Marie-Clémence?" Michaela asks.

"Yes. I opened the door to find MC spread out naked on my desk with Brock sitting on my chair, eating her out."

"Oh my God! What did you do?"

"For a long moment, I just stood there as my brain tried to compute what I was witnessing. Since her eyes were closed, MC was unaware I had caught her red-handed."

"Unbelievable," Michaela says.

"By the time Brock made her come, she was calling out all the saints up above. When Brock stood up—buck naked, unsheathed cock on alert—he froze in shock when he caught me standing there, staring right at him."

"Holy shit!" Michaela says. "He must have been freaked out."

"He was as white as a ghost and his rock-hard cock turned limp, just like that!" I snap my fingers. "MC must've sensed my presence because she opened her eyes. She panicked so much, she nearly rolled off my desk when she saw me."

"How did they react to being caught?" Michaela asks.

"They went into this pathetic song and dance of, *it's not what it looks like*, but I didn't have two shits to give."

"You caught them naked, and you heard Marie-Clémence begging Brock to make her come. That's pretty black and white."

"Exactly. I called security to have them escorted out of the building. I revoked Brock's security card and made sure every security guard knew he was persona non grata. I was livid."

"Of course you were angry with them. They betrayed you."

"They were doing a lot more than sleeping together. They were conspiring against our company."

Her eyebrows hit her forehead.

"What do you mean?"

"I was pleasantly surprised by MC's interest in what I did and how I was adapting to my new responsibilities. It's such a departure from her profession, but she was full of questions every time we were together, and she seemed to soak up every detail."

"She was playing you?"

"Just like Brock was."

"How did you find out?"

"I couldn't prove it then and I still can't now, but I'm certain Brock was feeding information to Ripley Madigan. I may not have proof, but I'm certain Marie-Clémence was feeding Brock intel."

"What makes you say that?"

"I made the mistake of allowing her to hang out at my place when I had to leave early for the office. Sometimes she'd come by the office and I'd hand her the key to my old penthouse when I was caught up in a meeting or on a conference call. It was casual, but I felt comfortable with her. I always brought files home. Left home alone, she was able to snoop to her heart's content."

"Why do you say you couldn't prove it? It sounds like you could."

"When I called my father and brothers to tell them I found my assistant fucking the woman I was seeing, Dad was puzzled I'd found them in my office, of all places. Why not a conference room or Brock's office? That got me thinking. They seemed at home in my office. A little too cozy. Dad demanded our tech team analyze Brock's computer and his company phone."

"Did they find anything?"

"Brock had several booked time slot entries in his calendar marked only with RM," I say in quotation marks. "There was also a string of texts from RM. All of them had cryptic messages like, '*I just texted you something. Check your other phone.*' Or '*You're sure she won't turn on us?*' Or '*Can she dig a little deeper?*'" I pause. "Turns out, RM was Ripley Madigan."

"You're kidding?"

"I wish that episode of my life was a bad dream, but it was more like a horrible nightmare."

"So why couldn't you nail Brock's ass to the wall?"

"We never found the other phone Ripley alluded to. My guess is any secret conversation they were having was happening on that other phone. Without it, we couldn't go after Brock or Ripley. 'RM' marked in a calendar would never hold up in court. Sure, we called RM's number from Brock's company phone and we confirmed it was Ripley, but that wasn't enough. There was nothing concrete we could use to pin Brock with corporate espionage, even if all the signs pointed to it. Brock was playing me, which explains why Ripley's team always one-upped us. I even hired a contact of mine who heads a topnotch security firm to see if he could find anything that could help us, but it was too late. By then, Brock and Ripley knew the cat was out of the bag, they had time to cover their tracks by getting rid of any evidence."

"Brock is such a tool," she says. "I still can't get over Marie-Clémence's betrayal. If she was more interested in Brock, why not just be upfront about it?" Michaela asks.

"After I kicked them out, she made sure to text me to let me know she was sleeping with Brock and me at the same time. I'm certain she was being spiteful. Realization hit me with the force of a Hulk-like blow. Her interest in my work made sense. She was another pawn in Ripley's game and most certainly paid very well for her role."

"They're awful people."

I nod. "Brock and MC made me look like a fool. It was humiliating," I tell her. "Because of them, we upped security measures by installing high-tech keyless touch-pad locks on the doors of every office on the executive floor. They're tamper-proof Wi-Fi-smart locks, which can only be unlocked via a secure smartphone app. Only Dad, my brothers, our head of security, Dad's long-time executive assistant, and I know all the combinations. That's also why elevators require a key card to access the executive floor. I will never underestimate anyone ever again. As far as I'm concerned, anyone can be a back-stabber."

"Smart."

"Fool me once, shame on me. Fool me and you don't get to

fool me again," I say. "Ripley must've dangled a golden carrot in front of Brock's face. He never had any qualms about being ambitious and since Ripley would sell his mother's soul to secure a business deal, it was a match made in heaven."

"I guess that explains why Brock works for Ripley now," Michaela says.

"Two weeks after I unceremoniously kicked Brock out of my office, I caught wind he was working for Ripley as a VP of boutique acquisition or some bullshit title like that. From my understanding, he heads the team that buys out family owned hotels looking to sell."

"Evidently, it pays to be a snitch," Michaela says.

"I nearly blew a gasket! That position was Brock's reward for allowing Ripley to profit from *our* hard work and strategic thinking. Six months later, as I was finally putting the MC and Brock debacle behind me, I found out they got married."

"Brock and his wife form the perfect couple—two venomous snakes in blissful marital harmony."

I can't help but chuckle at her comment. "Well said."

"It's been a recurring prayer since yesterday morning, but I'm so grateful Daddy didn't hand me over to Ripley," Michaela says. "I know he had no intentions of marrying me, but the thought of being his captive prisoner is nauseating. From everything you said yesterday, I'm sure he would've treated me like a whore."

She's right. He would've. In Ripley's world, women are disposable cunts meant to be used. Nothing more. Nothing less.

I reach across the table and open my hands, silently asking for hers. She obliges. I squeeze them before bringing them to my lips and dropping a soft kiss against them.

"Your father made the wager of a lifetime with the most

precious person in his life," I say. "I'm the lucky guy he trusted. Looks like his gamble paid off for both of us."

"Looks like it," she says.

Something passes between us and this fake marriage doesn't feel so fake.

"Not to mention, I'm fairly certain you make for a much better lover than Ripley," she says.

I like where this conversation is going.

"Speaking of which, I made you a promise after that brilliant performance, Mrs. König."

She cocks an eyebrow. "I might need you to refresh my memory. So much has happened tonight, I can't keep track anymore." Her flirtatious tone doesn't go unnoticed.

I stand up and round the table.

I extend a hand. "Let's go inside. I'll remind you."

"Shouldn't I know what I'm getting into?"

My gaze burns over her exposed shoulders, and my nostrils flare. "I'm going to fuck you hard in nothing more than your heels, your wedding ring, and the necklace I gave you to show my appreciation for having my back tonight."

She grabs my hand, her green eyes veiled with lust.

Chapter 27

Michaela

With each step, I'm more and more aroused.

My pussy tingles at his filthy promise, wetness pooling between my lips as my body anticipates what's coming next.

Yes!

Phoenix guides me to the bedroom, his hand never leaving mine, until he stops. Something flashes in his eyes and my stomach tightens with excitement, going straight to my core.

"Strip!" He lets go of my hand and pulls open the curtains. "I want you naked." That's not what I expected to come flying out of his mouth.

"Wh—what?"

I'm sure I misheard him.

"I'm going to fuck you in front of the window," he says.

I guess I heard him correctly the first time. Still, it doesn't lessen the shock. My brain swirls like a whirligig at the full impact of his words. My eyes bounce from the window to his.

"There are hotels and apartment buildings across the street," I say. "Someone will see us. Why can't we use the bed?"

"Predictable," he says.

"And that's a problem how?"

"Kitten, the first time we fucked it was a few hours after we tied the knot up against a wall. The second time was my father's garage while our guests were mere feet away. The third time, you gave me a stellar blow job on my private plane. Let's not forget that scorching hot episode in my office before we got married? A bed? Why would we lower our standards?"

"Phoenix, this is outrageous."

He caresses my cheek. "That's why it's so good, kitten."

I'm desperately searching for a retort, but I can only shake my head.

"You don't want me to make you come?" he asks.

I narrow my gaze at him.

"You're putting words in my mouth."

"I'd rather put my cock in your mouth, but you're shaking your head. You're sending more mixed signals than a drunk air traffic controller."

Cocky asshole.

"Of course I want you to make me come—"

"In that case, you'll do as you're told," he says.

My eyes shift from left to right.

A weird energy bubbles inside me—a mixture of dread and... anticipation?! No, excitement!

Whoa.

"If you prefer to use your fingers. I'll understand—"

"That's not fair! What kind of ultimatum is that?"

"Are you saying you *need* me to make you come, kitten?"

I should wipe that smug smile stretching his lips by French kissing him... but he's right.

I hate that he knows that.

Until six days ago, I was more than content with my solo sessions. Unlike sex with ex boyfriends, I always came. That's before Phoenix came barreling into my life. The man knows my body better than I do. He rocks my world with his long fingers, his skillful mouth, and his beautiful, thick cock. Having to use my fingers when we're sleeping in the same bed is a cruel punishment.

I scour the room over his shoulders.

The lights are low, but still bright enough to give a clear view inside the bedroom.

Would anyone really see us?

And if so, would they recognize us?

Would they take photos? Nah. That's crazy.

Would they watch? Ooohhh! That would be very naughty.

It's not like paparazzi is posted across the street, waiting to snap the money shot.

What to do? What to do?

"Tick tock, I'm still waiting, kitten."

I meet the hazel-blue eyes I've come to know almost as well as my own, including how they flare with smoldering heat when he's turned on... like he is right now.

I let out a long breath.

I might regret this, but my body is humming with desire. It's this hungry mass of volcanic fire, his dare teasing my flame.

I turn around so my back faces him.

"Can you help me with the zipper," I ask.

Resisting what I desperately need is futile and pointless.

"You're going to give me what I want?"

"Yes." With that one word I offer him my full submission.

"I love it when I get my way with you," he says, amusement lacing his words.

The zipper on my dress hisses as he slides it down. When the dress pools at my feet, I step out of it, balancing myself with a hand on his forearm.

Without even asking, Phoenix unhooks my strapless bra.

He snatches the expensive designer dress off the floor, struts towards the plush oversized chair in the bedroom and drops it with the bra. I barely have time to blink, and he's standing in front of me naked and ready.

Since the clock is ticking on our relationship, I make it my mission to commit every chiseled muscle to memory. Who knows if I'll ever be with a guy with such a perfect body ever again?

With a hand already stroking his cock, Phoenix approaches me.

My eyes are riveted on his mighty erection. All the veins stand out on alert. My pussy clenches in delicious staccato pulses at the sight, and my mouth waters.

God, that's as hot as fuck.

"You want to take this cock for a ride, kitten?"

"Yes."

"You're going to ride it like your life depends on it?"

"Yes."

"Good because that's the only way we do things—hard, rough, and dirty." His fist pumps between his legs, up and down, up and down. "Tonight, we have the added benefit of an audience to make things even raunchier."

Good Lord, I'm soaking wet.

The man's mouth might be his most beautiful feature and that says a lot considering his long list of attributes.

My eyes are transfixed on his cock as his thumb swipes over the slick head.

I lick my lips.

I want to drop to my knees to suck that beautiful cock dry.

"Turn around."

I obey his order.

In the reflection of the glass, my diamond earrings and

necklace glint like shiny stars against a midnight blue sky. Even my eyes seem to sparkle.

"You're a vision, kitten. I'm sure you already caught a poor schmuck's eye." I shift my attention, peering over my shoulder and I watch as Phoenix stalks towards me, his hand still working his cock.

I move my gaze back to the city line.

All those buildings... all those eyes...

The thought sends thrilling tingles down my spine.

Phoenix's heat and the banging of his heart against my back only amplifies how fucking turned on I am.

"They can look, but they can't touch," he says, low and firm, into my ear.

Those words travel straight to my clit.

Oh God.

I'm no match for his masterful dirty-talking.

He presses his front to my back.

I revel in the closeness and soak up the warmth of his body.

Three days of wedded bliss and I'm already addicted to this man.

"I wonder how many men will jerk off while watching you getting thoroughly fucked from behind," Phoenix says before his teeth graze my shoulder.

He nips my earlobe.

I gasp.

"You're going to come hard for me, kitten?"

"Yes."

"I want your hands against the window."

My pulse hammers against my throat in anticipation.

I lift my hands, pressing my palms against the window.

"Good girl." He traces a languorous finger from my nape, down my spine, and all the way to the seam between my butt cheeks. "Damn, I love your ass," he says before invading between my cheeks with a forceful hand. “I’m looking forward to claiming all of you.” He presses a finger against my sacred hole.

My breath itches.

His promise causes me to clench my cheeks together.

“Not today,” he says. “You’re not ready yet.”

I let out a sigh of relief.

I don’t think I’d refuse him, but I struggle to understand how my tight, virgin ass will adjust to his impressive size when my pussy can barely handle it.

“Tonight, I just want to lose myself in your slick pussy,” he murmurs against my ear.

“I want that too.”

The words slip from my lips without my permission.

“Spread them wide,” he says, kicking my feet apart. “Keep your hands on the window, or I’ll redden your ass.”

“Okay.”

Exhibitionism is one thing. BDSM 101 on the same night might be pushing the envelope.

My eyes scan as far as they can on the horizon, already searching for peeping Toms and peeping Tammys.

“You must really want to come because you’re not fighting me,” he says, groping my breasts.

His fingers pinch my hard nipples, and I bite my lower lip to curtail a cry. My breath hitches when he twists them.

“I love when you surrender to me. I can’t tell you what it does to me to know you trust me enough to give me everything.”

Take it. Take it all. It’s all yours.

“Your gorgeous tits are perfect, Michaela.” He toys with my nipples, sending jolts of pleasure straight to my clit. “Your nipples are so sensitive.” He squeezes them harder. “I bet I could make you come just by squeezing these babies.” He presses his cock against my back as he pinches my nipples hard.

I'm this close to losing my mind.

Oh God.

This is so obscene.

And erotic as all fuck.

I could lie to myself, but I love being this exposed. The forbidden thrill of being watched is so kinky.

I only expected what was promised to me from this marriage—regaining control of our family hotel, debt free. This man's feral appetite and his desire for me are beyond the realms of anything I could've hoped for.

Phoenix slides his hand down my stomach until he reaches my pussy.

Slap!

I choke.

Did he just slap my pussy?

Slap!

"Holy shit!"

Pain and pleasure fight for dominance. To my shock and dismay, pleasure wins.

My husband is turning me into someone daring and bold. And, I like her.

"I own this pussy," he says, cupping my tingling lady parts.

My legs tremble in response.

I didn't know there were levels to his alphaliciousness.

He glides two fingers between my pussy lips and pushes them knuckle-deep in a forceful thrust inside me.

I fold in half from the impact, and my hands slide down a few inches.

"Jesus!"

"Fuck, you're ready for me."

He doesn't give me time to catch my breath.

Phoenix fucks me deep with his long fingers.

I curl my hands into fists and bang them against the window.

Slap!

"I said, your hands remain on the window. Don't disobey me again."

"I won't."

I splay my fingers against the window.

"Good girl."

He resumes his mission.

With great effort, I manage to keep my hands on the window, never breaking contact and never allowing them to slide. By a miracle of God, they remain in position even when Phoenix rubs his cock against my clit. And my hands don't move when he glides his cock around my hole in mind-blowing circles, while fucking me with his fingers.

"You're going to scream out my name so loud when I take your ass, they'll hear you in Idaho. It won't be from pain, it'll be from ecstasy."

I moan in delight.

His filthy words trigger a series of strong contractions against his invading fingers.

"That's it, kitten. Show me how much you appreciate my fingers inside your sweet pussy."

Clearly, he controls my body, because my pussy clenches again on command.

"Oh, fuck, I need to be inside you," he says.

His strong hands grip my waist, forcing me to bend over. With a loud feral grunt, he thrusts inside me, balls deep, taking my breath away. All my senses shut down except for where our bodies meet. He's buried so deep, I'm about to beg him to never come out.

He powers into me like an oil-drilling rig, pumping harder and harder.

He shows me no mercy.

And, I welcome every punishing thrust.

I meet his gaze in the window's reflection.

His eyes are veiled with so much lust and desire, an expression that enters me deeper than his cock.

One of his hands leaves my waist and the next thing I know, he places it behind my head, forcing my face against the window.

I grunt as if he's pushed all the air out of me.

I'm trapped.

He loses it.

He fucks me with a vengeful force that nearly makes me delirious. He's almost cruel and careless with my body, and as God is my witness, I love it.

"More!" I tell him.

"My demanding, dirty wife," he says, driving into me like a savage.

"Oh, yeah. Oh, yeah. Oh, yeah." I can't stop chanting.

"Fuck, your pussy was made for my cock," he says.

"Don't stop!"

He fucks me deeper. Faster. Harder.

I close my eyes, relishing what this man is doing to my body.

Phoenix slides a hand down my stomach.

"Come all over my cock," he says in my ear. "Come hard for me, kitten."

He glides two fingers between my lips, flicking my clit. With every stroke, he chisels away the remainder of my resolve. One more flick and he obliterates the barrier between the waiting climax and me.

Ha!

A familiar buildup curls inside my tummy, causing my eyes to roll to the back of my head.

With one last hard thrust, Phoenix hits that spot inside me that sends me off like a rocket. A burst of bright light explodes behind my closed eyelids. It takes me a second to register the voice crying out is my own.

My body is engulfed in overwhelming sensations as I ride this sublime orgasmic wave.

"Oh, Phoenix," I say over and over again as my release gushes out of me.

"Fuck, yeah, kitten, give it to me." He doesn't stop fucking me. On the contrary. My climax seems to trigger his, and he fucks me harder.

I come, and I come, and I come, sobbing incoherent prayers.

The embarrassment is long gone now. Phoenix doesn't mind if I make a mess. Why should I?

"Oh, kitten. Fuck—" His body stills and his hands tighten around my waist. A feral grunt escapes him as his cock pulses with release, shooting his load deep inside my pussy.

With the last ounce of strength I possess, I clench my muscles hard, milking every drop of his warm cum, sating my every desire.

We pant heavy, unable to speak.

Seconds tick away.

"I guess we were someone's live porn stream tonight," I say, struggling to regulate my breathing.

"No one saw us," he says against my earlobe.

"You're just saying that so I don't freak out at the thought I just became an exhibitionist."

"I'm saying that because the windows are tinted."

What? "Tinted?"

"Yes," he says. "All the penthouse suites on the top floor

have tinted windows from the outside. People across the street can't see inside."

I turn my head, meeting his eyes. "You tricked me?" I'm not sure if I should be outraged or relieved.

"Stop kidding yourself, kitten," he says. "You enjoyed letting the bad girl come out to play. And trust me, I loved playing with her."

"That may be so, but a heads up would've been appreciated."

"A heads up would've prevented you from coming that hard. And that's unacceptable to me," he says. "As your husband and your lover, my job is to push you off the damn cliff every single time I fuck you."

Well, I can't argue with that logic.

We remain wrapped up like this for a while, neither of us in a rush to break the connection.

"Mine," he says out of the blue in a low voice, tightening his embrace around my tummy.

Oh wow.

Should I keep a level head to avoid drowning in this man? Probably. After all, nothing real can come out of something that started out as a sham. But right now, I don't give a damn.

It may only be for a year, but nonetheless, Phoenix König is mine. And I'm his.

Chapter 28

Michaela

My eyes spring open as the recollection of a disturbing memory stirs me awake.

"OhmyGod! I know where I've seen Brock before!" I sit bolt upright in bed as I blurt out those words. I look down at Phoenix. He's peacefully sleeping on his back. *Well, that won't last.* I shake him. "Wake up."

"Kitten, I fucked you not long ago," he says in a groggy voice. "Give me a chance to recharge, woman."

I roll my eyes.

"No, that's not it. Wake up!" I shake him harder.

"I don't have to be awake for you to suck my cock. Knock yourself out!" He pulls the sheet off his body, exposing his morning wood.

I thought he wasn't ready to go.

"For the love of God, Phoenix, wake up! This is serious."

He opens one eye. "What is it?"

"Brock. I remember where I've seen him before."

A sleepy Phoenix looks up at me, puzzled. "Where?"

"At the Villiers Grand."

"What?"

"Yes."

He sits up, pulling the sheet to cover up.

He's wide awake now.

"When?" he asks.

"Late afternoon on the day I was set to leave for Nepal."

"You're sure?"

"I am. I stopped by the hotel to say goodbye to the staff and grab a pair of old sneakers I kept in my office to use at the hotel gym that were perfect for trekking in Nepal. I figured I'd grab my shoes first. Then, say my goodbyes to the staff. As I was leaving my office and rounding the corner, I heard Thana's annoying voice. I ducked because I wasn't in the mood for a stepmommy-words-of-wisdom moment. I would've ignored her altogether, but she said something along the lines of, *'I pride myself in knowing a few ways of dramatically lowering the value of any company...'* I had no idea what she was talking about, but it piqued my curiosity, so I peeked out to see who she was talking to. Her back was facing me, but the man was looking straight at her. Since he seemed riveted by the conversation, I was able to check him out. Four things jumped out—he had the darkest eyes I've ever seen, his height, the pronounced scars left behind from severe acne, and that permanent self-righteous smirk he sports."

"That describes Brock to a T," Phoenix says. "Didn't he see you?"

"When he noticed me, he stared right at me. He narrowed his eyes, his gaze menacing. Every cell in my body was prickling and not in a good way. Before he was able to alert Thana of my presence, I fled, running down the stairs of the emergency exit. I weaved my way through the hotel until I reached the parking lot. I can't explain why, but I felt the pressing need to get the hell out of there. Fast. I jumped into my car and headed back to my father's house to finish packing."

"If he was staring right at you, why didn't he recognize you last night?"

"I was wearing a baseball cap and my *long brown* hair was loose," I tell him. "Since I didn't wait around for Thana to turn around and identify me, she had no idea who was standing there."

"How come you didn't recognize him last night?"

"The beard."

Phoenix nods.

"I guess it all came to me while I was sleeping. I'm going out on a limb here." I pause, unsure I should continue.

"I'm listening," Phoenix says.

"Given his position, Brock was most likely scoping out the hotel."

"I wouldn't put it past him."

"Ripley had everything he needed to manipulate Daddy to sell the Villiers Grand for much less than its value. How did Ripley get all that private info?"

Phoenix's eyes grow wide as realization sets in.

"Goddammit," he says.

"Ripley had leverage. He had Thana... who was probably in cahoots with Brock."

Chapter 29

Phoenix

After the shocker Michaela dropped into my lap, I needed to make an urgent call. After a quick shower, breakfast, and coffee, we're both seated side-by-side on the sofa, our eyes glued to my iPhone placed on the coffee table as it rings.

"Hey, Phoenix!" Bryce says when he picks up.

"Hey, Bryce. I hope I'm not calling too early?"

"Not at all. Are you calling to reschedule our dinner plans?" he asks.

I wouldn't call Bryce Van Der Linden a close friend. He's more of a secret weapon. He used to live in California. He now lives in the Big Apple. It just so happens we're both in Paris at the same time. We were set to meet later this week for dinner with Michaela, but this can't wait.

Bryce runs one of the most important internet security companies in the world. We've been using his services for years. On the tail of a fairly high-profile case surrounding his wife, he branched out, and now he also specializes in all sorts of white-collar crimes. He and his team of experts can track anyone, anywhere. He saves us several millions of dollars every single year with his cyber-intelligence.

"No, we're still on," I tell him.

"Good. I'm looking forward to meeting Mrs. König."

"Speaking of which, you're on speaker phone," I tell him. "Michaela is here with me."

"Ah, the new bride," Bryce says. "It's a pleasure to meet you, Michaela."

"It's a pleasure to meet you too, Bryce," she says.

"I can't wait to meet you in person," he says.

"Same here. Phoenix speaks highly of you," she says.

I wink at her.

She smiles.

"I'm honored," he says. "Congratulations, Michaela, on snatching a certified bachelor."

"Takes one to know one," I say.

"I'm not even going to argue with you. No complaints on my part. I love my wife," he says. "So, how can I help you?"

"I may have a situation on my hands," I say. "In fact, I'm certain of it."

"Words I love to hear," he says. "I'm all ears."

"Do you remember Brock Litoris?"

"Yes, the assistant who was feeding company information to your biggest rival and sabotaging your credibility," Bryce says.

"The one and only," I say, sarcasm weighing heavy.

"Is he back in the picture?" Bryce asks.

"He'll always be in the picture given who he works for—"

"I hate that we were never able to nab him or Ripley," Bryce says.

"The sneaky rats were miles ahead of us."

Years go by, but the sting doesn't lessen. Nor does the crushing humiliation of being blindsided.

I despise Brock Litoris.

And I darn right hate Ripley.

I'm sure Brock told Ripley we contracted Bryce's services. This gave them a leg up. Few con artists outsmart Bryce and his team. The Three Stooges—Brock, Ripley, and Marie-Clémence—knew from the get-go to never share any incriminating information on our networks.

"So, what did Brock do now?" Bryce asks.

Bryce signs a DNA with all his clients, so I have the peace of mind of knowing this conversation isn't going anywhere.

I tell him about bumping into Brock and MC last night.

I turn it to Michaela and she recounts what she told me this morning.

I tie it all together by telling Bryce about recently purchasing the Villiers Grand Hotel. Of course, I leave out details about our fake marriage.

"It seems Brock has moved on," Bryce says when I'm finished.

"I'm not so sure about that," I tell him.

"Why do you say that?" Bryce asks.

"We have a leak within our organization. Again."

Bryce grumbles. "Well, this time it's not Brock, which means there's another weasel playing you."

"I can't shake the nagging feeling Ripley has his tentacles in one of our board members."

"That's a bold accusation," Bryce says. "Board members are supposed to be on your side."

"You would think," I say.

I tell him all about Potter and what my father shared.

"You're right, he knows too much," Bryce says.

"Way too much."

Chapter 30

Michaela

With an impatient flick of the wrist, I peruse the pages of the French *Vogue* magazine I grabbed from the stack to keep myself busy.

Flip.

Flip.

Flip.

I let out a long sigh.

I check the time on my phone and go back to being a bored, Stepford wife.

"It's already six-thirty. When will he get off that darn conference call?" I grumble to myself.

I didn't expect this morning's revelation to topsy-turvy Phoenix's day.

He's been locked up in the office in our suite on back-to-back conference calls. He had me sit in on his calls with his father and brothers. All three men share Phoenix's acrimonious feelings for the duplicitous couple. Once we updated his family —minus Roman, who really doesn't need to deal with this shit right now—he suggested I contact the art buyer for the hotels in France, Spain, and Italy.

Victorine Ardant was expecting my call. Giddy at the prospect of stepping into my new role as Art Director and Principal Art Buyer for König Imperial Holding, I met up with her.

Victorine gave me a tour of her studio and the storage room packed with art located in the basement of the Pompadour, Saint-Germain hotel. After the meeting, I called Phoenix to see if he was available for lunch. He was in work mode, so I invited Victorine instead.

She's so very French. Her personality is as effervescent as her name. It's wild to share your first name with a famous Louis Vuitton luxury monogram wallet. I already know we're going to get along famously.

Contrary to Marie-Clémence, Victorine isn't a stuck-up snob who looks down at people because they only speak one language. Victorine didn't mind my accent or the fact I couldn't remember certain French words.

We had a really great time getting acquainted with each other better.

After lunch, I returned to the suite to find Phoenix still wearing his CEO-slash-COO hat. I knew this would be a honeymoon-slash-work week, but I was hoping we'd spend more time together.

Bummed out, I plopped myself on the sofa with my phone in hand. To keep myself busy, I called Keira to catch up and share all the details of my post-wedded bliss in Paris.

Then, I called Daddy. I told him about Brock and Thana. He shared his unpleasant conversation with Potter. The call with my father was supposed to be all shop talk, but it ended as an emotional thank-you-for-choosing-Phoenix-as-my-husband-instead-of-selling-me-off-to-the-dirty-old-man heart-to-heart. I told him about Ripley's disturbing perversions.

Daddy was horrified. We were both crying by the end of the call.

Since there was still no sign of my husband emerging from his office, I headed out to comb the streets of Paris, soaking up the unique atmosphere. I could've hit the shops to give Phoenix's credit card a good workout, but there was something more pressing on the agenda. French desserts.

I could snap my fingers and get the pastry chefs at the hotel to deliver a scrumptious assortment to our suite, but it's not the same as pastry shop hopping. Not to mention, if you have to walk from one pastry shop to another you burn calories, which means you can keep stuffing your face silly. As a result, I indulged in way too many lip-smacking sweets. Full and riding a sugar high, I hopped in a taxi and made my way from Saint-Germain-des-Prés to the Pompadour.

So, here I am, waiting after my husband.

Phoenix promised his last conference call of the day would be quick.

He lied.

An hour later, he's still locked up, and I'm still sitting on this sofa. Alone.

I'm starting to feel deprived.

Four days into my marriage and my husband is already ignoring me.

Well, we'll see about that.

I set aside the *Vogue* magazine and make my way to that darn office.

I rap my knuckles against the door and wait.

He opens the door and waves me in.

I step inside and he closes the door.

"Hey," he says in a theatre whisper.

I tip my head back to look up at him. "Hey." I match his hushed tone.

My eyes shift to the six serious looking faces on the screen of his laptop.

He leans into me. "The camera is covered with a Post-it note," he says. "I tend to pace a lot during long conference calls, and that drives people crazy."

"Why not select not to let the app use your camera?"

"The Post-it note lets everybody know I'm growing impatient."

I nod. "Got it."

"Sorry. I didn't expect this call would take this long," he says, rubbing his temples.

He must be having quite the day because he's still unshaven, which is unlike him. Even weary and drained, he's still as gorgeous as ever.

A man with a deep voice and a British accent launches into an explanation of the revised renovation plans of one of the Pompadour London hotels.

Phoenix isn't paying attention. Instead, his gaze is fixed on me. His blue eyes drop to my white designer heels and drag up my bare legs, up my body, pausing at my breasts before rising to my face.

"You look fucking hot," he says before dropping a soft kiss against my lips.

I changed into a pretty dress before going out shopping. I had to bring on my A game because I'm in Paris. I love-love-love this iconic Diane von Furstenberg knee-length wrap dress. The black and white print stands out, and the electric-blue background resembles the Adriatic Sea.

"Thanks," I whisper, with a coquettish smile.

"Did you go shopping?" he asks, making a move to untie the sash at my waist.

I shoo his hands away.

"What do you think you're doing, Mr. CEO-COO?" I say in a low voice.

He chuckles.

"Come!" He grabs me by the hand.

I follow him to the desk.

"Do you want a drink?" I ask. "It's cocktail hour somewhere in the world."

He nods.

"Whiskey or wine?"

"Wine. Red."

"Okay."

I make my way to the mini bar to locate a good bottle. I still can't get over the fact there's also a full bar in the living room area. The Pompadour is the height of luxury.

As I move about the room, I'm keenly aware of Phoenix's eyes on me. I peek over my shoulder.

His attention lingers on my ass, eyebrow cocked in interest.

I smile.

He doesn't.

He just stares at me. Or should I say, he devours me with his eyes. He runs a hand over his stubble, and my stomach flips as I long to feel it between my thighs again.

This conference call is becoming more of an annoyance with each passing minute.

Thank God for wine to pass the time.

I grab an exceptional Syrah I've had the pleasure of sampling before at Rhys's place. I pour two glasses and sashay back to my husband.

"Thanks," he mouths, grabbing the glass.

"No problem," I mouth back.

I sit on the sofa across from his desk and cross my legs.

I lift my glass in salute. "Cheers!" I mouth.

He mirrors my move.

I take a long sip of wine, enjoying every nuance of the punch of flavor that greets my taste buds.

My eyes glance over to Phoenix's to confirm if he shares my contentment with the wine, but the lovely Syrah is the last thing on his mind.

His attention is on my legs.

Ooohhh!

I uncross and cross my legs, each time making sure the bottom of the dress rides a little higher up my thighs.

Phoenix narrows his gaze.

He's onto me.

The newfound temptress in me takes over.

I position my leg so he gets a peek of the Promised Land.

He cocks his head to the side to get a better view.

The man with a deep voice and British accent stops talking.

Phoenix bounces his eyes back to the screen. "Thank you very much Gordon for the update."

I giggle.

I doubt he heard half of what Gordon had to say.

Phoenix's face contorts in a warning expression.

That only makes me giggle even more.

"Is there anything else that requires my urgent attention?" Phoenix asks the group of six.

"Actually..." a woman says. "Can we talk about increasing the budget for the two Spain renovations?"

"And I have a few things I'd like to go over about the Milan location," another female voice says.

Phoenix rolls his eyes.

"Sure," he says.

Good God, this conference call will never end.

I tune out the women's voices, preferring to focus my attention on the exceptional wine.

From over the rim of my glass, I catch Phoenix staring at me.

I point to the laptop, indicating he should be focusing on the conversation.

He shakes his head and points at me.

I frown.

He cups his crotch and bites against his lower lip.

My pussy clenches in response.

Oh, someone wants to play.

I drop the wine glass on the side table, get up, and sashay over to him.

Something in his expression is dangerous. I can't tell if it's a warning or a dare.

Dare, it is.

I pull the tie at my waist and unwrap the dress to reveal an Agent Provocateur mesh bra and matching retro high waisted panties in a flattering ocean-blue shade. The little red bow nestled in between my breasts and the one right below my bellybutton on the panties adds a touch of naughtiness to the sexy combo.

His eyes light up.

"Holy shit." The words drop from his mouth.

"Holy shit, what?" the woman with the Spanish accent asks.

Phoenix cringes.

"Holy shit, that's informative," he says. "Keep going."

Good save.

The woman keeps talking.

I shrug out of the dress and kneel in front of him.

He reaches out and strokes with his thumb over my lower lip. "Bad girl," he mouths.

"I am," I mouth back.

I reach behind me and unfasten the bra. I let it slide down my arms and toss it to the side.

Phoenix's gaze drops to my bare breasts.

Fueled by desire, I bring my hands to my breasts and flutter my fingertips over my stiff nipples before squeezing them.

The blissful sensation travels all the way to my clit.

He shakes his head, as if he can't get over my brazenness.

Neither can I.

Phoenix practically rips the shirt off his body before kicking off his shoes and removing his socks. With impatient hands, he makes quick work of his belt buckle and zipper. He lifts off the chair just enough to slide his pants over his ass. I reach out and help him remove them all together. He does the same with his boxer briefs and his cock springs to life.

Yes!

I wrap my hand around his beautiful erection.

When his hand covers mine, squeezing both our hands, we barely stifle a groan.

"I'm hopeful these renovations will get us even more nominations for next year's HEEA," the woman concerned about the Barcelona renovation says.

"Hear, hear!" The other five people on the conference call cheer.

"Don't you agree, Phoenix?" a man asks.

"We can never have too many HEEAs." His voice is gruff.

I lean in and drag one nipple over the tip of his cock.

"God, yes!" His body jerks.

"It goes without saying this can only happen with the grace of God," a man says.

The poor guy has no idea how off he is.

Phoenix and I share a complicit smile.

I push his hand away from mine.

He doesn't fight me.

I lean in and lick him from balls to tip before wrapping my lips around the head of his cock, sucking him in deep.

"Oh, God, yes!" Phoenix clamps a hand on the back of my head.

Heat flares at my core.

"I have to say, I didn't peg you as such an overtly religious man," a woman says.

I'm not sure who's talking. I lost track.

"Oh, well, you know..." Phoenix says. "God is good—"

I bob my head up and down his cock, making sure he hits the back of my throat each time.

I gag a little, but that doesn't stop me.

Phoenix grunts.

"Are you okay, Phoenix?" A woman asks.

"Yes. More than okay," he says. "A bit dehydrated from the flight. That's all."

I bet he is.

"The sensation of being as parched as if you'd been walking around in the desert for weeks is absolutely dreadful." Gordon's British accent gives him away.

"It is," Phoenix says.

The discussion resumes, as the participants move on to another topic.

I suck Phoenix deeper. Faster.

I'm turned on like crazy by the kinkiness of our naughty play. The group of six can't see us, but they can hear us. And it wouldn't take much for that Post-it note to drop from the screen.

God, this is filthy.

Almost as if he could read my thoughts, Phoenix reaches out and pinches my nipple before twisting it hard.

Fuck, this hurts so good.

I choke around his cock.

My eyes fly up to his.

He's sporting a devilish grin that speaks volume.

He points to his cock.

Bastard!

I keep sucking him off, lost in a sea of hedonistic pleasure.

Phoenix grips the hair at the top of my head, pulling me far back enough for his cock to drop from my lips.

I shoot him a questioning look.

"I need more," he says in a whisper.

I wipe my mouth with the back of my hand and nod. "Me too."

He lifts me up and drops me on his lap.

I straddle him.

I don't know what possesses me, but I lean forward and give his neck a small playful bite.

He groans low in his throat.

I do it again.

He pinches my ass.

Ouch!

I pull away from him.

"Behave," he mouths.

I giggle.

He reaches between us, lining his cock up against my entrance.

I lower myself onto his long, thick cock.

I'm so wet, he's inside me in one powerful thrust.

My head lolls back as my body welcomes the invasion.

"Hell, yeah!" Phoenix says.

"I'm glad you agree," a woman says. "I knew you'd be satisfied."

"Extremely satisfied," Phoenix tells her.

This is so debauched.

We're fucking to an unsuspecting audience.

"Phoenix, can we talk about—"

You've got to be kidding me.

He reaches for his laptop and closes it, putting an end to this interminable conference call.

Thank you, God.

"Enough!" he says.

Slap!

"Ride me hard, kitten."

I obey.

He clamps his hands under my ass and helps me glide up and down his cock.

Faster.

Deeper.

Harder.

"Fuck, yeah." I clench my inner muscles around him.

"Fuck, yeah" he says.

I bounce up and down on his magnificent cock.

"Harder! I want to feel your fine ass against my balls. Each. And. Every. Time."

I do as I'm told.

Every time I land on his balls, a surge of ecstasy shoots straight to my brain.

"My hands are full," he says. "I need you to take care of that beautiful clit of yours."

"Okay."

My fingers glide over my clit at a feverish pace, as he takes over the reins, fucking me senseless.

He brings a finger to his lips before sticking it inside his mouth.

What is he doing?

I get my answer when his hand finds my ass and his finger glides up the edge of my butt crease.

"Relax," he tells me.

He eases his finger inside.

I gasp, all my nerve endings jumping to attention.

"Damn, you're so tight." He reaches for my pussy with his other hand, pushes my hand aside and dips his fingers deep into my wetness, scooping up my juices. "Let's try again."

His gaze bores into mine. "You trust me?"

"I do."

"Don't fight it. Enjoy it."

"Okay."

He probes my tightness again, but this time, his finger slides inside me.

The sensation is so foreign... but nice.

"Keep riding my cock and playing with your clit while I finger-fuck your ass, kitten."

His command makes me wetter and to my surprise, I don't protest, nor do I tighten my ass in refusal.

I'm beyond turned on at the thought of being at his mercy while he fills me—front and back.

My eyes drift closed, my mind focusing only on Phoenix's naughty touch.

Parts of me I didn't even know exist, awaken.

I work my fingers faster against my clit.

This is so, so good.

Between my hypersensitive clit and his finger in my ass, I'm nearly flying.

"I—I'm close," he says. He tightens his grip around my waist, controlling the ride while finger-fucking my ass with determination.

"Oh God..."

"You're close?"

"Yes."

"Come hard for me, kitten."

His wish is my command.

Every muscle in my body tightens and I scrunch my eyes shut as pleasure shoots through me.

"Oh, Phoenix!" I shout his name over and over again as I freefall.

I lose myself in the most intense orgasm of my life. And that says a lot, considering my new husband has been more than generous.

Phoenix picks up the cadence.

Thrusting hard against me.

My muscles clench and clench, pushing him over the edge.

"Goddammit," he says as his hips lift off the chair, taking me with him.

I wrap my arms around his neck, holding onto him.

"Jesus. Kitten. Oh, fuck, your pussy is so fucking good! Fuck! Take my cum. Take it!"

He comes roaring, spilling his cum deep inside my pussy.

We stay tangled this way for a long while, both of us desperately trying to catch our breath.

"God, that was intense," I tell him.

"It always is between us," he says.

We're a match made in heaven.

He pulls away from me. "Thank you for saving me from that boring conference call."

I run my hands through his messy hair. "My pleasure."

"I'm sporting freshly fucked hair?"

"You are," I let out a small laugh.

"So are you, my naughty queen." He leans in and bestows a tender kiss on my lips. "You're the perfect wife, Michaela."

He said those words to me yesterday, but they didn't cause this unfamiliar pang tugging at my heart.

Four days into this marriage, and I'm starting to hate our fake arrangement.

I was willing to play along yesterday. I was willing to

believe I'd be okay with him being mine for a short while—and me being his—but now I'm not so sure. This thing with Phoenix feels more real with each passing day. It's not only the explosive, mind-blowing sex. It's also about this undeniable connection we share.

Gah!

How maddeningly unfair this man I'm married to can only be mine for a year when I want more—

Dear God, I can't be falling for him.

Stupid, stupid, Mikki.

Get your head screwed on straight. You're a means to an end for Phoenix König. You're not a real wife, or a real life partner, and you're certainly not his real queen. A year from now, you'll be nothing more than a distant memory.

Pissed off at myself for forgetting what I'd signed up for, I untwine my legs from around his and try to get up.

Phoenix tightens his grip around my waist. "Hey, what's wrong?"

"I'm fine."

"Fine? You just came your head off and you're fine? Clearly, my cock is broken."

"That's not it. Sex was good." His eyebrows shoot to his forehead. "It was great. It was incredible."

"Why the frowning face, kitten?"

"It's nothing."

"Bullshit."

"I'm fine. Really."

"You just said fine twice. That's a red flag that you're anything but," he says. "Talk to me."

"Never mind."

He fixes me with a stern gaze.

I lower my gaze.

"Other than a handful of people, we're lying to the world.

We can't lie to each other. Why the sudden change of mood, kitten?"

I really shouldn't put myself on the line like this, but his soft voice is my breaking point. I run off at the mouth and the verbal diarrhea ensues. "I went from hating you, to despising you, to swearing on a stack of bibles I'd never marry you, to walking down the aisle to save our hotel, to liking you, to—Gah! I'm not sure how I feel about you anymore."

He stares at me.

I cringe.

"You're not sure or you don't want to be honest with yourself?" he asks.

My eyes snap up to his.

"I'm just being silly—"

"I'm not sure what's going on between us either, but it's not what I signed up for," he tells me.

Great. Just great.

I'm so fucking stupid.

"You were supposed to be a crucial chess piece in my ascent to the throne," he says. "I wasn't supposed to like you this much, Michaela. And it's not just because of the off the chart sex."

My eyes widen in shock.

"You..."

Whatever he says next is swallowed by the thunderous pounding of my hopeful heart.

Then, it hits me.

"Wait a minute!" I hold up a hand. "What do you mean by, you weren't supposed to like me this much?"

He traces the contour of my jawline with his fingertips before tapping the tip of my nose. "Somewhere between our first naughty encounter in my office and this trip to Paris, you became... more."

I'm floored by his admission.

"You mean, you like-me like me?"

He nods. "I like-you like you. A lot."

My heart gallops out of control at his sweet confession.

"I like-you like you, too, Phoenix," I tell him. "So, what does this mean for us?" I ask, a tinge of insecurity knotting my stomach.

"Now that we've established our language skills have reverted back to that of kindergarten kids, let's cut out the bullshit."

I laugh. "Okay."

"I haven't dated many women. And the ones I did see for longer than a fling, I never shared so much of me with them," he says. "I'm an open book with you. It's so unlike me."

"Same here," I say.

"Fuck the arrangement. I vote we ride this out for all it's worth. No foot on the brake. No holding back."

With that one sentence, he kills me in a million different ways... each more elating than the other.

"I like the sound of that." I smile wide.

He captures my lips.

He kisses me soft at first and I cling onto him and press my body against his. The kiss turns ravenous and his cock swells inside me.

Holding me tight, he stands and carries me across the office.

"Where are we going?" I ask.

"The sofa," he says. "Time for round two."

Chapter 31

Michaela

It's Sunday lunch at the patriarch König's Malibu Colony Beach house.

Holy Mc Mansion!

This house is the size of Vatican City.

Phoenix, Slate, Wilder, and Soren are working the barbecue while talking sports.

Typical men.

Wilder is back in LA. Since Phoenix's younger brothers are certified bachelors, I'm the only girl. As the men were going on and on and on about last night's basketball game, I excused myself and headed to the bathroom. On my way back to the deck, I spot a beautifully appointed room. A wall decorated with myriad photos stares at me.

Curiosity wins.

I venture in. Since the door is open, I'm not being a busy body.

The space is bright—too bright for it to be a reading room. It's also too neat and organized to be a study.

This is a family shrine.

The aroma of fresh flowers tickles my nose. There are bouquets in every corner of the room, adding a spot of color to the gray-on-gray décor. Save for a couple large armchairs, there's a row of floor-to-ceiling bookshelves with glass doors filled with awards, old books and mementos. The rows of picture frames tell the story of a family—a legacy.

There are several black and white photos, and many colored ones that seem to have faded with time. I squint as I take in Phoenix's great-great-grandparents, great-grandparents and grandparents.

"Oh!" I say when I spot the official photos of Phoenix and me from the HEEA.

The König Hotels cleaned house that night. They won an embarrassing number of awards compared to the competition. Brock and Marie-Clémence's sullen expressions were priceless. They didn't get a chance to step on stage to represent Ripley Madigan's hotels. Boo woo woo.

I stroll to the wall of photos that caught my eye.

My gaze peruses the many photos of four smiling boys and a teenager. I recognize Phoenix, Slate, and Wilder. I'm guessing the shortest boy is Roman. The tall teenager must be Barron. My eyes move to another photo of him as a man. He was as handsome as his brothers.

Yup, it's in the König genes.

I check out photo after photo of the four surviving König men. Each time I land on one of Phoenix's, my ovaries explode.

Damn.

I cradle my stomach, wondering not for the first time what our babies would look like.

Sigh.

"There you are, Michaela."

I jump in fright at my father-in-law's voice.

I turn around to face him.

"I'm sorry," he says. With his hands in his pockets, he approaches.

Since Soren is as tall as his sons, I have to tilt my head back to meet his gaze.

"I thought you'd got lost. Arguably, the house is massive," he says.

No joke.

"Either that or you got bored with our sports talk," he says with a laugh.

"This wall caught my eye as I was leaving the bathroom," I tell him. "I didn't notice it two weeks ago when I was here last."

"It was your wedding day, sweet girl. There was a lot going on," Soren says.

"True." Guilt gnarls at me. "Maybe I shouldn't be in this room," I say, afraid I've made a gaffe.

"Nonsense. You're a König. You *belong* in this room." Soren offers a genuine smile.

"Okay." I return his smile.

Thank God he's not upset I'm snooping around.

"Speaking of which, congratulations, Mrs. König, on your two-week anniversary." Soren winks.

"Thank you." I wink back.

The rest of the Paris trip flew by in a blur. A lot like the last week and a half since we've been back in LA. There are so many perks to being married. Copious amount of sex tops the list.

"This is a special room," Soren says, changing the subject. "I had it built after Daniela died."

"I can't imagine how difficult it must've been for you to lose your wife a year after losing your oldest son."

He nods. "I didn't think I was going to survive their deaths. My four sons kept me going."

"I'm glad they did."

"So am I," he says. "Roman's accident brought back a flood of fear. The worst part was, I couldn't fly to Hawaii to see my boy—I still can't. Thank God he's alive and thank God for modern technology. Our video calls bring me peace of mind."

"Of course."

He points at two photos. "I desperately miss Daniela and Barron, though."

"She was so beautiful," I say.

"She was," he says. "I'm not destined to love again. Daniela was the love of my life." Sadness veils his blue eyes. "The moment I caught sight of her, she was it for me. Cliché, I know, but it's the truth."

That's such devotion.

"I love this photo of her the most." He points.

Daniela is wearing an elegant black hat with a wide brim. She has a Hermes scarf wrapped around the band. She's sitting near the pool, an e-Reader in hand, smiling and waving at the camera. Everything about Phoenix's mom screams style.

"It was one of the better days during her treatment." Soren rakes his hand through his salt and pepper hair. "The hat was to protect her from the sun and to hide the telltale signs of the ravages from the chemo. She had lost her long, dark hair. Still, she was my beautiful, fighting queen." His voice breaks.

My heart goes out to him. I place a comforting hand on his forearm.

He places his hand over mine and squeezes. "You know exactly what I'm talking about."

I nod, fighting back tears, as sad memories of my mom's courageous fight assail me.

"It's so hard to lose someone you love like that," I say, wiping away tears. "You're nothing more than a powerless spectator and there's nothing you can do to stop the hurt... or the tragic ending."

"And trust me when I say this, even when you have all the money in the world, it's still not enough to get the pain to stop."

A moment of silence passes between us.

"Which of your sons is the most like your wife?" I ask, shifting my gaze to the wall of memories.

"Barron," Soren says without hesitation. "In terms of personality, my oldest son had his mother's temperament. They approached life in a similar manner. They even had the same laugh." He pauses. "That's why it was so hard for Daniela after Barron's death. She felt she lost a part of herself."

"I was lost for a long time after Mom died," I tell him. "So was Dad."

He nods. "I'm still lost, quite frankly," he says.

My heart breaks for this man.

"Phoenix has the same particular shade of blue eyes as Daniela. Roman has one hazel-blue eye. Phoenix and Wilder are a mix of both of our personalities. Whereas Slate is a mini me. Roman is our wild card child. Who knows who he takes after?" He chuckles.

I laugh.

Soren's eyes move to the photo of his oldest son. His lips curl up in a sad smile. "Dear Barron..." his words trail, as he traces the frame. "Being at the helm of König Imperial Holding was his dream and destiny. He wasn't supposed to die this young. I didn't see the signs and I have to live with the guilt every single day." Another pause. "I never expected Phoenix to rise to the challenge the way he has, and I didn't think he was going to handle the additional responsibilities after my heart attack and Roman's accident. He surprised me."

"He's quite the astute and badass executive. I'm proud to stand by my man." I laugh.

My father-in-law doesn't.

"I might just be a nosy and hopeful old man, but watching

the two of you... I reckon it's more than just a fake arrangement. You don't have to impress anybody today. It's just family. Everyone present is in the know. Yet, Phoenix and you can't keep your eyes—or hands—off each other."

My cheeks burst into flames.

My father-in-law laughs.

"You, my dear, just gave yourself away."

"In a moment like this, I wish I had a poker face," I say, patting the back of my hands against my warm cheeks.

He taps the tip of my nose. "You're real and genuine. That's what won Phoenix over and that's what won Slate, Wilder and me over," he says. "Roman will fall under your charm when you two meet." His expression changes to something unreadable. "You're good for my son."

I'm not sure what to make of his confession.

"Phoenix is good for me, too."

"It's like your father had a sixth sense," Soren says.

"I agree."

"Niels orchestrated a big production. It was a gamble to bring together two complete strangers living on opposite sides of the country in the most unorthodox way. Yet, it seems it was meant to be."

I can only nod.

His words make me dizzy with hope, drunk with possibility. My throat tightens, as the wave of emotion takes over me.

Thud.

Thud.

Thud.

My stupid heart trips.

"What are you telling my wife, Dad?"

Startled, I turn around.

My gorgeous husband is standing there, a huge grin stretching his beautiful lips.

"Just a little daughter-in-law-slash-father-in-law talk. Butt out, son."

Phoenix struts towards us with a confident step.

"Not a chance. I'm here to rescue Michaela." He wraps a possessive arm around my shoulders and pulling me close to his muscular body. Even with the apron, he's still the consummate alpha. "I hope I'm not too late. God knows what damage you've already done."

A small grin touches Soren's face.

I let out a girlish giggle. "I know every sordid detail of your life."

"Lies. All lies!" Phoenix says. "Don't believe anything my father just told you!" He waves a warning finger at Soren.

"I was telling your wife, that despite your fake beginnings, destiny brought you together."

I stop breathing because holy fuck that's a big statement, and it's out there.

"In my humble opinion, Michaela and you belong together"—Soren pauses for a beat—"*for real.*"

My worried eyes snap up to Phoenix's.

For a long moment, he doesn't answer. He stares at his father, dumbfounded.

"Am I wrong, son?" Soren asks.

The air is so thick with crackling tension, I have to remind myself to breathe.

Phoenix cradles my face in his strong hands and drops a soft kiss against my lips before saying, "I reckon you're right on the money, Dad."

Chapter 32

Phoenix

After a great day and evening at Dad's with Slate and Wilder, we're home.

"I still can't get over this level of luxury," Michaela says as we step out of the elevator that opens into the penthouse. "And I get to live here now."

"Get used to it," I say. I'm just about to tack on, *for the next year*, but I don't. Those words leave a bad taste in my mouth.

"*Tu casa es una casa enorme, elegante, y magnífica, hombre*," Michaela says with exaggerated hand gestures.

"*No, mujer, mi casa es su casa—nuestra casa*," I say, waving my finger between us.

I may not be fluent in Spanish, but living in LA and employing a number of staff of Hispanic origin, I get by.

"*Bueno. Nuestra casa.*" She smiles. "Your enormous, elegant, and magnificent penthouse is *our* home."

I wink.

There was no time for her to move to my place after the wedding because we were flying out to Paris, but since our return, Michaela and I have been living together. The highlight of the move was when she discovered her walk-in closet jam-packed with designer clothing, shoes, accessories, and jewelry. Thanks to the astute buyers at our hotel boutiques, I was able to replace everything she lost in the fire. I even had Niels ship her family heirlooms. The irreplaceable jewelery is stored in a safe in my home office. She was jumping up and down, clapping her hands together for a solid five minutes.

Phoenix König shacking up with a woman.

Unbelievable.

I didn't know what to expect, but contrary to what I thought, I don't feel like I'm suffocating. The few times Marie-Clémence stayed over at my former penthouse while we were seeing each other, I always knew there was a way out. It wasn't permanent. But I'm married to Michaela. I thought for sure living in such close proximity with a woman for an extended period of time would drive me to jump off the roof of this building. That would be the stupidest thing, considering I have sweet heaven right between Michaela's legs.

"Wanna hit the hot tub before I ravage your body?" I ask her.

She shoots me a glance.

I should be able to read her expressions by now, but I'm stumped.

"You could ravage me *inside* the hot tub?"

My eyebrows shoot to my forehead.

Her suggestion throws me off.

"You were balking at the idea of sex in front of a window in Paris, but now you want me to fuck you outside in the hot tub?"

"What can I say?" She shrugs. "You've corrupted me."

"I'm always down for kinky, kitten, but no way am I allowing anyone to cast their eyes on your heavenly body," I tell her. "Not to mention, we're only two weeks into this marriage.

In other words, we're still fresh meat for the paparazzi. Let's not take a chance."

"Okay, we'll keep it to the bedroom." Her tone drips with effrontery.

Who is this woman?

"Who said anything about the bedroom?" I ask.

My phone rings.

So does hers.

What a coincidence!

"It's Keira," she says, her eyes moving from her screen to mine.

"It's Slate," I tell her.

"I'll go up to the bedroom," she says.

"I'll be on the balcony," I tell her.

"Hey, Keira," she says, answering the call.

It's a great effort to peel my eyes away from her delicious ass to answer my brother's call.

"We just left Dad's place. You miss me already, little brother?" I ask him.

"You wish," he says.

I open the glass door to the balcony, step outside and close the door behind me.

An illuminated LA stretches out under a dark sky.

I never get tired of this spectacular view.

"What's up?" I ask.

"That's why I called. I want to know what's up with you."

I frown at the phone.

"You lost me," I tell him.

"Granted I'm no expert on fake relationships, and maybe you two are really great actors, but you and your wife seem... more real than fake."

I pace around, buying myself some time.

"You still there?" Slate asks.

"I am."

"If you're not answering, I'm guessing I hit the nail on the head."

I let out a long sigh. "I'm not sure it was fake on our wedding day. Not for me, anyway."

"Whoa!"

My words shock him as much as they shock me.

"I'm not going to lie. When a desperate Niels showed me Michaela's photos, I was instantly smitten. When she came barging into my office, she had me by the balls. Then, there was that first kiss..." I let my words trail. "We only kissed twice before we got married, but it could've been a thousand times and it would've been as effortless."

"Let me guess. The marriage isn't platonic."

There's no point in lying. "It's not."

Slate sighs. "I hate to be the voice of reason, but what in the actual fuck?" His sharp tone cuts through the night's quietude. He continues before I can answer. "Mixing business with pleasure is always a recipe for disaster, big brother. It's a textbook CEO 101 case."

"It's—"

"You said this was a business deal. Now, you're thinking with your dick?! What if you piss her off? What if she walks out on you? If this blows up in your face before the board appointments another CEO, for the first time in history, we're going to have to answer to an outsider. Do you really want to be the König who loses the throne?"

Anger building in my chest. "I resent the implication."

"Get it together, then!" he says. "It's only one year. Keep it simple. Jerk off. Watch porn. And if all else fails, go to Dark Compulsion, sit your ass down in a voyeur's room all night long, jerking off to live fucking, then go back home and jerk off some more. So what if you end up with carpal tunnel? As long as you keep your eyes on the prize."

His insulting words are crude and an assault to my ears.

"Who says I can't have the throne *and* the girl?" I ask him.

"That's overly confident, even for you."

"Fuck off, Slate!"

"No, fuck you, Phoenix! We made the decision as a family you were going for the CEO position. If you didn't have the balls to see it through, you should've said so. You should've stepped aside and let me marry Michaela."

I see red and I'm filled with unshakable jealousy. He's my brother and my blood, but damn him if he thinks Michaela was meant to be his. He has no claims on her. None whatsoever.

There was talk of Slate becoming CEO because the board is more accepting of his personal life and his playboy image isn't as hardcore as mine. That talk died pretty quickly when Niels showed me Michaela's photo.

"I would've kept my dick inside my pants for the sake of the family legacy." He's not finished with me yet. "You have God knows how many rooms in your penthouse. You don't have to share the same bed."

I'm surprised by the animosity in his voice.

"I know what I'm doing!" I tell him.

"Michaela is a distraction!"

"Michaela isn't a distraction. Securing our legacy is my top priority—"

"You could've fooled me," he says. "Wait until Roman, Wilder, and Dad find out your status has changed to arranged marriage *with benefits*. They're going to be as pissed off as I am you're willing to jeopardize everything for a piece of ass—"

"Watch your goddamn mouth, little brother," I say. "She's more than a piece of ass, you fucking moron. FYI, Wilder has known since our wedding day there was more between us, and Dad figured it out on his own. He even brought it up today—"

"So Roman and I are the only two kept in the dark?" His aggressive tone irritates the hell out of me.

"Roman's main priority is to recover, not keep up to date with the intricacies of my marriage. As for you, I would've told you, eventually."

"Great." He lets out a sarcastic laugh. "Potter might get his wish after all."

"Fuck you, Slate! Fuck you!"

I end the call, pissed off to no end.

"Asshole!" I shout even though he can't hear me.

Chapter 33

Phoenix

Unless we're away on holidays, Dad, Slate, Wilder, Roman, and I kick off the week with a seven a.m. 'König' two-hour meeting—no VPs, directors, or executive assistants—either in person or via a video call. We usually hold a ten o'clock meeting with the board members afterwards, so this is our time to discuss openly behind closed doors. Since Dad had a doctor's appointment, it's just the three of us. I may be the interim CEO, but my father has been at the helm of this company for a long time. He's given me the reins, but now that he's back on his feet, he likes to be kept abreast of everything that happens.

"Good call on requesting an audit on the budget for the two Spain renovations," Slate says, wrapping up the meeting. He's careful not to meet my gaze.

Since last night's call, things are icy and tension is more real than it was between the United States and the Soviet Union during the Cold War. I'm in no mood to justify my relationship with my wife to my own brother. He may not have much faith I can pull this off, but I know I can do it with Michaela by my side.

"I agree," Wilder says.

"If the renovations in three locations in Italy can come within the allotted budget, why shouldn't it happen for Pompadour, Barcelona and Pompadour, Madrid?" I say.

Granted, during the conference call in Paris my wife's sexy, naked body straddling mine was distracting, I still made a mental note to circle back with the VP of our Spanish locations at her request for more money.

"On a different note, did Bryce get back to you?" Slate asks.

"His team is still busy following the breadcrumbs," I say. "He tends to hold back information until he has the full picture. That said, he promised a call at six p.m. today with an update."

"Should we sit in on the call?" he asks.

"That's a good idea," Wilder says.

"I agree. This impacts all of us. We'll patch Dad on the call as well."

As a board member, Potter doesn't work for us. So, tapping into his work computer or his company phone was off the table. In order to find out what the weasel has up his sleeve, Bryce's team had to go at it the old-fashioned way—surveillance.

"I can't wait to find out what kind of dirt he was able to find on Potter," Wilder says.

"I hope it's enough to kick his ass to the curb," Slate says.

"From your lips to God's ears," I tell him.

My phone rings.

My eyes drop to the screen.

I snatch my iPhone off the conference room table and accept the call.

"Good morning, Niels!"

"Good morning-slash-good afternoon from New York City," he says. "Am I catching you at a bad time?"

"I'm just finishing up a meeting with Wilder and Slate," I say. "How can I help you?"

"Are they still with you?" he asks.

"Yes, they are. We're sitting in one of the conference rooms."

"Can you talk or would you prefer I call at a later time?"

"No, now is fine."

I swing an apologetic gaze towards my brothers.

They nod their understanding.

Wilder points to the door.

I shake my head and gesture for him to wait.

"I just hung up with the lead investigator you so generously hired to help figure out who was behind the fire that incinerated my house to rubble," Niels says.

This should be good.

"Niels, is it okay if I put you on speaker phone? I want my brothers to listen in on the conversation. Dad isn't here, but I can fill him in later."

"Absolutely!"

I place my phone on the conference table and tap the icon on the screen.

"You're on," I say.

"Can you hear me okay?" Niels's voice booms through the speakers.

"Loud and clear," I tell him.

After a round of greetings, I cut to the chase.

"So, what's the verdict?" I ask.

"There's no arguing. The fire was a crime. The insurance will kick in and I'll will get the money."

"Good news."

"You can say that again." Niels lets out a long breath. "It

was Thana. She was charged this morning. The lead investigator confirmed it."

She's been sitting in jail since the fire because she didn't have money to post bail.

All signs pointed to her, but this is America. You're innocent until proven guilty. Now, we get to nail the bitch for shattering my wife and her father's life.

"She was so infuriated at me and so gung ho on revenge, she did a piss-poor job of covering her tracks," Niels says. "She knew I had canceled the home monitoring security service because I couldn't afford it anymore. Here's the kicker. I never bothered telling her the company granted me an extra month as a courtesy for being a long-time customer. There's irrefutable video proof placing her outside and inside the house. There's also..." his voice trails.

"Also, what?" I ask.

"In some of the footage, the callous bitch was laughing her head off while pouring gasoline all over my house."

"Jesus," Slate says.

"She's a nut case," Wilder says.

"The woman is psychotic."

"She's deranged, for sure," Niels says. "She didn't even bother renting a car. She parked her Toyota Camry right in front of the house, so there's video footage of her license plate. Thana made it easy for the police. Stupid bitch."

"Thank God you were still at the hotel," Wilder says.

"I doubt she would've cared." The harshness in Niels's voice doesn't go unnoticed. Not that I can blame the guy.

"We can nail her ass for arson?" I ask.

"Yes," Niels says. "The neighbors that flank our house will also press charges since Thana caused them to lose everything."

"Added to the other charges against her, she'll be in jail for a long time," I say. I already have a dream team of lawyers working with Niels on making sure that happens.

"There will be even more charges," Niels says.

"What else did the investigators find?" Slate asks.

"She set my house on fire because that morning, I told her I was onto her, which is why I had served her with divorce papers. Soon after she came barging into my office that morning, things escalated. She was livid. Freaked out, my executive assistant called 911. Thana was removed from the premises. You, Phoenix, quickly came into action and hired a team of bodyguards. The hotel was secured, so she couldn't come back unnoticed. Ian urged me to stash her desktop and laptop computers—which were company property—at his place. I'm glad I listened to his advice."

"Were the investigators able to find more incriminating information to further your other cases against her?" I ask.

"You're not going to believe what they found," Niels says. "I was dumbfounded."

My brothers and I exchange a look.

"Try me," I tell him.

"It's no wonder Potter knew so much private information that was never divulged—"

"No way," Wilder says.

My eyebrows shoot to my forehead.

"Thana and Potter know each other?" Slate asks the question before I do.

"Yes, they know each other *very* well," Niels says.

His words send chills down my back.

"Motherfucker," I say.

"Thana had a series of meetings with Potter," Niels says. "My financial debacle was pillow talk."

"What are you talking about, Niels?" I ask. What he's implying doesn't even make sense.

"I'm well past being embarrassed by my soon-to-be ex-wife's indiscretions, but for all intents and purposes, Thana was sleeping with Potter."

The news has the same impact as a bomb detonating.

"Jesus Christ!" I say.

"Some of those emails are pretty explicit and leave nothing to the imagination," Niels says. "It was there in black-and-white."

"What about her lover?" Slate asks.

"Yeah, what about him?" I ask.

"Thana was sleeping with multiple men at the same time."

My eyes widen in shock. "Whoa."

"I really should say she was *prostituting* herself," Niels says.

"Okay, you're going to have to translate that," I tell him.

"These key men needed favors or information. Thana had a price. According to numerous exchanges—I would prefer to still be oblivious to—the financial kickbacks were a given. The sex was to seal the deal and because... I wasn't adventurous enough in bed." He lets out a sarcastic laugh. "The things she let those men do to her... disgusting. Adventurous, my ass. Thana is into twisted kinks I wanted no part of."

Good God. "Un-fucking-believable."

"Oh, but there's more," Niels says, bitterness lacing his words.

"What more?" I ask.

"She was sleeping with a third man—"

"Three men?" I ask.

"Probably four," he says. "She was courting this vendor for God knows what reason."

I'm incredulous. "What the fuck?"

"From the emails I read, it seems she tried to lure Brock,

but he reminded her numerous times he was married. And faithful."

"How honorable?" I say. "The backstabber decided not to cheat on his cheater wife."

"Among the men, Thana was sleeping with—"

A knock at the door interrupts Niels in midsentence.

Dammit.

"Give me a sec, Niels," I say.

"No problem."

I swing my gaze to the door. "Come in!"

Lydia pokes her face through the door.

"I'm sorry to interrupt, Phoenix," she says.

"How can I help you?" I ask.

"Bryce Van Der Linden is calling on the landline. He's been trying to reach you, but it goes straight to voicemail. It's urgent."

Chapter 34

Michaela

My phone rings just as I step out of the elevator.

I rummage through my crossbody bag and check my screen.

Shoot.

"Not now, Daddy. I'm on a mission." I let the call go to voicemail and place the phone inside my bag.

I stroll, coffee in hand, to the dedicated art storage room in the basement of the Pompadour Beverly Hills hotel.

This is my second official week as König Imperial Holding's Art Director and Principal Art Buyer, and I'm loving every minute of it. For a person with a double major in art history and business, this is a dream job. I have my own office on the executive floor, but a bunch of paintings Phoenix suggested I buy last week while we were in Paris via the online auction of a renowned New York City gallery for the Santa Monica hotel reno arrived this morning. I can't wait to see them.

I swipe the key card against the security pad and push the door open.

The moment I step inside, the lights turn on.

There are motion sensors hidden underneath the floor. So high tech.

I scour the space, a huge grin stretching my lips.

I'm surrounded by pristine art that could rival any top gallery in the world.

It doesn't get better than this.

Humming a little tune in my head, I stroll to the back of the storage room with a spring in my step. The shipping and receiving manager for the hotel called not long ago to announce the arrival of my shipment. I instructed him to have one of his guys deliver the thirty paintings to this location, since I had made room for them.

I'm so giddy.

I drop my coffee on the top of a tall wooden crate, pull out a retractable utility knife from my crossbody bag, and get to work. For the next long minutes, I unwrap canvas after canvas. Once I'm done, I discard the mountain of protective wraps. I stand with my hands hooked to my hips as I admire the finest art money can buy.

Wow.

I ready myself to inspect each painting to make sure I received exactly what we purchased when the door slams shut. I didn't hear it open.

I turn around and stretch my neck out.

Footsteps clank against the cement floor.

I'm just about to ask who's there when a man's voice echoes in the space.

"Okay, I can talk now," the man says.

Who's that?

"It has to be quick, though, because the board's weekly meeting is about to start," the man says.

Potter?!

"I'm in the art storage room in the basement," Potter says.

How did he get in here?

Given the value stored in this room, Phoenix assured me there are only a handful of people who have a key card. Potter's name wasn't on the list.

"I snatched the former art buyer's key card. She thought she lost it and blamed her forgetfulness on pregnancy brain. I never had to use it until today. All my usual hideaways are buzzing with activity."

Weasel.

"Sue me. I had to be creative. I needed to find another private place inside the hotel to talk so I can report back to you every time you snap your goddamn fingers!"

Who is he talking to?

Why would Potter need such privacy?

What's going on?

"You keep asking me to do sketchy things," Potter says. "Hence, putting me in situations where I'm flirting with the wrong side of the law."

Huh?

"No, Ripley. *You* listen to me."

Potter knows Ripley?

"Things aren't looking too good for any of us," he says. "My source just informed me, we're in deep shit. The fire that destroyed Niels's house is about to cast a dark cloud over our heads."

Huh?

"Instead of telling me to calm the fuck down, you need to figure out a way to shut up Thana for good. If not, the stupid cunt will be our demise."

Thana?!

As in Thana, my soon to be ex-stepmother?

"You told me to seduce Thana Annunziata to get her in our

corner. You said she was a sure thing. Guess what? You were wrong, Rip," he says.

I can't believe my ears.

Potter knows Ripley and Thana?

Why was he seducing her?

What the hell?

I hide behind a tall crate so I can listen in on the conversation.

An idea pops to mind.

With trembling hands, I fumble for my phone, unlock it, and activate the voice recording app. I'm not sure if I'm going to be able to capture anything at this range, but by God, I wouldn't be able to live with myself if I don't try.

"Yeah, you're right on that front," Potter says. "The whiny bitch was useful when she was on her back or on all fours."

What is he talking about?

"The fact she begged for me to double-fist fuck her filthy cunt, gag her, choke her, and fuck her ass instead of her pussy were the only good things about the woman. Other than that, she was a giant pain to deal with."

Dear God, the imagery is disturbing and disgusting.

"Thana lied to me," Potter says. "She was fucking another guy—a crook and potential pedophile enabler—while she was fucking me!"

What?!

"I wouldn't be surprised if she was still fucking Niels, even though she said she wasn't." Potter's words have the same effect as a wrecking ball.

Thana was cheating on Daddy with two men—one being Potter?!

What the fuck?

"She was probably fucking you and another guy at the same time. I'm willing to bet my fortune on it. The woman has zero allegiance. For the right price, she'll let any cock fuck her."

Thana was fucking Ripley?

And Potter?

And potentially other men?

And she had a lover?

And she was married to my father?

Oh. My. God.

Oh. My. God.

Oh. My. God.

"I pleaded with her not to burn Niels's house down."

Potter knew?

"I told her such a rash decision would not only be criminal, it would expose us and make us vulnerable."

Dear God.

"But no, Thana wouldn't listen. She wanted revenge so bad, she flipped the middle finger to the consequences... and to her partners in crime—us."

Nausea churns in my stomach at Potter's shocking revelations.

"In the meantime, her offshore accounts were lined with money she diverted from Niels upon your request on top of the money you paid her for her willing participation in your demonic plan." He lets out an audible sigh. "How greedy can you get?"

Apparently, a lot.

"Thana's reaction made no sense whatsoever since she didn't even love Niels. She was using the poor bastard."

I knew it!

"She played him like a fiddle, and then she robbed him of the last thing of value he possessed. She should've been joyfully skipping all the way to LAX when she was served those divorce papers, not plotting to further destroy Niels." He lets out a derisive laugh. "Stupid, stupid cunt. Get out of town. Lie low. Shut your fucking trap. Enjoy your payout money. End of story."

The woman is evil.

"I told you from the get-go, Thana was volatile," Potter says. "But you didn't care because you were so intent on getting your hands on Niels's hotel at any cost. There are other family-run hotels in prime locations in New York."

This conversation explains so much.

"Right, not like that one. Not located in a heritage building," Potter says. "I hope you're happy now. One, Phoenix König owns the Villiers Grand, not you. Two, you didn't get your hands on the pussy you so desperately wanted to fuck since she belongs to King König. He gets to enjoy fucking her ass, you have to make do with your new eighteen-year-old girlfriend and the rest of your harem."

Shock reverberates through me.

"I still have my suspicions about that speedy marriage, but it's too late now," Potter says. "And three, Thana—your slutty pawn—just became a liability. She was charged for arson."

Holy shit!

"I might have to disappear for a while." Potter keeps talking. "It's not going to take much for her to sing like a canary to save her own skin or lessen the severity of her sentence, Ripley. Eventually, the police are going to link Thana to you, Brock, and me, and our plan to sabotage Niels. Then, they'll keep digging. It won't take investigators long to find out you make a habit of playing God by getting a pawn to weaken the position of a family-owned hotel you set your sights on so you can swoop in like a Goodman white knight savior and offer to buy them out at a discount, knowing full well they're desperate."

Jesus Christ.

"You have enough money to buy your way out of this

cluster fuck of a mess, Ripley. I don't have infinite funds. No way am I ending up in the slammer."

I have to warn someone.

I end the recording and place my phone back into my cross-body bag. I take a step back, but bump into something.

Shit.

The cup of coffee that was sitting on another crate hits the cement floor in a loud splash.

"What the fuck?" Potter says. "Hey, who the hell is in here?"

He stomps towards the back of the storage room.

Panic settles in.

I have to get out of here. Now!

My eyes land on the exit sign.

I don't think twice.

I plan my escape, but I bump into something else.

The clattering noise that ensues is deafening.

Fuck!

When I peek up, Potter is starring right at me from where he stands at a distance.

His eyes are murderous.

Dear God.

"Fucking bitch! You were listening in on my conversation?"

Sheer terror robs me of my words.

Run, Mikki! Run!

On trembling legs, I take off, bolting through the doors.

"Come back here, bitch!"

I race towards the stairs and take them two at a time.

Thank God I'm wearing Chanel Ballerinas and pants today. There's no way I could escape in heels and a pencil skirt.

Potter's loud steps grow closer.

I run faster.

He swears up a storm from behind me.

I keep running.

I grab hold of the handle of the door leading to the lobby of the hotel. I open it with such force, it goes crashing against the wall, making a ruckus.

Myriad pairs of shocked eyes stare at me as I bolt into the lobby.

"I said, come back here, you bitch!" Potter yells behind me.

Agitation and commotion run through the guests.

People gasp.

Someone shouts. "*Stop him!*"

I let out a murderous scream.

A bunch of people yell.

"*Call the police!*"

Frantic, I bolt towards the security desk.

"Help! Help me!" I yell at the top of my lungs.

Chapter 35

Michaela

Five days later

When the elevators to the executive floor open, I step out, my eyes glued to my screen.

"Unbelievable." I re-read the jaw-dropping headlines. I shouldn't walk and read at the same time, but I can't help it.

'RIPLEY MADIGAN UNDER INVESTIGATION ON SEVERAL FRAUD CHARGES.'

'DIRTY OLD MAN: RIPLEY MADIGAN'S HAREM OF YOUNG LOVERS EXPOSED!'

'KING KÖNIG'S EMPIRE TO SUE RIPLEY MADIGAN'S.'

'SHOCKING SCANDAL IMPLODES INSIDE KING KÖNIG'S KINGDOM.'

'MICHAELA KÖNIG'S EVIL STEPMOTHER UNDER SUICIDE WATCH.'

That last headline is the most shocking one of them all. I hate everything about that manipulative woman, but I feel for her. The backlash has been brutal. The media has stoned Thana to death with their less than flattering exposés.

You brought this on yourself, dear stepmonster.

I was in a lunch meeting with the director of an art gallery when the shit hit the fan. One minute, I'm enjoying a delicious *salade niçoise*, the next, the name König is breaking news on the large flat screen TV behind the bar. I had to cut the lunch short and rush back to the office. With my eyes still transfixed to my phone, I type in the code to my office with my free hand. I'm still reading as I walk into my office. As I close the door, my thumb swipes across the screen.

'MILLIONAIRE POTTER MACCAAK ARRESTED AT THE MEXICAN BORDER!'

"They finally caught you, asshole," I say in a low voice.

"They did!" a voice says.

I jump in fright.

My eyes meet Phoenix's.

"What are you doing in my office?" I ask him.

"I needed to see my wife. Since I have the combination, I let myself in," he says.

"Next time, give a girl a heads up. You almost gave me a heart attack."

He responds with a cocky grin.

He's sitting behind my desk, as comfortable as if this were his office. With his hands interlaced together, supporting his chin, he resembles a ruler pondering the fate of a disloyal subject. Since he isn't wearing a suit jacket or a tie, I'm going to guess he came to the office straight from Soren's house when the news broke. Suit or no suit, he looks good enough to suck.

"Make yourself at home, why don't you," I say.

"I already have," he says. I smile despite myself. "Did you miss me, kitten?"

I could be cheeky, but what's the point?

"I missed you a lot," I tell him.

He stands up and comes to sit in front of the desk. He licks his lips, as if he were a predator about to devour me.

Yes, please.

"Get over here," he says.

I close the space between us.

I toss my phone and my handbag on the desk and peer into his gorgeous blue eyes.

"I'm here," I say, standing between his parted legs.

He runs his index finger from my wrist to my shoulder.

I shiver.

He reaches out and grabs me by the back of the neck, bringing our foreheads together until they touch.

"I missed you too," he says.

I take a step back and cross my arms across my chest. "Oh yeah, prove it," I say. So much for not being cheeky.

"I will in a minute," he says, placing his hands on my shoulders. His expression turns serious. "But before that, I want to give you an update on a few things."

The past five days have been intense. The König men have been bouncing from their lawyer's office to my father-in-law's mansion, strategizing a plan of attack. To say they were angry with Ripley Madigan and his puppets would be putting it mildly. They were breathing fire. As a result, Phoenix was out the door really early in the morning and he wouldn't come back to the penthouse until very late. As much as I missed him, I didn't complain. The enormity of what he was dealing with was all-consuming.

"I haven't opened up much about this shit fest because I was protecting you." The sincerity in his words is touching.

"I understand," I say.

"Dad, Slate, Wilder, and I are going for the kill. Roman supports our decision."

"You're going to sue them?"

"We're going to annihilate them," he says. "We have the best lawyers money can buy on our team. We're going to sue the hell out of Ripley, Potter, Brock, and Mrs. Pisier-Litoris. By the end of this ordeal, those crooks won't have much left to their names. Ripley might still have a cushiony stash of cash, but he's going to learn the hard way, he isn't untouchable. Contrary to popular belief, not all publicity is good publicity. Our PR company will play an important role in his demise. With enough bad press, Ripley will be exposed for the callous monster he is. I'm not sure it's enough to crumble his kingdom, but the blow will peg him down by several notches and damage his reputation. All that bad press will trickle down to his hotels, and ultimately, his wealth. That should wipe the permanent smug smirk off his fucking face for good."

"I'm sure a lot of people will think twice before choosing one of his hotels," I say.

"Let's hope so."

Once the security guards detained an infuriated Potter, they called Phoenix and the police. The three König brothers arrived on the scene like warriors ready to declare war. Phoenix was so enraged, he lunged at Potter, pure hatred shinning bright in his eyes, fists flying, and cursing up a storm. Both Slate and Wilder had to hold their older brother back. Giving Potter leverage would be detrimental because the asshole would find a way to turn it to his advantage. There's no way out for him. He'll have to pay for his crimes.

The recording from my phone was too faint to make out much of Potter's conversation with Ripley. I was devastated my efforts were in vain. It turns out, it didn't matter. Millions of dollars' worth of art require a twenty-four-seven high-tech security system that includes video surveillance with sound. The second Potter started talking, every word was recorded. There's no way he can dispute that kind of proof. Same for Ripley.

"It's going to be a long legal battle ahead, but I'm confident things will turn in our favor," Phoenix says.

"I have no doubt they will."

"Have you talked to your father?"

I nod. "Yes, we talked this morning before my lunch meeting. Thank you for doing that. You've already been so generous, but this takes the cake."

"Thana handed us everything we needed on a silver platter. A publicity campaign is exactly what the hotel needs to ward off any potential bad press by association. It's irrefutable, your father and you had nothing to do with Thana's pedophile enabler lover. Plus, now that the public knows you were jilted by her callous and criminal actions, they have sympathy. No one will dare to cast the first stone."

"Daddy is so grateful—and elated—we get to keep the name intact. So am I. The Villiers Grand Hotel lives on!"

"Just the way it's supposed to be," Phoenix says.

I shake my head as emotions bubble up.

"A little less than six weeks ago, Daddy and I were on the verge of losing everything." I let out a loud sigh. "And now, there's hope. Mom must be throwing a big party up in heaven. Our family hotel gets a happy ending after all."

"Speaking of happy endings, I need to show you how much I've missed you these past few days," he says.

"That's an abrupt change of subject," I tell him.

"Not really," he says. "It falls right in line with our conversation."

I shoot him a dubious look.

He reaches and grips my chin. He stares into my eyes as though he's peering into my soul. "So you missed me, kitten?"

"I've already confessed that much."

"Just checking."

"It was hard to fall asleep alone in your massive California King bed."

"It was hard falling asleep next to your warm, sexy body, and not wake you up," he tells me.

"Why didn't you?"

"I knew it was a temporary situation and it wouldn't have been fair to wake you up at three in the morning for sex!" He taps the tip of my nose with his finger.

I smile.

"I have a gift for you," he says.

"Oh! What's the occasion?"

"Do I have to have an occasion to buy you a gift?" he asks.

"No," I say. "It's unexpected, that's all."

Something dangerous veils his eyes.

"Lucky for us you're wearing the perfect outfit for the gift."

I frown and glance down at my pretty, feminine white blouse and hot pink midi skirt combo.

"I don't follow."

He gives me a onceover. "Pants would've made things a lot more... complicated."

"I get it's cocktail hour somewhere in the world, but surely you're not drunk." I laugh.

He doesn't.

"No. I'm not drunk."

That pantie-melting look again.

My senses tingle.

"What are you up to, Mr. König?"

"It will all make sense in a minute, Mrs. König."

"Okay."

"I got you this." He shifts on the desk and grabs something behind him.

"What's—" I stop midsentence when he produces a small bottle of lube and a small cone-shaped object. "Is that what I think it is?"

"I don't read minds, kitten."

"Is that a butt plug?"

"It is," he says, a wicked grin stretching his lips.

I let out a shuddering exhale.

"Oh, okay..." I hesitate. "You bought me a toy, and you came to my office to announce we're going to have some kinky fun later tonight at home to make up for the last five days?"

"No. I came to your office so we can give it a test run," he says.

My jaw drops.

"Now?"

"Yes, right here, right now."

"Have you lost your mind?"

"Five days without fucking you, Michaela? Yeah, you could say that."

"Shouldn't we wait?"

"Why?"

I tilt my head to the side. "The location..."

"The door to your office is locked. The rest of my afternoon is clear and so is yours. I checked your schedule with your executive assistant."

I stare at him, dumbfounded.

"You can deny it all you want, but we both know you came

so hard you nearly forgot your own name the last time we had some fun in my office. This is no different."

It's not like I can deny it. He knows the illicit nature of office sex is kind of a turn on for me.

When I remain silent, he sweetens the pot. "I'm horny as fuck and I want you so damn much, I can't think straight, kitten." There's nothing but lust in his hazel-blue eyes. "Waiting until later isn't a consideration."

Oh. My. God.

It's unfathomable how he feels about me.

No one has ever wanted me with this much intense fervor.

He reaches out and brushes the back of his fingers against my breast. "Tell me you want me as much as I want you."

God, the man's raspy voice has an effect on me.

I release a harsh breath, but it doesn't have anything to do with trepidation or nerves. Not even close. I should be ashamed at how fast my body—and mind—switches gears.

How can I crave him this much?

"I want you. I need you."

With a growl, he pushes off the desk and crushes his lips against mine.

Good God.

The smoldering kiss intensifies, kicking up a storm of low moans from both of us.

When he pulls away from me, I claw at him because I don't want this kiss to ever end.

Phoenix spins me around.

"I want to fuck you on your desk—my cock pumping your sweet pussy and your ass full with my new gift." He grips the back of my neck and presses my body down until my breasts touch the desk.

I gasp, stumbling on my heels, but he steadies me.

"Do you trust me?"

I'm thrown off by this new level of supreme alphabadass-ness. His dominance is my drug. I want him to stick his big, fat cock deep inside me while he explores my ass. And, by God, I don't want to wait.

I drag my tongue across my lips, clenching my ass cheeks in anticipation. "Yes, I trust you."

He kicks my feet apart.

His hands drift down to the hem of my skirt before lifting it and exposing me in the middle of my office.

I draw in a sharp breath when he yanks up the fabric to my waist. I shiver all over, trembling from the yearning skittering up and down my entire body.

His fingers find what they were looking for—my lace thong. He brushes his languorous fingers across my pussy.

"Fuck. Me. My beautiful wife's pussy is dripping. My filthy, perfect wife."

"You make me so wet, I can't stand it."

"Hearing that makes me even harder."

Phoenix curls his fingers around the fabric of my thong and rips it apart, granting him full access to my needy pussy.

I gasp.

Dear God, this is kinky.

"I can smell your desire, kitten. You're desperate for my big cock."

"I am," I tell him.

Fuck, I'm getting off on this naughty play.

I wiggle my ass against him as he holds me down, gyrating my hips like a bitch in heat.

Fuck, he's so hard, so mouth-wateringly hard.

Slap!

I grunt.

"Patience, kitten." His gruff voice rolls across my skin.

"You'll get my cock soon enough." He lifts his body off mine and already I miss his warmth. "Don't move."

"Okay."

The hiss of Phoenix's zipper sounds ten times louder in the quiet office. The cool air caresses my exposed, bare ass, but it does little to lessen the raging inferno burning inside me, the hammering beats of my heart, making me anticipate his touch—and his cock.

He caresses my ass cheeks and takes a deep breath. "Fuck."

When his finger rims my asshole, my body writhes on the desk.

"You're not going anywhere, kitten." He clamps his free hand against my back. "You're about to find out what it's like to be fucked with both your holes filled."

A rush of juices floods my pussy, trickling down my thighs.

He grips my hips and pulls me down, lining my hipbones flush with the edge of the desk. He coats my asshole with lube. I welcome the cool sensation of the slick liquid.

Lining up his cockhead, he slides the tip between my pussy lips, teasing me mercilessly before delving into my slickness.

Yes!

I hold my breath and close my eyes.

He tortures me like this for a few blissful long seconds before pulling his cock out, tapping it against my ass.

"Nice and easy," he says as he eases the butt plug inside my ass.

I squirm.

"Relax," he says.

I really try, but I continue to shake as he pushes past the tight ring of my ass.

This is much bigger than his fingers.

The next thing I know, the entire length of his hard-like-steel cock rams into my pussy, his fingers digging into my skin.

Surprise washes over me when he inserts the last few inches of the butt plug into my ass.

Jesus!

The pressure knocks the air out of me and it takes everything in me not to writhe on the desk.

Pain and pleasure course through me at lightning speed.

Nothing could've prepared me for this ecstasy.

My mouth is wide open, but my scream is silent, my heart thundering against my chest.

"Christ," he says. "You're so impossibly tight with the plug in your ass. Jesus, I may never want to pull out."

Blinding pleasure takes over when he starts dominating me, fucking in and out of my pussy like a man possessed. I clench my ass muscles around the toy, drawing it in even deeper.

Holy Jesus!

Phoenix responds by fucking me harder.

And harder.

And harder.

At this rate, this desk isn't going to make it.

There's no stopping my husband as he takes me fast and furious, plunging his cock in with full abandonment.

Slap!

He ratchets up this hedonistic fuck by spanking my ass with every third thrust, a reminder he controls this ride. His hunger is savage. Almost barbaric. I fucking love it.

"Oh God." I jerk up, taking several ragged deep breaths.

Phoenix had his finger in my ass before, but being double stuffed like this is different. The way his huge girth stretches my desperate pussy while the toy fills my ass is sinful. I'm so aroused, I swear my juices must be coating the desk.

In and out.

In and out.

My desire spins out of control. I'm nothing more than a mess of small pleas and low moans.

He leans into me, pressing his chest against my back.

"You. Belong. To. Me," he says near my ear, thrusting into me with each word.

His shirt is unbuttoned and feeling the warmth of his chest heightens all my senses.

"I belong to you," I tell him.

"Don't you ever forget it."

"I won't."

"And I belong to you."

I'm caught off guard.

My heart stops for a beat.

I soak in his words, relishing them.

"You belong to me, Phoenix."

"Fuck, yeah, kitten."

I fight a smile threatening to cross my face.

"Now give me what I want." Sweet Phoenix just left the building. My demanding, domineering husband is back.

If I thought he was fucking me hard before, I was wrong.

Phoenix transforms into a power machine. I feel every inch of his long, thick cock as he slams inside me so hard, I'm shoved up the desk, my feet leaving the ground.

Oh. Oh. Oh.

What a beast.

And if I don't love every second of it.

With every savage thrust, I become a little more delirious.

"Take me. Take all of me," I tell him.

"Damn right. I'm taking what's mine."

I said that out loud?

He bites the back of my neck with a low growl. My pussy tingles as anguish turns into sheer ecstasy, and another intense round of electricity skitters into every part of me.

Phoenix curses low in his throat, driving into me with determination while he presses my face against the desk with more resolve. The cold metal sensation of his titanium wedding ring against my cheek makes me wetter.

My husband, the consummate lover.

I arch my back, jutting my hips up.

I'm there. Oh, fuck, I'm there.

I squeeze my legs together. Trapping my swollen clit between my pussy lips, I choke on a breath. Stars now float in front of my eyes, and I shudder as my orgasm rips through me.

"Yes, oh, yes—"

Phoenix places a hand over my mouth, muffling my climactic cries.

I clench my pussy hard around his cock, forcing him to dive off the cliff with me. He pumps once, twice, three times into my quivering pussy, and he lets out a deep growl as his body jerks forward. Hot cum spews deep inside me, filling me.

Branding me.

Claiming me from the inside out.

Marking me as his.

I clench my pussy hard, and I come again, my juices flowing down my legs.

God, each orgasm keeps getting better and better.

How is that even possible?

He places his forearms against the desk as he drops his weight on top of my body. I place my hands over his as an anchor.

Phoenix's hot, labored breath tickles my skin, causing my pussy muscles to clench again.

I try to speak, but I can't.

I can only focus on breathing.

For a few long beats, neither of us moves as the scent of raw and unbridled sex permeates in the office, filling my nostrils.

"I'm glad we never used condoms," I say after a long while.

"Why's that?"

"Feeling your cum shoot inside me is the hottest thing ever," I tell him. "Ditto for the way you grunt like a beast as you drive inside my pussy in punishing thrusts. The filthy sounds of your cock fucking my soaked pussy is so hedonistic. And, the sublime sensation of clenching hard against you, begging for more... God."

He lets out a breathy little chuckle. "It's amazing that hot-as-all-fuck rough sex gets you off like that."

"Until you, I didn't know those things turned me on," I say. "I didn't know I needed a man to take charge of all of me."

Another long silence stretches between us.

"You were fucking made for me, kitten."

I open my eyes.

"I love you, Phoenix." My brain is as foggy as my vision. That's the only explanation for allowing that confession to escape from my lips.

No sooner do the words leave my mouth, I panic.

Shit. Shit. Shit.

What have I done?

I needed to keep my big mouth shut.

He doesn't say a word.

Oh, God.

This is horrible.

Things were going so well. I fucked everything up.

Sure, we've agreed to explore things deeper, but blurting out those words is the kiss of death. It's not like I can take them back.

Tick.

Tick.

Tick.

Long seconds stretch between us.

My anxiety grows to paralyzing proportions.

"I—I mean, I love the way you fuck me." My pathetic attempt to save face is laughable.

In one swift movement, he pulls out of me, removes the butt plug from my ass, tosses it on the floor—where it lands near my destroyed thong—stands up, flips me over, and forces me to my feet. My skirt falls into place, hiding any signs of misbehaving. I watch in amazement as he yanks up his pants and boxer briefs before zipping and buckling up. His black shirt is still open and his hair is a beautiful tousled mess.

"What did you just say?" he asks.

I bring my arms to my chest, crossing them at the wrist, almost as an armor. "I love the way you fuck me?!"

He narrows his eyes at me. "No, smart ass, before that."

I sweep a hand in front of my face. "I wasn't thinking."

"So, those words were meaningless?"

Err...

I avert my gaze.

"Michaela, I asked you a question."

"Post-coital hormones took over my brain." I let out a nervous laugh. "Don't mind me. I was just being silly."

"So, you don't love me?"

I open my mouth to lie and tell him he misunderstood, but nothing comes out.

"I guess I shouldn't tell you I love you, too."

My gaze snaps up to his.

My jaw drops and my eyelashes flutter so fast, I'm surprised I don't start floating.

He rubs his thumb across my lips. "I love you, Michaela." The conviction in his words breaks me.

"You do?"

He nods. "I love you, kitten."

"Really?" It's crazy to ask that question when this gorgeous man repeated his declaration three times.

"Really," he says. "Somewhere along the line, this fake relationship became real for me." He offers a warm smile. "You said the words first, but it doesn't mean I don't feel the same way you do."

"This is surreal. We've only known each other for a short time."

"So?" he asks.

"So..." I bore my eyes into his when I say, "I'm happier than I ever thought I could be with a man I hated at first sight."

He chuckles.

"Same here, kitten. I'm happier than I ever thought I could be with a hellion."

I smile, my cheeks reddening.

He bursts out laughing.

"What?" I ask.

"A month ago, you came barging into my office, spewing fire, swearing up and down you'd never become my wife, then you bolted out of here, leaving a trail of flames behind you. I'm surprised firefighters didn't show up."

I giggle.

"Look at you now, my little dragon. In love and all..."

"Guilty as charged."

His expression turns serious.

He pulls me into his arms. "Just so we're clear, I'm not letting you go, Mrs. König."

"I can live with that, Mr. König."

He presses his lips against mine in a scorching hot kiss, our tongues tangled, thrusting against each other wildly.

It's everything I need.

He's everything I need.

Epilogue

Phoenix

Five months later

The König clan and extended family are gathered in beautiful, snowy Aspen, Colorado.

My father, brothers, and I spend Christmas here or at the family house on Catalina Island. It's our first Christmas together, and since Michaela has never been to Aspen, it was a logical choice. Dad owns a cabin here, Slate and Wilder share one, and I bought Barron's cabin to keep it in the family and because I always loved his place. All three cabins are in close proximity of one another. It's the same for our cousins' cabins.

Dad is chilling at his place—no doubt nursing a glass of smooth whiskey in front of the fireplace while enjoying a gripping crime and thriller book. Slate and Wilder headed straight from the private jet to the ski slopes upon arrival this morning. Roman should arrive in a few hours. He's still wary from his surfing accident, so for the first time since he was three years old, he's not hitting the slopes.

I'm skipping skiing. My wife doesn't ski. I suggested the

kiddy slopes, but the flash of panic glinting from her eyes had me changing my mind. Lucky for her, there's no shortage of other outdoor activities to enjoy in Aspen.

"I usually dread snow, but out here, it's so beautiful," Michaela says, shaking off the snow as we enter the cabin.

"That's because New Yorkers are pussies when it comes to a little snow."

"True." She removes her pale pink cashmere hat, matching scarf, and mittens before shrugging out of her puffy white down coat. She runs manicured fingers through her hair, her wedding ring and band glimmering under the light. I've grown accustomed to seeing them on her finger, but it doesn't lessen the pang of pride that hits me every time.

This gorgeous, feisty, vivacious woman is mine.

She spikes the end of her hair for style. "I must look like a wet cat."

"No, kitten, you look hot."

She offers a bright smile.

She's still sporting jet black hair and her trademark pixie cut. She considered growing it out, but when I told her how much I loved her hair short—and the easy access to her slender neck—she reconsidered.

She toes off her boots.

I follow her lead and shrug out of my winter clothes.

"Snow in Aspen two days before Christmas. You can't ask for much more," she says, entering the living room.

I follow right behind her.

"Absolutely not! I love California and I would never live in Colorado year-round, but snow on Christmas Day goes hand-in-hand."

"I second that!" she says, rubbing her hands together.

I grab them into mine and bring them to my lips, kissing them softly.

"You're still cold?" I ask.

The temperature has been unseasonably low in Colorado this December.

"'*Baby It's Cold Outside*'." She sings the bridge to the icon song.

I chuckle. "The wind was biting," I say. "Not to mention, it was a long walk."

"It was, but I'm so happy you took me. What an incredible, picture-perfect winter wonderland."

"Nothing compares to Aspen at this time of the year."

She trembles, her teeth chattering.

"Let me light up a fire," I say. It's warm in the cabin, but clearly, it's not enough.

I took Michaela on one of my favorite trails. It offers enchanting scenery of the area, but it's a good trek through the snow and the trees.

As we were ending our discovery walk, we spent another hour doing really rugged outdoor stuff—making snow angels, throwing snowballs at each other, and attempting to make a snowman. That got cut short when the wind picked up and snow started to fall hard.

Since Michaela couldn't feel her fingers and toes, we retreated to the cabin. By the time we reached the door, snow had blanketed our footsteps.

"Thank you," she says.

It doesn't take me long to get a fire going.

"Nice and toasty," Michaela says. "I still can't get over the magnificent penthouse in Los Angeles or the mansion in Malibu, but this..."—she opens her arms out—"The obscenely rich have a different definition of the word 'cabin'," she says with air quotes. "This is the lap of luxury."

"It's cozy."

"Right." She nods. "As cozy as the yacht, private plane, chauffeur, personal chef, cleaning lady... and the list goes on."

"There's nothing wrong with living well, when you've worked for it, kitten. And, don't forget, you get to enjoy all of this *coziness* as well."

She offers a dazzling smile. "I've said it before, the life of a billionaire's wife is nice work if you can get it."

We both laugh.

Six months into this marriage, and she's still a fascination. She appreciates the life I offer, but she never takes it for granted. Thank God she hasn't transformed into one of these obnoxious-stuck-up-entitled women who ride on their husband's fortune.

She doesn't have to work, but she shows up every day. And, every morning as she strolls through the lobby on her way to the executive floor, she makes it a priority to greet guests and employees with a huge smile. She says it's something her mother instilled in her, something ingrained in her DNA. I respect that about her.

"It's getting warm in here now." She fans herself.

"Too warm?"

"Nah, I'll just remove some layers."

She pulls the powder blue cashmere sweater over her head before removing her insulated pants. There's nothing provocative or overly sexual about the way she removes her clothes, but my cock stiffens. She's now dressed in a form fitting white camisole and black leggings. After six months in LA, her creamy white skin is now sun kissed. She's a true Los Angelina. My eyes brush down the length of her sexy ass body. One glance reveals she isn't wearing a bra and I don't see any panty lines.

I approve.

God, my desire for this woman is off the Richter scale.

No matter how many times I fuck her, it's still not enough to satisfy the insatiable pit inside me.

She folds her clothes with care, walks back to the foyer and drops them on the wooden bench.

"Kahlua hot chocolate and homemade cookies?" I ask her as she reemerges.

It's late afternoon and we're going to have a copious dinner at Dad's cabin in a few hours with the whole family, but there's always room for cookies.

"Yes and yes!"

"Make yourself comfortable and I'll be right back," I say.

I head to the wall-mounted iPhone dock in the hallway that controls the multi-room system offering surround sound throughout the cabin. I place my phone there and strut to the freezer. I pull out an assortment of frozen cookie dough, place half a dozen balls on a cookie sheet, and then slide them into the oven. I get to work on the hot chocolate. I'm no wizard in the kitchen, but Mom taught all her boys how to prepare kickass spiked hot cocoa.

Seventeen minutes later, I return to the living room, a large tray weighed down with sweet treats in hand.

"OhmyGod!" she says. "You've been hiding things from me!"

"Not really. I just needed the perfect setting." I drop the tray on the coffee table. "Drinking hot cocoa in LA makes no sense. In Aspen, it's a necessity on a wintery day like today."

"You have a good point."

I hand her an oversized mug.

Her eyes grow wide. "Thank you. I expected a splash of booze, but this is a work of art."

I sit next to her on the sofa before grabbing the second mug.

"Marshmallows slathered in salted caramel and a drizzle of

melted chocolate finished with a touch of the flame from a blow torch go a long way."

She cradles the mug with both hands and takes a long sip.

"Mmmm." She closes her eyes and moans. "This is insanely delicious." She shoots me a side gaze. "You, Mr. New CEO, have some wicked skills."

She's impressed.

"Granted, you just discovered my talent for preparing kickass hot chocolate, but I was a CEO when you met me."

She shakes her head. "You were an *interim* CEO," she says. "Now, you run the show."

"I do. And it's a pretty fucking amazing feeling!"

She lifts her mug. "Here's to teamwork!"

"Hear, hear!" I clink my mug with hers.

She takes a small sip of her drink, careful not to burn her tongue.

"Oh, you could get drunk on this," she says.

"By the time you finish your drink, you'll be pretty mellow," I tell her. "Two of those back-to-back, and you'll be knocked out."

"Noted." She drops her mug on the coffee table and reaches for a cookie.

I do the same.

"These are as scrumptious as the ones from the Pompadour!" she says around a bite, pointing at her white chocolate and macadamia nut cookie. "Please tell me you didn't prepare these."

"I didn't. I made a special request to the head pastry chef at the Pompadour."

She's addicted to them, but I won't point that out.

"You're a good man, Mr. CEO."

It's her new favorite word.

It also happens to be mine.

It's official.

As of yesterday, six p.m., the board of directors named me CEO of König Imperial Holding.

What a fucking amazing Christmas gift.

I didn't count my chickens until all the votes were in. You never know. With Potter out of the picture, there was no opposition. The votes were unanimous. The other board members always felt I was the man for the job—not because of my last name, but because I've worked damn hard to earn the title.

I was elated and relieved. So were my father and my brothers. Slate and I made peace a long time ago over the outburst that created a rift between us. He even went as far as to apologize to Michaela. Even with that, he took me aside right after I was appointed and apologized again for ever doubting I could pull it off and have the girl.

After an impromptu office party, my gorgeous wife showed me her enthusiasm over the joyous news in the most unforgettable way. She lured me to my office and gave me the ultimate gift—her naked on her knees, cupping her tits as an offering. I eagerly titty-fucked her until I jetted my cum all over her chest and face. Then, I showed her my appreciation by eating her out spread open like a sumptuous meal on my desk while finger-fucking her deep until I hit her sweet spot and her juices came gushing out with force. I came from the thrill of watching her dissolve like that under my tongue and touch. I didn't even need to touch my cock. It was that powerful.

Damn.

Between furtive glances, we polish off our hot chocolate and eat half a plate of warm cookies.

Michaela leans back against the seat, rubbing her stomach. "I don't think I'm going to be able to eat a bite at your father's place later."

"I'm sure you'll manage. Trust me, it'll be worth the effort.

Tonight's dinner is catered by one of Aspen's top chefs. Dad booked him five months ago."

She lets out a dramatic sigh. "Oh, well if you twist my arm, then I guess I'll have to."

"You're taking one for the team?"

"Something like that," she says. "Speaking of taking one for the team... what should we do until dinner?" The suggestive tone in her voice doesn't go unnoticed. Neither does the way she stares at me with hungry eyes.

God, I want to pull her on my lap and devour her, but not yet.

"Actually, I have something for you," I say, standing up. "Give me a minute." I throw that over my shoulder as I rush up the stairs.

"You can't give me my Christmas gifts two days before Christmas!" She shouts from downstairs.

When I arrive in the bedroom, I change into jeans and a t-shirt. I grab what I need and race back to the living room.

"It's not your Christmas gift," I tell her.

A pair of confused green eyes drops to the large envelope I'm holding.

"What's that?" she asks.

I head to the iPhone dock, open the music app, do a quick search until I find the song I downloaded specifically for this occasion. I press play.

I turn around to face her.

She frowns and then her beautiful face contorts in a grimace.

"I know you're older, but surely you're not that old," she says.

"You know exactly how old I am."

"So, what's up with the dated music?" she asks.

"It's circa nineteen-seventy-two, baby!" I approach her doing this little dance reminiscent of the era.

"*Dated*," she says. "Who's singing?"

"Al Green."

"Who?"

"Al Green. He's a R&B and soul hit singer from the early seventies—"

"You weren't even born in the early seventies," she says. "There's nothing else on your playlist that's more contemporary? Heck, the top hits from the last two decades will do. I can roll with that. No need to go that far back in time." She does a classic disco move.

I grip my chest, feigning outrage. "That hurts, smart ass."

"Please tell me this song wasn't part of your repertoire during your boy band days. If so, I'll have no other choice but to tease you mercilessly until the end of time."

I roll my eyes. "No, it wasn't."

"Then, why are we listening to it?"

"Are you even listening to the lyrics?" I ask.

Her eyes shoot up to the ceiling and she finally, finally pays attention.

"'*Let's Stay Together*.'" She sings the words out loud, but it doesn't seem to register. "Ooohhh!"

By George, I think she's got it.

"'*Let's Stay Together*'," she repeats. This time recognition shines bright in her eyes. A huge smile stretches her lips.

I take a seat next to her and hand her the envelope.

"What's that?" she asks again.

"Open it and you'll find out."

She does.

She scans the contract.

Surprised eyes snap up to mine.

"Phoenix..." My name comes out in a whisper. "Oh my

God." With her mouth gaping, her gaze bounces from mine to the papers she's holding. "Is this for real?"

"It is." I nod.

"I don't understand. When we discussed this arrangement, I thought it was two hundred million dollars in exchange for me becoming your wife for a whole year, at which point the Villiers Grand would become ours again. It's only been six months. Are you renegotiating the terms?"

"You could say that. I don't want anything between us."

She furrows her eyebrows. "What do you mean?"

I point to the ceiling. "The song selection isn't by accident, kitten. That's hours scouring YouTube, searching for the right one that says everything I feel here!" I tap my heart.

"Oh."

"If you notice on the last page, there are blank spaces in front of and after your first name."

She flips the pages. "Why is that?"

I run my hands through her hair and grip her by the back of the neck. "I want you well past the one-year mark, Michaela."

"Oh."

"I want you to want me—just for me, as much I want you—just for you. I don't want to hold anything over your head, and I don't want you to think I have any leverage over you. That's why I'm handing over control of the hotel back to you. The Villiers Grand is debt free and the new management we have in place will remain, regardless of your decision..."

"My decision?" she asks.

"Yes." I run my thumb over her lips. "You can let me know if you want to continue our journey together by telling me which name goes on the contract. Miss Michaela Knight Villiers or Mrs. Michaela König Knight Villiers?"

A heartbeat of silence pounds between us.

Finally, she shakes her head, and smiles. "Had you not prefaced your declaration with that little musical flash from the past, I might have been inclined to think you were serving me with divorce papers," she says. "After all, you got what you wanted. You're CEO—"

"That's not all I want, Michaela. I want you, too. I want you in my life forever."

She responds with a huge smile. "To answer your question, Mrs. Michaela König Knight Villiers goes on the contract." There's not a shred of hesitation in her answer.

"We're staying together, kitten?"

She tosses the contract over her shoulder before grabbing a fistful of my t-shirt and pulling me to her. "Damn right we are, König."

"Fuck, I love you, kitten."

"I love you so much."

She wraps her arms around my neck as my tongue sweeps into her mouth, and I kiss the living daylights out of her. The fire crackles and sparkles in the background as I pull her onto my lap, our passion burning hotter than ever. I growl, taking her breast in my hand, groping it with avarice. Needing more, I lift my pelvis, grinding my hard cock between her legs.

She moans into the kiss.

She pulls away from me when the next song starts to play.

"Back Door Santa."

Well, that was a stroke of genius.

Shock is evident on her face.

"Is that a message, Mr. König?"

I don't remember downloading the song, but I'll run with it.

"Not long ago you were inquiring about what we were going to do until dinner." I allow for a pregnant pause. "Now, you have your answer."

"Please be gentle," she says.

"I'm not going to make promises I'm certain I'll break."

Lust flashes bright in her eyes.

"Filthy girl."

She offers a shy shrug.

"Let's go upstairs to the bedroom, Mrs. König. There's a big bottle of lube with your name on it." I stand up with her in my arms.

Her legs straddle around my waist.

She doesn't balk.

She doesn't protest.

She doesn't even whimper.

She snakes her arms around my neck, pulling me closer.

"I can't wait." She murmurs those sweet words low in my ear.

My perfect, dirty wife.

Bonus Scene

Gage

After the worst week of my life, I planned on going home to my Beverly Hills mansion, diving to the bottom of one of the top-shelf vodka bottles I have in my freezer, and drinking the bad memories away.

As I was stepping out of the courtroom, my buddy Phoenix texted me and invited me to join him and Shane for drinks and dinner.

Although Phoenix sits at the helm of a conglomerate of luxury hotels, the CEO and magnate needs some breathing room. Something that's impossible to do when he's in one of his hotels, restaurants, or lounges.

The Quintus Hotel is our hangout, so that's where he's hiding out.

There's nothing like a public trial and the slandering of your good name to make a man irritable as fuck. To say my fuse has been short in these past few months would be an understatement.

I get out of my chauffeured Rolls Royce and stalk towards the Quintus's entrance. I step inside the luxury hotel and make my way to the elevators. I don't have to wait long for a car to reach the lobby.

I invite a group of women to step in before me.

A couple of them check me out.

With a polite smile, I park myself at the back of the elevator as more people file in. As we ride up, I pull out my phone and check the latest headlines.

'GAGE HOLLINGSWORTH FALSELY ACCUSED OF SEXUAL ABUSE AND HARASSMENT.'

'TALENTLESS WANNABE ACCUSES STREAMING MOGUL GAGE HOLLINGSWORTH OF BLACKMAILING HER AND THREATENING TO RAPE HER. ALL LIES.'

'SALLY BROUGHTON AND BOYFRIEND CON AMERICA INTO BELIEVING THEIR FILTHY LIES.'

'19-YEAR-OLD SALLY BROUGHTON'S ATTEMPT TO RUIN GAGE HOLLINGSWORTH'S REPUTATION. ALL THAT FOR 15 MINUTES OF FAME.'

'SALLY BROUGHTON. SHAME. SHAME. SHAME.'

'OPEN LETTER TO SALLY BROUGHTON: WHEN LIARS WITHOUT SCRUPLES CRY WOLF, IT HURTS REAL VICTIMS.'

'VERDICT CLEARS GAGE HOLLINGSWORTH'S NAME. CASE CLOSED.'

I shake my head and tuck my phone away.

I let out a long sigh, my eyes lifting to the ceiling, silently thanking God and my parents for watching over me.

By the time the elevator reaches my floor, I'm the only one left.

I exit and stroll down the corridor.

I check my Ballon Bleu Cartier watch.

Seven.

After a week of not being able to eat because of the stress over this trial, I hope tonight I'll be able to enjoy food.

I step inside Moonlight.

"Good evening, Mr. Hollingsworth," the maître d' says.

"Good evening."

"Mr. König mentioned you'd join him and Mr. Dennison for dinner."

"Indeed."

The maître d' leans into the high desk and says in a mere whisper, "Congratulations. I hope you sue them for what they did to you. That was disgusting."

He pulls away.

"Don't worry. They'll get what's coming to them."

"Good." He responds with a firm nod. "The boyfriend has money—"

"And he's about to lose a lot of it." My voice is so cold, I'm surprised ice pellets don't float in the air.

"Leave him with only the shirt on his back."

"I don't think I have it in me to be that generous."

The maître d' flashes me an evil grin.

I respond in kind.

"Mr. König is at his favorite table. Let me take you."

"I know my way."

"Very well."

With that, I stride through the restaurant.

It's a full house.

No surprise.

There's a reason, Zagat coined Moonlight "casual fine dining at its best". Leave it to Larkin Gallagher for hitting it out of the park. Everything he touches turns to gold.

I spot Phoenix and Shane at an isolated table near the floor-to-ceiling windows.

My friends stand up to greet me.

"Hey," I say, taking Shane in a bro hug.

Phoenix receives the same treatment.

After the customary greetings, I unbutton my suit jacket, and sit down.

From their half empty tumblers, I'm guessing they got here not long ago.

"I would've expected you guys to be hanging out at the whiskey bar," I say.

"We were there," Shane says. "The bar menu wasn't enough for me. I needed real food."

"No food at your house, Dennison?"

Shane chuckles. "There's plenty of food. Collin and I were in Vegas all day. It was non-stop. We had a few interviews with a morning show and a daytime entertainment show mid-day. Afterwards, we were whisked away to a new hotel that carries our equipment for a ribbon cutting. In other words, we had a full day in Sin City."

Levi Aldridge and his wife are Collin and Shane Dennison's business partners. They co-own Fit Thonix Sport Challenge Equipment. These four went from zero to multibillions in sales in the bat of an eyelash.

"Where's your brother?" I ask.

"He had to fly to Miami," Shane says. "Since I have to be in San Diego in two days, we had to divide and conquer."

"Got it." I nod.

A waitress approaches our table.

I place my drink order. Phoenix and Shane top up theirs, and we order an assortment of appetizers.

It doesn't take long before the waitress is back with our drinks and a ton of food.

I lift my glass in salute.

Shane does the same.

"Here's to the bad guys going down," Phoenix says.

Shane lifts his glass a bit higher. "Hear, hear!"

"I can drink to that," I say.

We clink glasses.

Phoenix and Shane take a sip of their drinks.

I gulp half of my vodka on the rocks. I welcome the icy coldness of the liquor as it coats my insides. It's not enough to erase the last week, but it's a good start.

"Slow down, cowboy," Phoenix says.

"You're right," I say. "I need some food."

I load up a plate with an assortment of appetizers.

Shane and Phoenix do the same.

The nervous energy I've been carrying with me all week dictates my every move. I eat like a man who stepped out of prison an hour ago. I empty my plate in a few bites and polish off my drink.

The weight of two pairs of blue eyes staring at me is unmistakable.

I meet my friends' bewildered gazes.

Shane opens his mouth to say something, but the waitress appears at our table.

"Another drink, sir?" she asks me.

"Yes, please."

"Holy shit, Hollingsworth," Phoenix says.

"If it wasn't for your text, I probably would be halfway down a bottle of vodka by now," I say. "Food wouldn't even be part of the equation."

"And you would've ended up with a helluva hangover," Shane says. "I guess you're taking the day off and you won't report for duty as CEO in the morning?"

"I'll report for duty, just not bright and early."

"When are you ever *bright*?" Phoenix says.

"Leave him alone." Shane comes to my defense. "The man was put through the wringer in the last week, and a different verdict could've sent his life spiraling."

Truer words have never been spoken.

The waitress is back with my drink.

After thanking her, I take a long swig. I'm tempted to polish it off in one gulp, but I resist.

Shane and Phoenix are staring at me as if I'm an alien.

"If you count when this nightmare began, it's been three months of hell on earth." I drop my tumbler on the table. "Today, was the accumulation of it all."

"I still can't believe this shit," Phoenix says. "Good thing you had Jordana in your corner."

"Loki's mom lives up to her reputation of being a wolf in sheep's clothing. On top of that, she handled the press with a lot more finesse and diplomacy than I ever could."

"It was a smart strategy for you to keep quiet," Phoenix says.

"After weeks of dodging a mob of entertainment reporters, bloggers, and vloggers, without so much as looking at them, I was able to make a statement. *I'm innocent.*"

"The two most critical words in our legal system," Phoenix says.

Ain't that the truth.

"Jordana's gagging order nearly killed me, but I'm glad I agreed. Everything that came out of those reporters' mouths set me off. I've never had to exert as much restraint in my life."

"They're pros at poking the bear."

"Phoenix is right," Shane says. "Good for you for not falling for their manipulation tactics."

"Anything you would've said would've played against you," Phoenix says. "And once it's on news channels' socials, it's a bitch to get it off the internet. It doesn't matter how many billions of dollars you have in the bank."

"Which is why I swallowed my anger throughout the trial," I say. "If that trial had lasted one more week, I would've ended up with a fucking ulcer."

"Glad it's over," Shane says. "You endured enough damage to your reputation. Thank God justice prevailed."

I lift my glass. "Here's to Jordana Berkshire!"

Phoenix chuckles. "Don't mess with that woman if you know what's good for you."

Shane nods. "Loki's mom is a force. She eats, sleeps, and breathes PR."

"She's the top gun of public relations crisis management," I say. "My dream team of lawyers would've gotten me off, but Jordana cleaned my public image. And that's priceless."

"These influencers make money so fast, it has little to no value to them." Shane shakes his head, disapproval etching his features.

I nod.

Phoenix adjusts his tie. "Their constant need for over-the-top sensationalism is irritating."

"They're not all bad apples," I say, "but those who push the envelope too far, fuck it up for the ones who walk the straight and narrow."

"Just because you made a name for yourself by using Photoshop to dupe people, it doesn't mean it should be your license to ruin other people's reputation and life," Shane says.

"You're going to sue them, right?" Phoenix asks.

"The maître d' asked me the same question," I say.

"And?" Shane asks.

Phoenix cocks a brow.

I take another long swig of my drink. "I'm going to make Sally and Chuck pay. They'll regret ever crossing me. By the time I'm done with them, they'll only have a pair of socks and dirty underwear to their names. Chuck may be worth three million dollars. I have *several billions*."

"Good," Shane says at the same time as Phoenix says, "They deserve to get their asses handed to them on a platter."

"I'm happy to oblige," I say.

Sally Broughton's twenty-year-old boyfriend Chuck Creeton is a YouTube star. Three years ago, he fooled everyone by posting a series of photos of him on his private jet, with Louis Vuitton luggage, decked out in head-to-toe designer wear. He was living the life at the tender age of seventeen.

He was sitting in his *parents'* living room. The background was Photoshopped. Same for the luggage. And the logos on the black tracksuit he bought at Walmart.

That little stunt was his springboard.

It also launched a new, lucrative business model. Piggybacking on the viral wave, an LA studio lets people look like they're on a private jet for an affordable sixty-five dollars per hour. It's a small price to pay to fake it. Appearing wealthy on social media has become its own industry, and the world has Chuck to thank.

Since that coup, Chuck has made a fortune by being a YouTube prankster. When his girlfriend—an inspiring violinist—got eliminated early on my talent show, *Jam Session*—think *The Voice*, but for musicians—Chuck decided to turn me into an experiment.

On *Jam Session*, you can only advance based on your talent. If the judges aren't blown away, they won't turn their chair around. As the competition advances, the public becomes judge and jury.

Sally took offense that none of the judges recognized her talent. Her boyfriend was willing to indulge her in her delusion. I was the scapegoat.

When people think you sexually assaulted a fifteen-year-old girl, it's the end of your life as you know it. Thanks to her boyfriend, Sally, who's a nineteen-year-old young woman and not an underage teenager, used fake ID to enter the teens category of the competition.

At the hearing, Chuck had the audacity to tell the judge it was all a joke and there's no such thing as bad publicity. Now, the joke's on him.

"Larkin came through for you," Phoenix says.

"He did," I say. "You can always count on Larkin."

My friends nod in agreement.

"The private investigators he referred me to did a stellar job. They were worth every penny."

"You still don't know how they retrieved the incriminating files from Chuck's laptop and phone?" Shane asks.

"No. They told me it's best if I didn't know."

"As long as you're in the clear, that's all that matters," Phoenix says. He lifts his tumbler. "Free at last!"

Shane and I lift our glasses and clink Phoenix's.

I polish off my drink.

"I hope you intend on celebrating your freedom by dropping by Dark Compulsion tonight," Phoenix says.

"It's theme night," Shane says. He drops his Rusty Nail drink on the table. "Those are the best because they bring in fresh faces."

"After dinner, I'm going home to change," Phoenix says. "My wife and I are attending. Beckett and Rhys—and their girls—will also be there. Rod is coming with Dominika."

"I'll be there," Shane says.

"I'll pass, guys," I tell them.

"If anyone deserves a good time, it's you," Phoenix says.

"Nah."

"Gage—"

"Phoenix, I said I'll pass."

He sighs. "Three years." He flashes me the appropriate number of fingers. "That's a fucking long time to punish yourself."

"Not that anyone has the right to tell you it's time to move on," Shane says, "because that would be insensitive and callous, but Gage, you're surviving. And surviving isn't living."

I narrow my eyes at him.

"The fury in your eyes is the same every time we attempt to broach the subject," Shane says.

My nostrils flare. "The topic is off the table."

These two are testing my patience.

I should've gone home after all.

"You two are done psychoanalyzing me?"

Phoenix narrows his eyes at me. "You've been locked in that tour of yours, aka your office, for so long. Being a brooding recluse is your new normal. If it wasn't for the fact you couldn't run your multibillion dollar empire from the comfort of your mansion, we'd never see you."

"Theme parties are off limits," I say. "I drop by Dark Compulsion when I need to. I don't want anything intimate—"

"Why not stay home and watch porn?" Phoenix asks. "You're paying a fortune for an annual membership to," he scours the room, "an exclusive adult club with some of the most beautiful female members—"

"There are club members willing to accept my unbendable rules."

"Jesus Christ, Gage." Phoenix runs a hand through his hair.

"You never take a woman up to one of the private rooms or one of the lounge rooms. Heck, you don't even go to one of the Peek-a-boo rooms with a woman."

Phoenix is a stubborn motherfucker.

That's why he's such a good businessman. But right now, he's grating on my last nerves.

"Those are too intimate for me," I say.

He rolls his eyes.

"I'm no MD and I don't pretend to play one on or off camera," Shane says, "but isn't it time you changed your ways?"

I give him a one-shoulder shrug. "If it ain't broke, why fix it?"

"Your mother wouldn't want that for you—"

I point a finger at Phoenix. "Leave my mother out of this!"

Shane soldiers on. "Aren't you tired of the unsurmountable walls you've erected around yourself and the tedious precautions you take so you can avoid intimacy at all costs?"

Phoenix crooks a thumb in our friend's direction. "What he said."

Shane isn't done dispensing unsolicited advice. "No one is telling you to date again, but what you're doing at the club with those women can't be all that... *satisfactory*."

My gaze bounces from one set of blue eyes to another. "Did you two win your medical degrees at the same carnival game?"

Shane ignores my jab. "Bring down your walls—"

"So now you're a fucking poet, Dennison?" I say. "Or did you pull that Oscar-worthy line from a goddamn Hallmark movie?"

"I'm a concerned friend."

I rub a hand over my face. "Everyone wants a piece of me. You guys are supposed to be in my corner. Instead, you're drilling me, pushing me to change my ways when I don't want to. I have one thing to offer a woman." I flash them a finger.

"One. It's a take it or leave it situation. It's enough for the women I hook up with, so butt out."

"Gage—"

I lift a hand, stopping Phoenix. "I've heard enough." I shoot to my feet. "Drinks and appetizers are on me, guys. Enjoy your theme party at Dark Compulsion."

With that, I storm out.

And they wonder why I'm always brooding.

That fatal day three years ago changed my life forever.

Don't fucking poke the bear and don't push him out of hibernation.

I don't need to thaw my frozen heart, and I sure as hell don't need more from women than I'm getting.

End of story.

Bonus Secret Chapter

For a bonus secret chapter about Phoenix and Michaela (Michaela overhears the Phoenix's response to Slate's accusations—her POV), subscribe to my newsletter!

www.MyRomanceAddiction.com

Who's The Next Filthy Rich Book Boyfriend in This Scorching Hot Series?

Gage Hollingsworth is next.

The brooding, grumpy LA CEO has built an impenetrable fortress around his heart. A soft-spoken virgin comes crashing into his life, wreaking havoc on his self-imposed rules. Unable to understand the power this stranger has over him, the sexy alpha billionaire does what he does best, he erects his walls.

No way is he letting a woman in...

Coming Soon: Billionaire Mogul—Gage

Beckett, Rhys, and Phoenix are part of a binge-worthy world.

The series is so unputdownable, you'll lose sleep over it. And no, I'm not sorry.

Each book in the **Billionaire Hotshots** series can be read as a standalone, but why miss out on a copious amount of sauciness by not starting at the beginning?

Billionaire Hotshot—Levi kicks off the series with a naughty ball that's so hot, it comes ***with*** a warning.

★★★★★ "Levi's story had me from the get-go, all the way to the end!"

Psst... you can read a sneak peek of Billionaire Hotshot—Levi at the end of this book.

Reviews are sweet as pie!

It only takes a few minutes to leave a review, which makes a huge difference for an indie author like myself.

Here's the link to leave a review for:
Billionaire Mogul—Phoenix

Scarlett's Book Banter!

Dear Sexy Reader,

I love, love, love Phoenix and Michaela. She went from, *"I hate him at first sight,"* to not being able to imagine not being his wife.

They're perfect for each other.

And let's talk about how dirty they are together.

As you know, my novels come in one shade––scorching hot. That said, I think I might've gone a little overboard with Phoenix's book. My new obsession of turning women into geysers/the Niagara Falls (please read between the lines) hit an all-time high with this book. Obviously, that's good news for you (wink-wink).

Note: I stole the term "turning women into geysers/the Niagara Falls" from Lauren Rowe. Sneaky Lauren.

Back to Phoenix and Michaela.

I promised you a lot of over-the-top drama, and I believe I more than delivered. Why have mundane when you can have copious amounts of craziness?

I hope you took notes. Phoenix has three other sexy brothers. Oh yeah, there will be more of these hotelier kings. I also hope you noticed Callum, aka Everly's cousin, is related on his mom's side to Phoenix. Pretty wicked. I know.

I first introduced Callum in Holt's book (**Billionaire Hotshot—**

Holt). Everly is the sexy donut shop owner that catches the former rock star turned record label exec's eye.

Billionaire Hotshot—Holt is a seductive single dad romance as intoxicating as a sugar rush.

It's Book 4 of the **Billionaire Hotshots Series.**

★★★★★ "This couple rocked it off the pages!"

★★★★★ "Holt and Everly are everything and more!"

★★★★★ "This book hits all the emotions of your heart."

★★★★★ "This book took my heart."

★★★★★ "Oh, and that ending! Had me laughing and crying."

★★★★★ "Scarlett has really outdone herself with this book."

Binge-read now: Billionaire Hotshot—Holt

If you want to color within the lines, you can always start with Book 1 of the series.

Billionaire Hotshot—Levi kicks off the series with a naughty ball that's so hot, it comes ***with*** a warning.

★★★★★ "OMG! Ms. Scarlett does it yet AGAIN! I love, love, love this book, and it was so, so HOT! She weaves a great story, great characters and lots of fun..."wink wink," in the process! She is my absolute favorite author. I devour all her books! Keep 'em "coming" Scarlett!" –JC

Binge-read now: Billionaire Hotshot—Levi

(Psst... make sure to read the sneak peek of Billionaire Hotshot—Levi at the end of this book.)

A couple like Phoenix and Michaela

Out of all of my couples, I'd say, Nikolaj and Ciara (**Billionaire Factor—Nikolaj**) share the same over-the-top passion as Phoenix and Michaela.

Billionaire Factor—Nikolaj is a whirlwind romance between a steadfast billionaire with the determination of a thousand warriors and a spirited heroine who fools everyone with her tough exterior, but inside, she has a soft heart and she yearns to find the one.

★★★★★ "OMG that was hot! I can't believe that book pulled me in and kept dragging me until the end! HOT! HOT! HOT!!! Didn't want it to end!" —Cassie

Binge-read now: Billionaire Factor—Nikolaj

Since Bryce Van Der Linden has a cameo appearance in Phoenix's book, you might as start with Book 1 of the series. I invite you to read Ciara's sister Sofia's provocative romance with alpha billionaire Bryce.

Billionaire Factor—Bryce is a provocative romance between a jaded billionaire who has written off love after being betrayed one too many times and a selfless soul with a fighting spirit.

★★★★★ "I love this book so much, I read it twice in a row." —Jacquie

Binge-read now: Billionaire Factor—Bryce

That's it for me.

Back to writing!

Much love,

Scarlett Avery

P.S. Reviews are always appreciated and let me know I wrote a swoon-worthy story! Thanks in advance.

P.P.S. I keep writing because of your hunger for my stories. Thank you for your fervor, love, and loyalty. I'm humbled and incredibly grateful. Without you, there's very little reason to keep coming up with new stories.

P.P.P.S. For access to an EXCLUSIVE Secret Chapter, go to the next page!

Get the Secret Chapter for Billionaire Mogul—Phoenix!

Thank you for purchasing this romance!

I have an EXCLUSIVE Secret Chapter to share with you!

For the Secret Chapter, you get a scene where Michaela overhears the Phoenix's response to Slate's accusations.

Trust me, you're going to love the extra tidbits.

When you sign up on my list, you'll receive an email with further instructions!

Sign up TODAY!

www.MyRomanceAddiction.com

***If you've already signed up to my list from previous books, you can visit the same page to download the Secret Chapters and/or Storyboard for this romance. ***

Billionaire Moguls Series

Billionaire Mogul—Beckett

Billionaire Mogul—Rhys

Billionaire Mogul—Phoenix

Billionaire Mogul—Gage

The Billionaire Moguls is part of the **Billionaire Hotshots'** world.

Billionaire Hotshots Series

Billionaire Hotshot—Levi

Billionaire Hotshot—Roderick

Billionaire Hotshot—Lochlan

Billionaire Hotshot—Holt

Billionaire Hotshot—Jace

Billionaire Hotshot—Jagger

These sexy as sin Billionaire Hotshots are notorious bachelors forever… that's until they cross paths with the women who bring them down to their knees.

You'll find **all my books** and **reading order** on my site: **www.ScarlettAvery.com**

I hope you enjoyed ***Billionaire Mogul—Phoenix***! Can't get enough of Phoenix and Michaela? Subscribe to my mailing list and you'll get instant access to an exclusive ***Billionaire Mogul—Phoenix*** secret chapter and/or storyboard. Just use the QR code below.

Already subscribed? You would've received the link in the first email I sent you. If you can't find it, you can email us. If you've changed your email address, simply resubscribe.

About the Author

USA TODAY Bestselling Author Scarlett Avery unapologetically pens all-consuming love stories featuring sexy as sin billionaires who have the determination of a thousand warriors. Her kickass heroines are smart and sassy. And you should always expect edge-of-your-seat twists.

Scarlett's stories are intense and passionate, emotional and steamy, and always leave you begging for more. In other words, they're the perfect blend of swoony and sinful.

Fair warning...

Once you start reading Scarlett's novels, there's no going back!